SACRED SINNERS MC
MOTHER CHAPTER

BINK CUMMINGS

23 HOURS

Copyright © 2019/2023: Bink Cummings
All rights reserved. No part of this book may be reproduced or transmitted in any form or by any means, electronic or mechanical, including photocopying, recording, or by any information storage and retrieval system, without written permission from the author, except for the inclusion of brief quotations in a review.
Thank you for respecting the hard work of this author.
Contact the Author:
Email: BinkCummings@yahoo.com
Editor: Mary Sittu-Kern
Cover Model: Alfie Gordillo
Photographer: Reggie Deanching
Cover Designer: Bink Cummings

For my readers, my true Sacred Sisters, who've been with me through it all. From loss to happiness and everything in between. So many of you have been there to lend an ear, give support, and show your love. I appreciate you for sticking it out and believing in me, even when I didn't believe in myself. This book, Gunz's book, is for you. I hope you love it.

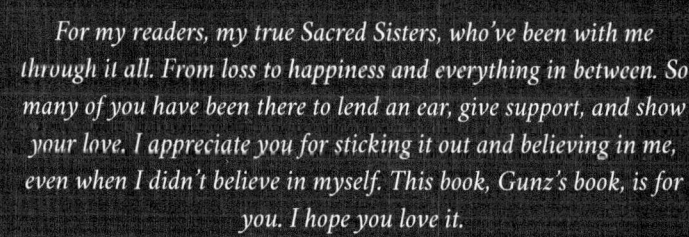

AUTHOR NOTE

This page is for those who need access to possible reading triggers. If you have none, please skip this page.

This book contains the following elements in varying degrees.

Rape.
Sex Trafficking.
Suicide.
Murder.
Cheating (mild).
Mentions of Child Sexual Abuse.

CHAPTER ONE

A string of blood splatters across the toe of my leather boot. An old grease rag that's been promoted to a gag muffles a shriek of agony. The head of a hammer *clinks* against the concrete as it lands on the floor of our shed, an omen of what's to come.

Welcome to the party.

I'm Gunz, your chaperone this fucked-up evening… the sergeant-at-arms of the Sacred Sinners MC, mother chapter. Ya know, the home of where it all began.

Before I break you in, we need to go over a few ground rules.

One—don't fuck with the Sacred Sinners. Two—if you neglect rule number one, your ass gets strung up naked in the middle of our prez's fun zone—the place men get taught lessons the hard way.

Pretty damn sure you don't want that now, do ya?

Three—Prez's old lady is off-limits.

Her name's Bink.

She's ours.

The daughter I never had.

If you haven't met her yet, she's the short, big-breasted blonde 'round these parts, who makes our lives run smoothly on the SS compound. She's also the mother to my grandbaby, Leech, whose first birthday is just around the corner. You touch either of 'em and you become worm food, no questions asked. Capiche?

Reaching into my cut, I extract a root beer Dum Dum and pop the sweetness into my maw before tucking both arms across my chest. With my back propped against the wooden wall, I watch Big Dick, our six-foot-eight, long-haired, bare-chested national prez, lose his last shred of sanity. If it were any other day, I'd stop him. Hell, I'd step in to take care of what needs done. Today's not that day.

"You think you can come to my home and fuck with my family!" Upper lip curled over his teeth, Big's fist slams into the skinny captive's stomach. He's been working him over for hours—breaking bones, making him bleed—reveling in his cries for mercy.

Happy to watch the torture unfold, I smile around my sucker stick. It's better this way. Someone's gotta pay.

"You think you can take away my old lady's innocence and there won't be consequences? Make her kill people! You think I'm a pussy? That I won't retaliate? You're gonna die. Your prissy-bitch friends are gonna die. I'm gonna kill every last one of you motherfuckers!" Each sentence is punctuated with the beautiful *thud* of fist meeting flesh. Air is torn from the man's body. His knees buckle, leaving his over-stretched arms to support his weight as Big pummels his torso, turning his innards to soup.

We're at war, if that much isn't clear. Ground zero for the latest attack. The first we've had here in close to thirty years. Big's taking it personally, as he should. We all are.

Less than twenty-four hours ago, a crew was sent to take us out by the infamous Remy Whitaker, sex trafficker extraordinaire, a sicko we've had beef with for ages. We've got ourselves an assassin on the side who takes his brand of disgusting off the streets and frees his merchandise. Remy ain't keen on us fucking with his business, and we're not down with the sex trade. Seems we're at an impasse. A bloody one that'll end one of two ways—us dead, and there's a fuckton of Sacred Sinners, or him and his crew buried six feet under. I'll let ya guess which one we're bankin' on.

Somebody pounds on the shed door from outside. It bounces on its hinges. "We good in there?" It's Kai, the new VP of our chapter. We added the oversized blond to our local brotherhood 'bout a month ago. He might be green here, but he's been running with the SS for half a decade. Before that, he was special ops in the Army. Real hardcore, classified shit. Stuff nobody's supposed to know about… besides me, 'cause I can find anything on the web, dark or otherwise. You wanna know about the bitch your husband's been texting? I'll find out in thirty seconds. Think I'm joking? Does it look like I'm laughing? Give me a day, and I could corrupt the entire US military system. Forty-eight hours and I could sell nuke launch codes to the highest bidder. It's a good thing I'm a goddamn patriot. Some would use the term hacker. I call myself a tech guy, 'cause I go beyond the coding, hacker crap anybody with half a brain could do in their brother's bug-infested basement.

"Yep," I reply to Kai 'cause Big's too busy unleashing his rage to answer. Sweat glistens across his blood-splattered skin. For what these assholes did to our Bink, there'll be hell to pay. Lucky for us, we've got two more of these bastards locked in the clubhouse basement whenever Big's gotten his fill with this bitch.

"You need anything?" Kai double knocks on the door, makin' sure we're straight.

"Kai! You talkin' to Gunz?!" a brother hollers over loud

rock music. It's coming from inside the clubhouse, through the shattered front doors they're workin' on fixing. Lots of glass and debris to clean up after last night's shootout. We're lucky nobody got dead on our side.

"Yeah, why?" Kai replies.

"Is Big in there, too?" Ah. I recognize that voice. It's Malcolm, the prospect.

Side-eyeing Big, I wait for my brothers to work out whatever needs to be handled on their end.

"Yes," comes from Kai.

"One prisoner wants a word," our prospect explains.

'Course they do. Bet I know what they want.

Our new VP ain't happy with the news when his usual laid-back tone lowers to a growl. "A word of what?"

Bein' new and all, there's no need for him to get mixed up in that shit. Not yet, anyhow, considerin' he's got a torso full of bruises. The idiot got himself shot half a dozen times yesterday. Good thing he was strapped with a vest. "I'll handle it, Kai. Just give me a minute!" I holler, then turn to the big guy, checkin' to see if he's worn out yet, or able to talk. By the firm set of Big's jaw and determination cast like granite in those blue eyes, I'd say he ain't stoppin' before sunrise. A bloody evening it shall be.

Take all the time ya need, brother—all the time.

When our VP doesn't respond, I check to see if he's left to deal with the fuckers. "Hey, Kai, you still out there?"

"Yeah."

I push off the wall and tidy up the floor with a random rag. Big's got bloodied nails scattered all over the place. Not wantin' a brother to get one through the foot, I toss them into a rusty bucket that sits on an old milk crate in the corner. "You wanna swap me places in here? Keep an eye on Prez?"

"Keep an eye on wh—"

Not in the mood for questions, I cut him off. "Clean up his messes, keep Bink out, make sure he drinks water... shit like that." Double checkin' the place is half presentable, I skim over the shed, bypassing Big's form and the fresh blood beneath our captive's feet. It runs down his legs in rivulets, thanks to the small holes Big inflicted. Kai hasn't been in here yet. Might as well give the man a good first impression. Torture has a way of making even the strongest men queasy. Let's hope Kai's military background has toughened his gut.

Satisfied with the presentation, I flip the eye-in-hook lock open and kick the door wide on its hinges for Kai to get his ass inside so I can handle the men in the basement. I gotta check on Niki anyhow, my favorite club whore. She's in my room. Been there a while and is probably pissed at me for making her wait so long for dick.

Liftin' my chin at Prez, I gesture to our VP. Not that Big's payin' a lick of attention. He's too busy snarling at the hanging cunt. "Big, Kai's gonna stay here. You get tired or need somethin', ask him." Bet he didn't hear a damn thing I said.

I look at Kai. Gaze meets gaze, so he knows I mean business. This ain't a joke or some immature game. "If he starts to act weird or anything, you call me or get him to bed. No matter what comes outta his mouth, you *don't* take him home tonight. He can sleep in his bed in the clubhouse. Got it?" Almost all of us brothers got our own houses in the back half of our compound, plus rooms at the clubhouse. For you newbs, I'll explain the finer details later. Ain't got time for that now.

Kai glances around me to eye Big and frowns. "Can't he make his own choices?"

What did I just say?

"No." I lay a hand on Kai's shoulder and squeeze, hopin' to imbue some sorta brotherly wisdom. "You'll learn this real quick. When Big gets in this mode..." I gesture to my best friend with a head tilt. "Where all he wants to do is kill, especially for his old lady, he's gonna need to wind down. If not, he'll worry her more by smotherin' her, and she don't need that."

Sometimes you gotta handle our prez with kid gloves. Ya stand back and watch him do his thing, violent or otherwise, and clean up the mess when he's through. Sometimes, you gotta step in and save him from himself. That's what brothers do.

Kai offers a single nod. "What I gotta do, then?"

"You take him to his room without his phone. Make him drink water. Get him into the shower and wait for him to finish. Then put him to bed. Club whores are always sniffin' 'round, so you gotta post someone outside his door, or one'll end up in his bed."

One of Kai's brows arches to his hairline. "Doesn't his door lock?"

Smartass.

I punch him in the shoulder, my eyes rolling. "Yes, genius. But there are keys, and bitches have their ways of gettin' what they want. You know how it goes."

Pickin' up what I'm puttin' down, Kai nods again. "Yeah. Just didn't think they'd be so stupid." A hand drags through his long locks.

"They are." All of 'em wanna piece of Prez, even more so now that he's with Bink. The behind-the-scenes club whore stories Niki tells me are hilarious. Big finds them amusing, too. We won't tell Bink about 'em, though. Don't want her any more pissed than necessary.

"Right. Think I got it."

"You'd better. Later." Delivering a final thump to Kai's shoulder, I exit the shed. It sits behind the brick clubhouse. Our treasurer, Blimp, is pissing in the blackened firepit as I pass by. We exchange chin lifts as I head to the only door out back—a steel-enforced fucker that opens into a rear hallway of the clubhouse where the bedrooms are.

Malcolm's waitin' on me inside, wearing his signature cowboy hat. The man used to be a drug dealer. Now he rolls with us. Sometime, in the next century, when Big gets over his snit, Mal will become a full-fledged brother. Until then, he's our bitch.

"Lead the way." I follow Mal through the halls lined with closed doors—each belonging to a brother. We've also got ourselves an infirmary and three offices—one for Big, one for our VP, and the other's mine.

Passing Mickey, he lifts a hand in greeting as his shadow, Gypsy, carries two overflowing plates of food behind him. They're probably going back to their bedroom for dinner. When we brought Malcolm on, we needed the extra space. Since they already housed together, sharing a room wasn't a big deal. Mickey's real fucked in the head. Got himself an eviler sexual deviant livin' in that skull of his than I do. Gypsy's his anchor. Been that way for years. That's why we don't make 'em go anywhere without the other.

I greet them with a shallow nod as Malcolm reaches the far door that leads to the basement. Catching up, I gesture for him to stay here while I take my time descending the steps. Every *thud* of my boot heel hitting an old wooden step sends an omnipotent echo through the hellhole, alerting the prisoners of my presence. This ain't a place you wanna be strung up.

In the center of the old, dimly lit room are two naked men. The twenty-something, skinny bastard has a bullet hole through his side that we didn't bother stitching up. It still oozes blood. His eyes are closed, his body swaying on piss-covered feet. The ancient, fat fucker beside him stares straight at me. Those deep-set brown eyes shoot venom with little effort. There's no doubt about it, this is the one who wanted to talk. His comrade's too busy dying to ask for anything but a bullet through the brain to ease his passing.

I stop close enough to feel the surge of anger from the big, hairy asshole. He's larger than me in both size and height. Got more hair than I do, too. Not that it takes much. I'm bald. My beard's better, though. More kempt, less gangly. Not like any of that matters. I'm biding time, waiting for him to speak first. I've got all day.

Seconds twist into minutes as we stare the other down.

Bullet Boy moans in pain, and I crack a closed smile, chewing on my empty sucker stick.

Fatty growls low in his throat, not liking my response.

Seems this dipshit doesn't know who I am. He must've expected Big to come barreling down here and fuck him up. Guess it's a good thing I'm a patient man. Always have been.

Tossing the stick on the floor, I pull another Dum Dum from my pocket, remove the waxy wrapper, ball it between my fingertips, and toss it at the man's feet, hitting a yellow toenail.

His nostrils flare, and his lips thin into an unpleasant line. Somewhere under that fat, his jaw might be set. Who knows?

'Cause I'm a dick, I smile at him, then wink, savoring the delicious mouthful of peach. It's that or light a cigarette, and I haven't smoked in God knows how long. Twenty years? Twenty-five? Shit, I can't remember the last time. The urge still lingers. That's what ya get when your mother got you and your brother hooked on nicotine even before you were a teenager—another long story.

Biding time, I check my phone for any messages I might've missed. He'll crack eventually.

> Niki: Where the fuck are you?

Head shaking in amusement, I chuckle to myself, hearing her voice inside my head jump a dozen octaves. Niki can be demanding when she doesn't get her way. I think I spoil her too much. Can't help it. I've got a soft spot for her. She gives me sex the way I want it, whenever I want it, without the added complication of a relationship. 'Cause I don't do romantic entanglements. Haven't in my fifty-plus years on this earth. Won't do it in death, either.

I skim through the list of unanswered messages from her.

> Niki at 7:26 p.m.- Gunz!

> 7:29 p.m.- I need your big, beautiful cock, baby. Please don't make me wait much longer.

I snicker.

> 8:03 p.m.- Gunz, I'm so horny.

> 8:14 p.m.- How much longer?

> 8:33 p.m.- It's been two hours. This isn't funny.

> 8:40 p.m.- My wrists are starting to hurt.

> 8:45 p.m.- God, I hate you!

> 8:49 p.m.- I'm sorry. I didn't mean that. Please come back soon. I'll suck your piercing as long as you want. Please!

> 9:05 p.m.- Goddammit!

> 9:12 p.m.- Asdfhasdfasdfasdfojasdfladfh!!!!!

Unable to help myself, I laugh out loud, not caring where I am. This woman ain't happy with me. Too bad my dick loves that way too much. He's perkin' right up at the thought of her red-faced, texting with one hand as she squirms to get loose. I've got issues.

> 9:14 p.m.- In case you couldn't understand that. It says I hate you.

Yeah. Gathered that.

> 9:35 p.m.- Please. If you care for me at all, send someone to take care of my pussy. It's been three hours. I can't take another. It's too much.

Knowing I gotta answer now, rather than later, 'cause it's been a few hours, my thumbs get busy.

> Me: You're fine. I'll be there whenever I choose to be. You'll wait because I said you'll wait.

Niki's gonna hate that, but she knows how I roll.

> Niki: Oh. Thank. God. You finally replied! What if I don't want to wait, baby?

> Me: You already know the answer to that.

> Niki: Refresh my memory.

Head shaking at her games, I snort.

> Me: If you can't wait, then you can call one of your club whores to set you loose. If you do, you know the consequences.

> Niki: The you won't touch me for a month rule?

Bingo.

> Me: That's the one. I don't play games. If I didn't want you spread out for me, ready and willing, then I wouldn't have tied you up in the first place. The club always comes first. I'm not gonna explain myself. You stay, your choice. You leave, your choice.

> Niki: Will it be much longer?

Ugh. More with the questions.

Someone's cruisin' for a reddened ass tonight. Cherry. Fucking. Red.

Keeping my patience in check, I give it to her straight.

> Me: You know I won't answer that. You're either willing to wait as long as it takes for me to handle club biz to get my dick, or you're not. Time isn't a factor.

Then I click off the message, 'cause I refuse to answer another. I'm not on her leash. She doesn't control this.

To see what the fat fuck's doin', I glance up from my screen. He's the same as before. However, he has balled his fists above his head. They weren't that tight before. Think he's sweating more, too. The rug of curly chest and stomach hair covering his overhung belly is wet as fuck. Droplets are making a small mess on the concrete floor.

I waggle a brow to see if he's gonna engage or not. It's a battle of the wills. Who's gonna break first?

Ignoring me for a beat, Remy's bitch glances over to his buddy, who's not lookin' so hot. His skin's gone from clammy and pale to a sickly gray. Bet ya a dollar, he'll be dead before I leave the basement. Whoever's left standing will have the honor of enduring the last of Big Dick's wrath. I should feel sorry for him, but I don't. Empathy's wasted on those who prey on the defenseless. Screw 'em.

I return to the task at hand.

Spotting who else texted, my face breaks into the biggest grin. It's our girl. Warmth lights up my heart just thinking of her and my grandbaby. I've never loved anything so much in my whole life. Don't think I ever could. If I wasn't here, handling club biz, I could be with them right now. After what went down yesterday, that's where I'd rather be, camped out on the floor outside her bedroom, for her protection and my peace of mind.

> Bink: Just put Harley down. Hope everything's okay there. Haven't heard from Big.

Not wanting to wake her, I check the time stamp on the message before replying. It was sent less than an hour ago, which means she's likely awake.

> Me: Handling stuff. Big's gonna be fine. He's sleeping here tonight. Don't worry.

> Bink: Okay. How's the clubhouse coming along?

> Me: We've got it covered. Now go watch a movie with Tati and get some rest.

Tati is Bink's latest project. A teen who was caught up in Remy's sex ring. Her big, bleeding heart couldn't let the girl leave. Now we've got ourselves a second survivor of the sex trade living on the compound. A single mother named Janie and her lil one, Dom, live with me. Another long story I don't wanna delve into right now. Life's complicated. How's that for an explanation?

"You talkin' to your bitch?" the fat man snarls.

Stowing my cell, I widen my stance and crack my knuckles, slow and deliberate, as I stare the fucker down, my lips sealed.

"I asked you a question, dickhead!"

On the inside, I'm jonesing to let 'er rip. On the outside, I appear bored. To push his buttons a lil more, I yawn, then snicker, when Fatty yanks on his restraints, testing their strength. When they give a little, he steps closer in challenge. I'm not gonna play into whatever pissing contest he thinks he just threw down. We've got the upper hand, and I have no desire to deal with false bravado bullshit. He's old enough to know better.

I fiddle with the heavy SS ring on my index finger and wait for him to make the next move.

I don't gotta wait long.

A sticky spray of spit varnishes my face. If this were Big, he'd lose it. Me, I pretend it didn't happen. Nice try, asshole. It takes a fuckuva lot more to get me riled up.

"Let me loose! I want a fair fight!"

I snort.

"Motherfucker! I said I want a fair fight! You a coward? Think I'll waste you? Come on. Untie me. Let's do this!"

Biting my bottom lip, I stave off a pleased smile. This guy's got guts, I'll give him that. Might've gotten his wish had Big been the one to come say hello.

When Fatty doesn't get his desired response, he loses his shit. Gripping the thick chains in his fists, he yanks and twists them to no avail, attempting to get closer. Not giving up, he kicks out and fails to connect with anything but air. Still, I remain in place as he has the adult equivalent of a toddler's temper tantrum, cursing like a biker, floppin' his blubber and puny cock every which way. It don't take long for him to breathe heavily. The police-grade cuffs dig into his wrists, trickling blood down his forearms.

"Argh! Come on! Let's fight!"

Unimpressed by his antics, I pull a small knife from my front pocket, flick it open with my thumb, and stab it into his left pec. When it hits bone, I keep going. Fatty Trafficker screams in surprise, then tries to scurry backward, but the chains don't let him get far. I drive forward, burying steel to the hilt. Eyes roll into the back of his skull before he passes out from the pain. Don't worry, I didn't kill him. No major vessels have been nicked. Close, but no dice. That's Big's MO, and I'm not about to steal it from him. This should shut the fuckwad up for a while. Maybe collapse his lung. No biggy. He'll survive long enough to die later.

Not wanting to inflict further damage, I extract the blade, toss it in the corner for Malcolm to clean later, and climb the steps back to the main floor.

The prospect is waiting on me like a good bitch at the top. "So?"

The door *clicks* shut behind me before I speak. "Make sure Big gets his time with the fat one in the next hour, two tops. If he wants to end the other's life, he'd better do it now. The guy might be dead already."

"Dead? Big said not to let either of them die on my watch." Malcolm trembles, hands shaking down at his sides.

I shrug. "Not my problem."

"Gunz, he's gonna kill me." His voice cracks.

"Naw." I pat the probies back. "He won't kill ya. Just rough ya up a bit." Leaving the prospect to deal, I navigate the halls 'til I reach the steel door of my bedroom.

Fishing the loose key from my pocket, I let myself in, ready to get my fuck on.

Sure enough, there Niki lies all trussed up with those lovely, bare tits ripe for the sucking as dark hair spills over the pillow. Her lean legs are spread eagle, thanks to the padded restraints cuffed around each ankle. Her wrists, done up the same. Gorgeous. Absolutely gorgeous. My favorite way to be greeted—cunt ready and willing. This is my idea of a perfect night.

"Gunz!" my favorite club whore gasps. A giant smile she reserves just for me steals across that beautiful face.

I lean a shoulder against the doorjamb, leaving it open for anyone who might wanna watch or join in. We're not shy. "Hey," I adjust my erection to keep it from pinching. One look, and he's rarin' to go. Whoever said ED happens to us fifty-somethings hasn't met me.

Niki wriggles on the bed, excited to get started. "Please."

"Please what?" I smirk, stroking my gray goatee as I indulge in Niki's palpable need. It's sweet, like fresh cherries and whipped cream.

Eager for touch, she tugs on the restraints, those eyes begging me to do naughty, naughty things to that body. "Fuck me. Dear God, fuck me! I need it."

"*You* need *my cock?*"

"Yes! God! Yes!"

Satisfied by her reaction, I push off the frame, stride to the bed, and stuff two fingers into her sopping wet cunt. Niki squeals in delight, her back arching off the mattress, tits jiggling. Adorable pink polished toes curl as her mouth drops open in the sexiest moan. Bet half the brothers hear her over the music.

'Cause I love her slick walls, I fuck her on my hand 'til she's writhing, ready to lose her goddamn mind. It doesn't take long. The girl comes like a champ.

"Gunz! Please!" She's on the precipice, but I've got other plans.

Withdrawing my fingers, I unfasten my SS buckle and jeans. My cock forces his way out of my boxers through the slit, eager for sex. Damn, my piercing is already coated in precum. I swipe the dew away with my thumb. Niki watches it all, her gaze hungry for action.

"You want this?" I show her the bead on the pad of my finger.

That sweet, sweet whore plays right along, licking her lips, nodding like an overeager bobblehead. "Please," she rasps.

The nice guy I usually am wants to give in to her desires. The bad one that comes out to play in the bedroom refuses to be good. Eyes on hers, I suck the precum into my mouth and moan, savoring the taste on my tongue. It never gets old.

Niki glares as I continue to relish the tang.

"Gunz!" That pouty bottom lip begs for attention. Nope, I'm not giving in. My favorite little whore might be hotter than a high-class hooker, but she can wait. I'll gorge on her splayed beauty and do whatever I want, whenever I want, however I fuckin' want.

To give her a better view, I shimmy my boxers and jeans down enough to expose every bit I've got to offer. I wrap a fist around my erection and jack myself slowly. More precum oozes from the pierced slit. I use it as lube and smear the rest into the skull tattoo above my dick, where pubes no longer exist. If you want whores to suck you off on a regular, you gotta keep the playground trimmed. I wax. It makes life easier. Call me Metro, but I bet you'd be the first to get on your knees to lick these smooth balls.

Niki attempts to scissor her thighs together for friction. They don't touch, not even a little. I laugh when she gets frustrated, trying to make it work.

"Havin' problems, babe?"

She yanks hard on the restraints, rocking herself on the

mattress. It squeaks in protest. "Touch me. Touch me. Goddammit, put that thing inside me!" Niki's chest heaves, desperation clinging to every inch of her form.

That's it, sweetheart, get ready. Nice and ready.

Someone clears their throat behind me. Not concerned about the intrusion, I don't stop gettin' myself off.

Niki's the first to address our visitor. "Hey, Viper," she purrs, battin' those long lashes. "Wanna give me some dick? Gunz is bein' stingy."

This greedy bitch has no patience. She's crusin' for a bruised ass tonight. If she keeps it up, she won't be able to sit tomorrow. Not that either of us will mind. Niki gets off on anything I wanna do to her.

I continue to stroke myself and turn to face my fellow brother.

Looking from Niki to me, Viper smiles like the deviant he was born to be. "You want me to take over?" His eyebrows bounce suggestively.

Like hell, he can. I didn't warm Niki up for him to work out her pussy by himself. "Take over? Why would I want you to take over when you could join?" Now get your mind outta the gutter. We share whores 'round here. It's a thing. Look it up. There's no shame in our game. We fuck what we want, with whoever we want. Swords cross, but don't touch… much. Watchin' a chick come apart on two cocks is a thing of beauty. You should try it sometime.

Viper shrugs off his cut and lays it on my dresser. Next goes the Harley t-shirt, exposing an impressive eight pack and an array of ink. "No can do, bro," he says. "There's some bitch goin' off on Dallas and Blimp at the gate. Says she knows you. That you need to talk."

You've gotta be shitting me. Now? When I could tag team Niki with Viper?

Fuck.

"Seriously?" I growl, tucking myself back into my pants and zippin' up as Viper drops trowel, knowin' damn well I won't leave Niki hanging when she's been such a good whore. If she wants biker cock, she'll get biker cock. From the looks of Viper's rod, he's down to take my place. Can't say I'm not salty about it, 'cause I am, but I've got business to handle. The club comes first.

"As a heart attack," he states, kicking off his leather boots, giving the room a front-row view of his bare backside. Niki whistles in appreciation. "She rode up in a lifted pickup 'bout fifteen minutes ago. Won't leave, and the brothers don't wanna hurt her. Figured you can work it out since we know she ain't armed."

This had better be life or death.

Ready to get this over with so I can join the tail end of the epic fucktacular, I don't bother saying goodbye when Viper climbs on the end of the bed and gives Niki a fresh lick from ass to clit. The bastard gets to have all the fun when I'm stuck bein' the responsible one.

Sexually frustrated doesn't begin to cover how I feel as I power through the halls on a mission, bypassing brothers and club whores alike. I punch the door to the common room open. More brothers mill about, cleaning up yesterday's mess like we ordered them to do. From the looks of it, they're about done. They propped a fresh door and frame against the wall, ready to be installed come sunrise. Beer bottles line the bar top as Buckcherry thunders through the jukebox. Jizz is gettin' a blowie from a whore on the couch. I give 'em a wide berth and beeline it to the hole we call an exit, where the double glass doors used to be. Bulletproof my ass. Those machine guns tore 'em up.

Standing at the mangled gate up ahead, lit by motorcycle headlights, are White Boy, Blimp, and Dallas. They step to the wayside as they see me approach.

I don't notice the chick on the opposite side of the steel until I'm upon them. That's when I hear her smooth, articulate voice first, givin' Blimp hell, before I get an eyeful of an inked-out, purple-haired woman with average tits and wide hips. Who, upon closer inspection, must be in her late thirties.

I stop next to White Boy, who looks like he could use some shut-eye.

"Can I help you?" I give her a second once-over. She's hot. A smidge older than I usually screw, but fuckable. Bet she'd look sexy trussed up in my bed.

The woman's arms cross beneath her breasts, her hip cocked. "You sure can. You can take care of your son. The asshole got himself locked up again for the second time."

Excuse me?

This lady is on something if she thinks I got a kid.

I glance at my brothers. They're snickering—the fucks.

To make sure I didn't misunderstand what she said, I cup a hand around my ear. "Come again?" It's a dick move, I know.

Unamused, her jaw tightens. "You deaf? I said take care of your stupid son."

Okay, so I heard her right the first time. This is a prank, it's gotta be… or a giant misunderstanding.

Trying to take the high road and be diplomatic, I take a step closer to the gate, to see each other more clearly. She mimics my movement, swallowing the last couple of inches. I rest a hand on a bar. It's chilly to the touch. "I caught that part. Sorry, lady, I dunno who you are, but I ain't got a son."

"Yes, you do. That's what I'm saying, and you're not listening. None of you are." Her angry gaze flicks to my brothers accusatorily before returning to me.

I peek over at Dallas. "Is that what she told you guys?"

Picking his teeth with a toothpick, he shakes his head.

"Nope. She said she needed to speak to you and wouldn't leave when we asked her to, repeatedly."

All right, so she's belligerent, stubborn, and drives a yellow truck on steroids—if the one parked behind her is hers. She also has a son in jail and dresses like a biker chick with ripped jeans and a Metallica t-shirt. Her shoes are plain ole flip-flops. She's ballsy enough to show up to a Sacred Sinners compound after sundown. Can't say she looks all that threatening. Though, I'm convinced she's batshit crazy. As a female, you don't roll up this time of night unless you want one of two things—to get dick, or you're lookin' for trouble.

Wantin' her gone before she draws a crowd, or Big catches wind and takes his rage out on her, I do my best to smooth over the situation. "Ma'am, please get back in your truck and go before things get unpleasant."

What does she do when I offer an olive branch? This broad plants her tiny feet and glares. I'm not sure if I should be impressed or pissed. My dick, he's a happy camper. We like ourselves spitfires, just not crazy ones who claim we got a kid when we don't. Me and my pecker gotta have a little chat about what's appropriate for hard-ons and what's not—in the future—when I'm not busy with bullshit like this when I could be fucking.

"Hell no!" Her nostrils flare in indignation. "In case you still aren't listening, things are already unpleasant. My son is in jail for the second time. *Your* son, Adam. He's almost twenty-two. You and I met at Sturgis twenty-three years ago, at the Black Falcon Saloon before they tore it down. I had brown hair then that reached my ass. We spent a day together." The woman drops her hand to show her hair's former length—to the hip.

"And? I've met and slept with a lot of chicks at Sturgis."

Three to six women every year for thirty-plus years. That's a lot of pussy I can't remember. Not that I should have to.

Her honey-eyed stare turns downright glacial. "You always bone 'em bareback?"

Blimp sputters a laugh, then chokes on it. *Asshole.*

Licking the front of my teeth, I massage the nape of my neck, so I don't go off on this woman for insulting me when she's already fired up. "No. I don't fuck bareback. Ever." Sure, condoms have broken, and I might've skipped out on glovin' up on a few rare occasions when I didn't have one handy, and the woman was too hot to pass by. But I haven't had a lapse in judgment in years… no… decades. With age comes wisdom. You know how that goes.

"Uh-huh." Her head swivels with attitude. Purple hair sweeps across her shoulders. "Bet ya tell all the girls that. *'I only go bare with you, baby, 'cause you're special.'*" The woman does a piss-poor job of mimicking the bass of my voice.

"I've never said that in my life," I growl, tightening my fist around the gate.

"No? Then how did I wind up giving birth to Adam nine months later?"

How's this my fault? She gets knocked up by some rando, and I'm the dickhead. None of this makes a lick of sense. Not her presence, her hostility toward me, nor the accusations. I'm through with the games.

"You realize that's impossible, right? Who shows up twenty-two years after givin' birth to a kid, to tell some man he's the father? What do you want? Money? That why you're here? I'll give ya fifty bucks to go on your merry way, ma'am. Sorry for the mix-up. Good luck with Adam." Too horny and aggravated to deal, I pull out my wallet, toss a wad of bills through the slats of the gate and turn to get the hell outta dodge. I'm done.

The bars rattle as I retreat. "My name isn't ma'am, dickface. It's Melanie... and I don't want money. I want you to talk to him. Make him get his life together. A-another charge like this, and he could be down for years." Desperation clings to her words, hollowing out my stomach.

I swallow hard.

Fuck.

Fuuuck.

Taking her sadness as my own when I shouldn't, I stop but refuse to turn around. I gotta draw the line somewhere, even if every cell in my body wants to help. It's fucked up, ain't it? A woman I don't even know rambles on about stuff that has nothing to do with me, and all it takes is for her veil of strength to drop, and I'm ready to rescue her. My mother sure did a number on me. May the bitch rot in hell.

Heaving a sigh, I reply when I should walk away. "Sorry to hear about Adam, Melanie. I am. I wish you the best of luck. Have a nice evening." There, I said my peace. Through with this whole fucked-up ordeal, I leave my brothers to handle her when I know I can't.

More gate rattling ensues. "Goddammit, asshole! Don't walk away from me! Gunz! Erik! You never knew my name, so you made one up. You called me Kit!"

Wait.

I stop halfway to the clubhouse, a smashed shell casing underfoot. "I called you—"

"Kit."

Scowling, I spin around to face everyone. "No." That's impossible.

"Yes." Melanie's chin lifts in defiance.

"No. That can't be right. That was..." I approach, racking my brain for any memory of a Kit. It sounds familiar, though I can't say why.

"Twenty-three years ago, this August," she explains.

I pinch the bridge of my nose, closing my eyes. Kit. Kit. Why does that hit a cord? "We—"

"Had sex," she chimes in unhelpfully.

We... Wait... Hold up... I think I got something... *Holy fuck.* That was the... No. This is her? *Kit.* The engaged bitch partying with her friends like Sturgis was the new Vegas vacation. They were outta place in a bar full of leather, wearin' sundresses and no panties. Sturgis was some rite of passage after college graduation before saying I Do. She was the drunk chick offering the goods to anyone who'd give her a ride. I stepped up when some greaseball from a club we don't associate with wanted to get up in that. I took over, lifted her dress, saw she was down, and we...

"At the bar," I fill in, vaguely remembering her back against the wood, her legs around my waist... "Wait... Blimp was there." I look at my brother. His face tells a different tale. He's half-smiling like a dumbass, half trying to hide it, stroking his long gray beard. Yeah, he remembers.

The fucker punches my shoulder. "Congrats, Daddy-o."

Nope, I'm not even gonna touch that comment. He can fuck right off.

I ignore him and address Mel. "Listen, just 'cause we had sex a dozen times, doesn't mean he's my kid." I'm not buyin' it.

FYI, in case you were wondering, I could use a cigarette right now, or an entire pack of menthols.

Juiced up on the news, my leg jiggles. I snatch another Dum Dum from my pocket and shove the thing in my mouth before I make Blimp give me a hit off the blunt he's packin'. I sigh long and hard as the strawberry bliss gives me the relief nicotine used to.

Melanie kicks a rock. It clangs against the base of the gate. "It kinda does when I have a test saying otherwise."

"Excuse me?" I keep my tone neutral, wanting to crawl outta my skin. Either she's a liar, or I'm fucked.

Her head cocks to the side. "How do you think I found you? I couldn't remember your name, much less the club you were in, so I put Adam's DNA spit sample in one of those fancy online ancestry sites, and Eli popped up as a close relative."

"My brother, Bonez?" Why would he submit DNA to a company like that? Hasn't he learned a thing from me?

"Yes. Him," she confirms, much to my horror.

"You talked to my brother?" If he knew and didn't tell me, I'll beat his ass.

"No." Melanie's nose crinkles like that's the most distasteful thing I could've said. "I wouldn't do that. I hacked his social media…"

She… How… *Argh!* Now I'm really gonna kill him.

"You what? You hacked his… You *hacked* Bonez's social media?" He's a biker, too. Sure, he rolls with the Corrupt Chaos, a more laid-back veterans club, but he's smarter than this.

"Well." She shrugs, all innocent and far too cute for her own good. "I borrowed his password for like a minute to find out more about you, since you're one of the few people on the planet with less online presence than me."

Fuckin' A. Hacker hotness shouldn't impress me, but it does. Even if I'm gonna wring my brother's neck for lettin' anyone get past his firewalls. Firewalls I set up for him myself. They're not top of the line, but they're nothin' to sniff at either.

"This is—" I begin.

Melanie waves a hand to shut me up. "Listen, I'm sorry for showing up like this. I didn't mean for any of this to happen. Can we talk somewhere? I'm here for Adam. That's it. I promise. I don't want your money, connections, or whatever you might be thinking." To prove a point, Melanie picks up the bills I threw at her, rolls them up, and sets them in a crumpled ball on the gate.

And just like that, I'm frozen, stuck in…mind-numbing limbo.

I must give some indication it's cool for the brothers to let her pass, 'cause the banged-up gate that got hit by two trucks yesterday opens.

Not giving me a chance to change my mind, Melanie strides toward the clubhouse, a sexy sway to those hips. *Damn.* As if I'm not already screwed, she's gotta show off the goods when I'm sex deprived. I want pussy, even more so now than before. Anything would be nice to distract me from tonight's surprises.

Closing my eyes for the count of ten, I take a breath and will my nerves to calm.

They give me the finger. Twice.

"Your truck." White Boy waves to her vehicle parked outside the gate.

"Move it. Keys are in the ignition," Melanie tosses over her shoulder, not missing a beat.

Feet rooted in place, I don't move. Can't. This is real. I might have a son… A son named Adam.

How the hell did this happen?

What am I supposed to do?

Fuck.

This could change everything.

CHAPTER TWO

KIT

This is for Adam.
This is for Adam.
This is for Adam.

The mantra turns in my head like a broken record as I put on a brave face and pretend, sitting across from the one mistake I tried to forget, isn't twisting every part of me up inside.

I had to come.

Or that's what I keep telling myself.

Anything for my son… *our* son. Try that wordage on for size. It sounds strange, even to me.

Being here is harder than I thought. Facing the music and anticipating it are two very different scenarios.

Across a table in the main room of a clubhouse they're renovating, I watch Gunz's face contort in a myriad of emotions, switching between confusion and anger. We're seated at a high top. My legs dangle off the stool as a bottle of water sits unopened in front of me. He cleared the place out for us to talk. Not that I'm sure what to say that hasn't already been blurted within ten seconds of meeting.

It shouldn't have gone down like this.

The two-hour drive should've prepared me better. It's not like I didn't go over what I wanted to say and how I wanted to say it a thousand times in a thousand different ways.

The weeks I spent picturing this moment should've theoretically made things easier, not harder. I wish that was the case, but it never is, is it?

I drove around for hours, debating if I should stop or not. If I should open this can of worms, I never intended to crack open. Now, here I sit.

I know what you're thinking. I'm an awful person for keeping Adam from his dad all these years. How dare I drop this bomb tonight of all nights. Truth? I'd think the same thing if I were in your shoes. Would it help if I told you I didn't know Gunz was Adam's father until my husband, now ex-husband, needed a bone marrow transplant, and we tested Adam as a match? Talk about a devastating blow to everyone involved when the results came back as they did. Especially for my son, who already grew up feeling out of place, apart from fitting in with a group of small-town hellions. I'd like to say it was the boys' fault—that their bad influence wore Adam down and turned him into a modern-day version of Evel Knievel or Robin Hood, depending on the incident. But I'd be lying. He's the ringleader. What you'd consider a bad boy. The kid you wouldn't want your daughter dating. For your daughter's sake, I wouldn't want her dating him either.

Perhaps the man with the dazzling pair of blue eyes that match Adam's will be the answer to my prayers. Not that I'm a religious woman. Agnostic is more apt, I suppose. Though, I'm sure you'll agree that you'd eat the grossest, moldiest, most rotten crow for your child if you thought it might save them from themselves.

That's why I'm here.

I visited Adam in jail today.

If you've never visited your child in the slammer, you have no idea how terrible it is. Sickness takes over the instant you walk through those front glass doors of the station. It worsens when you hand your driver's license through a security window to get those precious fifteen minutes with your son twice a week. You give them money to put on his commissary because you know the food is awful and he needs things. Things you can't bring him. Then you wait with all the other loved ones on long, metal benches that have seen better days, for the buzz of a steel door and an officer to let you inside a dark room lined with stools and plexiglass booths. Old phones hang on the wall for you to talk to your child. There's no touching. No hugging. There you wait, once more, for your kid to enter the box in his gray sweats. You're grateful for those sweats because you know where the men wearing the orange jumpsuits are headed. In sympathy, you flash those families closed-mouth smiles. They return the gesture in kind, their eyes hollow from loss.

Tracing a nail over the grimy tabletop, I wait for Gunz to say something. I deserve to be yelled at. I deserve everything and then some. It's not his fault, or Jeremy's, or my ex-husband's, for what I've done to them. It's mine. I take full responsibility for sowing my wild oats with my girlfriends when I was engaged to be married. When I found out I was pregnant, I didn't even consider the hot biker could be Adam's daddy. I didn't consider it when Adam was born with blue eyes when I have hazel, and Jeremy has brown. I also didn't consider it when Adam looked nothing like Jeremy or his family. It wasn't until…

"How long have you known?" Gunz tears me from my innermost thoughts.

I blink to refocus on my surroundings, namely the handsome man sparking up the conversation. I'll tell him anything he wants to know. It's the least I can do.

"Known what?" I ask.

Another sucker slips between his goatee-encircled lips as Gunz leans back on the stool and drums his fingers against the edge of the table. "That I might be his father." Those very words cause his cheek to twitch before he looks away like he can't stand the sight of me. Not that I blame him. This isn't my proudest moment.

Holding nothing back, I pull up my big girl panties and give him what needs to be given. "I knew my husband... ex-husband, wasn't his dad when he was fourteen."

Gunz flinches, and his nostrils flare at the news. "That was eight fuckin' years ago."

The scorching flame of regret, self-loathing, and remorse licks up my spine—a stark reminder of what I've done. A knot of shame coils low in my belly, forming into a jagged rock battering my insides.

I suck in a sharp breath as I push the tender spot with my hand, hoping the pain subsides soon.

Then I forge ahead, hating what the news must be doing to Gunz, too. I force my feelings down deep, to deal with later when I have time to reflect. This isn't about me. This is about Gunz and Adam. About owning our truths.

"I know," I agree with a solitary nod. To some, eight years seems like a long time. To me, it doesn't. Not when you're a single mom. Not when you have to pick up the pieces of your life after your husband up and abandons his family in the middle of the night, never to be heard from again. The house, the cars, parenting, all of it was left for me to handle on my own. With Adam and his issues, eight years feels like the blink of an eye.

With practiced ease, Gunz removes his leather vest and hangs it on his stool. "*Why* did you wait eight years to contact me?" His intense gaze sears into mine, seeking a valid reply. Not an excuse. Not a bullshit sob story. My past isn't his problem any more than his past is mine. I'm not here to be a victim.

I rest my elbows on the Formica, my hands clasped together, and keep things simple. "Eli came up as a match a few months ago. I didn't know how else to find you, or I would have." It was happenstance, a one-in-a-million chance of finding Adam's father. I was grasping at any straw I could find. Doing what I had to do. Pretending the best I could that my son's life wasn't already circling the drain.

He chuckles without humor, eyebrows pinched in the center. "Please excuse me if I don't buy into this shit."

Fair enough. That's his right.

"I understand." And I do. Whatever he's feeling must be intense. Rightfully so.

"Do you really?" His head tilts to the side as he scrutinizes me, to draw his own conclusions. There's an intensity there, an intelligence dissecting every word I say, every movement I make. I try not to let it get to me, but it's difficult.

I begin to sweat, the back of my old band t-shirt sticking to my spine and shoulders.

"Yes. I would feel the same if I were you. I do have the paperwork in my truck if you want to see it." In hindsight, I should've stuck it in my back pocket the moment I climbed out of the truck cab.

"I'm gonna need more than that."

"When Adam gets out, you can do whatever you need for confirmation." More DNA testing, more of anything he wants, I'm happy to oblige. If I wasn't already certain, I wouldn't be here. Trust me, just looking at the man is evidence enough.

He nods as if what I said is good enough for now. A heavy, emotional breath expels from a set of full lips. "So, you're here for..." Trailing off, Gunz runs a palm over his bald head. Some things never change. When I first met him, he looked the same as he does now—inked and gorgeous with well-kept facial hair and a wicked smile that would make any woman spread her legs. Like the finest wine, years have done him well. Very well.

Doing my best not to stare, I keep my tone easy to avoid sympathy for what I'm about to say. "When my ex found out Adam wasn't his, he... didn't just divorce me. He left us both. It was like he didn't care that he'd raised Adam for years. He couldn't get past what I'd done."

The eyebrow crinkle is back and joining the party, as is a small bulging vein in his forehead. "Seriously? He just left his fuckin' kid." Jerking upright, Gunz's shoulders tense as he growls his contempt on Adam's behalf. I'm grateful for the outburst more than I should be. It's more than I deserve.

"Yes." Picturing that awful night in my head, as if it happened just yesterday, I scratch the top of my jeans, rocking in my seat, hating the way Jeremy's loss unearths ugly, catastrophic feelings I don't wish to relive. "It was bad. I didn't know Adam wasn't his until he did. After that, Adam just... Well, he started getting into a lot of trouble. He was always different from the rest of us. Always tinkering with things. Always moving. Too smart for his own good. A daredevil of sorts."

The once anger is replaced with a cool biker nod as Gunz repositions himself on the stool—relaxing. "Okay... Go on."

"I had to pull him from school his sophomore year for hacking the school's computer system and planting a virus that made the bells go off every sixty-nine seconds. They only agreed not to press charges when they needed him to fix the issue, since they couldn't." Homeschooling took precedence after that, but he did graduate with passing grades. I made sure of it. Long nights were spent at the kitchen table.

Gunz chuckles and strokes his goatee in a way that suggests he likes what he hears. "Smart guy."

"Too smart, like I said."

"Then what happened?"

"Are you sure you want to hear all this?" I didn't come here to take a stroll down memory lane. Not this soon anyhow.

"He's my son, is he not?"

My heart warms at his admission. "Yes. But I didn't mean to rehash his messy teenage years. Only ask that maybe you could visit him in jail and talk him into getting his life together." Anything to keep him out of trouble. When you're a kid, things aren't taken as seriously as they are now. Adam's adult record is already sprinkled with misdemeanors. Can you imagine what it'll look like in three years, or ten, if he keeps going at the rate he is?

"What'd he do this time, and how long is he down for?" Gunz sounds genuinely concerned.

I open my bottle of water and take a swig. Elbows on the table, I cup both hands around the chilly container. "Sixty days. He's served almost half already. It was stupid, like it always is. He thinks it's funny to do stupid stuff."

"What kind of *stuff*?"

If only he knew the entire, colorful, and illegal laundry list of Adam's *stuff*.

Might as well give him a taste of what's to come, if he ends up wanting to meet his kid. "The receipts at every store within twenty miles of where we live printed *fuck you, have a nice day* below the total." Pressing my lips together, I stave off a smile. To be honest, it *is* kind of funny. Not legal. But a *Jackass*-worthy prank. Adam was proud of himself, even when they raided his friend's apartment to find his computer and the programs he used to hack into the systems. I wish I could say it was this well-thought-out plan. That he'd been setting up shop for months to pull this scale of a prank. Unfortunately, I can't say anything of the sort. The dumb kid decided the day before it went down. Like with most things, Adam is a fly-by-the-seat-of-your-pants troublemaker, who gets sick joy out of the weirdly stupid shit he pulls.

Gunz's head rears back, eyes blowing wide. "Oh hell, that was him?"

"Yes."

A devastating smile passes over his features. If I didn't know any better, I'd say it's one of pride. "I heard about that." The tiniest of chuckles breaks free.

I bet he did, it was all over the news.

An attractive woman, twentyish years my junior, saunters into the room through a doorway at the rear of the space. "Gunz," she calls to him, an erotic lilt to her voice.

Messy brown hair brushes the tops of her erect nipples as she approaches, wearing nothing more than a lace thong and a smile. She doesn't pay me any attention when she climbs into Gunz's lap with her perfect body and straddles him. Perky tits press against his chest as the curve of her back kisses the edge of the table.

I stare with bug eyes and a closed mouth. It's impossible not to. This isn't my scene. The biker life is so far from my wheelhouse that it might as well be another planet. Sure, I have tattoos everywhere, and I dye my hair. That doesn't mean anything more than I like ink and the color purple. I'm a boring online college professor—coding is my specialty. Unlike my son, I abide by the law. I don't ride motorcycles or wear leather vests. My truck is jacked up and has Boss speakers because I like it that way. When Jeremy left us, I embraced my real self. Stripping away years of sundresses and polite smiles was what I needed to survive the aftermath.

I found *me* in the rubble he left in his wake, and I like me... despite the guilt I live with for the twenty-three hours I spent with a man who made my pussy sing like a canary. If it wasn't for Gunz and that dashing smile, I wouldn't have Adam... And I'll never regret that. Not ever.

Gunz

Fuck. If it's not one thing it's another.

I grip Niki's hips to keep her from grinding against my cock. The dumbass in my pants is already prying at the zipper, hungry for a hole to hide inside. It's not all my fault. Her naked body isn't helping matters. Nor is the strong scent of sex coming from her soft, silky skin. The twinkle in those naughty eyes turns my crank hard. Just not hard enough for me to forget Kit... Mel... whatever her name is.

"Niki, what're you doin'?" I scold, unable to decide if I wanna bury myself in her cunt and forget about today—about Kit and Adam, about what Bink had to do, about the clubhouse in flux—or, if I wanna shove her off my lap, 'cause I'm worried how my son's mother will perceive this display. For all Kit knows, she's my old lady. Not that I should care. But I do.

Niki toys with the collar of my shirt, running a finger back and forth along my skin, dipping a nail inside to scratch my collarbone, knowin' exactly what that does to me. "Come back to bed," she purrs, batting those sexy lashes for added effect.

If only it were that simple. Trust me, I'd love to go to bed, but that's not possible.

"Can't you see I'm busy?" I lift my chin at the purple-haired hottie. Though my eyes are otherwise occupied with

Niki's killer body—mapping every inch of skin I've tasted and came on countless times.

Not caring about the other woman present, Niki nips at my chin. "So?" A soft tongue laves across my lips, tasting the sweetness left by my sucker. She hums in pleasure, her nipples grazing my pecs through the cotton of my t-shirt. The seductress is good, too damn good.

I bite back a groan.

"Didn't Viper take care of your needs?" We know he did. Niki's here 'cause she heard I'm with another female and wants to stake her claim. If I didn't wanna fuck her every day for the foreseeable future, I'd lecture her on how I'm not her property, and she's not mine.

Growing impatient, Niki delivers a stern look.

"No," I scold, but to be the nice guy, I kiss the tip of her nose. "Not right now."

"Please." Bringing out the big guns, she nuzzles against me, body heat to body heat. My cock pants for goddamn action. Throbs for it. It's a good thing I can control myself, unlike some of my brothers who're led around by their dicks.

To get my point across, I spank a bare ass cheek in time with my words. "I'm. Busy." This isn't some game. My son's in jail. His mother's here asking for my help, despite not wanting to do so. Lord knows I'm the kinda man who gets off on helpin'. How fucked is that when I don't even know if she's tellin' the truth? This hero complex I've got is a damn pain in the ass.

"With her?" The softest lips graze my neck, traveling to the lobe of my ear where she nibbles. Goosebumps sprout across my arms and my dick bucks. Which he can do all he wants. I'm still not changin' my mind.

"Yes. With her. It's important," I rasp, then swallow my arousal like a hot branding iron.

"More important than these?" Pulling out the biggest

guns, Niki leans back, cups her pale, perky breasts, and shakes them at me as if that'll help. It won't. They're sexy, and I would love to get my mouth on those tight, sensitive buds, but I've got more pressing matters to handle that don't include sex.

"Yes. More than those." There's no use in lying.

Not pleased with the truth, Niki whines my name under her breath.

Enough.

Peeling her off my lap, I set Niki on her feet and hop off the stool. I wrap my arm tightly around her waist and escort her from the room to get her as far away from Kit as possible. "Sorry. Be back in a sec," I call over my shoulder.

When Viper passes us in the hall on the way to my bedroom, I punch him in the shoulder, bro style. "The woman who's in the common room, babysit her for a bit, will ya?" I don't await his confirmation when we continue our journey to get Niki dressed and gone. The quicker she's outta here the better.

We pass Kai in the hall outside Big's room. His back rests against the wall as he plays on his phone. When I hear water running, I stop, then backtrack a few steps to check on Prez. Niki comes along for the ride, glued to my side, practically vibrating with lust. "What's Big doin'?"

Kai doesn't look up from whatever he's swiping on the screen. My guess—a stupid game. "He's in the shower," he mumbles.

That's what I figured. Then why isn't he in Big's bedroom keepin' an eye on him? Isn't that what I said to do?

"Did you take his phone?" I check.

Kai stows the cell in a pocket to give me his undivided attention. "Did I what?"

Christ, is he an idiot?

"When you brought him back here, did you take his cell?"

I ask, as Niki rubs a tit against my arm and tries to slip a hand down the front of my pants. Not letting her get far, I seize her wrist and don't let go. She moans, thinking this is our brand of foreplay. Truth be told, it can be. Just not now.

"Why would I do that?" Kai glances at Big's door with guilt, knowing damn well he screwed up.

Right on cue, the pitter-patter of female steps echoes against the floor of the hall. I'd know that sound anywhere. Their owner comes into view a moment later. Her hair is tied up in a messy bun. Dark circles encase familiar eyes. She's in pajamas—one of Big's oversized Harley shirts that reaches her knees, and striped bottoms. Placing Niki against the wall, despite her whiny protests, I go to my favorite person in the world and pull her into a hug. She fits perfectly against my pecs, her cheek resting there.

"Hey, Baby Doll." I pepper the top of her head in kisses, then sigh in contentment as her warmth and love seeps into me, calming my racing heart.

"Hey." Bink yawns.

The door to Big's bedroom crashes open and the tall, tattooed, asshole is buck naked when he steps into the frame. Big reaches out for Bink's forearm and I release her before things get ugly.

"Sugar Tits," my oldest friend groans as he wraps his old lady in his arms and drags her into his bedroom like a caveman. The door slams shut in his wake, the lock clicking into place, as I turn my annoyance onto Kai, who looks surprised by the turn of events.

I point to the closed-door evidence. "See. What did I tell you?"

"He texted her." Kai sounds defeated.

Ding. Ding. Ding.

Fisting both hands down at my sides, I wanna punch him in the mouth for not following direct orders. "Yeah, dumbass.

He did. And she loves him, so she'll let him smother her all fuckin' night long, no matter what. This isn't what she needs." What she needs is an old man with his head screwed on straight. Not a needy Big. Unfortunately, that's exactly what she's gonna get tonight. She'll be lucky to leave his sight to pee, let alone do anything else. Her female parts will be raw come morning.

"I didn't know." Kai blinks in confusion.

Bullshit.

"Yes. You. Did. I fucking told you. Didn't I? I walked you through the whole thing," I grit when I should be handing him his ass for the stunt he just pulled. VP or not, I've been here longer and know a helluva lot more. He should be taking cues from me, not acting like he's some hotshot know-it-all. Not that he does, or thinks that, per se. Kai's a stereotypical surfer boy—chill to the core. Too chill sometimes.

"It was a mistake," he amends with a singular nod and look of remorse, as if that'll wash away his indiscretion.

"You might be new, Kai, but we can't afford mistakes. *You* let Bink kill people. *You* didn't take her in the house. *You* didn't protect her. *You* put her in harm's way. Now Big's fucked up 'cause of it, and he's taking it out on her 'cause you didn't take his cell phone." That's reality. The bitter ugly truth of it all. He can swallow a slice of humble pie, or he can't. The choice is his. It's nobody's fault but his own. He found her roaming the grounds in the middle of an attack when she was trying to bring her Sacred Sisters back to her house for protection. Little did she know men were infiltrating the walls of our goddamn compound. According to them both, Kai carried her back to her place over his shoulder, intent on getting her to safety when shit hit the fan. Thus putting her in the line of fire. When he could've taken her into the nearest house—Deke's.

Not appreciating the truth exploding in his face, Kai's head rears back. "You can't blame me for this." He rubs with the edge of his cut between two fingers, his chest pistoning for air. "She was out there by herself last night. Don't pretend Bink's innocent here, Gunz."

"Not anymore she's not!" I growl, taking a step forward, ready to make him pay for his sins, fist to flesh. Pain on pain.

Butting her nose in where it don't belong, Niki steps between us like she's afraid I'll beat the tar outta Kai. She ain't wrong. "Babe, I think you need to calm down." Her palm flattens between my pecs and I swear I see red. It's a blip, a mere second, but it's there. The rage, the frustration, everything I do my best to keep in check fades out and rushes back in all within a breath. It scares me, but not enough to relent. Not from this.

"I don't need to do shit, Niki." My tone icy, I pry her hand off my chest and push it back at her. "Mind your own business, please."

Mindful not to provoke me, Kai gestures toward my bedroom. "Walk it off, bro. Walk it off. Get your head straight."

Like hell either one of 'em are gonna tell me what to do. I can make my own choices. I have more than twenty years on each of them. When they've run with the SS as long as I have, been through what I have, seen what I've seen in and out of the club, they can give me life advice. Until then, they can…

"Fuck off," I snarl, my upper lip curling back.

Not wanting to make things worse, Kai lifts both hands in childish surrender. "Gunz, come on, man, chill out."

"Why? 'Cause you're the one who fucked up? 'Cause you're new? You do realize you're lucky as hell Big didn't take you into that shed tonight and make you pay."

"He wouldn't do that."

I laugh. It's low and cruel, but nothing less than what he deserves for his stupidity.

"Wrong. If you think he wouldn't do that 'cause you're a brother, you need to rethink your importance here. She's his. Has always been his. Will always be his. If he had to pick between saving a bus full of children and saving her life, he'd pick her every time. Your actions are what did this to them. Not hers. Everyone knows Bink's impulsive and stubborn. That she doesn't always listen when she should. But everything she does is out of love. What you made her do is inexcusable. Big may forgive you, but I'm not sweepin' this under the rug. Not when you can't take a simple goddamn order and follow through. If you don't get your shit straight, you won't be VP here. We'll find someone more qualified." I'll make sure of it.

Through with the bullshit, with Niki's neediness, with the strong possibility of fatherhood looming overhead, with Kai, and everything I can't fucking fix yet want to, I turn to face my favorite club whore and lay down the fucking law. Tonight's not the night to toy with me. I'm a patient man. It takes a helluva lot to knock my world off its axis. Consider it knocked the hell off. At this point, it's rolling down the highway to hell with no end in sight.

"Go home, Niki," I order.

Hand flying to her mouth, she gasps. "Why? I thought I was staying?"

"No." My head shakes in firm side-to-side jerks. "You're going home. I have shit I need to deal with, and you're a distraction." *And Mel...Kit doesn't need you prancing around here naked. I'm not gonna let you screw up a chance for me to meet my kid. If he's my kid.*

"I'll stay in your room. I promise." Niki drops to her knees at my feet like submission will change my mind.

This should please me. It should make me painfully hard.

Any other night, I'd relish the sight. But I can't muster a single desire to fulfill her needs or mine.

I cross both arms over my chest to keep from touching her and giving the wrong impression. "No. You won't. You want my dick, and I don't have time to give you my dick. So, there's no use in you staying."

"That's okay. We don't have to have sex." Peering up at me, Niki fixes her hair over her shoulder as her lips pucker in a silent plea.

I sigh to myself.

It's sex or nothing. We aren't friends with benefits if that's what you're thinking. It's mutually beneficial fucking. Nothing more. She's a club whore who likes to spread her legs for bikers. That's the status quo and I have no desire for more, even if something beyond lust fueled my veins when I was around her. I've never been in love, don't know what it feels like. And if my incapable heart could feel it, it wouldn't be with her.

"Not the point." I slice my hand through the air when she opens her mouth to argue. "Please get your things and go. Since Big's taken care of for the evening, Kai can see ya out."

Taking my leave before Niki gets a chance to piss me off, I flash Kai a look that says he better not screw this up. He nods as if reading my thoughts loud and clear. Good. We're done.

Needing a moment of solace, I go straight to my office and shut myself inside. I click on the small lamp next to my computers. Yes, plural. *Computers.* My office space isn't used like Big's, or anyone else's for that matter. This is command central for the Sacred Sinners' money flow. I'm the man who finds it, washes its digital imprint, and adds it to our line of investments we launder money through. It's taken years to get us to this point, but my mad tech skills have it running like a well-oiled machine. This is where I go to get my happy, besides the bedroom. This is where I'm most useful. Apart from the surveillance and securities I run.

I take a seat in the leather chair behind my L-shaped desk and count to ten. When that doesn't suppress my ragged nerves, I open a drawer and pull out a glass. Setting it next to my backlit keyboard, I open an expensive bottle of scotch and pour two fingers deep. It was a gift from Big ages ago and I'm the only one who's ever had a taste.

Leaning back in my chair, I sip the liquor, enjoying the warmth it spreads from the center out as I scan the room I've called mine for years. Gray walls, a black desk, and a recent picture of Bink, Harley, and me, rests on the only other piece of furniture I have—a shelf that holds the extensive collection of old vinyl records I've collected since I was a kid. Mostly rock albums with a bit of other tunes tossed in. On top, next to the picture, is where I store the player. Not that it gets much use. Nostalgia isn't lost on me, but neither is the convenience of digital music on my phone and the wireless speaker I can take anywhere.

If I had the energy to get up, I'd select some Tom Petty and the Heartbreakers to relax with. "Don't Come Around Here No More," would be the perfect fuckin' backdrop to the day I've had.

What a day that was, huh?

Don't think it could've been any bigger of a shit show.

Moving the mouse to wake up my computer, I type with one hand to find what I can about this Melanie and her son Adam. There's little to go on, considering I don't know their last name, or much else. Then I remember his receipt stunt and Google that instead. Within minutes, I've got my son's mug shot, his birth certificate, social security number, address, and everything else you can think of on my screen. If there was any doubt before that Kit was lying, it's vanished. Adam's the spitting image of a younger me with hair and no goatee. The eyes, the smile, the broadness of his shoulders... it's like looking in a mirror thirty years ago.

I sigh, wearing a small smile as I take in his darker hair and sun-tanned skin—a stark contrast to the blueness of his gaze.

Adam McLeod.

A Scottish last name... interesting.

Curiouser, I dig up dirt on Jeremy McLeod and his now ex-wife Melanie. He's remarried with two kids, living in Utah. Works as an insurance adjuster. Snooze fest. Finding stuff on Mel proves to be more difficult than I expect. Though she did say, she lacked an online presence. It shows. She's scrubbed herself well from the online world. I'm impressed. Why she didn't do that for Adam too is bizarre.

Not having anything better to do, I sip scotch and do what any good father would. I wipe my son's questionable cyber presence clean. The articles about his poor life choices, more specifically, getting caught doin' them, I skim to fill in the blanks before making it all disappear. Sure, I could do the same for part of his record, but that'd appear more suspicious to the authorities. So, I let that slide and handle the rest for his benefit and his mother's.

When I'm halfway through, a light rap sounds at the door.

"Go home, Niki."

"It's not Niki. It's Melanie."

Fuck. I know I haven't left the best impression on Kit by leaving her to fend for herself in a strange clubhouse with Viper. Not the best decision.

When I don't reply right away, Kit knocks again. I like that she respects boundaries and doesn't just come inside. Most women aren't like that from my experience.

"Do you... um... want me to go, too?" she asks timidly through the door.

That's the last thing I want.

"No. Sorry. Come in." Finished with my scotch, I pour myself another to get through whatever's about to go down.

Taking her time, Kit enters and shuts herself inside. You barely hear the closing *snick* before she turns around to face me. And… what a sight. The light from the small lamp casts a delicate glow over her features and a shadow on the wall behind her. She's even more beautiful now—if that's even possible.

Out of politeness, I get up from my chair and offer it to her, since it's the only one I've got. Nobody enters my domain for me to need a second. Not even Big. They know I value personal space and honor that. But I don't mind her here. It's kind of nice to share it with somebody else. Maybe I'll grab a folding chair in the future, for times like this.

Eh. Then again, maybe I'm getting ahead of myself.

Hands twisted in front of her, Kit doesn't move from her spot inside the entrance. "It's getting late. I think I should get going. Maybe I could leave my number to discuss more tomorrow… if you're up for that?"

"You're leaving? Now?" I don't fuckin' like that idea.

Kit's posture stiffens. The tops of her fingers slip into her front pockets. "It's well past midnight, Gunz. I do need to sleep. It's been a long and emotional day for me. And I'm sure you still need time to process. I didn't want to skip out without saying something beforehand." Her forehead crinkles deep in thought. "I think his name is Viper… he suggested I leave my number with him before I go."

I'm sure the asshole did. Probably thinks she's another club whore I've got on the side. Pushing that thought from my mind before anger seeps back in, I check the time on my computer screen. "Damn… You're right, it's late. Will you stay here? We've got room." It's the least I can do for the mother of my son. Plus, I don't want her to go. Maybe she'd never come back and won't answer my calls. I'm not fond of tracking people down if I don't have to.

Kit nibbles her bottom lip. "I don't think that's a good idea."

"Would it help if I said I believed you?" I gesture to the computer screens, then wave her forth. She takes a tentative step forward, then another until she can get a solid view of the display by half leaning over my desk. "I did some digging and found stuff on Adam. You were right when you said you didn't have much of an online presence. Can I ask why my son does, if you don't?"

My son. Christ.

Kit wraps her arms around her middle to keep from touching my things. "Adam didn't clean it for himself, so I figured he wanted the stuff to stay."

Dammit. She has a point. If he's smart enough to do the shit he has, he's skilled enough to wipe his online imprint if he wanted.

"Is it bad that I did it for him?" I nod to the screen she's busy reading. When she's through, her eyes lift to meet mine.

"All of it?" she asks.

"Most."

Kit grimaces for half a beat before schooling her features, and I feel like a complete dick for overstepping. "If he gets mad, then that's between you two. Not me. I'm staying out of it. I've already meddled enough in his life."

Thigh pressed against the side of my desk, I sip my scotch. "Does he know who I am?"

"No. I didn't want to get his hopes up. Not that he'd say he was excited, but I know better."

Fair enough.

"Do ya think I can meet him soon?"

"You mean, while he's still in lock up?" Her spine

straightens and that sass I remember outside comes back in defensive form.

Not wanting to rile her up by pushing too hard, I play it subtle. "Yeah." I shrug a shoulder. "It might be easier through glass the first time."

"For him or you?" She's wary, and my respect grows another inch for the woman I barely know.

"Both?" I hedge, and back down the moment Kit's eyes start to glaze over in deeper thought—the kind chicks get when they're playing a thousand scenarios in their head, most of which are over the top and illogical. To nip this in the bud before she reaches the point of no return—with notions of me kidnapping her son and forcing him to be a Sacred Sinner, which will turn him into a killing machine—all untrue, in case you were headed down the same path, I jump in to bypass this inherent female process. "Hey, if that's not what you want, I'll follow your lead. You're his mom. I'm... just me." I take another sip of my drink, reading Kit's body language.

She tucks a stray hair behind her ear, blinks to clear her overprotective thoughts, nods once, then looks at me straight on. "No. No. I'm just a little shell-shocked by all this. You're taking this better than I expected."

She's gorgeous, isn't she? And smart... and mature. Is it bad I can't stop staring? Observing? Wanting to know more?

I smirk. "How did you expect me to take it?"

"Badly. Name calling. Disowning him. Bad. But you've been very mature about it all. I'm still processing that part. It kinda feels like a dream."

My heart thuds in an unfamiliar way and I disregard the feeling. "I'm not a twenty-year-old kid, Kit, who just found out he knocked up his one-night stand. I'm an old man—"

"Who just found out he knocked up a less-than-one-day stand, over twenty years ago," she cuts in.

I nod in agreement, my smirk twisting into a full, tooth-filled smile. "We did have sex. A lot of it if I recall. All over the place." In the bar more than once, the alley, the… hmmm… I know there's more.

Kit chuckles, her posture relaxing. "So now you remember?"

"Some. What do you remember?" I finish my glass and set it on the desk for later.

"Everything, or almost everything."

All right then. Not what I expected to hear. "How's that possible? You were drunk off your tiny, little ass."

She chuckles, light and sweet. My dick takes notice of the sound and the way he likes it, a lot. "Drunk, yes. Too drunk to remember, no."

Again, I step to the side and give her space to sit down. I don't like her standing here talking. Not when I have so much more I wish to discuss. Sure, it's late, but I haven't wanted to talk to someone like this in… ever. It's different from when I shoot the shit with the guys or chat with Bink about her life or the insignificant things Janie talks about. Even Beth, another woman I'm friends with, we don't do this. Apart from my brother, Kit's the only person I have an outside connection with—beyond the Sacred Sinners and all that surrounds my world here. Don't get me wrong, I love the MC life. Wouldn't trade it for anything. But I've never had any piece of my world that wasn't about the lifestyle. Growing up, my dad was a Sacred Sinner, and my mom was a former club whore turned old lady. What a shit pairing that was. Kit's presence is an unexpected breath of fresh air.

"Please sit." I do the gentleman thing and twist the chair to make it clear this is where I want her. Chivalry isn't dead in my book.

This time, she acquiesces, and I move some paperwork out of the way to prop my ass on the edge of the desk, close enough to Kit, I can see the flecks of gold in her eyes, but far enough, I don't invade her personal space. There's a delicate balance here I don't wanna fuck up. Not when I've got peace and quiet in a place nobody will bother us in unless they wanna visit the shed.

"Thanks." Kit smooths the tips of her fingers over the curved chair arms. I watch in rapt fascination as does my cock which twitches but doesn't thicken.

Keeping my need in check, I help the conversation flow. "Anytime. So, you gonna tell me what you remember?"

"We had sex a dozen times, I'm sure of it." Humor dances in those fine eyes.

"No way," I counter. "Even then, my dick couldn't handle that." I'd have blisters from that much fucking. If you don't have a dick, you don't understand what happens when you go that many rounds. Not only do you shoot blanks after the first few—as in no cum—you also get sore. Doesn't matter if you're a porn star or not, we're only equipped to come so much. A chafed dick isn't a happy dick.

Charmed by my brashness, she grins, and her cheeks twitch as if holding back a laugh. "Well, maybe you didn't have sex with me, but we had a form of sex."

Ahh... that makes more sense.

A blurry, fragmented memory bubbles to the surface of a Harley and a sexy woman with her legs draped over my shoulders. "I ate you out on the back of my bike."

Cheeks suffusing with my new favorite shade of pink, she nods once. "You did."

"And you loved it."

Not the least bit shy, Kit adds, "I did. It was my first orgasm."

"Ever?" I choke, then clear my throat so I don't sound like a fuckin' tool.

Clearly enjoying our exchange, she snickers. "No. From oral."

"Holy hell. Now that's some news. One point for baby daddy." Smiling, I lick my finger and mark the air with an imaginary point. It's not every day a man gets to add first oral-gasm to his list of life accomplishments. Not that I keep that kinda shit. But, for my son's mother, I'm gonna jot that down for safekeeping.

Kit laughs with her entire body. I take another mental note to make her do that more often. If I thought her chuckle was erection worthy, her laugh is downright sexy personified. "You're ridiculous. It was good, though."

"If I remember right, your friend wanted us to have a threesome." Said friend wasn't hot like her. Not even close. She was needy, too. Almost whiny. An image of Niki takes root, and I wince internally. Why I put up with that from her and not a chick who wanted a threesome, I couldn't answer. Perhaps Niki's grown on me. Maybe my patience has matured since then. A lot changes in twenty years.

"But you said your cock was broken from all the sex."

Too bad I don't have the heart to tell her my dick would've worked had I wanted him to. Maybe. Possibly. I'd give it the good ol' college try. Having sex with her friend wasn't on my priority list. I don't have to remember every second of the day to know that to be true.

"We were at our campsite. In a tent, I believe." In our younger days, we camped traditionally. Now that we're old fucks and have the dollars to spend, we rent RVs. A whole slew of 'em.

She nods. "Yep. We were."

"And she was naked." Big floppy tits, no ass. Ergo, not my type.

"She was and so was I."

"Right. No tats then... like you got now." Crossing my

ankles, I jut my chin at her colorful forearms. "Didn't she eat your pussy, too? After we had sex?"

"Yes. See, you remember quite a bit up here." Kit taps the side of her head, sounding pleased as punch. And I'm pleased 'cause she's pleased.

"It was fuckin' hot." I flash her a wink.

Watching her get tongued out by a chick was the hottest part. Not who was doin' it. Think I might've had a hand in that, too. Said something to the woman about gettin' her friend off for me after I'd blown my load inside her. Yes, now I remember doing that. Reckless on my part. Couldn't tell ya why I let it happen, only that it did. Hence, Adam.

Kit's blush intensifies as her fingers continue to rub along the arms of my chair out of nervousness, or to give her hand something to do. I don't know nor care. I just wanna watch. "It was the best sex I've had in my life."

"Seriously?" I arch a brow and will my pulse to get under control. I shouldn't like this news as much as I do.

Don't get me wrong, it's not the first I've heard I'm the best. You know women, especially club whores, they'll say anything to boost a man's ego. Kit admitting it, I know isn't for my benefit.

"Yes. Unlike you, I got married a month later. Jeremy was the second person I've ever slept with."

I swallow hard. "Making me number three?"

"That is correct." It's her turn to return the wink.

Massaging the nape of my neck, I digest that nugget of information, my stomach tight. "Fuck. That's some news." I chuckle awkwardly. Just when I think she can't surprise me anymore, I learn I'm the third in a very short line of partners. I'm willing to bet there's been less than a handful after Jeremy. Probably less than that even. Not that I'm gonna ask. It's none of my business. Her body, her choice. I fully support that, even if I put a kid in her, and hate the idea of anyone else putting their dick where mine's been. Where my son came from. Irrational? Fuck yeah, now ask me if I care. I don't.

I clench my fist on the desk and take a deep breath to cleanse the unwanted thoughts. It's been an off kinda day, between this and the club attacks yesterday. Then the stuff with Niki, I'm not exactly running on normal.

Kit doesn't seem to notice my internal struggle when she throws in, "I'm sure it is, considering your lifestyle." She's not judging. It's a simple comment.

"Does that gross you out?" I counter, hopin' she's not offended by how I live.

Her head tilts to the side. "No. Should it?"

"I did have Niki on my lap half-naked in your presence." While it might not have been the best thing for her to see, it's best Kit knows the score now before Adam gets involved and she's suddenly shocked how we live. Better to lay all the shit out there and let the cards fall where they may.

"According to Viper, that's a common occurrence around here."

My head bobs in agreement. "That's true. We have a lot of regular club whores who put out." Niki bein' the only club whore I bed on a regular. The rest bore me. The others are too young. Sure, gettin' my dick wet in a twenty-year-old would've been fun fifteen years ago. I may like 'em young, but not that young.

"I asked him if she was yours," Kit says, and I chuckle.

"Did he laugh at you?"

"A little," she admits with a small smile. "He looked at me like I had three heads and said he'd just gotten done fucking her in your bed. Then went on to explain Niki and you."

Sounds like Viper.

"That I'm her favorite." I am. By far. Big used to be her second favorite before he got with Bink.

Kit crosses her legs. "Basically." She shrugs a shoulder. "Evidently, you have a sexual chemistry that none of the others have with her, and that's why she's been hanging around for years."

Fuckin' Viper. Kit doesn't need to know all that. Sure, it's true. But damn... Way to throw a brother under the bus.

Dropping my chin to my chest, I pinch the bridge of my nose, clench my jaw, and blow out an irritated breath. "Christ. He doesn't know when to keep his mouth shut."

"It's fine." When I glance up, Kit's waving me off like it ain't no thing. "That's your life. Not mine. If you think that's going to change my opinion of you meeting Adam, it's not. I just appreciate you not making my life a living hell over this. It's not like I kept him from you on purpose." She chews on her lower lip, and I swear the softness of her voice combined with that type of vulnerability is what the best dreams are made of.

Not wanting her to think I'm ever gonna hold this against her, I say what I should've said an hour ago. "If ya need to hear it, I forgive you. You can't change the past. There's no use in making you pay for it when you're trying to set shit straight now."

Kit practically melts into the chair in relief. "Thank you. You don't know how much I needed to hear that."

Now that that's outta the way, we lapse into an easy conversation about anything and everything. I learn she's an online professor and Adam can't keep a job to save his life—a rebel to the core, like his father. She explains Jeremy's part in her past and how he left. The fucked-up shit she rationalizes pisses me off to no end, but I don't let it show. The bastard doesn't deserve them as far as I'm concerned. She's where she should be, here.

Not wanting things to appear one-sided, I fill in what I can about the club and my part. I even tell her about Janie and Dom living with me. About my brother, Bonez, who's a chiropractor by day, a biker by night, among a handful of other things I conveniently leave out for her protection. The more we share, the warmer, lighter, I feel. She smiles... a lot. Yet, I don't get hard, not once. It's a damn miracle.

When Kit's eyes start to lower from exhaustion and she yawns adorably, I keep the conversation flowing, not wanting this night to end, needing her to talk more. To hear her voice one more time. Slowly, I watch her drift to sleep, sitting up, and my heart clenches at the sight. I think this was the most I've talked to a woman in my life at any given time.

Soaking up her presence a few seconds longer, I memorize the wave to her hair, the paleness of her flesh, the curve of her breasts, and the colorful ink wrapped around her arms from fingers to shoulder. When I've had my fill, I hop off the desk to get her to bed. She's not going anywhere at this hour. It's four in the morning.

Scooping her into my arms proves easy enough. Her face tucks into the crook of my neck as she mumbles something. I smile, not tired in the least. If anything, I'm energized.

Opening the door to exit, I jostle Kit a little to get a better grip, not wanting to drop her. I take her to my clubhouse bedroom to get some shut-eye. The door's unlocked, and when I push it open with armfuls of hot baby mama, the sight I'm met with takes every ounce of me not to lose my cool. Asleep on the bed is Niki. Kai, once again, didn't follow orders. Either that, or she snuck back in like a naughty whore. I'll bet money on the latter. He isn't stupid enough to fuck up this bad again. At least, he'd better hope not.

Screw it. I'll deal with this later.

Blowing out a breath, I leave the door as-is and readjust a sleeping Kit in my arms before carrying her to the backdoor of the clubhouse. Again, I try not to wake her as I open the damn thing. She stirs for half a second as we step into the night. The stars are out in full force as I carry her from the front of the compound to the houses in the back—my house. The home I share with Janie and Dom.

I take the front steps of my place two at a time and see us inside without hitting her head or feet on the doorframe. It's a miracle she doesn't wake up when I finally lay her in my bed. Sweat drips from my forehead from exertion. It's worth it. Every bit of it. Not a single club whore has been in my house. Until Janie and Dom, I rarely used the place. There was no need when my bedroom at the clubhouse is adequate.

Looking down at Kit tucked onto her side on my side of the mattress, I brush strands of purple hair off her forehead. She's stunning—cute nose, sharp cheekbones, and the beginning of lifelines in places all of us tend to share when we age. I sweep my thumb across her jaw and her eyelids flutter from stimulation. It's sweet.

For half a second, I wonder if I should change her clothes, then think better of it. The last thing I want is to offend her. I decide to remove her shoes instead. It's the least I can do. I sweep my gaze down her body and the sandals she was wearing are missing. *Shit.* They must've fallen off on the way. I'll deal with that in the morning.

Backing away from her twists my stomach in knots. It gets worse when I stand in the doorway, watching her sleep on my blue comforter. Not liking this view, I round the bed and fold the blanket in half to keep her warm. There, that should do. Kit's cheek snuggles into my pillow as she adjusts to get comfortable. Unable to help myself, I do something I know I shouldn't and drop a single kiss on her temple. My lips linger there, eyes closing as I inhale her fruity scent—peaches and cream.

My cock thickens as I drag my mouth down her cheek to press another kiss there.

Inhale.

Pause.

Her pulse beats under my touch, offsetting mine that rushes faster.

"Goodnight, beautiful," I whisper and tear myself away before I make things worse.

To avoid temptation, I shut my bedroom door quietly. In the living room, I remove my shirt and shitkickers before sprawling out on the couch. I tuck an arm behind my head and hit one of Dom's toys. Chuckling at the plastic alligator, I set it and all his other items on the floor to get some shut-eye.

It eludes me.

For hours, I lay awake, staring at the white popcorn ceiling—thinking.

I grow hard, then soft, and hard again as fond memories and shameless thoughts tumble through my mind on a constant reel of good and bad. The sun eventually casts an early morning glow through the blinds, and I can't seem to care.

Today, I became a father for the first time. A real father. If I go to sleep, the day I learned of Adam will fade, as will the memorable night I spent with his mother.

I want it to last.

It's not every day you're given a gift.

There are very few I can count.

The day my mother died.

The day my father died.

The day I joined the club officially.

The day Bink came into the world.

The day Leech was born.

And today... The day I found out I'm a dad. Even if it's twenty two years too late, I'm gonna make the rest of 'em count.

CHAPTER THREE

GUNZ

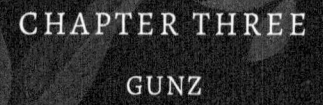

Standing in front of his chair, Prez slams a gavel on the large oak table with the Sacred Sinners emblem burned into the center to commence church before he takes a seat. The room is packed wall to wall with brothers. I sit to the right of Big at the head of the table. Kai, as a VP probie, takes Big's left. As treasurer, Blimp's beside me.

Getting down to business, Big dives straight into the hard shit we gotta navigate. "The attack on the compound must be met with power!" His lip curls back in feral hatred, and the side of Big's fist comes down hard on the oak. The pens go airborne for half a beat from sheer force. "We won't sit idly by and let Remy's shitbag crew come into our home and fuck with our family," he growls.

Prez's statement is met with a chorus of approving grunts.

He keeps going. "I propose we start sendin' members from all chapters to the locations Bongo scouted for us. Take 'em out in high numbers. No more of this small-time shit. It's time to put 'em to ground, for good. It'll be tricky to keep the law outta our way, but I don't give a damn. My old lady killed those motherfuckers on our land. Remy's shitbags will *never* get within a mile of her or any of our old ladies again. Am I clear?" Too agitated to sit, Big pushes to his feet. His chair flies at Viper and he stops the thing before it slams into his legs.

Nods and loud, eager grunts echo throughout the windowless space, giving Prez all the support he needs to make this happen.

"The first set of runs will start in four days. You decide among yourselves who's goin' first. I want six brothers from our chapter goin'. Kai will help organize where you'll be. Gunz has the specs."

On cue, I stand and slide thick packets across the table for everyone to read. Brothers along the wall are handed sets by the officers at the table. The space goes quiet as they ingest the goodies I've provided, which includes Remy's training grounds for his crews and the new spots they're peddling flesh in and out of the US and Mexico ports. There are three in Florida, two in Texas, another in Southern California, two in Maine, one in North Carolina, and six in Mexico we've pinpointed with recent activity. That's not including the large compound they just opened in the mountains of West Virginia. Those weasels so much as cough and we know. That's why the attack on the compound was a surprise. We should've been prepared. We should've seen them comin' from a mile away. Now we're paying the price for our negligence. Bink's paying the price. Big, too. That's unacceptable.

Before all this went down, our Texas chapter and Rosie handled Remy and his crew. Big made a deal with Rosie years ago to let her run things how she saw fit as an unofficial club affiliate. Now that it's escalated to this level, we're bringing in big players, as it should be. You don't have the prez's old lady killin' people on our compound and send a couple knives to battle.

"Any questions?" Big addresses the room, giving them a chance to speak.

White Boy, the young blond of our brood, steps out from behind Tripper. "When we free their merchandise, how's that gonna work?"

Big's gaze sweeps to me. "Gunz already talked to Whisky, and they're prepared to handle the influx of newcomers."

"And we've got safe houses stationed all over the US to assist in overflow," I add on his behalf. There are gonna be a helluva lot more freed people than we think. Whisky, my brother's club president's old lady, and my brother himself, rehabilitate the captives, but they can only take on so many without raising suspicion. The other spots will serve as temporary quarters until they can process them.

"I take it we're goin' to war then," Dallas pipes up.

"Yeah, brothers, we're goin' to war." Big thumps the president patch on his chest.

"It's about damn time," comes from Mickey.

"Hallelujah. I get to kill these motherfuckers," Viper announces.

Before church turns into a blood-lust confessional, I give Big a look. It's a simple one I've used a thousand times before to request unspoken permission to address the brothers. He nods once and retakes his chair, effectively giving me the floor to do what I gotta do. We might as well get this over with before the rumor mill fires on all cylinders.

I raise a hand in the air and the chatter ceases. Just like that, all eyes are on me. I force myself to breathe as my heart beats a little faster. I rub my palms on the front of my jeans before I pull a Dum Dum from my cut and pop the sweetness into my mouth. It takes the edge off. I sigh in temporary relief.

Blimp taps me on the elbow in support, knowin' what I'm gonna say after yesterday.

"There was a woman at the gate last night. She drives the yellow truck you've seen parked out front." I checked in on it before church. It's safe. White Boy took care of it.

I wait for someone to throw a sexual innuendo. When it doesn't come, I scan the room of my brothers, of the men I've had at my side for decades. This should be easy, not hard like it was for me to leave Kit in my house when I came to handle club business on no sleep. I left a note for Janie and one for Kit in case I wasn't back before they woke. God knows what's going on there right now. I wish I knew.

Kit

Stretching both arms above my head, my knuckles hit a wooden headboard as I yawn and pry my eyes open.

I fell asleep in Gunz's office last night. I remember that much. This place is too nice to be a clubhouse bedroom—white walls, blue comforter, and dark oversized manly furniture. There's a die-cast motorcycle on the dresser beside three family pictures—one of a man who looks like he could be Gunz's brother. There's the same blonde from his office picture in another and a tan girl with black hair with a baby in the third. That must be Janie and Dom. The nightstands flanking the bed are strangely neat and tidy, with brushed nickel lamps and white shades. Whoever decorated this room knew what they were doing. Is it weird that I pictured Gunz's bedroom covered in naked posters of women and Harley emblems? Stereotypical, much?

"Morning," a soft, accented voice whispers.

I nearly jump out of my skin. "Shit!"

In the doorway, with an auburn-haired baby boy on her hip, is Janie. I quickly sit up on the bed and tuck the blankets around my waist. "Hi. Sorry, you startled me." Out of habit, I comb my fingers through my hair to straighten out the inevitable bedhead.

"I'm Janie." She waves. It's awkward, like she doesn't know what to say or do with me. The feeling's mutual. Out of politeness, I wave back.

I'd planned on staying in a hotel in town last night. Now, I'm here, in Gunz's house. In his bed, no less. Not what I expected. None of it has been. Not the meeting, not the long and easy-flowing conversation last night. Not a thing. I've been living on my own for years, now that Adam has decided crashing on his buddies' couches is more fun than dealing with Mom or having a stable roof over his head. I live a mundane life that revolves around keeping my kid out of trouble. Obviously, I'm doing a bang-up job of that, too. Sleeping in a strange man's bedroom when I haven't kissed a man, let alone slept with one in over three years, is... unsettling.

I lift the edge of the blanket to my nose and inhale deeply. My eyes flutter closed in pleasure. *Mmmm...* Spicy men's cologne and rain detergent—orgasmic.

"Gunz left a note for both of us." Giving me a funny look, Janie points to mine on the nightstand. I quit being a weirdo and release the blanket to peek at said note. It's on a ripped half sheet of paper, written in small, messy handwriting, signed Erik, not Gunz. I smile at the sight, even if it's ridiculous. We're not some long-lost lovers and he's left me a sweet note. I think I've watched one too many Hallmark romances. Those are a secret obsession of mine, especially the Christmas ones.

"Thanks." I lean over without falling off the bed, pick it up, and rest it on my thigh to read after she leaves.

Janie bounces the boy on her hip as he gnaws on one of those cookies for kids. "There's food in the kitchen if you're hungry. The bathroom's just here." She thumbs to the hall outside the bedroom.

Out of politeness, I force a closed-mouth smile. "Great. Thanks."

Offering a nod of goodbye, Janie exits, and I'm left to my own devices in Gunz's very clean bedroom. I know, I already said that, but it still surprises me. There's not a sock on the floor. Not a smudge of dirt on the wall. Sure, there's a pair of old leather boots by the dresser, against the wall. Even those are mud free. Adam could learn a thing or two from his father.

His father.

Jesus, I can't believe I'm here. On a biker compound, in a biker's bed, and he's the reason I have a son. It's surreal.

Shaking the thoughts from my head, I take it one step at a time.

First things first. Read the note.

Kit,

I smile at my name scrawled diagonally across the top. Apart from Mel, short for

Melanie, nobody's given me a real nickname aside from him.

Don't worry, your virtue remains intact. I laid in the living room after I carried you to my place. I lost your sandals somewhere along the way. I'll find them when I can. I have a meeting with the brothers in the clubhouse this morning. It might run long. If you're up before I get back, please don't leave.

Mi casa es su casa.

Janie knows you're here. I promise she doesn't bite. I can't say the same for Dom. He's an ornery fella.

There's food and drinks in the fridge. Help yourself. If you need a shower, you're welcome to mine. I'm sure there's something in my closet that'll fit you, even if it's too big. Borrow whatever.

Looking forward to seeing you again,

Erik

PS Again. Please don't leave. I will track you down, so save us both the headache and relax for a while.

Okay. I'll stay. That works for me. I've got a few days off, and I don't have to visit Adam in jail again until tomorrow at the next available visitation.

Climbing out of bed, clothes fully intact, I take his lead and pad across his plush, feet-loving carpet and pull the door of his closet open. Once again, I'm met with a shock. It's clean. Shirts are hung by color and style—mostly black with a few other variations mixed in. Another pair of boots and a pair of black Converse rest beside yet another dresser. I pull open the top drawer and find jeans all nicely folded. The next yields shorts and more jeans. The bottom is where the pajamas are hidden. Let's just say it's a sparse collection of pjs, which leads me to believe he either sleeps in boxers or nude. I'm hoping the former 'cause I don't think my brain can digest the latter. Gunz naked twenty years ago was incredible. I imagine it's not much different now. Maybe even better. Not that I plan to find out.

Confiscating the nicest pair of pajama pants with a drawstring waist, I also snag a random t-shirt from a hanger. There are clothes in my truck I could wear, but I'm going to assume a stranger walking around on her own on a biker compound isn't advised. I don't know the rules, so I'm going to follow Gunz's lead. Fewer problems for me and him if I do that.

Draping the outfit over my shoulder, I remake the bed before slipping from the bedroom into the bath to wash. I find a towel under the sink to go about my business. By the time I'm through, I feel refreshed and ready to take on whatever the day brings... even if I'm dressed in a large Harley t-shirt from a dealership in Texas and bottoms so long and baggy, they cover my toes. It works, that's all that matters, as does my bra. At my age, I'd rather lose a toe than walk around people I don't know without one. Hell, if I had sex, I might not even take it off. Let's say, after breastfeeding a nine-pound newborn and sliding over the forties plate, my boobs are less than stellar.

Standing in front of the mirror, I wipe the fog away to see myself. There I am. Not bad. Not great. Just me. Purple hair to hide the gray. I got tired of dying it to keep my natural color, so I decided it didn't matter anymore. Purple's better. Life is too short to care what other people think. This age line on my forehead doesn't matter either. I massage it with my finger, and it smoothens out only to return when I quit messing with it.

There I am... me.

Melanie. Mother. Professor. All around decent human who doesn't smoke, rarely drinks, and is mildly addicted to tea, loud music, and wearing leather bracelets, like the one I'm re-tying on now—simple strips of black cord with a single heart charm dangling from the middle. Adam gave it to me for Christmas when he was in high school. It's a favorite of mine.

Fingering my hair, 'cause borrowing someone's brush without their permission is inappropriate, I do the best I can with what I've got. Next, I refold my clothes in a neat pile and exit the bathroom to set them on the edge of Gunz's bed for safekeeping. Now, it's really time to face reality.

The hall is basic enough and opens into a living room where Dom's playing on the floor with a blonde baby girl and old-school blocks. The oversized flat-screen television is on with a cartoon I don't recognize. Not that I would. I'm out of practice with the baby thing, now that Adam's a grown man, or tries to be.

I step around them and their toys and find myself in an adjoined kitchen, dining room combo where Janie sits at a small, four-person table within eyeshot of the kids. With her is the same blonde from Gunz's photos. Bink, I think her name is. He explained her a bit last night. There's also a brown-haired teenager wearing a huge sweatshirt that hangs off one shoulder, exposing a hot pink bra strap.

They look up at me all at once as if I interrupted a conversation, probably about me. That's how most women work. Gossip is their lifeblood.

Bink lifts a chin in hello. How very biker chick of her. She has bags under her otherwise beautiful eyes, high cheekbones, and she's gorgeous. Prettier than her pictures.

I return a half-awkward wave thingy.

Janie's the first to break the silent stare-at-the-new-woman moment. "Bink, Tati, this is Kit. Kit, Bink, and Tati," she introduces in a mild Spanish accent, her eyes sweeping from me to them and back a handful of times, gauging reactions. She's an observer, this one.

"That's me." I rock back on my heels and point to the kitchen. "Gonna grab a drink if that's cool. Gunz said to wait for him here. I didn't mean to intrude."

"Sure. Help yourself." This comes from Tati, the teen. She smiles my way when the others don't. If anything, they look like I'm infecting their turf with an imaginary fungus and want me gone.

Fantastic. This is going swimmingly.

Drink, then hide. That's the plan. I skate by the table and find what I need in the kitchen. Tea bags are in the fifth overhead cupboard, mugs in the second. I add hot water into a motorcycle-printed cup, microwave it for a minute, and dunk whatever tea Gunz has on hand in the liquid. I'm not picky. Tea's great in all forms—hot, cold, iced, sweetened, unsweetened, black, green, and flavored. I'm a fan of it all.

Blowing on the top, I rest a hip against the counter and look out the large front window that faces the street. Houses line the rear of the compound, all single-story with well-kept lawns. Nothing fancy. Very midwestern, nineteen-fifties suburbia. At the end of the road, there's a sort of cul-de-sac. In the driveway of the last house sits a pink-and-black classic muscle car. From here, I can't make out the model, but it's a nice one.

Across the way, a curvy woman, with brown hair, a bedazzled shirt, and wild print leggings, blows bubbles with her two kids on their front porch—a toddler and a girl, elementary school age.

It's nice here. Much different from what I expected. When you roll up to a biker compound with a mangled gate, you don't imagine women and children living beyond the walls. And you definitely don't consider how normal their lives seem.

I take a sip of hot tea and sigh to myself, wondering how long Gunz will be.

If I hide in his bedroom all day, I'll go stir-crazy. Sitting still isn't my forte. I'm a busy bee. Always working, cooking, cleaning, watering my neighbors' plants… you get the gist.

What if Gunz is off plotting a way to get rid of me?

Maybe he didn't feel the kinship I did last night.

I shake my head to purge such thoughts. He wouldn't have written the note the way he did if he didn't want me here. He's not some young stud trying to add another notch to his bedpost by appeasing the baby mama. The man clearly gets enough tail that he doesn't need to play games.

Waiting it is.

Is it weird I kind of miss him already?

I sound fucking pathetic.

Get a grip, Mel. He's hot, mega hot, and those eyes might be dreamy, but get out of fantasy land.

Gunz

Facing my brothers, I fill in the deets about our special visitor. "The woman's name is Kit, and she's the mother of my son."

The bomb's dropped.

It takes a second for it to explode and reality to sink in.

Mickey steps forth, and Gypsy grabs his bicep to reel him back. "Your what?"

"You got a kid?" Bulk asks, scratchin' his bald head.

"Is she free-range pussy?" This comes from Jizz—dick for brains.

Seizing control of the conversation before it gets outta hand, I keep talkin'. "I knocked her up—"

"We ain't givin' that lyin' whore money," Runner interjects with red-faced hostility as he steps up to the table and tosses the packet of papers back into the middle. They land with an ominous smack and everybody looks to see what I'll do.

Teeth grinding teeth, my hackles rise, as they always do around him. He screwed a dear friend of mine, Beth, over. She loved him. Wouldn't give away her virginity like he wanted, so he took club whores to bed, not caring how that would affect her—a chick he claimed to care for. In my book, if you care about someone that way, you don't mess around. Cheating's for cowards.

Nostrils flaring, I lift a chin in challenge. "Shut your fuckin' mouth, Runner, unless you want this night to end with me bashin' in your ugly mug. She ain't here for money. She's here for Adam, my son. He's in jail. Got himself locked up for doin' dumb shit." That's as much as the young prick deserves to know.

"So, he's grown?" Big asks from his chair, genuinely interested in the news.

"Yes."

"And the bitch kept a kid from you." Runner runs his idiot mouth a second time, inchin' closer to a mouthful of blood and a visit to the dentist. Nobody calls Kit a bitch.

"Again," I growl. "It ain't like that."

Dallas steps up and slaps Runner in the back of the skull. He scowls and flips Dallas the bird. Findin' it funny, I chuckle, as does Big. Runner doesn't care for our amusement at his expense and turns his rude sentiment in our direction. Well, mine. He doesn't wanna poke the bear. Big's in no place to handle any form of disrespect. I smile wide at Runner on purpose, to fuel the childish anger he brought upon himself. I've never liked the prick. For some reason, Big brought him into the club on account of his father bein' a member way back when. Seems the biker gene skipped a generation.

Blimp, God love the man, steers things back where they should be. "Then what's it like, Gunz? Where's she at now?"

"She's at my place." Which he knows, but the others don't.

As if shit isn't already weird enough, Viper's flip switches from chill to aggressive. "With Janie and Dom? What the hell were you thinkin'?"

Bonding with Janie and her boy a dozen and a half times does not make them his. This motherfucker needs to slow his roll. They're mine to care for. Mine to protect. This young-buck bravado needs a serious reality check. First Runner, now Viper—children, the whole lot of 'em.

Not havin' any lip, I put the man in his place. "I was thinkin', asshole, that it's my house and I can let anyone I want sleep there." To further cement my point, I double-tap the Sergeant-at-Arms patch on my chest.

That does fuckall to quell Viper's outburst. "Not with Janie and Dom there, you can't."

Has he even stopped long enough to think maybe I know what I'm doing? That Kit isn't a threat. That I wouldn't let her in my home if she was. I get he's overprotective after what went down, but I'm not the enemy here and neither is Kit. Emotions runnin' high or not aren't an excuse to be a punk.

Keepin' my cool, I arch a brow, when I'd rather roll my eyes at Viper's misplaced bullshit. "Says who, Viper? You?"

Said brother steps forth like he's about to start shit.

Kai cuts a hand through the air. "Hey. Hey. Hey. Calm down. Gunz is talkin'. Show him some respect," he interjects, and everyone shuts their judgmental mouths.

I deliver a chin lift of appreciation.

He returns one in kind.

Undeterred, I continue where I left off. "As I was sayin', Kit's here, and she's gonna stay here 'til I say otherwise. You're gonna show her respect and be nice. No tryin' to fuck her. No tryin' to get her on the back of your bikes. I know we're on lockdown and at war. This ain't the most convenient time to deal with this shit, but I got a son, and he's gotta be a priority, too."

Big stands, using the table to get up, and pounds the top of my shoulder with his giant fist. "Congrats, brother. You do what you gotta do. We're gonna support whatever you decide. Ain't that right?" His intense stare sweeps the small room, his intent loud and clear. *You gotta problem with it, fuck the hell off.*

Blimp also stands from his chair with an old-man groan. "That's right. We got you, brother." His elbow nudges mine.

"Congrats on the kid," Brew, one of Bink's brothers, says.

"Whatever you need, I'm here." Kai thumps his heart twice, then points to me, effectively gettin' himself on the low end of my shit list.

Scratching the base of his neck, Viper wades around Big to slap me on the back of my cut. "Sorry. They're right. Whatever ya need. You know I'm there."

I know he is.

All's forgiven. No hard feelings. Next topic.

Prez does what he does best and jumps back into club business. Kit and Adam are quickly forgotten as we discuss the up-and-coming run, the lockdown, who's on patrol, how we're gonna run our auto shop while on lockdown, and the line of repairs needed on the compound. Blood lust stinks up the room 'cause everyone's eager to take the first run, but we can't spare the protection here. Six guys. That's the deal. One I agree with. We can't let the mother chapter go undefended. Too much is at stake.

"Gunz, you want in on this one?" Kai's got his pad of paper out to take notes.

Going wasn't on my agenda, but I'm not opposed to a run. Probably best I go, considering Kai's too green, and Big's got Bink and his daughter to think of. "If you want. Sure."

Kai scribbles on his pad. "With your tech knowledge and other skills, I'd like to put ya down."

Fine by me.

"If this ain't gonna interfere with your son," Big adds, leaning back in his chair, the eerie picture of calm. I can't imagine the emotional shit he put Bink through last night. Seems whatever her magic touch does, worked. Thank fuck.

"He's got another month in the slammer. What we thinkin', two weeks, a month?"

"Somewhere 'round that," Kai replies.

"And Viper's stayin' back to help with Janie and the kid." My eyes sweep to the man who nods the affirmative.

"I'll take care of them," he vows, and I trust him to do just that. It shouldn't be Bink's job to care for all the women on the compound when their men are gone. I'm happy he's gonna step up.

"He'll be on the next run," Kai adds. "I've got Blimp, White Boy, Mickey, Gypsy, and Runner this time 'round."

My nose crinkles in distaste at the latter name mentioned. "If that shithead can keep his mouth to himself, then I'll go." I point directly at Runner, not givin' a damn if he don't like it.

He rubs the side of his face with a middle finger. "Don't worry, Gunz, I don't wanna blow ya." Gee…subtle and charming, and he wonders why he's gotta beg whores for action. Nobody wants to ride a whiny, oversensitive bitch, when they could fuck a real man. Not a wannabe in leather.

Shaking my head, I don't give him the satisfaction of a real response. "Not what I was referring to."

"Alright, fellas." Big claps his hands. "I think that concludes today's business." Prez picks up the gavel and slams it on the table to end church and the brothers filter out, besides the six leaving in three days, Kai, and him.

Those standing take chairs, and we dive in for a solid hour, goin' over every inch of the run. By the time I'm through, it's past lunchtime and I start to feel guilty for leaving Kit at my house that long with people she doesn't know. As for Niki, I haven't had time to address her poor behavior either. If all that wasn't stressful enough, I've gotta pack for a month-long trip and break the news I'm leaving to Janie, Bink, Beth, Niki, and Kit.

Fuck. That's a lot of women to come clean to.

Pray for me. I mean it. Hell hath no fury like a biker chick worried about her men. The claws are bound to come out.

CHAPTER FOUR

GUNZ

Kicking off my shitkickers when I walk in the front door, I hang my cut on the hook behind it for safekeeping. In the living room, I nod hello to my resident teen, who's too engrossed in the television to speak. Leaning over, careful not to ruin her view, I peck Dom's forehead. He's fast asleep, sprawled across his mama, sucking his thumb. Then I seek the one person I'm dying to lay eyes on before I take a siesta. After church and finding Niki gone, I'm ready to wind down. This no sleep is startin' to catch up.

When I don't find Kit in the main living areas, I check out the only place she could be. At the threshold of my bedroom, I pause as I catch a hottie propped against the headboard of my bed, her body tucked under the blankets, wearing one of my older shirts as she indulges in one of my favorite pastimes.

Happy to watch her all day, I rest my shoulder against the frame and stifle a yawn. "Whatcha readin'?" I prompt when she doesn't notice my presence.

Kit startles, eyes jerking up from the pages. "Oh. Hi. Um. Hey... A book." Holding her spot, she lifts the evidence. "I promise I wasn't snooping. *Much,* anyhow." The beauty shrugs, wearing a coy smile like she's trying to decipher if I'm gonna get angry or let her nosy ways slide.

Even if I was in the mental state to care, I don't see a reason to be upset.

I grin. It's lopsided and half-assed on account of exhaustion. "You were bored, huh?" I tease.

"I was. Sorry." Kit lays the open book on her lap, pages down, to give me her undivided attention. I appreciate she cares enough to give a damn I'm here. Most would keep on keepin' on. Janie does. Though she's a teenager, and this is her home. Different circumstances, I guess.

"Nothing to be sorry for." I scratch my forehead and blink a dozen times to stay upright. "I'm just glad you're still here. You know you could've sat in, oh, I dunno, the living room." I thumb that away in reference.

Kit tucks a strand of hair behind her ear as she looks up at me through her lashes—innocent and uncomfortable. "I don't think outsiders are welcome here." She chews her bottom lip.

I frown.

Whatever gave her that idea? Did something happen? Was Janie not inviting, as I explicitly stated she should be in the letter I left this morning? Guess that's another thing I'll have to get to the bottom of later.

Not liking how the word *outsider* forms on Kit's lips, I let my feelings be known. "Outsiders, no. You, yes. So, how you likin' the book?" I flick my chin at the well-worn black-and-red cover. It's my favorite of the series. Read it half a dozen times already.

Wearing a thoughtful smile, she caresses the spine with two fingers. "It's very good. I'm kind of surprised you have it."

I'm sure she is.

"Why? 'Cause I'm a man?" I wink.

"It's a romance."

Eh. Sorta. Kinda.

"And men don't read romance?" I bait, loving how our conversations bob and weave, regardless of the topic. No judgment. No bullshit.

Readjusting on the bed to get situated, the corner of Kit's mouth twitches in barely concealed amusement. "Not really."

See, that's where she's wrong.

"The series is about badass warrior vamps who listen to rap music and carry weapons to protect their species. It's not just sex and romance. There's action and a well-thought-out plot. Nuff said."

"It's still romance," she counters, her lips spreading into a brilliant ha-ha-gotcha smile.

Oh, she wants to play it that way. All right. I'm down.

"It's not romance. It's the Black Dagger Brotherhood. Not the same thing."

"Romance." Her nose turns up, all highfalutin' and shit. It's cute. Funny, too. She's lovin' this banter as much as I am. Nobody else knows about my reading habit. I keep it on the DL for good reason. The brothers would have a field day with the material I enjoy.

"Fuck. Fine." I sigh loudly, for show. "It's romance. But it's a badass romance. Not sappy shit."

Satisfied with my forfeit, Kit winks. The blush that creeps up her cheeks is sexy. Especially when she's wearin' my shirt, and God knows what else underneath those covers.

"Where'd you find it?" She gestures to the book.

I run a hand over my bald head and yawn. "Katrina, an old lady from the Texas chapter, mailed everyone books for Christmas last year. She used to be a librarian. I got that book, *Dark Lover*. When I asked her old man if it was a joke, he said to read the damn thing. I did..." At night, when I wasn't busy fucking Niki or another random club whore. It's always nice to wind down with a good book.

"And now you read vampire romance."

Here we go again.

"It's not like that."

By the tilt of her head, Kit's not convinced. "It was hidden in the bottom corner of your closet with ten other books from the same series." For emphasis, she holds up both palms, her fingers splayed apart to highlight ten.

Yeah. There's that. They were there, under a folded sheet. If she hadn't been looking through my stuff, she would've never discovered them.

"That you found by snooping."

Those hazel beauties widen in indignation. "I wasn't snooping. I was smelling your shirts. I was bored."

Well…okay. Shit… Not what I was expecting. This woman sure knows how to throw a mean curveball.

"Smelling my shirts." Christ. I love the sound of that, as do other parts of my anatomy.

"Yes." Her head swivels in defiance, and a shot of high-octane lust roars through my veins. "Is that not okay? Are you opposed to women smelling your shirts?"

"You like the way they smell?" My voice is husky, even to my ears. I'm gettin' hard despite my need for shut-eye.

Kit, mother of my son—in my space, wearing my clothes, smelling my shirts, reading my books, and lookin' mighty fine doing it. Damn, this is a fantasy I never knew I wanted—with a woman I shouldn't be attracted to, much less envisioning spread out naked on my bed, reciting *Dark Lover* with that smokin' hot voice of hers.

It's a good thing she can't read my thoughts when she sasses back. "That's a stupid question for someone as smart as you, Gunz."

Touché.

To be closer to the fox, I push off the doorframe and approach the bed. I tear my t-shirt over my head and drop it on the floor at my feet. Her eyes round to the size of hubcaps, and I'm over the moon, watchin' her ogle my chest, abs, and the array of ink with wonder. Since before Christmas, the brothers and I have been workin' hard to stay in shape and eat right, except for alcohol. We're never givin' that up. Not that I was a schlub before, but the renewed effort shows. Even for us old fucks.

"Why don't you scoot your sexy ass over so I can join ya?" 'Cause I know she likes the view, I run a palm down my stomach and over the trail of gray that runs from my chest to the treasures beneath my Sacred Sinners belt buckle. With a quick flip and pull from the loops, it, too, hits the floor with a heavy thud.

"J-join me? What for?" Kit swallows hard, and I delight in makin' her uneasy. The good kind that has her chest rising and falling with laden breaths. The kind that's makin' her panties wet. She may not admit it out loud, but she's a little turned on. Nervous, too. What a heady combination.

"So you can read to me." Playing it chill, to not spook the woman, I remove my club ring and rest it on the nightstand before gesturing to the book.

"W-w why would I do that?" Her voice quivers as I pull back the covers and climb in, close enough to feel her warmth. My head meets the pillow, and I prop an arm behind it, elbow out. It brushes Kit's side. She sucks in an audible breath but doesn't pull away.

Mmm. The closer, the better.

Naked from the waist up, my eyes slip closed of their own volition as I melt into the mattress, letting days of endless stress fade into oblivion. Stuff will sort itself out later.

"'Cause I'm exhausted as fuck," I explain. "I didn't get any sleep last night, and I wanna lie beside you and have you read to me." Can't be any more candid than that. Can I? From my experience, sugarcoating and half-truths don't get you far. No use in pretending I don't want her here when we both know I do.

"But there's sex. I can't read the sex aloud."

I rub her side with my elbow in encouragement. "You already know my secret. I'll keep yours if you blush reading about Wrath and Beth gettin' it on."

"I won't blush."

I peek at Kit through one eye and smirk at what I find. "You already are."

Hiding a smile behind her hand, Kit pokes me hard on the shoulder with the other. "Shut up." Amusement dances in her tone and across what little of her face that's exposed as she watches me.

"Read, woman." I snap my fingers for her to get on with it. Then I return to my dream-readiness state—eyes closed, body relaxed, and dick hard. The latter will go away soon enough. He's just pissed he hasn't gotten off in a while. Not yesterday, not today, and probably not before I leave, if Kit's around. It's not like I'm gonna pull an asshole move and bang Niki when she's here, and I don't masturbate if I can help it. My cock can wait for the real thing. Sure, he's not the most patient. Guess it's a good thing his owner is. Quality is always better than quantity.

"Anyone ever told you you're bossy?" she fires back.

"Never." Another yawn slips free. "Now, put me to sleep with that sexy voice of yours."

"Fine." Kit harrumphs, playing into this banter. "As you wish. But I want it known I'm doing it under duress."

"I'm alright with that."

"Knew you would be."

I snicker. "Glad you're here, Kit." A sense of lightness fills my chest as the hottie ignores my statement and begins to read from where she left off. Kit's voice is smooth, like water running over rocks in a tranquil river. It doesn't take long for me to drift off beside the woman I wanna get to know better, even if it's for the sake of my son. Having her here feels right. Dunno why that is. Not gonna fight the urge to be around her, either.

Wrath removes his wraparounds to show his old lady his eyes, and sleep drags me into its darkened abyss.

CHAPTER FIVE

KIT

Popping another grape into my mouth from the Ziplock baggy I'm holding, I stick with Gunz as he gives me the nickel tour of the SS compound. Why he chose to do this, I couldn't say.

Back at his place, I'd fallen asleep beside him not long after he did. The man doesn't breathe loudly let alone snore. It's a little creepy, to be honest. No movement. No noise. Only a hand that twitched every so often after it migrated to my leg and stayed. When I woke up, he was gone—as in out of bed, but in the same house—playing with Dom while Janie showered. When she was through, he got the bag of spare clothes from my truck. While I love wearing Gunz's jammies, I'm happy to be back in a pair of ripped skinny jeans, a plain purple t-shirt, and my flip-flops he tracked down.

It was bittersweet watching him with Dom, knowing he missed out on those important milestones of Adam's life. You could sense the connection he has with the little one. The joy they experience in each other's presence is undeniable. You can tell a good man from a bad one by the love he shows those he cares for and more importantly, to strangers he doesn't—like me.

This. What we're doing now is a ten on the good-guy scale. Every minute with Gunz is like looking through a window into a different life with a man, unlike anyone I've met before. He's genuine and smart. An odd combination if you've been single as long as I have. Not saying I haven't attempted to date. I have. It's horrible. Sure, when you're in your twenties, it's easy, and every man wants to bone you. When you hit your forties, men your age want younger, sexier women like Niki. Those even older than you also want younger, sexier women like Niki. There's a reason Gunz and her are together, whether it be in the traditional sense or not. That's what men want. What he wants. She is gorgeous.

I offer Gunz a grape. He pops it into his mouth and delivers a panty-melting smile that could light up Broadway. It's hard to look and not experience the effects. Everything about him affects me when it shouldn't. I've had at least a dozen mental orgasms since he returned to the house after his meeting. Between wanting me to read, to the flirting, and taking his shirt off.

Holy hell...

Mind blown.

Ovaries gone.

"This is the infirmary." Gunz opens the door and flicks on a light, but we remain in the hall, on the edge of the threshold.

The room's what you'd expect a sterile space to be. Nothing special—if you can ignore the fact it's inside the clubhouse of a motorcycle club and not a hospital operating room. From the looks of things, it has high-tech equipment and a shelf full of medical supplies.

Unsure what my reaction should be, I bob my head and look ridiculous doing it. "This is nice." I toss another grape into my mouth to give my body something to do besides stand here, looking into a room not all that exciting.

Shoulder resting against the wall beside the door, Gunz unwraps a sucker and studies me. I do my best to keep my attention on my food, the room, and my feet, to avoid eye contact. "You've said that about every room I've shown you."

I shrug. "They *are* nice."

The clubhouse kitchen is where he plied me with fruit after trying to feed me more. I'm not comfortable mooching off people, even if it's just a sandwich. The room itself was industrial in size, clean, and well-stocked. The main room has a new set of front doors and was cleaned of debris at some point today. The pool table, table and chairs, couch, bar, and jukebox all remain the same, as do the signs on the walls and the overall biker den feel.

"You're bored." Gunz twirls the sucker stick between his lips before it settles in the corner of his mouth, rounding out his cheek. He rolls the waxy wrapper between his fingers, turning it into a ball.

"I'm not bored." Not really. He's here and watching him is far from boring. If anything, it gives my dull life something to focus on. When you eat dinner standing in your kitchen, over the sink, you realize your normal has reached an all-time low. Spending time with Gunz in any capacity trumps anything I could be doing in the studio apartment I rent, after losing the house and cars when Jeremy disappeared. One salary could only weather so much. With Adam gone and no desire for stuff to clutter my life, it was economically sound for me to downsize. I'm happy in my shoebox.

"This is uninteresting." He gestures to the infirmary before turning out the light and shutting the door.

Maybe a little, though I'm not about to tell him that.

"It's fine. You wanted to give me a tour."

"Guess there's not much to see, huh?" He smirks, his eyes

crinkling at the edges. It's a good look on him, as I imagine everything is. If you bet me a month ago, I'd meet a man who, after fifty years on this earth, could put thirty-year-old fitness models to shame, I'd have taken that bet and lost... happily.

In the middle of a vacant hallway, I nibble the edge of another grape. Sweetness bursts between my lips, wetting my tongue before I pop it into my mouth to finish. "It's a building with rooms," I note between chews, for no real importance other than Gunz seeing my thoughts laid bare. The more honest I am, the better it is for our budding friendship. With the fiasco of Jeremy in my rearview, I refuse to put Adam through another heartbreak like that. If I can keep this world steady for the both of us, I will.

He contemplates my words for a beat before replying. "Most women are dyin' to see every part of the clubhouse."

I nod, saying nothing because I'm sure they are. Most women here are looking to land a biker, or already have one. That's not my intention, no matter how attractive the motorcycle man in front of me is.

"Do you like dogs?" he asks out of nowhere and pushes off the wall, stowing the trash ball in a front pocket.

I chew thoughtfully. "Is that a trick question?"

"No. Why? Do you not like 'em, or are you more of a cat person?"

Felines and I do not mix. We had a tabby growing up, I'm positive was Satan's right hand. Since then, I've sworn the furballs off.

"Does it matter?" I return, hoping he's not secretly obsessed with cats like he is suckers. There are bowls of them everywhere, and I do mean *everywhere*.

Raising both eyebrows, he strokes his goatee. "Maybe?" The hint of a devilish grin hooks at the corner of his mouth and is gone a breath later.

"Gunz..." I groan, waiting for him to tell me why he's curious.

"Deb raises and trains dogs here."

"To fight them?" I guess, considering the source of where we are. It isn't too far out of character for an outlaw motorcycle club to run a dog-fighting ring, is it?

Scratching the side of his head, Gunz looks moderately offended by my assumption. "God. No. To sell 'em to people who need dogs for protection. Not for fighting."

Whoops.

Gunz

I'm fuckin' this up. Can't say this has ever happened before. Kit wakes up, sits with me and Dom in the living room, keepin' to herself, and I struggled with ideas for us to do while she's here. We can't go on a ride—it isn't safe. Can't fuck—too messy. I don't trust the brothers around her, and I definitely don't trust the Sacred Sisters. Bink's been blowin' up my phone with questions about my lady friend since Big told her who Kit was. I've not responded. As much as I love Bink, this part of my life is mine. I'm not gonna defend it to anybody. I expect them to respect Kit, not because they wanna, but because I demand it. My choice, my business. If I thought she could play nice, I'd give Bink the opportunity to meet Kit again after Big exposed her identity. I know better. She's overprotective. Anything she'll say will only cause problems I don't need right now.

I'm also a selfish bastard.

Sharing Kit's time means less one-on-one. Less learning about Adam and her. And I'm likin' that a whole helluva lot.

To quit boring her to death, I escort Kit out the back door

of the clubhouse. I even do the gentlemanly thing and hold it open, to get a spectacular view of her butt in those tight jeans as she steps into the grass. I'm an ass man. Sue me.

We say little as we cross the road that runs through the middle of the compound to visit Deb's kennels. The dogs are running in their outside pens as we approach. They bark in welcome, then sit without being told as Kit reaches in to scratch a blue nose -pitbull on the head. His tongue lolls out the side of his mouth in excitement, yet he doesn't move an inch as he enjoys Kit's ministrations. She coos on and on about how great of a boy he is, and I swear an unfamiliar piece inside my chest starts to unravel. I'm also half jealous of how sweetly she talks to him.

In comfortable silence, we hit all ten kennels with the same result. The one on the end holds Debbie's newest recruit—a short, brawny French bulldog with blue eyes. I heard Dallas talkin' to his old lady about the breed—how she's trying 'em on for size, for people who want companionship with watchdog capabilities. More bark than bite. He sure is a cute fella with pointy ears and a flat nose.

He snorts in pleasure as Kit kneels outside his pen to love on him.

"You're the cutest little guy, aren't you? So sweet. I just wanna take you home and give you lots of cuddles."

I want her to take me home and give me lots of cuddles.

Shit.

I shake my head to clear such thoughts. Not the place, and definitely not the fuckin' time.

In response, the Frenchie's ass waddles, and I smile at the scene. Might even snap a couple pictures when she's too preoccupied to notice. They'll come in handy on a lonely night.

One of Deb's boys, who helps run the business with their mom, exits the side door of the building and waves. "Hey."

"Hey." I lift my chin in greeting as the lanky kid joins us.

"He's so cute," Kit croons, lookin' between me, the teen, and the pup, unsure where to set her sight.

Deb's youngest pulls a treat from his pocket and drops it into the pen. Vibrating with pure excitement, the Frenchie swallows it whole. "He's Mom's new favorite."

"What's his name?" Kit asks, scratching behind the pup's speckled bat ears.

Kneeling too close to my lady for my liking... I mean, Kit... the kid reaches in beside her to pet the pooch. "Unofficially, we've been callin' him Chibs," he explains as I watch to make sure his fingers stay on his own side of the pup, not getting anywhere close to hers. When they damn near touch shoulders, thanks to Chibs rolling onto his back for belly rubs, my teeth clench down on the sucker stick, my abs drawing tight as I resist the urge to snatch the kid up by the scruff of his neck and force him to leave. If I thought Kit wouldn't get pissed, I'd do it.

I scuff my toe in the dirt to get this... whatever is goin' on in my head, under control.

"Like the Scotsman from *SOA*?" Kit inquires, oblivious to the kid's proximity. He's a red-blooded male, and she's hot. She smells good too—peaches and cream. Don't act like he don't know what he's doin'. He's a teenager. They know. They always know.

"Same one," he agrees on a nod, and I come up empty, knowin' nothing of which they speak.

Kit twists around to look up at me from her spot on the concrete pad, all smiles and beauty. Fuckin' A. I damn near have to catch my breath. "Wasn't he the club's sergeant-at-arms, just like you?"

Good question.

Eyein' my patch, I shrug. "I dunno. Never watched the show."

"Wait…" Her scratching stalls under the Frenchie's chin as that honey gaze sears straight through me, passing judgment. "You read… you know what, but you won't watch a biker show?" Tilting her head to the side, she tries to figure me out. It's cute and a damn waste of time, 'cause she'll never figure shit out. Nobody has, apart from my brother. Not even Big.

"I don't watch TV." Apart from when Bink was little and the rare occasion with Janie and Dom, it's not my thing. Not that I pay much attention. Television puts me to sleep. See, I've got nothin' against biker shows, or any shows for that matter. I just don't watch 'em.

A pair of full lips round in shock, not enough I could fit my cock through them, but enough my brain went there.

Christ.

"Ever?" She gapes, shufflin' her body enough to keep lookin' up at me without getting a crick in her neck.

"No time."

"Seriously?"

I don't think she believes me. Guess that's what happens when you've got better things to do than get lost in a fantasy world with actors and actresses. Running a club, for instance, or caring for people. There are also bikes to wash and wax, boots to shine, systems to hack, and money to be made. Leisure time doesn't exist in my world. Apart from the quiet nights, when I'd rather be reading, fucking, or drinking.

I deliver a flat smile. "Seriously."

"You're saying you haven't seen all the *Terminator* movies then?" Chibs has grown impatient with Kit's lack of attention. He rolls back over and shoves his nose into her palm. Deb's son chuckles and gives the dog a final pat before standing to his full height—not much shorter than me.

I keep talking as he sees himself home across the grass and out of our personal space. It's a relief to get her alone again without prying ears gettin' in the middle of our business, even if it is a stupid discussion about my lack of movie knowledge. "Nope," I respond to her Terminator question.

My answer is met with wider eyes and supple lips parted in a way that shouldn't look hot yet turns my crank. A crease runs from the corner of her brow into her hairline. Her skin flushes a rosy color as she ties her hair into a low bun, staring, thinking, obviously confused. If it wouldn't cause problems, I'd snap a picture of Kit's expression, to savor it. It's one you never wanna forget. Like the way the sun glistens off her purple hair, highlighting the flecks of white-gray that's lost its color. How her pale skin reacts to the simplest things—expressing her innermost thoughts without words.

She inhales deeply.

It's comfortable, the sound of air leaving her lips, her probing gaze that lands on every inch of me like the soft dance across skin.

The sound of motorcycles rumble in the background as my brothers do their thing. Dogs groan and sniff. Then there's her, breathing, blinking, looking more beautiful than anyone I've met before. Brilliant colors dance up her forearms and across her hands. I watch it all, every movement, every tick, as she overthinks like women often do.

A solid minute, maybe two, passes before she breaks the silence. "No, *John Wick? Iron Man? Avatar? Bloodsport? Resident Evil? Fast and the Furious?*" she rattles off, still not buying my ignorance. I smile at her cute ramblings and step up to unlock Chibs' cage before he licks her hand clean off.

Eager as a beaver, he dives headfirst into her lap, knocking Kit onto her ass. A sweet, melodious laugh rings through as I step off the slab into the grass, watchin' him wiggle with joy. Kit doesn't disappoint when she returns his enthusiasm with a carefree brand of her own. I smile wider, just watchin' it unfold. It's the best sight. Right there. Him and her, in their own world, doing what they want, how they want, with no worries. This is why real life is better than television.

Once the excitement has died and Chibs is content to cuddle in Kit's lap, I return to our conversation. "No, I haven't watched a single one."

She whistles or tries to as she catches her breath. "Woo wee." The back of her hand swipes across her brow. "Adam is gonna have a field day with you."

Tucking my arms loosely across my chest, I square my stance. "What's that supposed to mean?"

Head tilting, Kit grins up at me as her back rests against the thick pole that supports the overhanging roof. She stretches her legs out in front of her, not caring if her ass gets dirty. "He's obsessed with movies, rock music, and riding his Honda. Those are his favorite things. Outside the stuff that always gets him into trouble."

My kid has taste and a rebel heart. I don't even know him, and I already like the guy.

"A Honda, movies, and rock music, huh?" I wink, lovin' how her face lights up just talkin' about him.

"Yes. He'd also love these dogs. He's a huge animal lover." Kit finds *the spot* on Chibs' belly and his hindquarter goes wild. I remove the barren sucker stick from my mouth and tuck it away to toss out later. I replace it with a fresh one—strawberry.

"Tell me more," I insist as I offer her a Dum Dum from the inside pocket of my cut. She accepts it with a grateful nod. 'Cause I'm a nice guy, I remove the wrapper and lean down to press the sucker to her lips. With a shy smile, Kit opens and steals the gift with the snap of her teeth. Yet she doesn't yank away. She just looks at me, the ball hidden in the depths of her mouth.

Still pinched between my fingertips, the stick slowly

slides free as our eyes meet, and I have to force myself to back away before I do somethin' stupid. My poor dick gives a cursory twitch, to see if it's time to wake up. *Sorry, bud, it's not.* Kit's now suckin' on one of my Dum Dums, the ones I've only shared with three women in my life—Bink, Beth, and now her. If that ain't tellin' on where my mind's at, then I dunno what is. I'm a private man. I keep everything close to the collar. Until now... for whatever fucked-up reason.

Cheeks puckering, she twirls the Lolli without a care in the world. "What do ya wanna know?"

I stuff my sucker into the crook of my mouth to give me room to talk. "What's his favorite food?"

"Cheesecake."

Interesting.

"His favorite food is cheesecake?" I reiterate for some stupid reason. Like her and me with the movies, I can't believe anyone would love cheesecake more than other food... like steak or shrimp, or some form of meat. What can I say? I'm a carnivore through and through.

"Yep. Sure is."

Now that we've established his favorite, let's hope he fancies somethin' better than plain ole cheesecake. Vanilla's boring, when there are a million other flavors to appreciate, in both food and other parts of life... if you catch my drift. "What kind does he favor?"

More twirling of the sucker. "All kinds. I bake him whatever flavor he wants for his birthday each year."

See... She's hot and a wonderful mom. Not that I ever doubted the latter.

"What's your favorite food?" I ask, 'cause I wanna know. Does she like strawberries or blueberries better? Dark chocolate, milk, or white? How does she take her coffee in the morning? Does she even take coffee in the morning?

Perhaps she likes tea. I like tea. It's the best cure for hangovers and when you need help gettin' some shut-eye.

Cheeks flushing watermelon pink, she shrugs off my question as her eyes leave mine to focus on a sleepy Chibs. "Oh. That doesn't matter."

Like hell it don't.

"It does if I wanna know."

She nods once as if accepting I give a damn, though I can tell she's not used to men caring about her that way. Bet her ex didn't appreciate the way her smile lights up the world, or how her cute toes curl when she's uncomfortable, like now. "I…Um… Okay… I like deep-fried pickles with ranch dressing." A blank statement with no inflection.

"Pickles and ranch." Again, I repeat what she says like a goddamn moron.

"Yessss," she draws, forcing an awkward smile. "Don't make fun."

"You mean…" Hating how closed off she's acting, I pop the sucker from my mouth and point it at her playfully. "Like the way you teased me about reading romance."

My sarcasm is met with a similar sugary ball directed at my face. "Fine. You win. Tease away." She snickers, pleased with herself.

"Don't worry. I will. Out of all the food you could choose, you pick fried pickles dipped in ranch." I roll my eyes, grinnin'.

Wouldn't be my first choice, but I appreciate she owns her likes and doesn't pretend to enjoy whatever I do. You'd be surprised how many chicks are like that. You love motorcycles and now they do. You have an addiction to grilled cheese sandwiches, and suddenly they can't get enough of 'em. You and I both know, some of these bitches count calories in every bite.

Not backing down, Kit adds, "We were poor growing up.

Every year, Dad would take us to the fair and let us buy one thing we wanted. My brother always picked the elephant ears. My sister, the funnel cakes. And—"

"You wanted fried pickles," I fill in for her.

"Precisely."

"Your family still around? Hey..." I start to apologize for bein' too forward when it's none of my damn business, but she moves on like I'm not a nosy bastard as Chibs begins to snore far too loudly for such a tiny creature.

"No. My parents are dead. My brother died in the military, ten, no, eleven years ago." She taps her chin. "My sister, we never got along. After she graduated from high school, she left and never came back... You have a brother named Bonez. Is that all?"

This queasy, fluttery sensation settles low in my gut when she asks me about me like she gives a goddamn.

I chew on the inside of my cheek and motion to the clubhouse across the street. "My family's here. But there's no other blood relation 'sides Adam and Bonez."

"He doesn't have any kids?"

"No. We're both too fucked up to raise kids." Ain't that an understatement? We'd do far more harm than good. The demons we live with don't just disappear. We're both smart enough not to put that on our own blood, or a partner.

She scowls. "I don't see how that's true. From what you said last night, you sorta helped raise Bink and you're doing a wonderful job helping Janie with Dom."

"Bink had Big, too, and Janie is a fine mother without my help." End of story.

"See. I don't believe that. You're a great guy."

No, I'm not. I'm really not.

It'd be rude to scoff, so I suck back the reaction for Kit's sake. "As a friend, sure. As a brother, yeah. As a father, no. As a husband, hell no. I'm not built that way. Our mother saw to that."

"Do you wanna talk about it?" Kit asks. The wave of soft-faced, open-minded sympathy she produces is downright stifling.

Fuck no, I don't wanna talk about it. I can't believe I said as much as I have, which is more than anyone else knows. This woman's doin' a damn fine job gettin' under my skin.

"I'd rather not." I'm polite, despite the chill I get when mentioning my mother.

Don't get me wrong… It's sweet Kit asked. Nobody does. 'Cause I don't give them a reason to, I guess. When you were raised like we were, it's easier to forget. People wonder why we're fucked-up deviants. Probably think it's genetics, since our mom, Cassie, was a club whore. The thing is… club whore or not, doesn't fuckin' matter. No mother makes her kids do what she made us. And ya wonder why relationships and us don't mix. Why Bonez can't decide whether he wants to be fuckin' a chick or submissive under a man. I know that bitch screwed him up more than me. Made him take it up the ass for money, to pay bills our father wasn't there to help with. He was too busy gambling and ridin' to care.

Bonez got sold to the cleanest-cut motherfuckers in the highest-class neighborhoods. Top-dollar teen ass. She broke him in first, then added me to the roster for lonely middle-aged housewives with rich husbands. Who doesn't want a rent boy who matured early for his age to plow you and tell you you're pretty? They paid extra for the flattery. An all-service buffet between the two of us. Mom was livin' the high life. Nice clothes, a new car, and what did we get? We fucked or got fucked twice a week for years. Even had couples who wanted foursomes. And the truth of it all? I liked it. No, I *loved* it. The power was all-consuming. I was addicted to the feeling of older bitches wanting to fuck me. Women who thought my dick was good enough. I was a God to them, makin' 'em come in ways you could never imagine. They made the teenagers my age seem like inexperienced children in my eyes. I wanted to learn from them. To worship them. To dominate them...

Have you run to the bathroom to vomit yet? 'Cause that's what you get when you skim the surface of my past. Sick shit all thought up by one devious, evil fuckin' cunt with dark hair and green eyes.

I hope you rot in Hell, Mother.

Kit reads my sour mood and snaps her fingers to pull me from the past into the present. She scoots her ass along with Chibs off the concrete slab, onto the grass beside me, then pats for me to join her. "If you do wanna talk, you know you can tell me. We might not know each other all that well or that long, but I'd like to consider you a friend. Is that weird? My son's father as my friend?"

"No. I feel the same." Gettin' my old ass to the ground, I groan when my knees pop and the back of my neck aches from stress. But I make it, close enough to smell her sweetness, but not enough to invade her space. Leaning a bit to get comfortable, I splay my fingers in the grass and sweep my sights over the rear of the compound, or what I can see of it.

"Then as your friend and the mother of your son, I have to say, I'm leaving tomorrow to go visit him in jail." Her shoulder bumps into mine and I wanna groan for a whole other reason.

God, what this woman does to me.

I force myself to focus on her words long enough to reply. "You mind if I tag along?" Tomorrow's as good of a time as any to meet Adam. I'd rather do it before I set south on a run. If I die, at least he can say he met me. Not much good that does.

"If you want," she replies.

"This is also the place I tell you, as a friend and sperm donor, I'm goin' on a run in three days." Not like Kit's gonna go crazy over the news. She can't know enough about runs to worry unless she learned too much watchin' *SOA*.

She kicks off her sandals and squishes her adorable toes in the grass. I watch every movement like some lovestruck teenager, which is goddamn absurd. "To where and for how long?" she asks.

I shrug. "Can't say. Even if I wanted to, I couldn't. That's how this works."

"Club business stays club business."

"Yes. Did you learn that watchin' *SOA*?" I sideways glance at Kit to read her reaction.

The blush creeps back in. "Maybe." She hollows out her cheeks and sucks mighty hard on the last bit of Dum Dum.

Fuck.

I close my eyes to stop lookin' at her and swallow down a groan before I spring a physical boner when my brain already has the biggest hard-on.

"Kit," I rasp.

"Yes?"

"Can I tell ya somethin'?"

"Anything," she breathes.

Goddamn, that simple skin-pricklin' word hits me like a sledgehammer to the chest.

"I-I'm glad you're here," I choke out, curling my fingers in the grass to get a tight grip. My nails sink into dirt, my forearms throb with tension, and my balls ache.

"Me, too," she whispers.

"When I'm gone, I'd like to keep in touch." Every day. After this, she'll be lucky if I let her outta my sight.

This is fucked up.

I'm fucked up.

What the hell is wrong with me?

"I'd like that, too," she agrees.

Just like that, things settle in my world as we sit side by side in the grass, almost touching but not quite. Scratching a sleeping Chibs in her lap, we watch the sun begin to set on the horizon. The oranges and pink hues are a perfect send-off to the day. Later, when we've gotten our fill of fresh air and alone time, I'll fix her dinner at my house. If she's anything like the woman I believe her to be, there's no way she'll turn down a hot grilled cheese sandwich and tomato soup. Then Kit will stay the night, in my bed, while I take the couch. But only after we finish reading *Dark Lover* together. To some that may sound boring as fuck, but after the weeks I've had, peace is all I want. And with her around, it seems to come in spades.

CHAPTER SIX

KIT

I'm not crying inside a gross jailhouse bathroom. Nope. I'm not sitting on top of a toilet, inside a stall, bawling my eyes out, and using the equivalent of tree bark to wipe my snot. That's not me. I'm not that woman.

Except… I am.

We're here.

I'm here… with Gunz.

He's out there on those same benches I told you about. The cold ones. The ones that suck the soul from your marrow. He's here with *me*. Melanie. Adam's mom. The woman who dropped unceremoniously into his life thirty-six hours ago. Nobody's ever visited this place with me. Not a single person. But he is, wearing a handsome smile that doesn't quite reach his eyes because he's having a small mental freakout about what we're about to do. He drove his truck behind me the entire way, then removed his Sacred Sinner vest when we parked in the lot across from the jail. They don't allow colors inside, and we don't need to draw unwanted attention.

There's a metallic screech as the outside door opens. Somebody clears their throat, and it's not female. The thud and scrape of heavy bootheels cross the cracked linoleum and stop beyond my stall. I am... or was, alone.

Another gruff clearing of the throat. "Babe?"

My stomach swoops and crashes at my feet, then I'm the one clearing my throat. "Y-yes?"

"Whatcha doin' in there?" He raps on the stall door with a solid *knock, knock*.

"Peeing?" I scrub both hands down my face to regain a semblance of composure. How embarrassing is this?

The same screech echoes ominously as another person enters the facilities and gasps at the sight of Gunz—tattoos, muscles, well-worn jeans, bald head, goatee—the whole biker package.

"This is for women," the newcomer chastises.

"No shit," comes from my visitor.

"We're in a jail and you're in here creeping on women."

The omnipotent sound of Gunz's boots scrape beyond my door. I catch a flash of skin out of the corner of my eye as he faces the lady with a bad smoker's rasp. His hand cuffs over the top of my stall. Trimmed nails attached to long, strong fingers and a skull ring relax there. Like a weak fool, I stare in wonder at them as I dab the remaining tears from my cheeks with toilet paper.

"No, ma'am. There is no creepin' to be had. I'm here with my old lady, takin' care of her before we go see our son. You gotta problem with that?"

I swallow hard as his words echo through the space. *Here with his old lady. Seeing our son.*

"Oh. Um. Sorry. No. No, problem." The woman coughs to cover her discomfort.

"Good." The fingers draped over my stall double-tap the metal before they disappear, and he moves toward the exit.

"Now, I'm gonna step out so you can do your business. Then, I'm gonna come back when you're finished. 'Cause, like I said, I'm here to take care of my woman."

My... woman.

Good God.

The stall beside mine creeks open. "Sure. Thanks," comes from the woman.

Gunz pushes the outside door and the white noise from the waiting room filters in. "I'll be back in a minute, babe, unless you wanna get your tears dried up and meet me outside. Don't think we want another jail visit tonight."

Right.

Right.

Of course, he's right.

We don't need him getting into trouble for my emotional mess.

I spread my jean-clad thighs and drop the paper in the toilet, then watch in blank fascination as the water in the bowl soaks in, turning it transparent. I breathe in and out, letting oxygen saturate my lungs just as the water does the paper. The tension in my shoulders dissipates on a harsh exhale. "Yes. Sorry. I'll... finish up."

"Take your time and don't apologize. You're allowed to feel whatever you're feelin'."

Is he real? I just can't with this.

As the door comes to a close, I slap my cheeks for good measure as the woman peeing in the space beside me thumps the wall between us. "You've got yourself a good man."

I do, don't I?

Gunz may not be mine, but he is one of the good ones... for Adam's sake at the very least. Let's hope this visit goes well today.

"Thanks," I reply as I right myself, flush the commode with renewed strength, and get on with this damn thing.

We're here.

Adam has a father now and we're about to blow this bitch wide open. There is no going back. Only forward.

As Tom Hanks says, "There's no crying in baseball."

Game on.

CHAPTER SEVEN

GUNZ

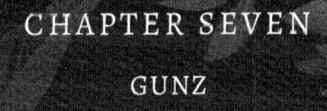

Kit sits her fine ass on the stationary stool in our booth as we wait on Adam to arrive.

Fuck, I'm nervous.

I stuff both hands into my front pockets and chew the inside of my lip. I had to empty these pockets before we came inside, or I'd have a Dum Dum hitching a ride in my mouth by now.

It's been years since I've been inside a room like this. Sure, it's common for brothers to be in and out of jail. I visited a few of them in my youth when they had a higher propensity of gettin' caught. Mostly Blimp and his hornball ways. We're smarter now. With age comes wisdom. Plus, money talks. Don't believe anybody who tells you any different.

Not wantin' to crowd Kit when I know she's nervous, I stand behind her and keep my distance. There's not much space to do that, but I'm tryin'. It's the least I can do after I found her cryin' in the bathroom. She hasn't said much since. I'm all right by that as long as she doesn't ask me to take a hike.

A line of stools flank either side of plexiglass, and old-school payphones hang on hooks to use for communication. The lighting's dim. Too dim. A guard takes his post beside the steel door we passed through as another does the same on the convict side. The bigger of the two is with the criminals. His back's propped against the wall, arms crossed over his chest as he waits for men to enter.

Sweat tickles down the nape of my neck before it soaks into the collar of my shirt. I ball my hands into fists inside my pockets and clench my teeth to calm the hell down.

Fuck.

It's about time.

I swallow thickly as the first tatted-up man enters in a jumpsuit and finds his family.

Fuck.

It's not every day you meet your son. Your flesh and blood.

Three more find their spots. The woman in the booth beside us does jazz hands when her scrawny boy in sweats waves at her through the window. I try hard not to smile and fail. They're excited to see each other, that much is evident.

In saunters a big, scary motherfucker who takes up half the aisle as he makes bedroom eyes at what I assume is his old lady on the far end. Her tits heave out of her low-cut tank top as she blows kisses to him from her seat.

Then the atmosphere changes.

The air thins.

Kit notices Adam half a beat before I do. Her body goes taut, and she blows out a low breath as he steps into his side of the booth.

Adam's eyes, the same color and shape as mine, meet his mother in hello then tilt to examine me like I'm an organism inside a Petri dish. They falter, as does his poker-faced expression when he realizes who I am.

Smart kid.

Tears well in my eyes.

They swim in his too as his mouth opens and closes in disbelief.

I tip my head in greeting and swear my heart nearly explodes when a lone tear begins its trek down my son's cheek before he swipes it away with the back of his hand just as quickly as it appears.

Kit tugs on my pant leg, and I finally break eye contact with Adam to look at her. She's smiling, despite the blotchy flush to her cheeks from breaking down in the bathroom.

Gorgeous.

Unable to control myself, I tilt her head back and bend to drop a kiss on her forehead.

"Best. Day. Of. My. Life," I whisper to her hairline.

She sighs a wispy, delighted sound that shoots straight to my groin.

I groan lowly in response.

My lips still attached to her warmth, 'cause I can't seem to let go. She touches the side of my face with gentle fingertips. I close my eyes and feel her there, smell her.

"I'm gonna talk to our son."

I nod.

Our son. *My* son.

Fuck.

A frog lodges itself in my throat, makin' it hard to breathe.

I'm a pussy. I get it. I'm a goddamn pussy. I'd planned what I wanted to say to Adam on the ride here. Down to the speech about gettin' his shit together and how I wanna help him do that.

Now look at me. I'm a mess.

If Big saw me now, he'd give me shit for goin' soft. Then

again, maybe not. He's got a daughter now. Things change when you become a parent.

"You can speak to him when I'm through, okay?" Kit traces my jawline in the barest of touches. My lips tremble against her forehead.

I nod again, once, knowin' I can't speak. Adam's watching us. Bet he thinks I'm a sorry fuck for a father, actin' this way with a woman I barely know.

"Can you let me go to talk to him—Gunz?"

Right.

Shit.

I release Kit and glue my ass to the wall, to keep my hands to my damn self. She delivers a faint, albeit sweet smile over her shoulder before she picks up the phone. Adam's already seated on his stool, receiver ready.

Their voices are low as they speak, yet Adam keeps looking at me and back to his mother every few seconds. He nods the same as I do when Kit says something that has his throat bobbing and eyes watering a second time. My kid fidgets, and his mom plays it calm. Not the bundle of nerves I expect her to be.

When they're through, she waves for me to take her seat, and I go without question. Her hand brushes across my shoulder before she retakes my place against the wall to give me a chance to...

Fuck.

"Hey." Adam's voice is rough through the phone, like he swallowed a bowl of gravel... like mine.

"Hey."

"So, you're my—"

"Father. Dad... Gunz. M-my name's Gunz." I sound like a complete moron, fumbling over words. Speakin' too damn fast. Not breathing.

I pinch the top of my thigh to reel in these stupid nerves.

"And you're a biker."

Guess Kit filled in a lot during their brief talk. Wonder what else she told him.

"I am," I confirm.

"Mom tell you I ride?"

I smile with pride. "She did."

Adam's lip kicks up at the corner. "Not a Harley."

"That's all right. Not everyone can have good taste in bikes." I wink, so he knows I'm just givin' him hell. Unlike many of my brothers, I don't care what you ride between your legs as long as you ride. Though, I'm not sayin' I don't think plastic bikes are bitch bikes... 'Cause they are.

He snickers, shaking his head in amusement. "She found you, huh?"

"She did."

"You didn't know about me, did you?"

Great. *Way to jump straight into the hard stuff, kid.*

"No." I'm honest. "Wish I had. Wanna know you now if that's something you'd want."

Adam pauses to digest my words. It feels like a lifetime before he speaks again, his tone somber. "Not sure what Mom told you, but I'm... a difficult person. I fuck up. I'm not perfect. My da..." Adam clears his throat and rocks back for a second before finishing his thought. "Her ex-husband didn't like me much."

Fuck that bastard for makin' him feel unloved. That sad sack of skin deserves to be worm food as far as I'm concerned. If he didn't have kids and an old lady, I'd call someone up to take him out. He's lucky I'm nice. A real mensch.

"His loss."

Adam cringes and scrubs the top of his head, messing up his hair. "You seem like a... um... a decent guy, sure, maybe.. but do yourself a favor and forget she contacted you. This isn't worth the trouble. You've got your own life. I... I'm... Listen, it was nice to meet you. But it's not—"

Nope. Hell no. Hell fucking no. We're not doing this. He's not puttin' me in the same goddamn category with the pissant he once called daddy. I am not like him, and I will never be like him. Adam is not a burden. He isn't a mistake. This self-preservation mode he's projecting, I get. Still, I'm not gonna let him think he isn't important. Not for any second of any day, ever.

"You are worth it, and I sure as fuck ain't goin' anywhere," I declare with the strongest conviction I can push through the phone when I'd rather hug him. "When you get outta here, I plan to see you and get to know you. On your terms, of course. Ya hearin' me?" I jab a finger at the glass separating us, hitting it hard enough to get my point across. "You're my kid." I point to my chest. "What you've done or haven't doesn't change shit. You. Me. We're blood. You're mine. I ain't going any-fucking-where. Yeah?"

Staring at his lap, Adam bobs his head along as if he heard everything but can't speak.

"There is no you and your mom anymore. There's us... Me, you, and your mom."

More bobbing and a tug at the hem of his sweatshirt.

"You gonna let that happen?"

A single-shoulder half-shrug.

"Mom says you got about a month left."

A firm nod.

"I gotta leave on a run with my club this week, but I'll be back by the time you get out. Can we agree you won't kick me outta your life 'til you've gotten to know me enough to decide that?"

Truth? I wouldn't let him do that anyhow. I can be a stubborn asshole when provoked.

Adam's head snaps up in panic, redness rimming his eyes, his bottom lip chewed half raw. "I'm not… That's not…"

I infuse gentleness into my tone to calm him down. "It's cool. We're good. Everything's good, Adam. We'll grab a beer and hang wherever you want."

"Sure."

A loud buzzer signals we've got a minute to wrap up goodbyes and my stomach turns over at the thought of leaving him. We didn't get enough time. No wonder Kit hates coming here.

I tap on the glass a second time. "Keep your nose clean in the meantime, yeah?"

A round of absentminded nodding ensues. "I will."

"Good man." Flattening my palm against the glass, I get up from the stool, unable to handle saying bye to my kid, not like this. Without a backward glance, I hand the phone to Kit and exit the area. There's no way I can watch him walk back into jail.

Needing the space to process shit, I weave through the benches and people waiting to see their family and hightail it outside where I can breathe easier. I cross the road, open the tailgate of my truck, and sit on it with my legs hanging over the edge.

I can't believe I'm a father.

A real father.

I have a kid who looks like me.

And I just fucking met him.

Not five minutes later, Kit joins me. She lays my keys, phone, and suckers beside my hip. Greedy for a fix, I rip open a Dum Dum and practically inhale it.

"That was a lot, wasn't it?" she prompts, swaying back and forth, hands clasped behind her back.

I shrug, not wanting to put my crap on her. "Yes and no."

"Well… what did you… You know?" She rocks back on her heels, a nervous gesture.

"He's mine. I'm gonna be there for him. He doesn't think I should be. I don't think he thinks he deserves it. It pisses me off that your ex did that to him. Parents have a way of doing numbers on us whether they mean to or not. Your ex, he screwed with Adam's head."

Kit blinks in surprise. "He talked about that?"

"He was trying to convince me to walk away."

"And you're not," Kit tests, as if she's got something to worry about.

"Not a chance." I'd have to be good and dead before anyone could keep me from my kid, or Bink, or Leech, or my brothers. Even her.

"I'm glad to hear that."

"It's the three of us now." I gesture between us, so she gets it.

That nose scrunches in adorable confusion. "It's what?"

Popping the Dum Dum from my mouth, I point it at Kit for emphasis. "You. Me. Him." Then I return the sweetness and crunch down on the last bit of sugar, breaking it into shards.

"You live on a compound with your biker brothers, Gunz. You have a family already. A teenager and her baby live in your house. They depend on you. There isn't anything close to an *us*."

Yes, there is. I think I already made that clear.

"If you think that, then you're crazy."

Kit heaves a long-suffering sigh. "Gunz—"

Shaking my head hard, I chuck my empty sucker stick to the ground. "Nope. We're not doin' this, Kit. Not now. I've gotta get back and pack for a run. While Adam handles his jail time, I gotta handle my club business, and you've gotta live your life. That's reality. But you're my family, too. He is my kid. You're his mother. There is an *us*. When I get back, I'll be the first to show you what that means."

The fierce lady comes forth and tucks both arms across her chest, no longer the picture of unease. "Then we do what in the meantime?"

"As I said… You do your shit. I do mine. We can text."

"Right. Okay." Her lips purse into a thin line as she looks anywhere but me.

Here goes that overthinking, staring-into-space bullshit women do. The kind that has her convinced I'm bailing. That I'm some asshole who talks the talk but doesn't plan to walk the walk. With her history, I understand the hesitance. That doesn't mean I'll tolerate it.

"Don't give me that look," I scold harsher than I intend, 'cause I'd rather her focus on me, not the red Toyota parked across the street.

Kit rolls her hot-as-sin eyes, and I swear to Christ, I pop a semi from the defiance alone. "What look is that?" she sasses, still staring into the great unknown of female bullshittery. Trust me, I know it well. Bink, Beth, and even Janie put me through this every damn week. The difference is, I'm not usually the subject of their hormonal mind fucks. I'm their outlet for 'em.

"That one." I two-finger point at her now scowling expression. "Let me make this clear before you continue to overanalyze everything. I am not going away."

"Okay." She turns her nose up at me like I'm the biggest liar on the face of the planet. It's equally infuriating and a major turn-on.

To keep a lid on things, I focus on my frustration, not my boner, and throw both hands up in exasperation. "Good God, woman, I'm not."

"I said, okay."

Women are such pains in the ass.

"No. Your face says you don't believe me." I remain cool. I'm the goddamn Dalai Lama.

The spitfire doesn't back down. She stares straight into my eyes, straight into my soul. I swear I feel her poking around in there, doin' Lord knows what to the junk drawers. "It doesn't matter what I believe, Gunz. This isn't about my feelings or my thoughts. This is about Adam. Now that you've met him, I just don't want you jerking him around. He's been through enough."

"I know." Still, I'm patient when all I wanna do is yell, *Of course, I fuckin' know that!*

"I love him. He's all I got."

"I know you do, and you've got me, too."

"Okay," she deadpans.

Enough. I'm done.

My stupid cock concurs when it bucks against my fly, hopin' to get some fresh air. If it wouldn't draw attention, I'd punch the thing into submission. He's screwing with my head and our situation.

Inhaling the deepest breath in the universe, my chest expands to the max. I blow it out slowly before I harness my voice in a way that keeps me from losing my shit, but still gets the point across. "That word needs to be washed from your vocabulary, woman. Lose it. No more of this *okay* bullshit. We are his parents. I'll text when I can while I'm gone. You will see me when I get home from the run." I speak deliberately, emphasizing each word.

Fixing her purple hair, Kit opens her mouth, and I know what sass this fuckin' female is about to spew before it even comes out.

"Don't do it. Don't you do it. Don't say that damn word. Say, I'll see you soon."

"Sure. Fine. I'll see you soon."

My nostrils flare in a heady blend of agitation and lust.

"Woman, you're infuriating."

"I'm sorry. I'm not meaning to be."

Like hell she's not.

"Get over here." I wave her closer.

The hottie doesn't budge.

Fuck it.

I hop off the tailgate with the swing of my legs and go to her, but I don't stop there. I do what needs to be done to get my intentions across. In the past week, my club was attacked, and I became a father. Kit handed me the best gift anyone has ever given me without even knowing it. To show her just how grateful I am, I grip the back of her neck and drag her closer. Our fronts meet, tits to abs, and I bend to take her mouth in a hard, knee-buckling kiss. She squeaks in surprise as her fingers grasp at the sides of my shirt.

Greedy for more, I claim a handful of that sexy ass and make her feel what she's doin' to me as I plunder that wicked mouth. And she lets me. Every bit of Kit submits to what I want. How I want it... Goddamn, if that doesn't make me wanna bend her over my tailgate and screw her 'til she can't walk straight. But I won't. She's better than that, and we've got our own bullshit to deal with... for now.

Instead, I'm content to inhale her sweetness and lose myself in her even sweeter taste. My cock throbs in time with my heartbeat as her tongue dances with mine.

Sucking her bottom lip into my mouth, Kit emits a needy little sound as my fingers dig into her jean-clad flesh. A growl rumbles in my chest, traveling up my throat, low and hungry. Losing myself in all that is her, my mind goes hazy, and the dirty, depraved fragments I reserve for those who can handle the darkness of my soul slip through the cracks.

Before I realize what I've done, Kit's back is flat on the bed of my truck, and I'm grinding between her legs, fucking her with our clothes on.

Her nails bite my shoulder blades through the cotton of my shirt, spurring the monster on. And he attacks as he always does, ripping through my tight-leashed control, swallowing the goodness only to leave behind the bad. This is what happens when I ride high on emotions for too long with no real outlet. This is what I get for depriving myself.

I grip a handful of soft, purple hair and yank her head back, exposing a milky strip of neck.

"Gunz!" she moans.

I freeze, my name still fresh on her lips.

Blink...

I look down and see what I've done. What I've allowed myself to do. What I've done to her, here.

What the fuck's wrong with me?

Easing my grip on Kit's hair, I pry her legs off me and sit back on my knees. She watches in stunned silence as a cold sweat breaks over my skin.

"I'm sorry. I'm so fuckin' sorry," I croak, watching her sit up and adjust her shirt, then comb both hands through her disheveled hair.

Those lips, the ones I want more of, are swollen and red. I did that.

The sick part of me revels in the filth and wants to split them open with my dick and force her to choke on it. To gag her 'til her eyes water and she begs for me to stop. Only I wouldn't, 'cause she wouldn't really want that. In my dreams, she'd want more. To swallow a mouthful of my cum. To lick it clean from my shaft.

Christ, I gotta go.

Shaking my head to clear the depraved thoughts before I follow through with them, I climb down off my truck.

Wordlessly, Kit does the same, and I help, not wanting her to fall. I brush away what little debris her shirt collected from the bed of my truck. It's purely platonic. Not at all aimed to check out her ass for a second time or touch it as I remove the invisible dirt from denim.

"Gunz." Kit sweeps her fingers over the back of my forearm, and I jerk away like she's on fire. And because I'm a total fucking asshole, I do one better and shove my hands into my front pockets to keep them to myself as the words *sorry, sorry, sorry,* tumble in my head like clothes in a dryer.

Jaw locked tight, I squeeze my eyes closed in shame.

I'm sorry. I'm sorry. I'm sorry.

"Gunz?" My name's a mere whisper on her lips.

I'm sorry.

Images of my childhood flood forth... of them. The women. The old housewives crying for more. Begging me to finish inside them. Telling me how much they loved me.

I fucked them how I fuck Niki. I treated them like I just treated Kit. With dominance and debauchery.

She's better than that.

Hell, I'm better than that.

Needing to get away before I lose her and Adam forever, I do the only thing I can think to do. I kiss Kit's cheek in goodbye and leave her standing in the parking lot as I climb into my truck and peel out.

I grip my steering wheel and crank the music up as I force myself to face forward and not look back.

It takes every ounce of strength to leave.

Every. Fucking. Piece.

But I do it.

For Kit.

For Adam.

For the uncertain future.

For my heart.

'Cause I think, for the first time in my life, the damn thing's breaking.

CHAPTER EIGHT

GUNZ

Still keyed up by how I left things with Kit, I blindly throw whatever clothes into my duffle bag that sits on the floor beside my clubhouse bed. I gotta pack. I gotta get shit straight. No more thinking of her. She's gotta be the furthest from my mind for what I gotta do... what we gotta do as a club.

What if she hates me after this?

What if goin' on this run ruins the friendship we're building?

Dammit, I can't think about that. I shouldn't even care. Everything happens however it's gonna happen. If Kit doesn't wanna look at me after I molested her in the bed of my truck, then I deserve what I get. It's my fault I crossed the line. My fault I put my lips on hers. My fault I got hard and continue to do so whenever I think of her. That shit's on me.

Kicking the bag, I curse the thing for no reason other than the need to release on something.

I'm unraveling. I can feel it, muscles tight, mind racing, stomach churning... and it scares me. Not for my sake, but everyone else's. I'm the sane brother. The levelheaded one.

On the run, they'll look to me for guidance and trust. If I can't lock down my emotions by the time we ride out, we're as good as dead.

Music blares from the common room, filtering through the back halls.

Mouthing the lyrics, I plug my phone in on the nightstand to charge. If I had it in me, I'd go home tonight and spend time with Janie and Dom. Maybe I'd seek out Bink and Leech for family time. Maybe I'd tell 'em all about my visit with Adam today. I'm exhausted. Too exhausted for any of that. They'll ask questions I don't wanna answer. I'd rather be left alone. We ride out in two days. Got plenty of time to say goodbye beforehand.

Toeing off my boots, I lay my cut on the nightstand and sigh.

I need sleep.

Hours of sleep. Days. Maybe a fuckin' month.

Out of nowhere, a sweet, floral scent suffuses my room. I draw in a deep lungful of air, knowing the familiar perfume well. Arms wrap around me from behind. Hands splay across my stomach. Tired of thinking... of... feeling... I grip her dainty wrist and glide her hand down the front of my pants.

Taking the hint, the sexy bitch strokes my budding erection to full mast. To give her more room to work, I unbuckle my belt, unbutton, unzip, and drop trowel, jeans and all, straight down to my feet, where I kick them off. Breasts grate against my back, hot breath puffing through the fabric of my t-shirt. Wanting skin on skin, I tear the cotton over my head and drop it with the rest of my clothes.

Wetness blooms up the exposed curve of my spine as she licks a stripe of flesh to the base of my skull, her hand never ceasing to stroke. I relish it and am beyond thankful for the distraction.

Precum beads on the tip of my cock and drips in a thin,

translucent stream to the floor, landing between my spread feet.

Staring at the spot, my mouth begins to water. I lick my lips, then moan without consequence when she grips me harder, nails raking my shaft, forcing sparks of pleasured pain straight to my heavy balls. Without shame, or thought, or any of that horseshit, I let go and free-fall into lust, into desire, into the dense, inky fuckery I try so hard to fight.

I'm weak.

Raw.

Torn up inside.

I have no fight left.

There's a moment, a mere blip of time, I pause to allow myself to experience disgrace for what I'm about to do. To be disgusted. Then I throw the unwanted emotions in the trash and take what I want, do what I want, and ignore the moral sting of fucked-up choices.

Pealing Niki's hand from my shaft, I turn and lift her into my arms. Those sexy legs wrap around my waist as I carry her to my bed and lay her on the mattress. I don't bother with niceties when I strip her leggings and tank off, leaving her bare to me, perky tits for the taking... and that's exactly what I do. Take.

Giving zero fucks, I tear open the condom I find in my nightstand, roll it down my cock, throw her legs over my shoulders, and pound her cunt, not caring if she's prepped or not.

Nails rake angry stripes down my back, that I'll wear as a souvenir for the weeks to come.

Every nuance of the outside world fades into nothingness as I succumb to my baser needs. To the hunger. Moans and groans soaked in raw sex play backdrop to the throbbing in my chest, in my cock. Nothing compares to the power, to the hedonism, to the need to consume. I bite Niki's neck, leaving a lasting mark as I wreck her pussy. Sweat drips off my bald head onto her face. Ecstasy rachets up my spine.

Tearing into Niki's bare shoulder like a savage, my eyes roll into the back of my skull.

A rough hand clasps my shoulder.

Words are spoken, yet I don't bother to listen.

Throwing Niki further up the bed, my dick falls free from her cunt as I turn to grab the bottle of lube and a handful of condoms from my drawer.

Viper's already undressed when he catches what I'm offering midair.

We exchange nods and closed-mouth smiles before I crawl into the middle of my mattress, toss Niki over my lap, her legs straddling my hips, and fill her full of cock in one powerful thrust. Her tits bounce as I seize those slender hips and force her to take whatever I wanna feed that slippery hole.

Joinin' the party, Viper scoots my legs together and pushes Niki forward to take her ass. Like a well-oiled machine, I spread her cheeks wide for him as she sucks at my neck, mewling like a crazed nympho, ready to be double stuffed by her two favorite bikers.

Viper glides two of my fingers toward Niki's ass to penetrate her lubed pucker, to get it nice and stretched for his grand entrance. I take little care in hooking my digits inside to pry her orifice apart.

"Fuck yeah," he hisses. "Open that bitch."

And I do. I open the whore with three fingers. The fourth leaves her writhing, her cunt greedily clenching my shaft. 'Cause the twisted fuck inside me gets off on it, I massage my shaft through the thin skin separating ass from pussy.

Niki loves it.

She always loves it.

Ready to enter the kingdom, Viper knocks his cock

against my hand. Knowing what he loves as much as her, I draw Niki's hole upward with four fingers to gape that beauty, and he slams in, sharing the space with me.

"Fuck yeah." My brother groans and seizes my wrist, to use me as a makeshift dildo. In and out, he fucks himself into our favorite whore alongside my four fingers. If I gave a damn, his cock touchin' me in any way would send me spinnin'. Thing is, I've fucked countless bitches with friends of mine, or Bonez. Sometimes swords innocently cross. Sometimes you gotta do what ya gotta do to feed your kinks. Viper wants Niki gaping. Hell, I want her gaping, too. Club whores are here to fulfill whatever depravity we can dream up. 'Cause there ain't no way any of us would ever consider doin' a fifth of our debauchery with someone we give two-shits about. Even I've got standards.

Good thing our bad girl Niki is always ready for anything we wanna give her.

"Call Kai," I tell Viper as Niki loses her mind in DP pleasure.

He slams deep and stops. Brushing Niki's hair outta my way, we make eye contact over her shoulder. "Kai? You want me to bring Kai in?" A pierced brow arches in question as Viper spanks our whore's ass with heavy-handed blows. The sound's music to my ears. Her wiggling on my cock between each smack is even better.

"You want another dick, sweetheart?" I ask.

Niki nods frantically and babbles a string of unintelligible words into the crook of my neck.

Just as I thought.

"See, she wants more. Maybe give her mouth somethin' to do for a while."

Viper turns her pale skin the perfect shade of red. "I'm not sharin' her ass," he growls.

No shit. He's a greedy bastard about that ass. It's his favorite hole to claim.

"Nobody said you gotta share, fucker. Just call him. He's probably readin' some *VP For Dummies* book in his office."

Viper snickers yet does as he's told. Climbing off the bed, he discards the condom in the trash before handling the call. Givin' my morals the middle finger and Viper a friendly screw you, I withdraw my fingers from Niki's ass and wrap her long brown hair around my fist. Don't worry, I'm not a complete douche. Knowin' she's too strung out to ride me herself, I sit her straight up on my dick and fuck her from below for a bit. Viper watches from his spot beside the open bedroom door, strokin' his shaft as he talks in hushed tones to our VP. When I know he's payin' attention, I slip out of her pink and into Viper's preferred hole.

Niki's eyelids flutter as she takes me to the hilt, her jaw slack.

"You like me in your ass, sweetheart?" I palm her tit and give it a hard squeeze. Her hole clamps around my rod.

"Y-yes."

"Gunz," Viper growls in warning from the doorway where he now stands beside our blond, fully dressed VP.

"What... the... Gunz?" Kai's eyes widen at the scene spread before him.

"Welcome, Kai. Why don't you come take Niki for a test drive?" I wave him over.

"I don't—"

Viper clasps our neighborhood beach boy on the shoulder. "Just put your dick in her mouth, brother."

"Guys, I—"

"Ask him, Niki. Ask Kai for his dick. You know you want it." To spur the blissed-out whore along, I massage her clit with my thumb, and she shoots off like a rocket. If the nice guy in me was awake and well, he'd let her enjoy her orgasm in peace. Thing is, I'm not that man anymore. I keep on rubbing that tender nub as I force the sexy bitch to take my cock up her ass. I'm not gentle, nor am I nice, as I force her to come a second time. Viper, done watching from the sidelines, straps up, straddles my legs again, pushes Niki forward, and penetrates her ass alongside my dick. It's a tight fit, but damn does it feel fuckin' good.

A stream of cool lube pours down both our shafts as Viper forces her off us long enough to get prepped for the brutal onslaught. She'll be lucky if she can walk straight tomorrow.

My cock bucks against Viper's at the thought of her trying to sit down and having to stand. Of her legs shaking like Jell-O with every step, 'cause we dicked her out to the max. Of her jaw aching from the abuse.

Fuck.

Yeah.

Laying her head on my shoulder, facing outward, Niki waves Kai closer. The man does as he's told, and fumbles to undo his pants before feeding his half-hard shaft to my favorite whore.

Niki moans loudly as Kai fills her throat.

Combing fingers through his long hair, our VP expels a shaky, uncertain breath before fulfilling his lifelong duty of wrecking Niki's mouth. It's a hard job, but someone's gotta do it. Might as well be him. She'll love it, and so will he. If we're gonna accomplish anything in this club with him as VP, we gotta bond, right? What's a better way to do that than share a whore?

From below, I keep Niki's head bobbing sideways on our VP's dick as Viper takes control of how our cocks get serviced. He angles her hips and guides them in time with his thrusts. It's glorious. The scent of sex hanging like heavy rain clouds in the air. Niki's garbled groans. Three club brothers takin' care of our needs.

Closing my eyes, I succumb to my darkness and let the unfettered pleasure wash me away. It's heady and addictive. Cocaine to my cock.

"Fuck," I grate when Viper releases my rod from the confines of Niki, unrolls my used condom, and replaces it with a fresh one before reuniting me with her wet cunt. All I do is lay here and enjoy. It's freeing—a slice of heaven drenched in hell.

The sex flows on and on... all of us desperate to hold our nut longer and make her scream a little louder.

Kai takes control of Niki's head and fucks her face with zero restraint.

She screams, and she screams, garbled and broken. Her heart races against my chest, sweat cementing us together as we take more from her willing body.

Viper is the first to pull out, rip off his rubber, and shoot his seed across her back.

I'm next.

Heels digging into the mattress, my body bows off the bed as I convulse in ecstasy, filling the condom.

Niki swallows Kai's offering last.

Without saying a word, my brothers gather their things and leave me with Niki for our time, the moments we spend together in the afterglow of animalistic sex.

Most days, I'd appreciate the space.

Today, I throw the well-fucked whore off me onto the bed and race to the bathroom to purge a chasm of guilt from the depths of my murky soul.

Tears matt my eyelashes as the goodness in me rears to the forefront with pictures of a beautiful woman with tattoos and purple hair.

Pissed at myself for feelin' anything, I yank the condom

off and throw the evidence in the trash as Niki's concerned voice penetrates my ears, and I throw up again.

Fuck.

This isn't normal.

I... *Fuck...*

Another heave leaves me listless, my stomach twisted in barbed knots.

"Gunz? You need me to do anything for you? Are you okay?"

"Leave. Please. I... I need my phone."

A kiss is placed on the back of my head and my phone set on the tiled floor beside me. For once, Niki leaves without argument.

Then, I'm alone.

Naked on the floor of my bathroom, sick in the head, in the soul, in everything.

Too weak to stop myself, I text her. I know I shouldn't, not after today, not after what I did...

I'm sorry. I can't wait to see you when I get back. Please forgive me.

CHAPTER NINE

GUNZ

Bouncing Leech and Dom on my knees to keep 'em occupied, Beth, a good friend of mine, talks my ear off on the couch cushion beside me. We haven't seen each other in weeks. I'm not much for phone conversations, and texts only convey so much. Guess Bink invited her for the club dinner, even though we're on lockdown. Tomorrow morning, we ride out.

Beth wiggles a finger at Dom, who gives her a big boy grin. She coos in turn.

"How's Jonesy," I ask, referring to her grandfather, whom she cares for. He used to run with the SS back in the day.

"Good. Still as sharp as a tack."

We carry on, sharing stories of her gramps and other insignificant stuff as the rest of the brotherhood does their thing in the common room, eating food Bink and the Sacred Sisters prepared, drinking, and shootin' pool. It's a typical family night. No club whores, they'll be by later, and I have no intention of staying for that after last night. Mindless sex is great and all when it doesn't end how it did. I've never had anything like that happen before. Throwin' up after fucking isn't my idea of a good time. Neither is the myriad of emotional torment that followed. I think it's best if I keep things as they are. It's safer that way.

Oh, yeah, and if you were wonderin' if my weak text to Kit resulted in a positive outcome, or any outcome for that matter, that'd be a negative on both fronts. No reply. Not a damn peep since I left the parking lot yesterday. I'm tryin' not to dwell on it, but my mind finds ways to screw with me even when I think I've got it on lockdown.

"Bink told us you have a son," Beth notes outta no-fucking-where. As if my thoughts on Kit weren't bad enough, she's gotta rub salt in the gaping wound that's formed.

Taking Dom into her lap, he snuggles against Beth's average chest and tugs on a stand of brown hair. Beth's pretty in a Plain Jane kinda way. Nothing about her is exquisite or striking. Bottom line, she's wholesome and nice. A good, albeit naïve, and too trusting of a woman, who had her heart stomped on by Runner. She's friends with Bink and became mine thanks to a bit of Big coercion. I don't need to bore you with the details.

Laying my sleepy girl's head against my shoulder, I pepper her soft hair with Grandpa Gunz kisses, and relax, enjoying the world's best medicine—Leech time. She's snuggly and beyond fuckin' adorable in her skull-print jumper as she lets me snuggle with my much larger, tattooed arms wrapped protectively around her teeny form.

Beth's eyes rest heavily on us as she permits me time to be with my girl without distraction.

It doesn't last long enough.

Once Leech zonks out and Janie comes to take Dom home, Beth doesn't let her previous question slide and probes a second time. "Soooo," she drawls, massaging the tops of her denim-covered thighs nervously. "You have a son."

Knowin' the Sacred Sisters, they sent Beth here for the deets. I haven't said a word to anybody about Adam since church. Don't think I have anything else to say on the matter. If Big asks, I'll tell him. Anyone else can kiss off. Adam and Kit are mine. For me. Not the club's and surely not a group of nosy old ladies' business. They do their thing, fine. But I don't want some unfounded, overprotective judgments screwing things up for me with Kit. 'Cause that's what'll happen.

What Beth says next confirms my suspicions. "Bink texted our group. That's how I know. She said he's grown, and his mom kept him from you. She said the woman stayed here this week, for a day. Do you think that's smart, Gunz? Havin' her here? What if he's not yours? What if she's here to hurt the club? What if—"

I hold up a hand for her to quit talking. These are not the words of my friend. Of the woman I've been there for... the heartbroken person who cried on my shoulder before fallin' asleep in my bed. These are not the questions and accusations founded by Beth. These have Bink and the rest of the Sacred Sisters written all over 'em.

I've had enough.

I'm done.

Spent.

Massaging the bridge of my nose, eyes closed, I rest my chin against Leech's hair and try my hardest to reel in the budding anger before I take it out on Beth, or accidentally wake my grandbaby. It's not her fault she's the pawn of the sisterhood. Alright, it is, but it's not intentional. She's not malicious. There's no doubt in my mind this is born of care and concern. However, I'm still fucking done. I don't have another ounce left in me to deal with petty bullshit. I'm going to war tomorrow.

Clenching my jaw, I swallow the sharp retort I wanna

unleash and formulate a better one. One I'd normally say under better circumstances—when I have a legitimate patience storage to siphon from. Too bad for them, those wells were sucked dry.

"Gunz, I'm sorry," Beth tacks on when she realizes I'm not in a good place.

"It's fine," I lie, then squeeze my grandbaby a little tighter to imprint her body on mine, to remember when I'm gone for days on end. I'm gonna miss this little shit. Dom, too.

She pats my knee in apology and rests her hand there. "It's not. I see you're upset. I didn't mean to make you upset. I promise."

"I know."

"The sisters are worried." Beth's nail traces anxious circles across my kneecap. I watch as it does, too caught up in my own head to pay attention to those around us.

"I know. They sent you to get information."

Out of my periphery, I watch Beth's body language and expression morph from blank indifference to guilty as her eyes mist over. Lettin' the guilt eat her from the inside out, she sucks in a sharp, emotional breath. "I'm sorry."

I know she is. If I didn't, I wouldn't say what I'm about to, so she has something to report back to the sisters.

"I do have a son. He *is* mine. He looks like me. And his mother never kept him from me. Her intentions of why she was here are our business. I would appreciate it if the sisters would respect my privacy on this. Everything's still fresh, and I'm leaving tomorrow. My head needs to be in the game, not on this sh—stuff."

The knee drawing persists. "That's good… understandable. I'll tell them."

"Thanks."

Her finger pauses mid-draw. "Do you want me to tell

them now?" Tucking a strand of hair behind her ear, Beth looks to me for guidance.

"Are they waiting on your report?" Wantin' a little less touchy-touchy, I remove her hand from my leg and set it back on hers. She frowns as I do.

"I'm guessing so. Bink has... um... never mind."

"No. Finish your thought. Bink has what?"

"She packed food for you to take on the road tomorrow. I'm supposed to go get it."

"Okay. You do that. But have her bring me the food when you're finished tellin' her I have a son, who is really mine, and I plan on keepin' him and his mother in my life." I reiterate the last bit so she don't forget. I need her to relay the message loud and clear for Bink's stubborn mind to hang on to, so she'll quit makin' my life difficult.

Beth doesn't fill the silence with a needless reply when she stands and heads straight to the kitchen. Breaking away from their men, the sisters join her beyond the swinging door. I smile privately to myself as I watch Pixie, Axel's old lady, carry an empty food tray in with her like that's gonna make her departure appear any less conspicuous.

Bulk, a fellow baldheaded brother of mine, drops his heavy ass into the spot Beth vacated. "Do they think we don't know what they're doin' in there?" Chucklin' to himself, he bumps shoulders with mine. "Damn women."

"I'm guessin' you know what this's about."

"I have the loudest old lady in the club. Yeah, I know. She's been rantin' about the kid shit all fuckin' day."

"She tell you they were gonna use Beth as bait?" I ask.

Bulk's foot bounces. "Not exactly, but Axel, Trip, Dallas, and I compared notes and shit before we got here."

"You sayin' you're a bunch of gossipy bitches, too?"

"Nope. Not at all. I'm sayin' we knew they were gonna start their gang mentality shit, and we wanted to be in front of it when it happened. In case they pissed ya off. We don't have time for games. But they can't keep their noses outta shit that don't concern 'em."

He's right. They can't.

"The brothers got an issue with me havin' a kid and Kit comin' 'round?" I test.

The big man heaves a sigh. "'Sides Viper's outburst in church and Runner always runnin' his punk-ass mouth, nope. We got your back and theirs too, without question."

Good. Glad that's settled.

Perching himself on the couch arm, Axel offers me a bottle of Bud. I accept it with a nod of respect, then sip the cold brew. The cold liquid feels mighty nice as it slides down my throat. Even better when I take a whiff of Leech's hair at the same time. Unconditional, no-bullshit love, and beer, it doesn't get much better than this. 'Cept maybe a beautiful woman sittin' beside me. In my head, I picture Kit takin' her own pull of Bud where Bulk's giant ass is. Gotta say, he's not as pretty as her. Don't smell as nice either.

When I open my mouth to tell him as much, Bink exits the kitchen, a bag of food in hand, headed straight for us. Knowin' what's good for 'em, my brothers scram to claim their old ladies who have rejoined the party.

Blonde hair pulled back in a ponytail, one hand on her hip, Bink sets the bag on the empty seat beside me and eyes her sleeping girl. I'm not breaking the ice first. I'll let her do that. If she's got somethin' to say, she's gonna be the one to say it.

Swayin' back and forth, she nudges my toe with her own, that beautiful face etched in equal parts concern and nerves. Most wouldn't be able to read Bink's emotions, but I've known and cared for her since birth. I know everything about this woman. Love everything about her, even the bossy, nosy, stubborn parts that irritate the hell outta me sometimes.

When she continues lookin' at me and Leech, her toe nudges mine again. I arch a brow. She knows what I'm askin' without me havin' to speak.

"I..." Bink's sentence falters, and she swallows thickly.

It's not like her to tread lightly. Neither is the lip chewing in my presence. By the way she's actin', she must think I'm pissed. Maybe that's what Beth told her.

Alright. I gotta nip this in the bud.

Knowin' exactly what my girl needs, I pat my thigh. It does the trick and Bink climbs straight onto my lap. Jostling her around a bit, I drape both of her legs over my other, her ass on my thigh, and tuck her head against my free shoulder. The woman practically melts into me, a sigh imparting her lips.

Unable to help herself, she strokes up and down Leech's back with soft touches as I wrap arms around them both. A kiss presses to the underside of my jaw. "I wanna get to know them both," she whispers so only I can hear.

Thank fuck.

I squeeze her a lil tighter in gratitude, my heart growin' six sizes. "Me, too, Baby Doll."

And just like that, all is right in my world.

It's funny how quickly pieces align when those who matter most give you something you didn't know you needed.

Bink in my arms beside her daughter is heaven. Her wanting to know my son and his mother, without puttin' up a fight, even better.

Tomorrow, the club comes first. Tonight, it's family, my family. Even if Adam and Kit can't be here, I'll carry them in spirit, in the cradle of my arms where Bink and Leech rest.

CHAPTER TEN

KIT

::Bang :: Bang :: Bang::

Beneath a spray of water, mid-shampoo, fingers massaging my scalp, someone pounds on my front door. Worried it's an emergency, I rinse off in record time, hop out, and quickly throw a towel around myself.

"Hold on! I'm coming!" I yell, dripping water halfway across my apartment to unlock the deadbolts and pull open the door without bothering to look through the peephole.

Securing the towel to my chest, one hand on the knob, I gasp when I come face-to-face with a bouquet on legs.

"Holy crap," I hiss, staring straight into a sea of colorful blooms.

"Delivery," the man laden with flowers says. "Sorry, I had to kick your door."

"Uh. Those aren't mine. They probably belong to Jessie down the hall." I point to her door with the seasonal wreath, even though the guy can't see me. Jessie's ex is a stalker, always sending her flowers, balloons, and chocolates once a week.

"You, Kit?" He shifts the large bowl vase as if he can't hold on much longer.

"No..." My brain freezes mid-thought, and I sigh, lips turning down into a frown. "Yes. That's me."

Fucking Gunz.

"I can't see. Maybe you wanna back up, so I can set them inside somewhere?"

"Sure." I slip away from the door to make room, streaking the small pool of water along with me. We don't want him to fall and bust his behind on my crappy linoleum entry.

The scrawny boy I saw walking on the street just this morning when I went out to get the mail, sets the oversized arrangement in the center of my coffee table.

"The water makes it heavy," he remarks as he dusts both hands on the sides of his jeans.

Unsure what I'm supposed to say to that when I'm wet and naked under a towel, inside my tiny apartment, with a stranger... I escort him to the door. "Thanks for the delivery," I fib.

The kid knocks on the doorframe twice, wearing a put-on smile. "You have a nice day now."

"You, too." I shiver at his creep factor but don't let it show.

Once the door's secure, I about-face, and there it is... the bouquet. No, it's more like a massive flower arrangement you see at funerals. The asshole bought me dead people blooms. With how the baldheaded jerk acted after the hottest moment of my life, followed by an idiotic text, this must be a goodbye gift. An our-flirty-friendship-is-dead-because-I-want-someone-younger send-off. A you're-my-baby's-mama-but-you-kiss-like-a-fish letdown. Why else would the world's largest funeral spray be on my coffee table? Why else would he have sped from the parking lot like I disgusted him?

I don't understand.

Not him.

Not men.

Nobody, it seems.

One minute, you like a man and he kisses you like you're his, like he owns you. The next, he runs away like a coward. Like he realizes it's you he's kissing and not someone hot, like his lady friend, Niki.

Ugh.

This is why I don't get caught up in those of the male variety anymore. The games are too much to stomach at my age. Been there. Done that. Have the T-shirt. I've got enough on my plate with Adam and keeping my head above water. I don't need Gunz's rollercoaster, too. I'm better than that, even if I don't believe *that* half the time.

Not bothering with the blooms or the card I see amid them, I return to the bathroom to finish my shower. I take my time—as much time as I need—and then more for good measure. Sure, my brain concocts a dozen implausible scenarios as to why I have that thingy in the living room. Nobody has ever bought me flowers before unless you count the dandelions Adam used to pick for me on his way home from the bus stop.

Double ugh.

Why did Gunz have to send them today?

It's been a week since I last saw him.

A week of unknown.

I was doing better, slowly getting past our kiss and the time spent together. Trying to forget the damn grilled cheese sandwich and tomato soup for dinner, where I laughed so hard, I cried. All thanks to a story he shared about his brother and him growing up. Who knew flamingo underwear was a thing, even then? Guess Bonez and Gunz fought over a pair. Silly kids.

I also visited Adam this week again.

He's excited to see Gunz when he gets out. The smiles he had when he talked about his father made me... I dunno. Let's not talk about it.

Now there are flowers.

How did he even know where I lived?

Triple-washing my hair and conditioning it, I then scrub every ounce of skin with a coffee-infused sugar scrub. It's supposed to fight cellulite. Not sure if it works. It's hard to tell under all the ink, but I paid a pretty penny for the jar. I'm not about to let it go to waste. At least it smells good.

Satisfied with the extensive washdown, I step out of the shower, my toes and fingers extra pruny.

From the rack, I use a fresh towel to dry and forgo looking in the mirror. I'm not in the mood to see all this looking back at me.

Hidden behind the bamboo partition that separates my living room from my bedroom, giving the illusion of a wall and privacy from the front apartment windows, I slip on a raggedy tank and boxers from my only dresser.

Then I groan.

Guess this is the part where I get over my snit and read the card.

Meh.

Do I really want to? Nope.

Okay. I'm lying. You know you want me to read it, too. We both need to know what it says. Bet you care about it more than I do.

Tossing my towel in the hamper, I pause and curse to the high heavens about men and their dickish ways. Once I've got that out of my system, I enter the living room and snag that stupid card from the plastic fork in my funeral flowers.

Tapping my foot on the carpet, I take a moment, a microscopic one, to appreciate the blooms. They're made up of Gerber daises, mostly purple and white ones. If those weren't nice enough, there are roses in three different shades, and what you'd consider filler greens. I wish I didn't have to admit this, but it's beautiful. Something I'd buy for myself if I did that sort of thing. And I hate all of it. Every square, heavenly scented inch.

Flicking a hardy bud, I glare at the thing for being too damn pretty, then roll my eyes for acting like a lunatic over flowers... Over Gunz. Over... Whatever.

Enough already.

I read the stupid, plain white card.

Baby Mama,

Roses are red. These flowers are purple. Sorry I stuck my tongue down your throat and ran away like a ... motherfucker. (No pun intended.)

- Erik.

Sorry.

He's... sorry?

Sorry he ran away, or sorry he stuck his tongue down my throat? Or both?

It sounds like both, doesn't it?

See, I told you I kiss like a fish, and this was goodbye.

Frustrated with the world, I toss the card back into the blooms and find my phone on the nightstand beside my bed. I sit on the edge, ankles crossing, and fume as I pull up Gunz's number to get this out once and for all. No more games. No more miscommunication. Things need to be said.

If only he were ugly.

Or stupid.

Or a horrible kisser with a black heart.

That'd make this a thousand times easier.

Fuck men.

Confusing bastards.

CHAPTER ELEVEN

GUNZ

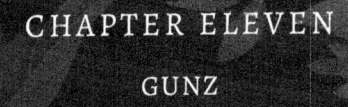

Strapped to the nines, huddled midday at the edge of the woods with a group of fellow brothers, I point to the intel on my phone, courtesy of Bongo. For once, someone else dug up what we needed for specs. It's nice not havin' to be the brains of every operation.

"The hotel's got two entrances. The main one out front and the one in the rear, through the kitchen." I draw a circle around the spots on our aerial image for better visuals, like a doctor does an x-ray, then I look up to make sure they're payin' attention. Their lives could very well depend on the data.

"It's a shithole," I add. "Probably got rats, mold, leaks, ceilings cavin' in, and weak floors. Do your best to stay on the studs. We don't need anybody gettin' dead besides Remy's crew."

"Bongo say how big the setup is?" Mickey asks.

"It's two stories. Fortyish rooms. Most of our visitors will be civilians here to take care of business, if ya catch my drift." My nose wrinkles in distaste.

"Fuckin' disgusting," a brother mutters under his breath.

I nod in agreement. "We haven't handled an operation like this before. Remy's changin' his tactics. Openin' popups for a bit of local underage fun. Might have five girls in there. Might have fifty. Can't say."

"The order from Big is to execute all predators, correct?" Blimp clarifies as he double-checks the clips in his guns.

"Yep. Anyone who isn't a victim gets dead on the spot. That means no game playing." To get the point across, I make eye contact with the biggest sicko of the bunch. "Kade."

The knife twirling between his fingertips halts, and he hides the evidence behind his back as if I didn't notice the damn thing in the first place... Or the dozens of times I've watched him do the exact thing before. "What?" Kade plays innocent, wearing a big, jovial smile complemented by his over-the-top eyelash batting.

I snort, half-amused. If I didn't like the guy, I'd give him hell about his antics. Good thing I've got a soft spot for Bear's boys. He's the president of our Texas chapter. A damn good man and leader. Kade's one of his.

Knowin' he follows rules well, given he wouldn't be here if he didn't, I arch a single brow to lay down the law. It's no secret Kade gets satisfaction watchin' people die in sick-and-twisted, fucked-up ways. This operation isn't about that. It's death and done. No muss, no fuss. We ain't got time for an elaborate knife circus.

Takin' orders without a peep, Kade dips his chin in respectful compliance. If he does a good job, I'm not opposed to lettin' him and his old lady take a souvenir home to carve up later, off the books, after we've gotten everyone to safety. Who am I to rain on their parade? We've all got demons to tame. Some more than others.

Positions are divvied up, to give everybody their spots to shine.

Here's what I know, so you're in the loop, 'cause shit's about to go down.

Four days ago, I left the compound to join forces with my other Sacred Sinner brethren. At our safe house, we caught wind of two major operations over the Mississippi state line. Yesterday, we collaborated to get our asses here to shut down Remy's newest streak of evil. The quicker we handle this, the quicker the victims are freed and sent to my brother for rehabilitation. And, honestly, the quicker we get to the next place, and the next place, and the next fucking place, to free the Janie's and Tati's of this vile trafficking world. A month will never be long enough to rid the earth of Remy's scum, but I will make damn sure I put a giant dent in it. It's the least I can do after he attacked our compound.

No more sideline sitting. The Sacred Sinners are gonna show these motherfuckers what real war looks like.

Stowing my phone, I pull a Dum Dum from my pocket and pop it into my maw to center myself, even for an instant. To let the world align and my thoughts remain on the task at hand. Not stray to Kit or my son. Not to the gaping hole in my chest for missing her, a woman I barely know. Of course, I don't think of purple hair, or her scent, or the kiss I'll remember for the rest of my days. No. I'm stronger than that. I've got my shit together. I'm focused.

Blimp steps up beside me and slaps my leather-clad back. "You ready?" He juts his chin toward our destination a quarter mile up yonder. The rest of our brethren have already dispersed.

"Yeah."

"Been a while since you were in the thick of things."

He ain't kiddin'. "I'm good."

"You sure? 'Cause you got a family now."

"I've always had a family, brother," I remind him.

"Not like this one. Not like her. Not like him."

Nope. We're not going down this path. I don't need to hear this crap when I've got a job to do. "I'm *good*," I emphasize, so he'll drop it.

Blimp chuckles and pats the holster under his cut. "'Kay, 'cause I won't say nothin' if you wanna hang back to keep an eye on things. Let the young bucks handle the kills." He winks. A cocky half-smile parts his long, gangly, gray beard.

What-the-fuck-ever.

Snickering in return, I shake my head and follow the same route the rest took through the woods. "Come on, Blimp, killin' is half the fun." I wave for him to catch up.

The pungent scent of pot drifts as he lights a joint. "This is gonna be fun."

Yes. It is.

Putting sick fucks to ground is the best part of our runs, 'cause it sure ain't leaving my woman behind.

I wonder what she's doin' right now...

Did she get the flowers I sent?

Picturing her smile like some lovesick idiot, I stumble over a fallen branch and catch myself on a nearby tree trunk before I bite the dust.

Blimp yucks it up at my expense. "Watch where you're goin', brother."

I flip him off.

A blood-curdling scream echoes through the trees, gunshots trailing a moment later.

Fuck. We're missing the action.

Charging through the remaining forest, Blimp at my six, my phone blows up in my pocket. I ignore it as we step over two dead bastards lying in a puddle of their own blood on the cracked asphalt parking lot.

More screams ensue.

Together, we kick through the front, mud-caked doors of the hotel, armed and ready for whatever's waiting for us on the other side. It's dark. The cloying stench of mildew and blood is a bitch on the senses. Our resident sadistic fuck, Kade, cackles his love for death somewhere in the bowels of this hell.

Staying close, Blimp obeys my hand signals as we hunt the sexual predators like a well-oiled machine. This ain't our first rodeo.

The first closed door we reach, I gesture for Blimp to cover me as I kick in the rusted handle. It caves easily, and wouldn't ya know it, a man stops mid-pump to look over his shoulder at us. Rays of sunshine filter through the cracks in the boarded windows as the monster's glassy eyes land on mine.

Pop.

A single bullet barrels through his skull. Blood sprays the wall like a modern art piece.

Sayonara, asshole.

The lifeless man drops to the side, landing half on top of what appears to be a younger female. I'll spare you the gory details as I shove his fat, hairy form off the girl and cover her with an old, disgusting sheet I find on the floor next to the bed. Her eyes are closed, her body deathly still as I check for a pulse on the side of her throat.

Alive.

A sigh of relief escapes me as I notice raw track marks littering both of her forearms.

My jaw clenches and I turn to Blimp.

"One down," he growls, his gaze flipping between me and the open doorway. "She's gonna be fine. Next one's mine."

A nod is all I offer.

Shit just got real.

CHAPTER TWELVE

KIT

Foot bouncing, I chew on the side of my thumbnail, impatiently waiting for a reply. It's been hours and not a peep from the father of my son. No explanation for the flowers. No middle finger emojis. Silence. It's eerie. Something doesn't feel right.

The hairs on the back of my neck stand on end as a diesel truck revs its engine nearby. An unusual sickness roils in my gut.

Staring blankly at the computer screen resting on the cushion beside me, I toss a purple throw over my thighs.

Call it Mom Intuition or crazy town. Either way, the world isn't normal.

The longer I sit in limbo... waiting... waiting... waiting... the urge to call the jail and check on Adam grows.

I check my phone for the hundredth time.

No Gunz.

The clock on the screen reads just past ten p.m.

Streetlights and a bright evening sky casts a low glow across my gauzy curtains. I watch the shadow of a spider spinning a web on the opposite side of the windowpane. Too antsy to sit still, I pick a flower from the funeral arrangement on the coffee table—a rose. One by one, I pluck silky pedals from their home and discard them onto the floor to clean up later. I can't eat. Can't sleep. Work eludes me, even if I have papers to grade.

The white noise of the refrigerator does little to calm my rising... whatever this is.

What if the texts I sent threw Gunz off? Were they too brash? Did I push him away? Will Adam ever forgive me if I did?

Dammit.

Why isn't he texting back?

He sent flowers.

Flowers. For. Me.

The stupid card stares at me in infamy from the bouquet.

I glower at the scrawl of his words. I've already memorized the poem. It wasn't difficult.

Yeah. Yeah. Yeah. I know what you're thinking, I'm thinking it too... Pathetic. What kind of grown-ass woman acts this way? Me. Apparently.

A muffler backfires close by, sending my nerves into a tizzy.

Maybe I need a drink. Something to calm me—tea. The sleepy kind. Something with chamomile. Yes. Tea. That should do it. No more of this waiting. Tea, then sleep. Tea... then sleep. Brilliant!

Not bothered by the current, not-so-clean state of my apartment, I dump the throw onto the floor with the petals. I'll worry about that tomorrow.

In the kitchen, I pull out my favorite mom mug and a random chamomile-flavored tea from the cupboard. I don't bother reading the labels, as they all taste good to me. I'm not picky. As I heat tap water in the microwave, I resist the urge to grab my phone and check it... again.

Lame.

Beyond lame.

Why do we women do this to ourselves? Obsessing over something dumb. Logically, I get I shouldn't care. If he wants to be in our lives, he will be. It's that simple. Yet, I can't shake this feeling, no matter how hard I try.

The microwave dings its completion just as a series of knocks rattle my door.

One. Two. Three.

"Hello?" I call as I retrieve my mug, set it on the counter, and drop a tea bag into the steaming liquid.

Nobody replies.

Two more knocks—an ominous racket compared to the quiet of the room.

"Yes?" I speak louder.

Silence.

Leaving the chamomile to steep, I approach the entrance.

Knock. Knock. Knock—slow and steady.

Knock. A definitive finale.

I poise my hand on the knob and lift onto my toes to glance through the peephole. A shadow passes, yet I make nothing out.

"Hello?" I try one last time.

"Ma'am?"

A sigh of relief deflates the tension in my shoulders as I recognize the voice—my neighbor.

Unlocking the door to see if something is wrong, I open my mouth to ask as much, when a bloodied face comes into view. Rivulets of crimson pour down his battered face, soaking into the white of his shirt.

My eyes widen. "Oh. My. God. Are you okay?!"

Only he's not.

His entire body free falls into my door, knocking it wide open as he collapses to the floor inside my apartment.

I don't...

What... the...

"It's like takin' candy from a baby," a familiar voice cackles like a villain.

Then... darkness.

CHAPTER THIRTEEN

GUNZ

Kneeling at the end of a cot, I rest a tiny, purple teddy bear upright on a little girl's legs. She couldn't be any older than eight, maybe nine. We found five women and children dead in the hotel we raided today. Fucking five. Violated, bruised, and *dead*. With nobody to hold them and tell them they were gonna be okay. Not like this shaky kid with brown, matted hair. The unfortunate thing looks at me with big green eyes and back to the bear, no doubt checking to see if I'm playing some sick-and-twisted game.

To prove I'm not a threat, I get down on both knees and sit back. Ain't none of us here gonna harm her or any of the survivors. Twelve were saved from the shithole. It's a start. Not good enough, but better than nothing.

Ten tiny fingers wring together as she overthinks about the stuffed present I've brought. Does she want it? Should she? What's the catch? I get it. My childhood might not have been the same, but you question everyone and everything when you've been abused. A big, bald, biker dude with tattoos sitting at the end of your bed isn't the most comforting. It will be, though. She'll learn soon enough. They all do. It takes time to earn trust.

"Go on." I lift my chin. "All yours, kid. You're safe now."

With a single glance over me and the room full of those we saved, she then watches my brothers mill about, handing out blankets, food, and clothes to the others. Our safe house tonight was a godsend. A friend of Bulk's old lady opened her outdated farmhouse to us, no questions asked. It's big enough to hold everyone for the night, before my brother Bonez finds stable homes for these women and children tomorrow.

The girl's nose twitches in distaste when she spies Blimp and his ugly beard carrying an armful of juice boxes out from the kitchen.

"He's not the best lookin', huh?" I snicker.

The tiniest grin forms at the crook of her mouth and vanishes a moment later. It's fucking beautiful. I'll take what I can get.

Rounding the room, Blimp offers juice to the survivors. The girl grows antsier the closer he gets, clawing at the blanket on her lap. I wave for him to skip her cot when he delivers a box to her neighbor. A look of understanding exchanges between us as he passes by. Blimp knows the drill. Some kids are more comfortable with certain people. Seems I'm one of those people. Most take to me easily enough. Not sure why. Probably the same reason I bonded with Bink so young and why Janie was happy to live with me. I'm the level-headed asshole of the bunch, go figure. Well, most of the time.

Once my brother lumbers into the next room, the kid visibly relaxes, and that's when it happens... she takes the bear. Crushing it to her chest, she sighs. It's a content sort of sound. Exactly what I needed to hear after a long, gory day. Four men got dead by my hand in the hotel, all of them scum of the earth, not fit to breathe the same air as me. The Devil better have himself a hay-fuckin-day with those bastards—tie 'em up and let 'em burn for eternity.

Not botherin' with hello, my blood brother joins me at the end of the girls' bed, kneeling as I do on the scarred hardwood. She takes one look at him and then continues to play with the bear. It ain't hard to see we're related. Kids in school often confused us 'til he beefed up.

"How's it goin'?" he asks, knocking a shoulder with mine.

"Fine."

I know what he wants—information—on Kit and Adam. Someone let the news slip of the kid and his mother. I haven't told my brother about them yet. Wasn't planning on it 'til I was ready. I'm still not ready. It's bad enough I ignored her texts all day. Haven't read a single one on account of what they might say. Don't think I'm ready to know. But this damn phone sure is burnin' a hole in my back pocket.

Reading my tone like any brother would, Bonez doesn't push for more and turns his attention to the kid. "Who ya got there? She's a pretty bear."

The cutie dances the toy in her lap and shrugs bashfully.

"You gonna name her?" he asks.

Another shrug is all she offers.

"I think she looks like a…" Bonez scratches his goatee in exaggerated thought. If he wasn't tryin' to put on a show for the girl, I'd smack him upside the head for the antics. Instead, I do what any good sibling would and play along.

Pursing my lips together, I scrunch my face in constipated deliberation as I join Bonez on the important search for the perfect teddy name.

"Theodore?" he suggests after a moment.

The lil one shakes her head, wearing the prettiest of crooked smiles. There's an adorable gap between her two front teeth.

Turning my nose up at the perfectly acceptable name, I roll my eyes at Bonez. "Try again, old man."

"Hey. Who you callin' old?" A shoulder collides with mine hard. Going with the flow, I topple over onto the floor like an overgrown oaf. Making it a bigger spectacle, I bitch up a PG-13 under-breath storm at the disrespect. Drawing all the attention in the room, girls and women alike chuckle at my expense. I eat it up, knowing this might be the first they've laughed in ages.

Still not finished with me, Bonez throws both muscled arms in the air with flourish. It's fuckin' spectacular. "That is what ya get for callin' me old."

Curling into a ball on my side, an arm propping my head up, I glare at him. "Oh yeah?"

He meets my glare with one of his own. "Yeah."

"It's not my fault you can't pick proper bear names," I taunt.

"Theodore *is* adequate." Faux offended, Bonez flicks the side of my calf.

I pretend to kick his advance away with a girlish gasp. "Real mature, Bonez. Real. Mature. I think you'd better ask the bear's owner what a suitable name is."

The girl in question touches her belly as she trembles in silent laughter, tears streaming down both cheeks. In the corner of the room, fellow brothers record our performance on their phones. Good thing this can't wind up on YouTube. This kinda fun isn't for worldly consumption, only those I trust and give a damn about.

Doing as he's told, Bonez waggles his eyebrows at the kid. "Fine. All right. Theodore doesn't work. What's the bear's name, sweetheart?"

Just like that… the room goes lax, the amusement fading to a simmer as we await her response. I get off the floor to rejoin my brother. The beautiful kid combs a nervous hand through her hair, knowing she's been put on the spot. All eyes look at her. I urge her forward with a smile. She's got this. I know it. The entire room knows it.

Her lips part, close, then part again. She peeks at my cut, reading my name patch letter for letter.

"Gunz," she mutters. "Her name is Gunz."

Good God.

My heart... I rub the damn thing as it explodes like a balloon full of glitter. The pink-and-purple kind, in case you were wondering.

Fuck.

CHAPTER FOURTEEN

KIT

The pain of a thousand spurs piercing my back sets my teeth on edge. I groan low in my chest as a violent chill rips through every cell. Palms flat on the cold, solid ground, grit embeds beneath my nails as I flex my fingers. Sharp pebbles imprint flesh. I blink to figure out where the hell I am—in nothing more than a sea of darkness. Inhaling deeply, mildew mixed with body odor and piss hits my nostrils like fresh skunk spray. Choking on the aroma, I blink twice more, but I still can't see the damn thing. Water trickles nearby. A fusion of whimpers and subdued cries fill the air. Nearby, someone shrieks in agony—a woman.

"Do we know her?" a voice mutters from feet away.

I lie still, now realizing I'm not alone.

There's shuffling.

An onslaught of whispers.

Alright… Focus. A man was at my apartment, right? He had dark eyes, I think. After that… I remember nothing.

"Please! No!" the shrieking female pleads, "Oh! God! Please! Stop!"

A different person cries quietly to herself. "Fu-ck. F-uck. Fuck," she stammers in fragments.

"Are you awake?" a third woman asks, far calmer than the rest.

Not knowing what to do, I ignore the throbbing in my spine and pretend they don't exist. I don't know these people. I don't know anything anymore.

A lone tear forms in the corner of my eye.

I ignore the traitorous bastard.

Nope. I'm not gonna cry. This is not the time for weakness. So what if I've been taken?

Shit.

Taken—like in that movie with Liam Neeson.

Is that what this is?

Wait.

What?

No.

I'm nobody.

I'm…

A masculine grumble carries forth, his footsteps godlike as they stop far too close for comfort.

"Please don't come in. Please don't come in," a nearby female chants to herself.

The door to our space opens with a rusty whine, and a hulking silhouette fills the frame, the light behind him forming a halo around his head.

Lying deathly still to avoid detection, I hold my breath and shutter my eyelids just enough to watch the asshole shove a naked woman into the room. She stumbles on wobbly legs before collapsing in the middle of an area not much larger than a walk-in closet.

A moment later, he's gone. The *thud* of a lock engages in his wake.

"Kit," the newbie rasps as we descend back into darkness.

It's her. I'd recognize that voice anywhere... Gunz's naked friend.

Dammit.

This isn't good.

CHAPTER FIFTEEN

GUNZ

Leaning against a porch rail in desperate need of paint, I stare into the tranquil distance. There's not a house as far as the eye can see. Not in the dark, anyhow. Cool, evening air fills my lungs as I continue to resist the urge to read Kit's texts.

Not knowin' when to leave shit be, Bonez joins me as Blimp smokes a bowl on a rocker in the corner. He and White Boy shoot the shit as our resident fuckhead, Runner, gets his dick sucked on the tailgate of one of our pickups. Guess he couldn't hold out like the rest of us. Had to call a random whore to get him off. Can't say I'm surprised. The asshole didn't learn a thing from the clusterfuck we handled today. It's not like we don't have a house full of sexually abused females. He ain't worried about what they might think if they saw him. 'Cause that'd mean he'd have to use the peanut-sized brain in his goddamn skull.

Whatever.

Ain't none of my business.

He's a piece of shit. Always has been. Always will be.

Barely visible, Kade runs the parameter of the grounds.

He's on security detail tonight, so the rest of us can catch some Zzzz's. As if that'll happen.

Bonez clears his throat.

I know what he wants.

When I don't play into the subtlety, he tries a different tactic. "Spill it, brother."

I chuckle without humor. "Nothin' to spill."

"You've got a kid now."

See. I knew he wouldn't be able to let this go for long.

Not in the mood to get into things, I shrug a single shoulder half-assed. "Yeah. So?"

"And?"

"And... what?" If he thinks I'm gonna offer up every personal detail about Kit and my son, he's got another thing comin'.

The rickety screen door opens, and a brother pops his head out. "Any you fuckers want a beer?"

Knowin' how the lot of us roll, I wave a dismissive hand. "We're good. Thanks." It's an unspoken rule in the mother chapter—no drinking on runs when we've got civilians to protect. None of us know what Remy and his crew might pull. It's best to remain sober. If Blimp wasn't already high as a kite every waking moment, I'd give him hell too. Guess it's a good thing he works best stoned.

"Just holler if you need anythin'," our brother offers before disappearing back inside.

A loud, "Will do," rasps outta Blimp between puffs.

The nosy giant to my left kicks a stone. It flies into an overgrown bush that flanks the porch. "Alright, Gunz." He sighs, annoying as fuck. "Don't make me beat it outta ya."

Funny.

I snort, unamused. "There's nothin' to say." So, I've got a kid. He's got a mom. What's left to review? If I wanted to share, I'd share. Now's not the time nor the place. We're away from home, doin' what needs done. This ain't social hour.

Meddlin' like only he can, Bonez meets my stubbornness with a dose of his own. "Uh-huh. 'Cept his name's Adam, right? And his mama dropped her hot, purple-haired, tattooed ass on your doorstep not long ago."

Ugh.

Teeth clenching, a low growl escapes my throat. I grip the banister and squeeze until the veins in my forearms throb. Someone has been running their mouth about my family without my permission. They're mine. Not anyone else's. Tattlin' to my brother is a giant fuck no in my book.

"See. I know shit," he tosses out like the smug prick he is.

Screw him.

Sparing Bonez a glance over my shoulder, dyin' to punch a hole through the nearest wall or his face, I grit a menacing, "Who told you?"

His graying eyebrows hike skyward. "First or last person?"

Red flashes behind my eyelids, my hold on the rail turning my knuckles white. "Christ. There's more than one?"

A nod. "Bink first. Then Big when he knew you were goin' on the run."

Bink *and* Big. Figures.

"It's not their fuckin' place," I seethe, not caring they're also family.

My asshole brother expels an exasperated breath. "Maybe not Bink's, but it is Big's. We both know that. He doesn't want your head in the clouds or you bottlin' crap up when we're doin' what we gotta do here."

True. Big doesn't butt in unless it could interfere with the safety of us all. I still don't gotta like it.

"Fine," I concede as I watch a bat fly overhead. "But there ain't shit else to explain."

"Except there is. You got a kid, brother… and his mom. You've never had a kid like this…"

Never had a real kid to begin with. Sure, I helped raise Bink. That's different. Janie and Dom haven't been around long enough to be mine. I care for them. Love 'em. That's different, too.

"Don't worry. He's grown now. Can't fuck him up like us." Can you imagine what that would've looked like? What kinda father I would've been?

Bonez nudges the side of my boot with his own. "What the hell? I wasn't thinkin' that. *You're* worried about that?"

Terrified.

Not wanting to scratch the surface of my deepest fears, I shrug and massage the base of my neck. "No… I mean… Fuck… His mom…"

"You like her." The asshole reads between the lines far too well.

"Sure. We'll go with that." I'm addicted. A full-on addict. It doesn't make sense to me. Not even a little. Doesn't make it any less true, though. I can't get the witch outta my head. Not for a single minute. She lingers there, under my skin, in my thoughts. Talkin' about her makes it worse.

"You never liked anyone like this woman." A statement, not a question.

Lost in thoughts of her, I bob my head like a moron. "Truth."

My brother's tone grows soft. "Then what's the issue?"

"You know…" I trail off, 'cause Bonez gets it. He always does.

"The childhood stuff? The kinks? What?"

All the above.

"We ain't right, ya know? 'Cause of that shit." You know what I'm talkin' about too. Not the prettiest picture, huh? Didn't think so.

"Your point?"

"I can't like her."

"'Cause of the—"

"Sex, childhood, all of it. I can't like anyone like that. She deserves better."

"Better than what?" Bonez counters.

Aggravated to the point of violence, I throw both hands in the air and face him. "This! Me! Better than me!" I slap the center of my chest. Doesn't he fuckin' get it? It's not rocket science. One plus one equals two. I'm the problem in this equation. Kit deserves heaven, not hell. Love, not motherfuckin' immorality.

Not down with my outburst, Bonez drops both of his hands on the top of my shoulders and squeezes hard enough to leave bruises. His nostrils flare. "You listen here, and you listen good. If you wanna be with someone, you will. You're loyal to a fault. You won't need the whores anymore. You know yourself. I know you. Do you really think you'd harm someone you care about?"

I'm not my mother or my father. I'm not like Runner or half the brothers who don't give a shit about the women they claim to love. All they care about is sex. Don't get me wrong, I do, too. It's part of me. The desires and twisted parts won't disappear. The itch to control and fuck always lingers. But…

"No," I reply and mean it, 'cause I'd never harm a single hair on that sexy woman's head.

Sighing, I twist from my brother's grip and close my eyes. There she is—again. Grinning this time, lying in bed beside me, reading.

Just like that… my dick turns to granite.

Ignoring the beast, I eject a rush of air and yank a Dum Dum from my pocket. The moment sweet bliss hits my tongue, it's relief in the purest form. Tension bleeds from my shoulders. My erection starts to subside.

Stepping up beside me, Bonez bumps his giant bicep against mine in brotherly affection as we watch a club whore right her skirt in the lot. Runner must be done.

"I've never been—" I begin.

"In love," he cuts in. "I get it's not the same for us. It won't be, 'cause of Mom. But you worrying ain't gonna solve jack shit. You'll love how you're supposed to love when you're supposed to love. There's no rule book on how that's gotta look or be." Bonez delivers another arm thump. "I can't believe we're havin' this conversation. Didn't see that one comin'."

I smirk, half-cocked. "Me neither." Not in this lifetime.

"Got me a nephew." The bastard puffs his chest with pride. "He look like us?"

Rolling my eyes at the ridiculousness of this conversation, I give my brother what he seeks—honesty. "Yeah, Bonez. He looks like us."

He chuckles in full-bodied childish delight. I share in the sentiment with a smile. It's small and lacks enthusiasm, but it's there.

The long-bearded asshole in the corner whistles loudly, drawing our attention.

"You ladies done yet?" Blimp's rocker creeks as it struggles to bear his weight.

We both snicker and join him on the far end of the porch. Blimp offers Bonez a hit. My brother declines with a respectful head shake.

"Suit yourself." Blimp tokes and holds it before liberating an impressive cloud of smoke into the night. Wearing a dazed grin, he rocks back in the chair and strokes his beard. "Maybe you can help us with somethin' important."

"Uh-huh... what's that?" I ask.

He looks to White Boy and jerks his chin. "You explain."

"I got a text from Hunter, Jade's boy. He was askin' if I'd seen his mom."

"Okay... And?" I gesture for him to keep on.

"He hasn't seen her since yesterday morning, and she hasn't responded to any of my texts or calls since then. I told him to check out my mom's place. He said she's not home either. Blimp hasn't heard from her since last night."

That's not exactly something to worry about with those two. "They're best friends. You sure they're not out havin' a girls' night or somethin'?" Probably holed up in some hotel, drinkin' cheap margaritas. They do that. Party hard. Let loose. Especially Loretta, White Boy's mom. She's the wild card.

White Boy sits up straighter and grips his knees. "We were thinkin' that, too. But Blimp called over to Mom's work, and they said she didn't show for shift tonight."

"And she never misses work," Blimp adds before I get a chance to ask.

The phone in my back pocket vibrates with an incoming call. I pluck it free and check the number. It's Prez.

"'Ello?" I answer, hopin' he's callin' for a status update and not what Blimp and White Boy are going on about.

"We've got a problem."

Fuck.

I sigh. "How big we talkin'?"

"Where you at?"

I glance at my brothers. They've stopped talking and are focused on me, concern etched in their faces. "On the porch of the safe house with Bonez, Blimp, and White Boy."

"Alright, we're gonna need privacy," Prez explains.

Fuuuck.

"That bad?"

"Yep."

Great.

Just great.

Leaving my brothers to fend for themselves, I don't bother explaining shit as I jog down the porch steps and find a quiet spot along the side of the house between two overgrown bushes. Kade's shadow passes in the distance. Once he's made it down the way, I lean against the worn wood siding. "Okay… we're good."

Big clears his throat in his I'm-pissed-off-ready-to-commit-murder way. I know it well. "Remy sent a crew to kidnap our women who don't live on the compound. We don't know where they are, but we know he has 'em. A text was sent from a burner phone about an hour ago with pictures." A slew of grumbled curse words follow his announcement.

For the sake of the club, I remain calm. That's how I roll when I'm not fucked up on fucking emotions. This is business. We ain't got time for sentiments clouding our judgment. "What kinda pictures?" I discard the empty sucker stick and replace it with a fresh blueberry one.

"The works—rape, naked, bound."

Fuck.

"Who?"

"Jade, Loretta, Niki—"

"Goddammit," I cut in.

"Beth, some other club whore I don't remember, and…" he trails off.

"And who?"

Don't you say it. Don't you fuckin' say it.

"You gotta promise you won't—"

"And who, Big?" I growl. "They already got Niki and Beth. Tell. Me. Who."

"Kit."

"No." My stomach bottoms out.

"Yes."

"No!" My heart seizes.

"Listen, you can't do what you wanna do. We gotta go a—"

Chucking my phone to the ground, I rip off my cut and throw it on the bush. Blood rushes through my ears. Sweat beads on my brow. Every muscle contracts at once.

They took Kit!

Her.

The one.

My one.

The mother of my son.

They…

Roaring to the inky sky, I punch the air and lose every ounce of control I have left.

It burns to ash at my feet.

The edge of my vision turns hazy.

The world goes black.

Rage prevails—its wicked tentacles an old friend.

Fists meet flesh.

Pennies coat my tongue.

I don't stop.

I can't.

"Christ! Put him the fuck down, Bonez," is the last thing I register before free-falling into the comfort of her bosom, purple hair tickling my face.

Kit.

There you are.

How I've missed you.

CHAPTER SIXTEEN

KIT

Knees pulled to my chest, back against the cool, brick wall, I listen to another woman beg for mercy... Something she won't get. None of us do. They're taking turns. Every few hours, somebody's pulled from the closet, kicking and screaming, then violated outside our room. The sounds will haunt my dreams for years to come.

I bite my bottom lip and squeeze my eyes shut as she wails in pain for the hundredth time.

"Just stop. Just stop. Just stop," an older woman named Loretta sobs under her breath as she rocks beside me.

Beyond helpless, I reach out and pat her shoulder.

We are in this together. All of us. Neither she nor I have been used yet. Perhaps they're saving us for last.

"Ohhh, Jade, I'm so sorry." Loretta quakes in misery. "This shouldn't have happened to you."

No, it shouldn't have. None of this is okay. None of us should be here.

There are six of us—Loretta, Beth, Niki, Jade, Julia, and me.

Our common denominator? The Sacred Sinners.

Loretta, from what I've been told, is White Boy's mother and Blimp's old lady.

Jade is Loretta's younger best friend and White Boy's friend too. I guess they're neighbors. She also works as an artist at a member's old ladies' tattoo shop. I think they said Pixie, but I'm not positive.

Niki and Julia are self-proclaimed club whores.

Were.

Dammit, Mel, get it together.

Against the farthest wall, Julia's body lies still. They brought her back to us after they strangled her to death.

It all happened so fast.

I still can't believe she's gone.

One minute, they ripped her from the room, kicking and screaming, the next, she went silent.

Gone.

Just like that.

Poof.

I shake my head to clear such thoughts as a shiver rolls down my spine.

Then there's Beth, who's related to a retired Sacred Sinner named Jonesy, has a messy past with a biker named Runner, and thinks the world of Gunz.

What can I say? You learn a lot when you're locked in the dark with five women for eternity, hoping this'll soon end. That, or I wake up from whatever fucked-up nightmare I'm having, and this will all have been nothing more than a sick-and-twisted dream.

I pinch the side of my knee and… yep… still here.

"Nooo!" Jade screeches.

A man moans.

I cringe.

Another tear sneaks free as I continue to pat Loretta.

It's almost done. She'll be back with us soon.

Then they'll come again... and again... until... I don't know when.

Resting my forehead on my knees, I think of my guys... Adam and Gunz.

When it's my turn, their memories will give me strength.

I will survive this.

I will.

I can't let these criminals win... no matter the price.

CHAPTER SEVENTEEN

GUNZ

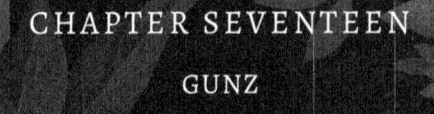

Pulling my gun from its holster, I don't bother with niceties like patience. I'm done. It's been eleven days since we got word our family was taken—that Kit was taken. Since then, my world has plummeted from unsteady to downright crumbling beneath the sole of these old leather shitkickers.

Aiming true at dull brass, I blow a knob clean off, before kicking the ancient door wide open. It smashes against the wall—the violent echo reminiscent of what's to come.

A darkened foyer greets me.

If they're not here, I'm killing Bongo myself—low and slow, with fists and no fucks. He's been running the show from his trailer in Texas. *He's* supposed to be helping us but hasn't done the job the way I would. His failures steal precious minutes. We don't even know if the women are alive.

Seven places we have raided.

Seven.

Yes, you heard that correctly.

Fucking seven.

One lead takes us to another and another. All dead ends.

Now here we are at another shitty house. It's quiet inside. Quieter than the last six.

It smells of mildew and old age as I step across the threshold, ready to shoot any bastard between the eyes.

"Gunz!" someone hollers, wanting me to wait for backup. Fat chance. I'm done waiting. Sure, we've freed other women, men, and children along the way. I've stained my hands in more blood than I care to discuss. It doesn't matter much now, does it? Nothing will until I get them to safety. I can't eat. I sure as fuck can't sleep. The bruises from my hazy night outside the farmhouse have faded. The brothers haven't said much about it. And… thanks to Kit, I can't even enjoy tea anymore without thinkin' of her. And thinkin' of her makes me rage.

This should've never happened!

Hot on my tail, White Boy, not faring much better than me, joins the crusade. The faster we clear this place, the quicker we get to the next on Bongo's endless list of bullshit.

Eyes sharp, I flick on light switch after light switch, not giving a fuck about their electric bill as I scour the place for signs of life. White Boy inspects the rooms I don't as our brothers stand watch outside.

Fresh clothes lie in a pile on an unmade bed upstairs. Fancy men's toiletries are lined up neatly on the attached bathroom vanity.

In the furthest room on the second floor, I find the corpse of a young, naked male, lying in the fetal position beside nothing more than dust bunnies. From the looks of it, he's been gone a while. I'll spare you the gory details.

Holding my breath, I back out of the room, and close the door. There's nothing I can do for him now. The stench of death has become a companion as of late. I barely notice it anymore.

The scrape of bootheels on hardwood greet me as I jog

down the winding staircase to join White Boy and Kade in the parlor. Our resident sick fuck from Texas twirls a Bowie knife like it's nothing as he sifts through a stack of newspapers on the coffee table.

He points to a date with the tip of his blade. "Looks like someone was here yesterday."

Not surprising. They probably caught wind of us in the area and bailed, taking their merchandise with 'em.

"There's a dead teen upstairs," I explain.

"Been there long?" comes from Kade.

"Looks like it."

"Kinda quiet here," White Boy throws out from somewhere in the house.

He's right. It's too still.

"Anyone check the outbuildings yet?" I rock back on my heels, ready to get this over with.

Runner steps into the parlor to join us. "The grounds are clear."

Super! Fantastic! Another motherfucking dead-end.

"Basement?" My upper lip curls in unspent wrath.

Somewhere a door squeaks, and White Boy hollers, "Last on the list!"

Stowing my gun, I scrub both hands down my face and curse and curse and goddamn curse until my anger ebbs long enough to join White Boy in a well-kept kitchen. He holds open a scarred door and flicks on a light switch. Sweeping his hand and bowing with flourish, he bestows me the ridiculous honor of checking out the bowels of this house.

It reeks of rot and piss, as I descend the creaky stairs with him on my tail. There's nothing to see beyond cracked walls, mold, and a small, stained cot in the corner. No signs of life. We turn a corner, and I push a ramshackle table out of the way. The drip, drip, drip of leaky pipes leaves a small puddle on the ground beside a closed door. I press my ear to the rusted steel and hear nada before testing the knob. It's locked.

White Boy juts his chin at the handle and aims a gun at the door. "You check. I'm ready," he whispers as if a werewolf's gonna break out and maim us. This man has lost his marbles.

Past the point of exhaustion, I sigh, and gesture for him to lower the weapon. It's pointless. What's he gonna shoot? A rat? Not likely. I'll end up with a bullet in my foot before any varmint gets offed. My brother needs sleep. He needs peace. Hell, we all do.

White Boy heeds my instructions but stays on alert as I knock the locked handle with the butt of my gun, once, twice, three times… before the thing gives way and falls on the ground in a chorus of too much damn noise.

Opening the door, I step straight into a goddamn horror scene.

Dried blood and a putrid stench, I couldn't explain if I tried to, rapes my senses. I gag and blink, then gag more. A thing shifts in a darkened corner—a person. There's a fuckin' person in here! What the hell is this place?

I pull out my cell and use its light to see better. A mop of reddish hair, and scarred, pale skin, is attached to a set of suspicious eyes as they glare at me from the dirty floor. White Boy gasps when he sees what I do. It's a kid. A boy. Yet not quite a boy. A young man. A buck ass naked one.

"Hey." I lift a palm to show we come in peace. Beside me, my blond brother does the same as he slowly stows his weapon.

The kid says nothing. Doesn't move. Doesn't do jack. Only his glare intensifies. Jaw setting tight, his entire body primes for a fight. By the looks of him, it wouldn't be his first.

"You wanna get outta this shithole?" Light lingering on

him, I take a step back to give the kid space to breathe. If I were him, I wouldn't trust me either, but I'd sure as fuck want outta this room. I'd want a decent meal and a hot shower. Then I'd wanna kill whoever left those whip marks all over my body. Remy and his crew are a magical bunch of pedos. This ain't the first time I've seen this kinda skin décor. Not even the first time I saw it this week. Lots of scars and brandings are left on his treasures. Mostly on the males we save. Now what does that tell you about the piece of shit? I haven't quite decided yet, but I'll leave you to mull it over as I get our only find of the day out of this disgusting place and into some clean clothes.

Leaning against the doorjamb, I pop a mystery Dum Dum into my maw and wait for the kid to chill out. The last thing I wanna do is fight the guy. We don't need that. "Me and my brothers are here to find our women who were kidnapped by the same asshole who did this to you."

When the redhead doesn't respond, much less move to leave, I keep talkin'. "We've freed a bunch of you lately, from bigger places than this." I gesture to his chamber. "We've got a safe place to help ya get back on your feet... You got a name?"

The kid relaxes against the wall but doesn't speak.

Thumbing toward the exit, I push off the frame. "I'm gonna head upstairs. You join us whenever you're ready. Ain't nobody here gonna mess with you." With a parting nod and a tight smile, I leave the young man to decide what he wants. I'm not in the business of freeing people who don't want it.

Hauling my tired ass up the stairs, I join my brothers in the parlor. To give the kid time, we shoot the shit and plan our next course of action. It doesn't take long for the scarred redhead to join us.

One more down…
All our women to go.
Fuck this shit.

CHAPTER EIGHTEEN

KIT

Soft fur sifts through my fingers. Chibs' perky ears twitch as I give him the best rubdown of his life. On the grass beside us, Gunz and Adam laugh together. It's a deep and beautiful sort of sound. I'm home with my guys. A real home. Not like before. Not like the shell I was. It's new… one of comfort and peace. One of…

I wince.

"That's it," a man moans, bursting through my internal defenses.

Squeezing my eyes shut, I inhale, then exhale calmly.

I'll get through this. I will.

They will not win. This is my fucking body, my fucking mind, my fucking spirit, not theirs.

Inside my dreamscape, a strong set of fingers lock with mine, bolstering my determination. "You're a badass," Gunz whispers, his beautiful blue eyes holding mine.

He's right. I am a badass. I am strong.

My body remains numb, every muscle pliant to a fault. The table is no longer cold at my back. Their unwelcomed gropes no longer punishment upon flesh.

"We. Should. Make. Her. Scream." The words penetrate in time with my rapist's thrusts.

A different man laughs his loud, joker-esque approval moments before my nipples are twisted and yanked in brutal glee. Yet, I breathe… and breathe… and breathe… calm and collected. Cool as a cucumber. Right as rain. The present fades like ash in the wind, and I float back into my safe space… where I long to live forever.

"I love you both." I lift Gunz's knuckles to my lips and press a sweet kiss upon the rougher skin. He grins, cheeks pinking in the most handsome of ways.

"I'll protect you for always," he vows.

"You already are."

CHAPTER NINETEEN

GUNZ

This damn well better be it.

It's been too many days since we rescued the kid in the basement. Each stop, each raid, has begun to blur into an endless blood-filled river of torment, of bodies and nameless faces, of violence and sleepless nights. They are out there somewhere, waiting on us to get our fucking shit together and save them. If that's even possible at this point. If they're still alive.

Fuck!

Seated on a rickety chair in our hotel room, elbows on my knees, I rub my temples, and suck angrily on a Dum Dum. My eyes are closed and my chest hurts. The bastard won't stop hurting. Each breath is more painful than the last.

"You need to eat." Blimp drops a tied gas station bag at my feet.

I don't need food. I need to kill. I *need* to find them. All of them... whole. Body parts intact. Blood still in their bodies. Breath in their lungs.

"He can't," comes from Kade, sitting on top of a dresser

next to an old black-and-white television, playing with knives like a child would toys.

Loyal to his core, Blimp doesn't yield. "The fuck he can't. He hasn't eaten in two days."

Truth, from 'em both.

"He'll just throw it up," Kade remarks.

Truth again.

Ignoring our Texas brother, Blimp nudges the toe of my boot. "Gunz, come on, brother, you gotta power up. If you don't, you won't be strong enough for this. The specs on this place are scary, even to me."

Kade chuckles darkly, liking the data far more than the rest of our crew.

Blimp's right. The warehouse is bigger than we've taken on before. Our numbers are solid. Our weapons are on point. The information we've amassed is extensive. I made sure of it this time. No more guesses. No more houses and small-time shit. This is it. It has to be.

Knowing this won't end without a fight, I heed Blimp and dig into the sack. Your standard fare of sandwich and chips rests on my lap as I remove my empty sucker stick from my mouth before taking a bite. Everything tastes like nothingness. It has for days. Just like Kade said, I'll puke it up later, when I don't have a roomful of family eyeing me like I'm two seconds away from ending up in the looney bin.

Walking into the room, White Boy sprawls out on a bed and tucks both hands behind his head. "When do we leave?" His words are slow, laced with exhaustion.

The entire room falls silent, awaiting my response to his question. They've been doin' that a lot lately. Somehow, I've become their anchor. As much as I get it, I don't like it. I'm in no place to lead. Not for this. Not in my condition. Not with this rage. Not with… this… *ugh*. I fuckin' hate war.

Not keen on speakin' at this juncture, I ignore them all

and continue to consume Blimp's offering.

Joinin' our party from the stoop outside, Runner props himself against the open-doorframe. "What'd Big say?" He chews on a piece of gum as a breeze from outside ruffles his hair.

"Tonight," Blimp answers between long drags from his joint, not giving a damn we're in a nonsmoking room, in some rinky-dink hotel on the outskirt of whatever this town is. "He thinks it's best under nightfall. The rest of the brothers Big called are already camped out, ready to rock 'n' roll whenever we give word."

After this is through, when I've got my lady and the rest of my family safe and secure, I'm calling in reinforcements to chop Remy up into tiny, little, microscopic pieces. I don't give a flying dogshit fuck if it takes me years to clean house. He's done. Finito. You can run your dirty operation under the radar. You can be a world-class sicko. Hell, I know my fair share of sickos. One thing you can't do is lay an unwelcomed finger on any person I care about and expect me, the usually reasonable one, to let it go. This old, baldheaded biker doesn't roll that way.

There will be blood.

Buckets of it.

Ripping a chunk of bread from the corner of my sandwich with my teeth, I lean back in the chair, my legs spread wide. "We ride at dusk."

"Shit yeah, we do." Eyes wild, Kade twirls his blade with far too much delight. "Dead fucks at dusk," he sings loud and proud.

Blimp snorts. "Dead fucks at dusk."

On a yawn, White Boy parrots their sentiment.

You heard 'em... Dead fucks at dusk.

Now if you'll excuse me, I'm gonna puke in the comfort of our grimy shithole bathroom.

CHAPTER TWENTY

GUNZ

Brick and steel stretch as far as the eyes can see. It all rests in the middle of a well-lit, black-topped lot, surrounded by dense tree cover on all sides. A single road leads in and out, a lane in each direction. Trucks, vans, and buses are parked everywhere—new, old, creepy white pedo types, expensive sleek beauties, and everything in between. This is the place. Their East Coast headquarters. We've hit the motherload. Big had better hope he sent enough reinforcements because we're not going in tactile and quiet like we usually do. This is brute force infiltration. There are far too many of us to stay under the radar.

Blimp parks our bulletproof SUV next to another one similar in size and style. A line of us roll in single file, each riding in our version of an armored truck. Hell, some of us are in actual armored trucks. Nobody's fuckin' around. We've got a med van standing by a few miles out as my brother, Bonez, has a fleet of vans waiting for whomever we free. This is the biggest operation I've been a part of… ever.

An incoming text vibrates on my lap.

> Prez: Be smart. Stay safe. Bring them home.

Popping a Dum Dum into my maw, I snicker around the stick, shaking my head in amusement. "Prez says for us to be smart and stay safe," I announce to the brothers riding with me.

Blimp chuckles, stroking his beard, on board with Big's sentiment.

"Says the giant fucker who stayed home," Kade singsongs from his bucket seat in the back as he double-checks his arsenal of pointy weapons.

"Yeah... annnd Bear or Ghost aren't here either," I tease. Big might be our national prez, but Bear and Ghost, Kade's chapter prez and VP, are also sitting this one out. I'd say it was their advanced age, but who the fuck am I to talk. I'm closing in on sixty, year after year. So is Blimp. Maybe they're the smart ones. 'Cause any brother riding with us today is out for blood. Trust me, nobody becomes a Sacred Sinner because they're normal. We don't do normal.

Deciding not to reply to Prez, not that he expects me to, I wait for the rest of our brigade to surround the warehouse on all sides—sixteen armed to the nine's vehicles and their inhabitants. Lace, a clinically insane brother from Texas, waves at us, having the time of his life, hanging halfway out of a rolled-down window as they pass.

"He's gonna have funnn." Kade two-finger salutes in return to his fellow chapter brother.

I smirk over my shoulder. "So are you."

White Boy clucks his tongue. "It's quiet. Too quiet," he observes from the rear bench seat.

"That's how all the places have been. The calm before the storm."

"Nobody's mannin' the guard shack. Nobody's out on patrol," he whispers more to himself than us.

"We expected this. Remember? All these vans and trucks aren't parked like this just 'cause it tickled their fuckin' fancy." It's strategic. Some of 'em are likely loaded down with explosives. Some might even have men inside, ready to engage when given word. With Remy's reach and how important this location is to his operations, I'm sure one of his minions caught wind of our not-so-subtle plans. The hotel and other raids haven't gone unnoticed. He knows what we're hunting. If he's smart, he's kept our women alive as a bargaining chip. Only time will tell.

Once our final pickup has taken its spot, all headlights shine like hot bacon grease on the side of the warehouse—the taunt of a biker. The promise of death. A welcome to Hell —Sacred Sinner style.

Setting wheels in motion, Blimp flashes our headlights twice, and everyone in our SUV places a tiny earpiece where it belongs. To make sure they function as needed, I test mine. "Coal, can you hear me?"

"Loud and clear, Gunz," he replies from somewhere in the parking lot. Coal and his crew rode in all the way from the West Coast for this.

One thing down, about a dozen more to go. Closing my eyes, I inhale the deepest, calming breath. This is what we've been waitin' for. We're here to save my woman, my family, and my friends. Today, we will reunite together. Death is part of life. The lives I may take are necessary. On a long exhale, a bone-deep Zen I've been missing for weeks enters me. For the first time in forever, I feel more like myself—ready, steady, and in goddamn control.

Palms flat on my knees, I reopen my eyes and look at Blimp. "It's time."

He nods.

One by one, I unleash war on the scum we've come to terminate. Brothers exit their vehicles in time with my instructions. Many scout the surrounding buses and vans while others set up shop in their posts, protected by tree cover. Gunfire bellows into the night sky as we quickly locate and eliminate our enemies from their hiding spots. No mercy is given, nor is it sought.

In teams of three, our Corrupt Chaos brethren break through every exterior door to gain us safe passage inside.

"Is it time yet?" Kade vibrates in excitement.

"Almost. We're the second wave."

This afternoon, I spent hours on FaceTime with Sniper, the Corrupt Chaos president I've mentioned to you before, to flesh out their involvement in today's war. I couldn't have done this without him, or any of the key players in today's raid.

"We're in," Smoke's thick, Scottish brogue confirms. *"Lots'a bloody fuckin' bodies."*

Out of my peripheral, I watch Kade ready his door handle. "Now?"

I turn to Blimp, then all the way around to see my brothers in the back. "Stay whole. Follow orders and stay in the truck, Blimp." I clap his shoulder.

Knowing his role as getaway if needed, Blimp dips his chin in understanding as the rest of us pull our weapons to fight. In front of us, lit by headlights, is an open doorway, ready to enter, flanked on either side by our armed Corrupt Chaos brothers. This section of warehouse is our closest guess to where they'd hold the captives. Whether or not our calculations are right makes little fuckin' difference. The three of us are on a mission.

Calling out my final round of orders through the comms, I smile wickedly over my shoulder to Kade.

The hunt is on.

Stepping into the unknown, the echo of gunfire greets us. High-octane adrenaline dumps into my system. Sweat beads on my brow. My muscles prime for a fight. Ready for anything. Kade and White Boy protect my six as I lead us into the bowels of our enemy's camp. Lights flicker overhead as gray hallways lead us down more dingy gray hallways. Room by room, we search, uncovering little more than stolen car parts and electronics.

"Need Doc. We've been hit," comes through the comm as we progress, focused on our task. I clear a room, Kade clears the next, then White Boy. Like a well-oiled machine, we remain alert.

At another bend in the hall, Kade presses his spine against the corner. A demonic smile parts his goatee, and he tucks two blades to his chest as a round of voices carry. I ready my gun. Our gazes catch in a don't-get-dead comradery. We chin lift as one. It's showtime.

"Come out, come out, you dead motherfuckers," he taunts.

Four young douchebags dressed in black jog around the corner. Bypassing Kade altogether, they come guns blazing, straight for me, and I'm ready. Dropping low, I avoid the spray of bullets as they chip away at cinderblock walls, clouding the air in chalky smoke.

In a masterful ballet of blades, my Texas brother engages, slicing and dicing in a blur. Crimson coats him, the concrete floor, and walls as I masterfully unload into our enemies. One thigh, two thighs, three thighs, four. Five thighs, six thighs... ooops, they're dead on the floor.

Not quite done, Kade plants his feet on either side of a corpse, slices open the man's cotton shirt, and removes his innards with far more precision than I care to witness. Heavy wetness slaps the ground as Kade performs whatever surgery his dark soul hungers for. It's not my place to judge. Not today. The guy's already rotting in Hell. Let bygones be bygones.

On a groan, I stand to my full height and dust off my knees.

"Mother wouldn't like this," Kade hisses to himself as I take his spot at the corner, to make sure we don't encounter any unwelcomed guests.

In a nearby room, White Boy whistles to get our attention. "You good?"

To be sure, I peer down the hall. It's clear. "Yeah."

"Well... I think I found something."

Leaving Kade to his devices, I join White Boy in a room close to our collection of corpses and...

What the actual fuck?

Hospital beds full of women line both sides of a long, dimly lit room. Down the center, there's a narrow path wide enough to roll a gurney through. Machines beep and chime their greeting as I pause long enough to soak in the scene. Over my shoulder, Kade observes the same and wipes his blades clean on the backside of his jeans.

Nose scrunching in revulsion, I shake my head. "What the hell is this place?" The angry vein in my forehead throbs.

On the other side of the space, White Boy aims his gun at two females lying face down on the floor, fingers threaded behind their heads. "Ask them." He gestures to the bodies with his weapon.

So, I do. Without moving. Because I don't wanna see this shit. I don't wanna be near it. I don't wanna think about it.

"Explain. Now," I growl.

This had better be good.

"It's our job," one croaks.

Right. Their job.

I scoff.

"To do what?" I know what, but I'm askin' anyhow. Consider me interested, 'cause we haven't come across this style of sick fuckery yet. Not from Remy, anyhow.

"Keep them alive," the other explains, less emotional than her counterpart. If I had to guess, she's the leader here. Her voice is far too steady to be anything else.

"They're pregnant," I observe aloud for no reason other than to cement this is real life in real time.

Fuck.

Positioned on their side, each victim is exposed from the waist up. Each wears a cannula for oxygen, an array of wires, and IVs. I can see their tits, their distended bellies, the stretch marks, the bluish tint to their skin. Nothing more than a thin, white sheet covers their bottom half in a room chilly enough to raise goosebumps to flesh.

"Yes," the composed one confirms.

"They're sedated." A statement, not a question. Bags filled with piss hang down the side of their beds as their eyes remain eerily shut. It doesn't take a genius to see what's going down here.

"Yes," the same woman confirms with cold detachment.

Unable to stop the questions from forming, I ask what I need to know… things that mean fuckall right now. 'Cause what is, is. Still, my brain needs to digest the ugly facts. "How long do you keep 'em like this?" I watch the rise and fall of chests as their bellies move with life.

"We get them close to delivery."

Christ.

I pinch the bridge of my nose and breathe before the Zen I've acquired goes *poof*.

"And then what?" I force through gritted teeth, jaw aching.

"He doesn't like used goods." More of that matter-of-fact monotone crap from the short-haired brunette.

Behind me, Kade curses and takes a walk to get some space. Can't say I blame the man.

The squelching of entrails resumes noisier than before from the hallway.

"You're gonna have to elaborate." I gesture for the woman to keep talkin', even though she can't see me.

"We perform c-sections, and he sells them."

Sells. Yeah, you heard her as clear as day. He sells babies.

Babies like Dom.

Babies like Leech.

I stow my gun and shove both hands into my front pockets before I punch something. "What about the mothers?" emanates more as a growl, than words.

"They are—" The redhead hiccups on a sob, her body shaking with emotion.

"They're, what? Say it!"

"W-we cre-cremate them," she finishes.

"It's quick. They don't feel any pain," the cold-hearted bitch tacks on as if that justifies anything.

I should throw her in with them, still conscious and breathing, as flames scorch her flesh and heat turns her insides to dust.

"And that's okay?" I seethe.

"We don't have a choice," the bitch defends.

Lies.

"Everyone has a choice."

"Are you gonna kill us?" comes from the one with a soul.

My head shakes, even though they still can't see me from their spot on the floor. "Not today. Not until my brother decides what to do with these women, then what to do with you." Once he speaks to the brunette, he'll come to the same conclusion I have. Death. If I'm lucky, I'll be there to watch. Male or female, evil is evil. Not caring that you take part in murdering new mothers… Well, that's evil as fuck, don't ya think? Only Bonez will be nice about it. Quick. Painless. Bleh. Boring. She deserves a nice long visit with Kade.

Knowing it's the right thing to do, I text my brother. He needs to know what kinda shitstorm they're walking into.

For an accurate figure, I tick off each woman bed by bed.

Twenty-two.

One less than the number of hours I spent with Kit the first time we met.

The night we conceived Adam.

Balling one hand into a fist, my head hanging low, I sigh.

I miss her.

I miss... fuck... no...*nope*... I don't have time for this. We've got a job to do. One thing at a time.

To ground myself, I yank a Dum Dum from my cut and devour the sweetness as I text Bonez.

Heads up. We have twenty-two sedated pregnant women.

Just as I hit send, Runner's voice cuts through the coms. "We found 'em." My phone pings with a location not far from us.

"On our way."

I'm comin', love.

CHAPTER TWENTY-ONE

KIT

Gunfire. Yelling.

A cacophony of ugly and violence. For a moment, I wish they'd stop, so I can think. So my ears could stop ringing.

Exhaustion erodes a trail straight down to my marrow. I sag into a stiff chair. Too heavy to hold it up, my chin bounces off my chest as I drift in and out of consciousness.

Frigid air bites my bare flesh. Gooseflesh pebbles.

I'm tied up.

No. We're tied up.

My sisters.

My friends.

Exposed.

In pain.

Blinded by whatever they've knotted around our heads.

The awful cotton in my mouth makes it impossible to swallow. Dry. It's so dry.

I try to move to get comfortable. It's futile. Abrasive rope holds me hostage—my tether to this horrible place, wearing divots into my ankles and wrists.

I hate this.

For me.
For us.
Again, I try to swallow.
Ugh.
I want to scream.
I want this to be over.
No more.
Please.
No more.

CHAPTER TWENTY-TWO

GUNZ

The heels of my shitkickers scrape across concrete as I pass brother after brother in the hall. Our chins lift in mutual respect as I'm guided from one corridor to the next, through a double doorway, and into a large office where a group of us have taken up arms, ready to kill whatever motherfucker gets in our way.

Next to a whiteboard, I leave Kade with Lace as I scope out the space alone, to get a clearer vision of what's about to go down.

Tables are pushed to the far walls. In the center of the room, each woman is naked and bound, seated in a row of chairs. A couple of feet separates one from the other. That seems to be the going trend around these parts—incapacitate. Above each of them, a single bulb sways to-and-fro in a morbid display of debauchery. Leaving little to the imagination, their vaginas are visible, bare tits splattered in what I assume is dried cum. Thanks to the fabric tied around their heads, they can't see a thing. Nor would I want them to. Not since Remy's crew has sheared their hair clean off, leaving them bald... as bald as me.

A growl rumbles viciously in my chest as my molars grind. Nostrils flaring, I do my best to keep my anger in check. Foolish action breeds deadly consequences. It could get them killed. It could get her killed. My Kit. The furthest from me. On the end. Chin resting on her chest in defeat, purple hair gone, skin pale.

I'm here, love.

I'm here for you.

In hopes she'll sense my presence, I channel the unspoken words in her direction.

Not much longer, sweetheart.

She doesn't move.

If it wasn't for the shallow rise and fall of her chest, I'd think she was dead.

I continue my perusal of the space. Calm, as if I'm bored. As if there isn't a line of brothers impatiently waiting for their moment to unleash. Many already coated in blood from battle. They bounce on the balls of their feet, necks cracking, as if they've taken a fresh snort of coke, and the world of death is now their oyster.

Fifteen, possibly twenty, men wait in the darkened recesses of the room, a mirror of our own. They've planned this well. If I wasn't here to destroy them, it might impress me. Only I'm not. Because you don't do this to innocent women. Women who've done nothing more than be a part of our world, nothing more, nothing less.

Staying focused, I don't look at any one female longer than necessary. I can't. Not if I wanna get us outta here in one piece. They're nothing more than bodies in chairs—faceless victims. I can't identify them and make this any more personal than it already is.

I step forward—out of our shadows and into the light. Enough to expose myself to the enemy. To become the key player in tonight's game. Power vs. power. Them vs. us.

They're about to become the pawns on my playground. Welcome to the show.

A man dressed in an expensive black suit and tie steps behind our girls. "Hello, Gunz," his thick, Russian accent articulates.

To appear less threatening, I relax my stance and cross both arms over my chest. "Hello, scumbag." My tone's flat as I tip my chin in slow greeting, my eyes meeting his in strength.

A smile splits the Russian's lips. He chuckles, dark and amused. "Ah, yes. Funny, American."

This is new. An outsider working with Remy. Perhaps his empire spreads further than I anticipated. Or... he brought in the big dogs to help in this fight. Either way, I'm ready for anything.

In a show of arrogance, the Russian rests a palm on Niki's shoulder and the other on Beth's as he stands between their chairs. A row of thick, gold rings shine under the lights. I wanna laugh at his antiquated mob boss routine. It's cute.

The scumbag arches a bushy brow in challenge.

See.

I told you he thought he had something there.

Arrogance only gets you so far.

I remain impassive and yawn because I can, my posture lazy, like I have all day.

If he were up against a man like Big, the room would've erupted in chaos by now. But I'm not Big. There's a reason I'm here, and he isn't.

The brothers behind me grumble their discontent as his faction mocks us in muted laughter from across the way.

Yuk it up, boys. You won't be smiling when your families welcome you home in body bags.

When I don't give the Russian the reaction he seeks, he does what any egotistical, small dicked bastard would and forcefully removes Beth's blindfold before he gropes one of her breasts. It's cold and callous. A silent tear treks down her cheek as she winces in pain. My gut tightens in response, dying to step in and help. But I can't. Not yet.

He arches that same brow again. What a cocky, cocky man. A sinister smirk follows at the corner of his mouth.

A brother curses behind me. Another snarls. I say nothing. Give nothing.

"You son of a bitch!" Runner bursts through the doorway and advances on the Russian, not caring about anyone but Beth. Stupid asshole. On instinct, I lurch forward to grab his cut and yank the jackass to safety. I barely get ahold of his back before he twists out of my grasp and powers on, giving zero fucks.

Beth's watery eyes widen in disbelief as she croaks around her gag, seeing him for the first time in forever.

"Beth!" he roars at the same moment the familiar sound of a gun discharging pulses through the air.

I dive for Runner. Hitting him from the side like a linebacker, we collapse on the floor in a mess of limbs, knocking the wind out of my goddamn lungs as I land on top of him. He doesn't move. I roll off and turn him onto his back. Blood seeps into the carpet, turning the blue an ugly shade of blue-black as it pools beneath us.

"R-un-Runner, where you hit?" I wheeze as I lean up to jostle him. He still doesn't respond.

"Runner!" I punch him in the shoulder, waiting for him to open his eyes, groan, something. To give me hell like the stubborn asshole always does.

He does jack all.

I press a finger to the side of his unshaven throat.

Blood trickles down the side of his forehead. That's when I see it, the hole just below the hairline. The specks of brain matter on the ground around us. In shock, I blink once to focus, then look down at the blood on my hands, at the blood on my shirt, and it soaking into the denim of my jeans.

He's dead.

Someone killed my brother.

An asshole he may have been, but Runner was still my brother. Will always be my brother.

A pesky tear finds its way from my eye before I swipe it away with the back of my hand. I lay a palm upon Runner's still heart and wish him a farewell. Emotions I don't wanna acknowledge unfurl in my chest—ugly, raw, and dangerous.

Closing both eyes for a beat, I inhale a single, profound breath and hold it there as the ache spreads, as my Zen sloughs off, and the glue holding my jagged pieces together melts into a puddle of nothingness. No longer held captive, tendrils of darkness leak into my vision. Most of the world fears our prez because he's the giant, the dick, the face of the Sacred Sinners… but they don't know me. They don't know what happens when I let go. The calm one. The rational one. The one with a murky past he won't talk about. The boy sold by his mother to the neighborhood whores. The one who unleashes his evil within the confines of depravity. On those willing.

I'm done.

Clenching my jaw, my abs, my pecs, I expel my breath in a rush and twist my head slowly to the side. The room falls quiet, watching the Russian watch me, waiting for a pin to drop. Fuck him. Fuck 'em all.

Smoothly dropping onto my back, half on top of Runner, I rip my gun free from my cut and shoot. You wanna fuck with the Sacred Sinners, you wanna fuck with me, you wanna kill my brother, you wanna touch my women? You're gonna die.

The first bullet hits the Russian bastard in the shoulder.

He staggers backward, catching himself on the top of Niki's chair in obvious shock. There's more where that came from.

In the confines of the office, brothers and enemies alike engage as I clamber off the floor to handle business. A group of bikers carry chairs laden with our women out of harm's way, doing their best to cover them with their own bodies as they run for safety, under a cloud of deafening gunfire.

Tables are knocked onto their sides as shields. Lace and Kade slice and dice their way through a throng of enemies. Trusting my fellow brothers to do their job, I focus on him—my prize.

"You killed my brother!" I loom over the Russian bastard as he squirms in pain on the floor, blood seeping from too many holes. "You did this."

His cronies wouldn't have ended Runner without his consent. They wouldn't have cut our women's hair off or tied them up without the orders to do so. They know the rules.

Watching his eyes widen in horror, knowing these are the final moments of his existence, I kick the son of a bitch in the side. He groans a high-pitched, pathetic sound. Unsatisfied by his reaction, by how easily he succumbs to his wounds, by his lack of fight, my upper lip curls back over my teeth in an ugly snarl. I spit on his face, varnishing it in my hatred. On a whine, the fucker clutches his stomach as tears trickle down the sides of his face. Pussy. I straddle his form, one foot on either side, and aim true, at the exact spot they ended my brother. "Fuck you!" The bullet carves a pit right where it belongs. The Russian's body jerks one last time before I watch the remnants of his soul escape, headed to whatever afterlife.

Good riddance.

The scent of pennies suffuses the air as the Grim Reaper stakes his claim one by one through the office. Those who live clear out, leaving behind nothing more than a brutal war field—a cemetery.

Checking for signs of life, just to be certain, I nudge bodies with the toe of my boot. Nobody moves. Not an inch. Not a breath. Good.

White Boy, coated in bodily fluids, sidles up to me as I flip a deceased biker onto his back and cut off his patch to take home to his family. I shove it into my rear pocket for safe-keeping. I may not know this man, Jimbo, but I respect his sacrifice.

I press my thumb to the center of his forehead. *Rest in peace, brother.*

"You hit?" White Boy asks as he flips another fallen Sacred Sinner onto his back.

I kneel beside the young male and press my thumb to the center of his skull, or what's left of it. *Rest in peace, brother.*

White Boy removes the guy's patch and hands it to me. It, too, joins the other.

"You hit?" the pain in the ass repeats when I don't answer the first time.

Can't he see I'm busy? I side-eye him, unimpressed. He raises a brow, challenging me. Fine. My bones crack like I'm a thousand years old as I stand long enough to get my brother off my ass.

With flourish, I scan my legs, shake 'em a little for show, then check my torso and arms. Everything seems just peachy, 'til a finger grazes my side, and my adrenaline begins to wane. I stumble forth and catch myself on the closest wall.

Shit. Fuck. Fuckin' shit.

Heaving a pained breath, I grip my side. Blood squishes through the hole in my cut, bathing my palm in red.

Goddammit!

White Boy turns me around by the shoulders and props

my back against the wall. Grabbing me by the chin, he forces me to look him in the eye.

"Let me see." He peels my cut to the side, and shoves my t-shirt up my abs, exposing the hole. It leaks steadily onto the waistband of my jeans, coating my belt. He reaches around my back to probe for an exit wound. No dice.

"You gotta see Doc," he confirms, doing an I-told-ya-so eyebrow wiggle, as if he saw me get hit. Who knows... he might have. But if he thinks I'm seein' Doc, no, the fuck I'm not.

I push his overbearing touch away and cover the hole with my palm, to staunch the bleeding. "I need to see the girls." All of 'em. The bullet can come out later. This isn't the first time I've been shot, nor will it be the last. I'm not dying today.

"After you fix that." He waves to the wound. "Bonez is already outside. The girls have been removed from their chairs. They're safe. You, not so much."

Rolling my eyes, I shove off the wall to go see them. To make sure Kit knows I'm here for her. That I came. I should've been the first face she saw when they removed the blindfold. I need to be there. I need to touch her. To hear her voice. To tell her Adam's okay. That Big's got him.

"Stubborn asshole." White Boy hooks an arm through mine and escorts me like an old crippled from the room, despite my grumbly protests. We hobble over several bodies before we reach a hallway teeming with brothers. Many of them mend flesh wounds with packets of gauze and tape on their own as others take a beat to catch their bearings. Can't say I blame 'em. It's been a long night.

"How's your mom and Jade?" I ask as we amble through the warehouse, pretending I'm fine.

"I don't wanna talk about it."

"Brother..."

"I knew whatever happened to them would be bad. Now it's real."

"They're still breathin'."

"Yeah. I know." He doesn't sound convinced. Truth be told, neither do I, but I'm not about to tell him that.

"We're gonna get 'em help." It's the best positive, self-help, mumbo jumbo I can muster at the moment.

Wind knocked outta his sails, White Boy shrugs both shoulders, nearly touching his ears. "I know." He sighs as they drop. "But what about Jade's son? He's gotta see his mom like this. Then Blimp and Mom... Fuck... He's messed up."

"That's why I told him to stay in the truck." There's no way on God's green earth Blimp could've witnessed his old lady tied up like that and not gotten himself killed trying to rescue her. Like Runner. For all his toked-up chill, he's protective. He's also the size of, you guessed it, a Blimp. Despite the fact he owns a gun shop, he's not stealthy. He's the backup man. The slow-and-steady blow-you-apart-with-a-sawed-off kinda brother. The one great for a lookout, or from a distance, but up close, when emotions run high, he's more liability than asset. I knew that going in, which is why I lied about the getaway driver. He's a smart cookie. He knew what I was doin' as I was doin' it. We've been friends most of my life.

"We did this," White Boy declares with too much vehemence.

"We didn't do shit," I return with just as much, if not more, intensity.

"They're like this because of us. Because of who we are." My brother pounds the center of his chest with a fist, stacking all the responsibility on his shoulders.

Not down with the martyr horseshit, I shake my head, and I do it well. "No. They're like this 'cause some sick motherfuckers prey on women and boys... and they don't like us meddlin' in their business," I rationalize to keep the kid's guilt in check. He doesn't need this kinda baggage. That's for us ancient fuckers to carry. We've got the grit to manage it. He needs to live his life to the fullest—fuck, fight, and have a blast on the back of his Harley, with the wind in his blond hair. Not nightmares of blood staining his hands. Pussy and booze. Smiles and rock-n-roll. The shit men sign up for when they become a Sacred Sinner. Violence might be a byproduct of our brotherhood, but it's not the heart of us. We do what we gotta do to make the world a better place for those we love and those who can't fight for themselves. I happen to think it's honorable. Maybe that's just me, though. I'm not some twenty-something, fresh-faced baby. I've bled Sacred Sinner far longer than many of these fuckers have been alive, including him.

We don't speak much as we finish navigating our way outta the warehouse, me grittin' my teeth with each step.

The parking lot's a circus as we exit the building through the front. The first thing I latch my sights on is Bonez's big head tending to Niki in the open bay of an ambulance. One of two they brought, parked side by side. I scan for you-know-who and find feminine, tatted arms embracing Loretta next to a wild-eyed Blimp, staring a possessive hole straight through his old lady. Never blinking. Not moving. Just lookin'.

Kit releases her friend when Blimp speaks to her. Rubbing something from her eyes, my lady turns and... fuck.

CHAPTER TWENTY-THREE

KIT

Those eyes. Those beautiful blue eyes. They tether our souls across the headlight-lit expanse as I stumble forth in oversized sweats like a newborn colt, nearly falling on my ass to get to him. Gunz's arms widen to catch me, his hands bathed in red. Not caring about anything but him, I dive into his embrace, arms locking around his middle. He staggers backward to keep us upright and groans as he absorbs me, wrapping me up tight. Warmth and him. Leather and comfort. Muscles and man.

Unable to control it a moment longer, my internal dam crumbles into a million pieces at my feet, and I weep into his chest. Vicious, full-bodied agony rips from the depths of my being. Fat, salty droplets soak into his shirt. He's here. We're together. I'm alive. He's alive. The torture's over. The relief's immense.

Gunz whispers sweet nothings against the top of my new beanie. The warmth of his breath bathes my bald head through the knit fabric. I clutch the back of his shirt until my knuckles ache, never wanting to let go.

"I've got you. I'm here now, love," he vows.

In response, I shudder violently, then hiccup as an all-consuming wail wrenches itself from the knot in my belly, up my throat, and through my mouth, needing to be liberated. I let it go because it doesn't give me a choice.

Just as he's been with me through it all. My shelter against the storm. My solace. Gunz holds me, strong and unyielding. I want to tell him how much this means to have him here but can't. Not yet. Another horrible noise erupts from my lips. I try to swallow it down, but it doesn't fucking care.

Stuffing my nose between his pecs, I breathe in the scent of death and him—of spice, laundry, and sweat. I close my eyes and relish the present. Not the past. Not inside the building. Not the emotions. I ignore the ache in my legs, as I struggle to stand for too long. I can't let go. Not yet.

I breathe.

In.

Out.

Calming myself.

When they cut us from our chairs, they dressed us, mended our surface wounds, and fed us protein bars. They didn't taste like much. It couldn't fill the void in my middle. The rot there, poisoning me from the core out, has changed me forever. No food could ever fix it. I don't know if anything can. Not for me, not for any of us women. Not after what we went through.

"Gunz." The breathy accentuation of his name comes from Niki. I do my best to tune her out. She's in love with him. We all know it. He's all she spoke about in the closet. He, too, was her solace. If I was selfless, I would let him go to care for her like he has me. But I can't. Horrible or not. Selfish or not. I just can't.

I know I don't know Gunz well. Not like Niki. Not like Beth or Loretta. Not like Jade. I'm new. He and I have spent a total of three nights together, just three, and look where we are. The first time, he gave me the biggest gift anyone could receive. The second, he gave me another. I couldn't tell you what it is or what it means. I just know he feels big... he's important. I should've known it the night we met all those years ago. How special he is. The rebel who fucked me into oblivion. For many years, I often wondered how he was. How his life turned out. In the parking lot of a warehouse, wrapped in his arms, now I know.

"Sweetheart." Gunz jostles me.

I rub my face on his shirt to dry the tears. "Yes?"

He breathes in, his chest expanding. "I gotta go see Doc. But I want ya with me."

I pull back just enough to look up at his face—pale skin, a grimace, sweat dripping down his forehead. "What's wrong?"

Beside us, wrapped in a cocoon of their own, White Boy rubs Jade's back. "He got hit," he answers for me.

"Hit?" Huh... how?

"Yeah. Here." Gunz peels back the edge of his cut, exposing his side. There's a hole through his stained shirt.

Brow furrowing, I take a small step back and watch blood leak from his body. "What... the... why didn't you say anything?" I glance down at myself. I'm stained, too, in his blood, on the matching side.

Not giving a single damn he's hurt, Gunz seizes my hand and folds his clammy fingers through mine. Those intense blues bore holes through me as he speaks. "I wanted to see you first. To make sure you know I'm sorry and I'm never fuckin' leavin' you again." The sentiment is sweet, his care palpable... but he's... hurt.

"Jesus Christ." I scrub a palm down my face. "That can come after we get the bullet out of you." Like right now.

Before I panic, I squeeze Gunz's hand in the tightest hold I can muster and drag his stubborn ass behind me, over to the ambulance where his brother's outside, stitching up another Sacred Sinner on the lid of a cooler. I drop Gunz's hand, throw up his shirt, and expose the wound to Bonez.

His brother's wide eyes, pursed lips, and head shake say it all as he motions for us with the flick of his chin to climb onto the back of the ambulance. Before we do, I help Gunz out of his cut and hand it to Niki to keep safe. She hugs it to her chest, her eyes pinched closed, and smells it. I do my best to ignore the jealousy it bubbles to the surface as I tug his shirt over his head. He trembles and loses his breath for half a second as I discard the ruined fabric into a nearby bin. Not causing any fuss, he uses the railing to climb into the ambulance first, leaving bloody fingerprints on the steel in his wake, me hot on his tail.

Ever so slowly, Gunz perches his behind on the edge of the stretcher as I sit across from him on the bench, out of the doc's way. Like he can't stop touching me, to make sure I'm okay, Gunz reaches out for me to take his hand into mine as he uses his other to cover the swollen injury. Gently squeezing his fingers in support, a slender, clean-shaven, white-haired man enters through the side door, takes one look at Gunz, and rolls his eyes heavenward. "You're a dumbass."

My injured guy... friend... whatever you wanna call him... tries to pull a smile, but it ends in a wrinkled scowl. My expression mimics his in sympathy. "I know," he wheezes out as his shoulders hunch forward in noticeable discomfort.

"This'll be the fifth I've dug out of you, boy. You'd think you would've learned by now," the older man half-chastises, a hint of humor simmering beneath the surface.

Holy crap... Five times. F-i-v-e.

I shake my head at the thought.

"It's been almost a decade, old man," Gunz grumbles.

"Since the last?" Doc fusses with supplies on the wall at the head of the bed.

"Yeah."

The male chuckles. "Well, alright, then. Guess you've learned a lil somethin', huh?" He pops open a small compartment.

Gunz looks up at me through dark lashes and rolls his eyes. "Seems so." Despite his misery, a tiny smirk twists at the edge of his lips, just noticeable through his unkempt beard. I deliver him a sunnier one in return, so he knows I'm here to stay. That he's gonna be okay.

"Now, who's this, pretty lady?" Doc flashes me a flirty smile over his shoulder and winks. Out of courtesy, I return a polite grin.

Gunz is not impressed. His deepening frown says as much. "No more questions, Doc. Just cut me open."

The white-haired man tsks his patient. "Now. Now. You talk. I work."

"She's my old lady."

Whoa. I'm… his…

I don't get a moment to contemplate whatever that means before the old man fires a high-pitched whistle and slaps his knee. "Damn. You gotta old lady now. Didn't think I'd see the day."

Patience hanging by a thread, Gunz chews his bottom lip for a long, painful pause before speaking. "Just cut the fuckin' bullet from my gut," he forces out.

If he's done, I'm done. Old lady or not, Gunz is hurt, and I don't enjoy seeing him this way. Sweating profusely, the hair curls on his chest, and his skin glistens in the overhead lights. Speckles of blood dot his face and bald head. I watch him breathe. Each respiration's more difficult than the last.

Doc lays a small bag on the floor beside Gunz's foot and digs around in the thing. "Might need to put ya to sleep for this."

"Just give me the morphine."

"We're out."

"Fuck. Fine. Numb the area then cut it out. I'm not goin' to sleep."

"It's gonna hurt."

"No shit."

Doc hums.

"Gunz, it might be better if you just—" I start, only to be cut off by an adamant biker.

"Not a chance, love. I'm—" His words are severed as a fast-working Doc stabs a needle into Gunz's bicep and expels a plunger full of liquid. Glaring at the doctor, Gunz curses up a shitstorm.

"Now, lay down." Not giving Gunz a chance to fight him, Doc grabs his brother's shoulders and forces him flat onto the stretcher. I move as they move, to keep our fingers entwined. Doc removes Gunz's belt with a mighty tug, unfastens his jeans, and shoves them down his thighs to get more space to work. Then he folds the edge of his boxer briefs down, exposing the skull tattoo at his pelvis, and disinfects the wound with a squirt of iodine. Enraptured by his no-nonsense way of getting shit done, I watch Doc as my biker stares away from the scene, straight at me. His eyelids flutter open and closed until they come to a solid rest. Once his patient is out, Doc places a pulse-ox on Gunz's finger, an oxygen mask over his face, and checks his blood pressure with a cuff from the bag.

"What'd you give him?" I ask as quiet as a church mouse, not wanting to disrupt the process.

"A sedative." Another one of those charming, toothy smiles flashes my way.

In the open bay, Bonez removes his dirty gloves, snaps on a fresh pair from a box on the wall and climbs in beside me. I release Gunz's limp hand to give his brother's large body room to maneuver in the smaller space.

In sync, Doc and Bonez work as two bodies, one mind—far better than any doctors I've watched on any trauma series before. Or perhaps I'm biased because I've never seen this in real life. Not as a professor. Not even as a mother to Adam. He kept the bleeding incidents to a minimum. Skinned knees and a couple of broken bones, which I assume is normal when parenting boys.

They speak in hushed tones as a group of Sacred Sinners, most of whom I don't recognize, gather at the open doors to watch them work.

"He's gonna be pissed you put him down," Bonez states.

"I don't care. It's better than havin' to hold him down and make his old lady listen to him scream." Doc opens a small refrigerator and extracts a bag of blood. He hangs it on a hook above the stretcher. Then he IVs the sleeping man like he's done this very thing a million times before and feeds the fresh blood into a vein as Bonez irrigates the wound with a syringe.

In quiet fascination, I curl up on the seat to watch them, and they let me. One pries open the wound as the other fishes a gloved finger into the hole to assess the internal damage.

"Nothin' major," Doc announces confidently.

I sigh in relief, and two bikers standing watch throw their arms up in celebration before high-fiving. Tucking my arms around my middle for comfort, I chuckle to myself at their antics. Gunz means a lot to many people. He matters. It's nice to see others care. Being a loner, it's been a while since I've witnessed this level of give-a-shit. Not since… I was married, I guess. Before our world went haywire and I started on this new path of finding myself. Becoming the real Melanie. Realizing I don't need anyone, but me and my son. Us against the world. My heart aches at the thought. Such lonely times.

Wrestling their way to the front of the crowd, Loretta and Jade signal to me with a wave of their hands. Not knowing what to do, I return an awkward wave in greeting.

"You need anything?" comes from a black-eyed Loretta.

Shaking my head, I mouth, *No thanks.*

"We're here if you need us," Jade adds, tugging the beanie further down her head, stopping just above her eyes.

Thank you, I mouth, my chest getting all weird and fuzzy. For no reason at all, water clouds my vision. Turning away, I swallow to stop the icky emotions from doing whatever they're doing. Jade and Loretta were my crew on the inside. I wasn't alone with them by my side. They made sure of it. Outside, they're doing the same. I love them for it and appreciate it more than they could ever know.

To get my crap together for Gunz's sake and my own, I close my eyes to do just that, and I'm transported back there —dark closet, cold floor, shivering, naked.

Loretta nudges my shoulder. "Kit, ya gotta eat." Her voice crackles with emotion.

Refusing to show weakness, I cup my sore vagina. Viscous liquid coats my palm, remnants of their fun. "I can't." Or I'll wretch.

"Just a bite." Jade presses a rough piece of bread to my cheek, trying to locate my mouth.

I turn away, my stomach cramping in hunger, in...

"Almost done," Bonez announces, hurling me back into the now.

I sag in relief, grateful to be here. Grateful to be alive. I shake my head to purge the raw memories.

Suction and irrigation run in tandem as they remove the final fragments from Gunz's abdomen. Before long, most of the blood bag is empty, and they're stitching him up. I watch every minute of it and ignore the *once was* in preference for the *what is*. I pretend I'm not bald, that my skin doesn't crawl

201

with every breath, that I'm not tainted. I'm grateful. I... am. I'm strong. I...

Straightening my spine, I focus on the bandage they place on Gunz's ripped stomach, over the perfect line of stitches.

Tossing bloodied gloves into a receptacle, Bonez turns to me. "Welcome to the family, Kit. I look forward to meeting my nephew real soon." An exhausted smile is the best Bonez offers before he stuffs a fresh box of gloves under his armpit and slings a bag of supplies over his shoulder. "He'll be up soon. Take care of yourself."

"Thanks. You, too," I call to his retreating form as the crowd parts and he jumps out of the ambulance, into the night. An angel to heal the less fortunate. A savior in leather. Right now, I couldn't be prouder my son shares DNA with that man. One of the good ones. An obvious rebel with a heart of gold. It gives me hope for Adam. For his future.

Just as Doc removes the mask from Gunz's face, those pretty blues flutter open and land straight on me. "I've got you, love," he slurs before passing out again.

Cleaning up, Doc's head shakes in amusement. "He's gonna do that for a bit."

Less than a minute later, the same thing happens. "Hey, babe."

"Hey back." I offer a tiny finger wave.

"I've got you..." Out he goes again, his head lulling to the side, mouth slack.

Wanting to be closer, I get up. "I've got you, too," I whisper as I lean over to peck his upturned forehead, letting my lips linger there.

He hums a deep, content kinda sound. "My... lady."

"Your lady," I repeat, to hear it in my own words, to let it sink in.

His lady.
Gunz's.

I don't know how I feel about that. Hell, I don't know what to think about much of anything. Staying alive, staying sane, has been the focus for… however long we were kidnapped. Yuck. I don't like that word.

A terrible prickle rises at the base of my neck, forcing a shiver down to the tips of my toes.

Eyes still closed, Gunz's lazy hand flops around, seeking mine. An itty-bitty smile peaks at the corner of my mouth as I rejoin us as one. His cool, damp palm in my small, warmer one.

The handsome man hums once again, squeezing our connection with far more strength than I expect. "Mine."

Yes.

Yours.

CHAPTER TWENTY-FOUR

KIT

Elbow perched on the window ledge, palm cradling my face, I sag against the door and watch a colorful world pass by. Trees and grass. Grass and trees. The most beautiful sky I've ever seen. Gunz squeezes my knee, a simple gesture that means everything. Soothing heat penetrates through the cotton of my sweats where his hand lingers. Grateful for the connection, I pat the top of his hand to communicate what words cannot. I don't know how or why, but he gets me. He knows what I need before I do. He reads between lines I didn't know existed.

I sigh loudly, one tick past the point of exhaustion, not the normal kind, the kind that makes your skin weigh a thousand pounds as it hangs off your bones. The half-gone Dum Dum in my mouth clinks against my teeth as I roll it to the other cheek. Peach. Another comfort from Gunz despite healing himself. Despite having been on the road for months, resting his head in places not home, eating fast food day after day. Not that you'd know it. He acts as if he wasn't shot, as if this is the norm. Stubborn, strong, stalwart man. Beautiful man.

Less than forty-eight hours ago, they freed us from hell. You'd think that'd mean the worst was over, right? Wrong. Wrong. Triple wrong. Nobody tells you what happens in the wake of trauma. You read books and watch movies where the girl gets banged up, then she's saved. The survivor. The resilient one. What they don't talk about is the edginess. The need to always glance over your shoulder, waiting for the other shoe to drop. When you close your eyes, you're there again… like an old, scratchy record player that gets stuck on repeat. You worry about your friends. Not the normal kind of worry. The obsessive, anxious kind. You wonder how they're doing. If they're experiencing the same. If they're sleeping. How they're healing. But you can't talk about it. Not with them. Not with anyone. Why? Because it's not their burden to bear. On the slight chance, they've moved on… if they're that woman in the movies, the resilient one who can pick up life where it left off, like nothing happened, you don't want to trudge up horrors. It's selfish. So, I live in the now for as long as I can before the eerie coldness reclaims me.

At the thought, I shiver, despite the warmth in the truck.

Once more, Gunz reads me like an open book. The hand resting on my knee squeezes longer than before, imbuing me with whatever magic he possesses. I calm as I always do, his enchantment weaving through me as I focus less on feeling and more on now. Loretta's in the passenger seat, holding her man's hand across the console. Rock music bumps lowkey through the speakers—enough to make out the lyrics but not enough to really jam like I used to in my jacked-up truck. Man, that feels like a decade ago now. A different life.

The rumble of tailpipes suffuses the air, a steady reminder we're not alone. Men in leather joined our motorcade an hour ago. Sacred Sinners in the front, Sacred Sinners in the back—an escort home. The promise of a safe return.

Brilliant streaks of the mid-afternoon sun gleam through

a cloudless sky as we roll past a freshly painted compound gate and matching guard station. Black. Matte black. Those on bikes guide us across a parking lot crammed with people. Blimp parks our SUV next to another and cuts the engine. I don't get a chance to ask Gunz what's next when my door's nearly torn off its hinges by a big-breasted blonde in an oversized Harley shirt and skintight leggings. I'd recognize the woman anywhere. Bink. One look at me, and *bam,* I'm hugged right out my seat. Having no clue how to react, I look over my shoulder for help, only to find Gunz climbing out behind me, wearing the biggest shit-eating grin I've ever seen, his eyes glistening in delight. A giant of a man with long, dark hair braided down his back shuts our door as I'm squeezed nearly half to death by a woman far mightier than she looks.

"Welcome home." Bink's voice trembles, her breasts mashing against mine. Stuffing my nose into the side of her hair, I squeeze her back. Not because I have to. Not for any other reason than... I think I need it. Wetness begins to leak from my eye sockets into her strawberry-scented trusses. Not at all disgusted by this, Bink holds me tighter, making it more difficult to breathe. We sway together in the parking lot, feet slotted between feet. I note her sniffles alongside my own. The giant man grumbles his discomfort at our display, but neither of us seem to care as she clutches the back of my sweatshirt and I let her.

A palm I know to be Gunz's, by touch alone, lays upon my shoulder. He leans in and kisses the back of my beanie, then shifts, and I hear him kiss Bink's head too. They exchange muffled words as his hand slides up and kneads the base of my neck, a reminder he's here and not going anywhere.

"Mom!" a voice I'd know anywhere calls above the raucous crowd of men and women, of bikes, and rock music pulsing from inside the clubhouse. "Mom!"

My boy's here!

Having heard Adam, too, Bink releases me. I turn just in time to be swooped up by my son, all six feet of him. Wrapping both arms around Adam's strong neck, he lifts me off the ground as if I weigh nothing. Spitting my empty sucker stick out, I pepper kisses across his cheek as tears of happiness rain down my face. I missed him. I missed him so much. He kisses me in return. The press of warm lips upon my cheek. Giving zero fucks how I look, or that I'm being a gross, icky mom in front of a parking lot full of bad boys in leather, he lets me love him. I accept the rare gift and kiss him until he begins to vibrate in full-body laughter at my ridiculousness. Heart full, I beam at his chuckles, at the way his chest quakes against mine, at his tangible joy. What an incredible feeling... a feeling I wasn't sure I'd be lucky enough to experience again.

Not caring if he minds, I wipe the remnants of my tears on his t-shirt-clad shoulder. Adam says nothing. Nor does he mind me squeezing him hard enough my muscles begin to twinge. Actually, the jerk doesn't seem to notice. My mom muscles are no match for his. He bulked up in jail. The hardness of his pecs and the roundness of his shoulders are evidence enough. He put on some weight. I open my mouth to comment as much but stop short when I realize he's talking to his dad for the first time outside of jail. Face-to-face, no glass between them.

"How ya holdin' up?" Gunz asks him as if he genuinely wants to know.

Our son's arms lock tighter around my center. "Good. Now that she's home safe."

Awe. He was worried. Quite the change in our dynamics when I'm usually the one concerned about him and what shenanigans he'll pull next.

Alone in our hotel room last night, Gunz explained that

Big, his president, picked Adam up from jail upon his release. Then took him to gather his things and brought him back to the compound to keep him safe. What that meant I didn't know, nor did I ask. I trust him. It was late, and we were exhausted from being on the road most of the day. Now that we're here and Adam's here, I'm suddenly more tired than I've been since I was cut from my restraints.

Yawning, I massage the bruises around my wrists over my son's shoulders. Adam takes the cue that I want to be set back on my feet. I slide down his front and land softly on the ground. Doing what moms do, I cup his cheeks and paste on the best smile I can conjure, regardless of how puffy my face and eyes probably look. He shakes that adorable head, liquid shimmering in eyes that match his father's. He looks tired. Like he hasn't slept in ages. He tugs at the edge of my beanie.

"No more hair." I shrug it off like it's no biggy. It'll grow back. It's hair. It has already begun to.

Adam frowns, a deep pinch settling between his brows. Not liking this side of him, I pull a silly face. One of the many I've perfected over the years when he was sad, when his not-father abandoned us, or when he broke my trust, and I forgave him as mothers do.

The lighthearted effect works like a charm when Adam drones, "Mommm," in the same youthful way he always has. A tear slips free and glides down the crease of his nose. I swipe the evidence away with my thumb and discard it on my shirt.

"I'm here. Now tell me all about your time at the compound." Weak from little sustenance, I sway on my feet.

Ever my savior, Gunz catches me around the waist and pulls me flush against his side. If I had the mind to swoon, I would. He feels nice. Warm and… him. Safe.

I sigh softly to myself.

"How about we do dinner at the house tonight? We can talk then. Your mother needs sleep," Gunz says.

Adam acquiesces with the simple tip of his head and the shyest smile. "Big gave me a room in the clubhouse. Either of you can stop by anytime." He chews the corner of his lip nervously, like he's unsure if this is good news or not.

Gunz grips my hip, forcing me to snuggle into his body. I turn into him just enough to rest my hand on his stomach, away from the injury. "He give you mine?" he asks our son.

Rocking back on his heels and stuffing both hands into his front jeans pockets, Adam nods. "Yeah. I hope that's okay."

"That's what I told him to do, so it's definitely okay." Gunz reaches out to clasp Adam on the shoulder. It's brief, but I watch our son's eyes round in surprise at the simple gesture.

A father giving up his room for a son he barely knows. That's something to digest at another time when I've got a solid twelve hours of sleep under my belt.

No longer wanting to hang in the clubhouse parking lot swarming with people, I keep my goodbyes to a minimum, to prevent unnecessary conversations. Adam pecks my cheek. I return the sentiment. A firm hand glues to the small of my back and guides me forth. Gunz and I wave to Bink, her giant of a man, and the group of women who've gathered as we slide past them, headed toward the rear of the compound, away from the chaos.

Focused on our mission, Gunz lifts his chin a handful of times to fellow bikers we encounter. Out of politeness, I offer closed-mouthed smiles. They chin lift to me as well. The comradery feels different, settling a new yet not unpleasant sensation in the center of my chest. I like it. I think.

It doesn't take long to pass a row of bikes, the brick clubhouse, dog kennels, playground, and enter the rear of the estate, where all the single-story homes reside. Including his.

Just past the entrance, I yawn loudly, lose my balance on an imaginary rock, squawk like a chicken on my descent to the ground, and am caught by a quick-footed biker before I bite the dust, all in the same breath.

Gunz snickers, righting me. "Almost there, love." He dusts off my side as if I'd dirtied it somehow. Thanks to him, I haven't.

Taking his hand into mine, I carefully place one foot in front of the other. I yawn a second time, not at all embarrassed by my lack of grace. Nope. Not me. That never happened.

The yawn elicits another snicker from my handsome companion.

A third yawn appears just as Gunz's front porch welcomes us.

Releasing my hand, he escorts me up the stairs by the curve of my back. A sense of home washes over me as we step over the threshold into his home. Cinnamon and clove. Masculine and calm.

I sigh, freeing my first real breath in... ages.

Finally.

Some peace.

CHAPTER TWENTY-FIVE

GUNZ

The house is different. Not the same as before I left. I press two fingers into the center of Kit's back as I escort her through the living room to the bedroom... our bedroom. It hasn't changed. The same blue comforter is on the bed. Clean and tidy, as I like it. Someone vacuumed. On Kit's nightstand, which used to be mine, *Dark Lover* rests, awaiting her return. Grinning fondly at the memory of our time reading in bed, I caress the book's cover as she climbs onto the mattress fully clothed and collapses onto her side, snuggling into the plush pillows. The sweetest of contented hums fill the space.

Careful not to cross any lines, I prop my ass on the edge of the mattress and rest a hand on her upturned hip. My lady hasn't talked about what she's been through yet. None of the sisters have. I asked Blimp about Loretta and White Boy about Jade. Nada. I've checked in with those in charge of keepin' an eye on Beth and Niki... still no dice.

Not knowin' if she wants company or to be left alone, I pull my side of the comforter over her as a shield and tuck in the edges to form a cozy burrito of security. It's not that I'd ever do anything to break her trust. I sure as fuck wouldn't do it on purpose if I did. But I don't want my presence to come off wrong. I want her to wear what makes her comfortable and talk about what she needs to whenever she's ready. I'm not gonna push, pry, or whatever the hell else people do to find out stuff that ain't none of their damn business. Fucked-up shit happens to the best of us. Kit's damn sure the best of anyone. Gorgeous. Smart... and finally, fuckin' here with me. Safe and alive.

My heart clenches to the point of goddamn pain at the thought of those dicks harming her. At what they did. At them touching this skin. My skin. Bruising it. Tying her up, cutting her hair off, and violating this body. It makes me wanna rip those bastards apart all over again with my hands. Slower this time to make 'em feel it. To experience what my lady did. Pieces of shit.

Nostrils flaring on a deep inhale, my jaw clenches as I release a low, agitated growl, hoping not to spook her. I hate this. Being helpless. Being here when I can't fix it. I can't fix anything. All I can do is be present... and you better fuckin' bet I'm not goin' anywhere.

Christ.

I rub the center of my chest with two knuckles.

Is this how Big feels about Bink? Overwhelmed. How Dallas feels about Debbie? Addicted. Bulk and Jez? Axel and Pix? The shit's intense.

Set on my need to be supportive, I keep my hand still on her hip and force it to remain there, just over the blanket and her sweatshirt. No rubbing. No movement. Not because I don't wanna do more. I wanna caress her skin. I wanna hold her and tell her it's gonna be okay. That we're gonna get through this. But I don't know what she needs or how far is too far. Less is sometimes more. I'm rollin' with that.

No words are exchanged as Kit drifts off with me by her

side. I watch her eyelids flutter in and out of consciousness until they relax long enough to slumber. Her lips part as she breathes—shallow puffs of air passing through. I remain. Watching. Ever watching. The persistent ache on my side doesn't matter. Not here. Not now. Bonez and Doc did a bang-up job fixin' me. Not that I expected anything less. In time, I'll heal. We'll both heal

Content, I wait. Patient. Soaking Kit in.

There's a tiny bruise on her cheekbone and imprints of fingertips around her throat. She's lost a lot of weight. Too much.

The phone in my pocket vibrates with an incoming text. I check it with my free hand, hoping I don't disturb her.

> Prez: We need to talk. Church.

Now?

I scowl at the screen and lick the front of my teeth, head shaking.

> Me: I can't leave her.

I type out with a thumb, careful not to drop my cell, and press send. Then I gaze upon my lady. Listen to her mini snores. Be with the mother of my child. With the woman I've spent weeks searching for. Hoping. Praying. Fuck. Look at her. Just look... have you seen anything so beautiful? So incredible? I...I don't think I have.

Swallowing thickly, I get mystified just watching her breathe in and out. In and out. Just as I did last night in the hotel. Her on one bed. Me on the other. Well, part of the night, out of respect. Once she was asleep, I was there, beside her. Inches apart, propped against the headboard. I slept maybe an hour. Enough to recharge a bit.

Prez: I know. I'm sending Bink and Adam.

Me: She's my responsibility. Not theirs.

Prez: This isn't a request, brother.

Asshole.

Giving in to baser needs, I lean in and peck my woman's bare cheek right on the yellowed spot. "I'll be back soon, sweetheart," I whisper, in hopes she hears but doesn't wake.

Kit hums adorably in response.

I pat her hip, kiss her again, and repeat, "I'll be back soon." Other words, words I've never spoken, roll up my throat and bang around in my mouth, in my head, in that complicated organ in my chest. I ignore them to translate later when I've got time. When shit's a little less real. When I can breathe normal again. Less heavy. Less… fuckin' everything.

I leave her without looking back. No lingering. If I don't go now, I'll never get outta this house. As a parting gift, I drop my Sacred Sinner ring on the nightstand, so Kit can see it the moment she opens her eyes. A reminder I'm nearby.

Having let themselves in, Bink and Adam loiter in the living room.

"I told him this could wait," Bink explains, her arms crossed in frustration. Her exaggerated huff that follows is sweet and much appreciated, but we both understand how this life works.

"Club business. I get it." It always comes first. Always has. Always will.

For the first time since I've returned, I glance around, noting the lack of life. No toys or little blankets. No sippy cups or DVDs under the television. "Where's Janie? Dom?"

"That's another thing Big needs to discuss," Bink says.

I figured as much.

"Why don't *you* tell me?" I gesture for her to do just that.

She nods as if that's fine by her. "Not sure if you noticed, but while you were gone, Big and the brothers poured a concrete pad behind Bulk and Jez's place and bought three trailers to put on it."

Nope. I didn't notice. Haven't had the time.

"Is that where Janie and Dom are?" I seek clarification because they've either been relocated to provide them independence—a space to grow. Or... the only alternative... Viper has overstepped his duties, and I've got another thing to wrangle. He is too old and too damn wild to claim Janie as an old lady. She's one of Remy's. Saved from his world. Forced to bear a child as a teen, against her own will. Yet, she's flourished here. Learned English as a second language, matured, began to heal, and has become an amazing mother to Dom. Watching her grow, and helping her when she's needed it, has been a blessing. Her leaving at some point was inevitable. Change doesn't bother me. But Viper... Not a chance. I've fucked far too many women with him. Seen too much.

Bink twists the edge of her oversized shirt. "Big figured with Adam moving here and Kit coming home, you might need the house to yourself." She signals to my son with the tilt of her head, then spreads her arms wide to indicate a quiet, clean home.

"Was that his idea or yours?" I don't have to ask to know the answer.

"Eh... A little of both?" Bink shrugs, fixated more on the ceiling than me.

Bingo.

Big's had far too much to deal with in my absence, with all the Remy shit poppin' off. Where Janie and Dom live has never been and will never be on his to-do list. Who lives on the compound, how they live, and where they live is a Bink thing. Even as a child, she had her hands in it all. Her bitch of a mother sure as fuck didn't care about the old ladies, even though she was one. Bless Debbie and Candy Cane for taking her in and doing their best to teach her the ways of the Sacred Sinner old lady. Look where she wound up. I couldn't be prouder.

"Thought so. And... Viper?" I grumble a bit... or a lot.

Fixing her messy bun, Bink chuckles, knowing exactly why I'm asking. "He's still in the clubhouse." Delight sparkles in her pretty blue eyes.

Thank fuck.

I flip my attention to Adam, who's focused on our conversation. "Mom's asleep. Make yourself at home. Just keep it down. Both of you." At that, my son says jack shit and literally drops his ass on our oversized sectional. His feet pop off the floor on impact and resettle a second later. Resting an ankle on his knee, Adam stretches his arms across the back of the sofa.

My attention swings back to Bink. "Where's my grandbaby?"

"She's with Tati, at the house. We didn't want her getting overwhelmed with all the people and noise. It's been a tense couple of months. You've been missed."

"Yes, it has," I agree. "I'm gonna need some grandbaby lovin' real soon." Tonight, if possible, only if Kit's keen on havin' some lil girl company. Gotta introduce them properly. Grandpa Gunz and... we'll figure out Kit's title later. No need to go rushin' things, even if part of me—a huge fuckin' part—is itchin' to claim. Put a... nope... Not goin' there. Not the time. Not the place. I just got her back. We barely know each other. It's the trauma bonding talkin'. That's a thing. I read about it last night, at the hotel, when I was sitting in bed next to her, feelin' far too possessive and needy for my liking.

"That's always available," Bink explains, and I gotta reflect for a beat to recall what we were talkin' about.

Harley. Leech. My grandbaby. Right. Family time.

Fuck. I'm a mess.

"Good." I extract a Dum Dum from my pants pocket, unwrap it, and shove the treat into my mouth post haste. "Now…" I wave between the two of 'em. "I'm guessin' you're acquainted."

Bink smiles fondly at my kid and winks. He returns a similar sentiment, like they're in on a secret I'm not privy to. "Adam's been spending a lot of time with us. So yeah… You could say that."

I dunno why but hearin' she accepts him bein' here, and the brotherhood accepts him bein' here, releases some sorta tension in my chest. Somethin', until this point, I didn't know was there.

"Good. Good." I nod far too many times to be considered normal. "I'm sure that'll make Kit real happy to hear when she wakes up." It makes me happy too, but I'm not about to say that. Shit's startin' to…

Bink hugs me—quick and unexpected. Full body, tits to abs, hard squeeze, then release, step back, and smile. Big, big, sweet smile. A twinkle in those eyes. Like she knows something I don't. Like she can read my fucked-upness. Knowin' her, she can. Obviously. I helped raise the woman. She's my kid. Maybe not conventionally, but my heart doesn't care about bullshit semantics.

"We've got things here. Go to church." She two-finger points to the door.

Go. To. Church.

Over my shoulder, I glance longingly down the unlit hallway.

That spot in the center of my chest throbs, pulls.

I swallow.

Expel heavy breath around the sucker.

Stare a beat more.

"She's asleep," I whisper to myself.

But she's mine to care for.

That's mine in there. On our bed. Under those covers.

The first fucking thing that's ever been *just* mine.

Alright.

I gotta go.

Church.

Fuck.

The brotherhood calls.

"I'll be back," I announce, then get the hell outta dodge before I do something irresponsible.

"We'll be here," Bink calls to my back as I slam the door to my house shut and jog down the steps, all the way to the rear steel door of the clubhouse.

Church, then home to her.

"It's good to see ya, brother." Kai pounds the top of my shoulder as I enter the room to get this meeting over with.

I say nothing and take my spot next to Big, at the head of the table, the last to arrive.

Standing in front of his chair, our prez raises his arm and down comes the gavel.

Let's get down to business.

CHAPTER TWENTY-SIX

KIT

Palms wrapped around a lovely, hand-thrown mug, I blow over the top of my hot tea to make it palatable. I tuck my legs beneath me. A cozy, knit blanket strewn over them, as I sink into Gunz's couch with one of my new favorite women and the boy I raised. They're keeping me company after a nap. It didn't last long, but I needed it.

Both of my companions throw their heads back and laugh at an oldie but goodie about Adam. One he doesn't remember, as he was too young. Yet, I do. Every minute of it.

Bink's amusement slows to chuckle when she speaks. "I can't say Harley has had one of those accidents yet." She swipes the remnants of tears from her face with the meat of her palms and discards the wetness on the top of her thighs.

"Let's hope you don't need a strainer if she does," I jest.

Caught up in the moment, Adam chokes on his merriment, folding in half at the waist as he gasps for air, coughs a dozen times, and punches the sofa cushion beside his leg. "Fuck. Mom." He wheezes. I chuckle more to myself at his red-faced enjoyment than the experience I had when he was a toddler. To capture a mental snapshot of this moment to tuck away for later, to draw from when times get tough, I blink. Then I blink again, just to be certain I got everything.

"I hope not, too. If she does, maybe we should have Adam come clean up the mess as payback," Bink teases, nudging my son's shoulder with her own. I can tell they've taken a liking to each other. Bonded amid chaos. She's good to him, and he needs a lot of good in his life. That's all I've ever wanted. Hell, that's all any parent worth their salt wants for their children. Goodness. Happiness. To feel loved and wanted.

Content to just be, I sip my tea and watch their banter unfold.

"I didn't poop in the bath on purpose." Adam rolls his eyes, still smiling at the ordeal.

"Says you." Her head swivels in good-natured attitude.

In an exaggerated display of ridiculousness only he's capable of, Adam's eyebrows waggle. "I'm givin' your daughter lots and lots and lots of prunes, so you'll need a strainer. I'll get you one for Christmas." He winks, slow and deliberate, a nostril wrinkling at the corner as he does.

Bink faux gasps, covering her mouth. "You are not."

Head held high, nose upturned, my son puffs out his rather broad chest. "Oh, ye of little faith." He speaks like a duke, terrible British accent and all.

Once more collapsing into peals of laughter, they soon lapse into stories of themselves as kids. Pivoting from poop in the bath to rainbow Band-Aids from Big Dick, the club president, now Bink's man. How that one came about, I don't know, nor is it my business. Adam shares his school shenanigans. The same ones that wound him up homeschooled. You know the gist of those.

"Your dad's a computer genius. It's no wonder you could do all that," Bink notes.

"My mom is, too."

Turning toward me, the blonde woman's eyes round. "You are?" She sounds skeptical.

I shrug a single shoulder, disliking the attention. I'm far more interested in watching them interact. It's been a long while since I've seen Adam come this alive.

"She codes and other shit," he answers for me and tilts his head back to take a drink of bottled water.

"Is that how you learned?" comes from a curious Bink.

Yes. He doesn't have to say it for it to be true. I never knew Gunz was the specialist he is, nor did I need to with Adam having me as a mother. I know my way around security systems and computers just fine. Adam spent a portion of his childhood watching me. Not that I ever expected that knowledge to soak in and compute to jail time. That's, in part, why I take his experiments to heart. They're a byproduct of my rearing. Not intentional, but still indirectly my fault.

Growing up, my father tinkered in the garage most days with me as his curious shadow. My mother and his relationship was strained, as was my relationship with her. She was callous and cold. Never one to show love. I told myself if I was ever to be a mother, I would never follow in her footsteps. I wanted more for myself. For my family. Our nights around the table were filled with silence. The dinners were always lackluster—the same foods night after night. They lived separate lives under the same roof until my father died of a heart attack many years ago, and she ended up in a home.

Thanks to the relationship I had with my ex, I stopped coming around prior to that. We phoned, my father and me. The conversations were obligatory. Nothing more, nothing less. The same five minutes of small talk on holidays. Adam never really knew them. It's for the best he only met them twice before age five and nothing thereafter. Not even a birthday card, or Christmas gift. Not that I expected different. My father was never one to rock the boat or push for more, and my mother never cared about me, let alone the child I bore. She acted the same with my siblings. No wonder my brother joined the military straight out of high school and my sister fell off the face of the earth. I haven't heard from her since the day she left. Not a peep.

That's why I swore I'd do better for Adam. We all do that, don't we? Promise ourselves that our child will never experience the same heartache we did as children. As if we won't fuck them up in our own special ways. We do. Oh, we do. My love for computers is why we're here. Why my son was jailed. How I found Bonez and, by extension, Gunz. It's crazy how the puzzle pieces fit together. One begets the other to form a picture. One you can't see clearly until you... can.

A hand waves in front of my face. I blink, glance around, blink again, and focus on my son.

"Mom." Adam's lips press into a thin line.

Uncomfortable with how my brain seems to wander these days, I deliver a similar expression. "Oh. Um. Hi?"

My kid retakes his seat. "You zoned out a bit. You need something?" He inches forward on the couch, his butt hovering on the ledge as if he's waiting for me to cry or worse. He has nothing to worry about. That's not gonna happen.

"No. Just thinkin'."

"Care to share?"

"Just the norm." I shrug. "How we're here today because of my choices. First, the wild night of sex."

Adam pulls the cutest grossed-out face. Well, it's cute to me. I'm his mom. You'd probably find it sexy. Who knows?

The tiniest of smirks hooks at the corner of my mouth, and I keep talking. "Then jail time because of what you learned from me." I lift the mug to my lips and take a long, calming sip of tea. The warmth rolls down my throat and heats a trail all the way to my belly. Adam stares at me as if I've lost my marbles. A blanket draped over her lap, Bink remains quiet and observant.

"You think *you* have something to do with my run-in with the law?" If his higher-pitched tone is any indication, Adam isn't buying what I'm selling.

"Yes." The *duh* I tack on in my head doesn't add to the conversation, but yeah... *Duh*.

"I'm grown."

"Not that grown," I counter.

Obviously.

"Grown enough to know what I'm doing." Adam gestures to himself as if that somehow changes the facts.

Grown, as in hit puberty, sure. Grown, as in mature, not so much. He has a long way to go in that department.

Not buying his *maturity*, I tap my mouth with a finger. "Hmmm... and yet, you still end up in trouble. Stupid, childish, trouble."

Taken aback by my words, my son's expression screws into an awful glower. "You seriously think teaching me how to code and work systems makes my choices your fault?" he growls much like I'd expect Gunz to. It's odd hearing it come from him.

"The fruit grows from somewhere," I throw out.

His cheeks redden, his jaw working overtime as I've struck a nerve. "What the fuck does that mean?" He speaks slowly, his head cocking to the side, assessing.

"It has to be planted first before it can grow," Bink illuminates for me.

I nod. "Exactly. I planted the seed. I tended it."

"This is a dumb analogy." His blues roll, but he plays along anyhow. "Sure, you took care of me. If I'm the fruit, I had to fall from the tree... and what I do with my seeds," he taps the side of his skull, "is no longer about the tree. It's about the fruit."

"But the health of the fruit is because of the tree," I, again, attempt to explain.

"Wrong. The health of the fruit is about nourishment from the tree. What happens to the fruit after it's been nourished enough to ripen is no longer the responsibility of the tree. You took care of me."

I did my best, and sometimes, that wasn't enough.

"Your father left," I note.

"No, he didn't. He's here." Adam looks around Gunz's living room, his brows raised in a cocky spectacle of his oh-really-Mom attitude.

It's my turn to deliver an eye roll. "I'm not talking about Gunz." Gunz is new. He wasn't there when Adam was a child. He didn't play daddy. This kid of mine knows exactly what I'm referring to.

"I am. Do you think, had I been Jeremy's, that we'd be happy? That I'd be less of what I am?"

"Yes." No contest.

Adam's head shakes. "Wrong. I hated him. Even before I knew he wasn't my real dad, I didn't like him. He was an asshole. I was happy, Mom. Fucking ecstatic to find out he wasn't my biological father. Jeremy is better off living his new life as an insurance salesman with his new family. We're better off how we are now. That's the truth. Blame yourself all you want, but now I'm happier I'm not stuck with him as a parent, stuck in that life."

Okay.

This is news. Maybe we're getting somewhere.

I stare at him pointedly. "Then why the rebelliousness? If it's not acting out, it's something." I'm calm. Far calmer on the outside than in.

"Have you looked in the mirror? Have you met you? Have you met Gunz?" he asks.

What's that supposed to mean? Didn't he *just* argue his actions are not a reflection of my parenting? Which, as we both know, I do not agree with. Now he's circling back around to say… what? Look in the mirror. As if he's a reflection of me. That's what I've been saying all along. Isn't it? Now I'm confused, and my brain hurts.

I massage my temple.

Wait… maybe he's trying to say I'm a "bad girl"? That I'm a…

"I'm not a rebel," I defend.

Adam snorts, not at all convinced. "Right, and the Pope isn't Catholic."

"I'm not, Adam." I'm really not.

"Look. In. The. Mirror. Mom."

"I have," I counter.

"No. Seriously. Go look in the damn mirror, Mom." He points toward the bathroom as if I'm somehow gonna get off this couch to do as he asks. This is getting out of hand.

"No," I bark.

Noting my tone and overall dislike of where this conversation has headed, Adam readjusts himself on the couch before speaking again. "Maybe you should because you'll see the strong woman who raised a strong man. A man who can think and act on his own. I've done far worse than I was arrested for. The pranks are always decoys."

Sure, they are.

I resist the urge to roll my eyes. "Care to elaborate?"

"They're meant to keep people off the actual trail. They're not the act of some child. They're deliberate."

"You *want* to go to jail?" Who the hell wants to sit in a cell or a bunk or whatever it is they do in county? That's insane. Not maturity. At least not from my perspective.

"Yes," is Adam's simple, shoulder-shrugging, calm, infuriating answer.

I grip my mug harder. "Why the fuck would you want that?"

"So I don't get caught for the bigger shit. If they're too focused on the silly stuff, they pay less attention to the subtle moves. The ones that make an actual impact," he explains, as if it's no big deal. As if it's logical.

Is it just me... or maybe don't do shit that requires police evasion or willful jail time? Ding. Ding. Ding... We have a winner. Don't commit crimes that'll do the time ... I know... I know... the irony of this moment isn't lost on me. I'm sitting on the couch of a biker, on a compound full of bikers, all of which are not law-abiding citizens. I'm aware. They're not Girl Scouts. Never expected otherwise. Adam's antics have nothing to do with Gunz or the Sacred Sinners and everything to do with life choices.

Not wanting to alienate my son by being a holier-than-thou bitch, I adjust my grip on the mug, take the world's largest breath, and calibrate my tone to give-a-shit-non-judgey-mom. "Like what?" The words drip like honey from my lips. I loathe them almost as much as I loathe where this conversation continues to go.

Stern as ever, Adam's head shakes back and forth. "I'm not sharing that with you. That'd make you an accomplice, and I'm already sitting here watching my mother drink tea from a mug with bruises around her neck, her wrists, and on her face. You've lost a lot of weight. They raped you. I'm gonna guess repeatedly. You wanna discuss my actions, fine. We can do that another day. Right now, you need to focus on you. On getting right with whatever the hell went down at that warehouse."

That sounds like a cop-out if I ever heard one. "Adam—" I begin, only to be cut off by my son.

"No, Mom. It's true. You're always concerned about me and everyone else, so much so, you don't live your own life. You're doing it now. Focusing on my shit, when I'm not the one who just got pulled from a fucking warehouse. We are worried about you. I was scared out of my damn mind."

Ugh.

I swallow hard and look away from them both.

I bite my bottom lip.

Maybe I don't wanna talk about the warehouse. Maybe I don't wanna focus on *my* stuff. I'm sorry I scared him. I didn't want that. I didn't wanna be there in the first place. I'm sorry we're here because of me. I'm sorry I couldn't help the women I lived in that hellhole with. All I could do was listen to them being violated day after day. At one point, I offered myself to our captors, so did Loretta, when Jade couldn't take another moment of pain. They loved her more than the rest of us. Big tits and ass, lots of curves—gorgeous. They wrecked her. I couldn't save her either. Only listen to the screams.

I'm sorry.

So… so… so fucking sorry.

For everything.

I just want my son to be okay. Not jailed. Not making dumb childish decisions.

I don't wanna deal with the rest.

I don't wanna think about it.

I don't wanna talk about it.

I'm sorry.

I'm sorry.

I'm sorry.

A lone tear treks down my cheek. I smear it across my face with my thumb.

Fuck.

I'm.

Sorry.

Gunz

The last to exit church, I close and lock the door behind me.

Fuck.

What a shit show.

Plans are made for Runner's wake. Big sent him to be cremated. More Remy findings. Despite my heated opinion, Prez wants me back at it tomorrow morning. Just my luck, hours behind a desk for the foreseeable future. Not even a day home, and I'm already picking up the broken pieces left by my lack of presence here. Money, security, and a laundry list of other shit has been added to the to-do list, none of which I wanna do. I'm old. I wanna kick back, relax, ride a bit, and rest. Spend some time getting to know Adam and Kit. Reconnect with my family. Cuddle Harley and Dom. The simple stuff. Maybe take up gardening, woodworking, or some other bullshit. Not be at war. Not spend hours in my windowless office.

Rubbing the pulsing vein in the middle of my forehead, I snort. Things change, huh? A year ago, I wouldn't have felt this way. I'd be content to spend my days working. I'd be happy to go on runs and takin' care of business. Funny how going to war, meetin' someone, having a son, losin' a brother, and gettin' shot can put life into perspective.

Heading toward the rear door of the clubhouse, I stifle a yawn. If the loud music from the common room is any indication, our homecoming party is in full swing. Booze, pussy, and a bar lined with alcohol. Brothers are hootin' and hollerin' already. Not much has changed. Same shit, different day. What isn't the same... me. I need sleep. About a year's worth, and I wanna do it lying beside a bald, tatted-up, beaut, who's waitin' on me to come home to her.

Turning left at the corner, I find Kai and a topless Niki arguing. Gripping his cut in both hands, her eyes bugged wide, Niki tilts her head back to look up at our new VP.

"Please! Kai! Please!" The woman shoves her tits at him, hitting him in the gut harder than I'm sure she intends. Kai rocks back on his bootheels to maintain balance. Havin' none of what she's offering, he raises both hands in surrender.

"Not happenin'. I'm sorry." Kai's head shakes on repeat, doublin' down on his stance.

If her flinch is any clue, that one stung a bit. She's not used to bein' passed over by single brothers. But that doesn't seem to stop her. In the next breath, Niki steels her expression and clenches her tiny jaw. "I've sucked your dick before. I can suck it again." She tilts her head to the side in challenge, those tits smashing against Kai's abdomen. Damn woman doesn't listen. That much is clear.

Red. Ass. That's what she deserves for this kinda behavior if times were different. If she hadn't been abused, and this wasn't an obvious display of some mental issues she's gotta work through. The woman needs help, not cock.

Giving zero fucks, Niki does what Niki does—drops to her knees and attempts to make fast, sloppy work of Kai's belt buckle. That's when my brother notices me watching from afar, trying to get a bead on what's goin' down. Looks like someone might also be drunk. Where her keeper is, I dunno. I'll find out later and kick their ass for not doin' their job by keepin' her outta trouble. Niki can't be left to her own devices. They raped the woman just like the rest of them. She wears the same bruises. This shit is messed up, even to me, and I'm usually down for this level of kink. Hell, I've participated in this exact scenario at least a hundred times. Face fucked a club whore in the hall, makin' her mascara run, as she chokes on my dick. She always played with her clit. Got herself off in time with me wreckin' her throat.

Christ.

This is… sad.

This is… just… fuckin' wrong.

Kai makes eye contact. Desperation clings to every inch of the stock-still man. He doesn't know what to do. Most wouldn't.

Handlin' business, 'cause that's how I roll, I approach and carefully remove Niki from pawing at our VP's privates. Kai sighs in relief and cards a hand through his long hair. Niki wobbles as I hoist her off the ground by her armpits. She sways even more when righted on both feet. She uses the wall to keep herself steady and snaps an infuriated gaze at me, ignoring Kai's presence. When she speaks, Niki's breath fans my face in moist heat and the potency of strong liquor. Tequila, if I had to guess.

"What the fuck, Gunz?" she seethes and stabs a finger to the center of my chest. I grab the digit and hold it there as I gesture for Kai to get lost by the flick of my chin. There's no need for him to stay. Whatever's about to go down shouldn't be clubhouse gossip. The fewer witnesses the better. I don't gotta tell him twice, and he's gone without so much as a parting word.

Niki. Niki. Niki… What am I to do with you?

The fury that emanates from this beautiful creature should be boner-inducing. Only I'm more concerned about her state of mind. Not what's between those thighs.

"What are you doin', Niki?"

"None of your fuckin' business, asshole." Niki yanks her hand free of mine and takes a staggard step backward, her other palm remaining on the wall for stability.

"You wanna go somewhere and talk?" I gesture toward my old clubhouse bedroom not far from here. Adam might've claimed it but gettin' her some place private where she can sleep off the alcohol is for the best.

"With you?" Throwing her head back, Niki barks a dark, humorless laugh. "Hell no."

Well damn. Someone doesn't like me much today, does she? I dunno what I've done to warrant this kinda attitude, but I'm about to find out.

"What's wrong?"

Her nostrils flare. "I wanted dick. You stole my ability to get said dick. Dick."

Knowing she's not in her right mind, I ignore the disdain. "Let's go to my room and chat. Sober you up a bit. Maybe sleep off whatever this is. Yeah?"

"No! I'm sick of all you bikers thinkin' you have a say in what I do, or I don't do!" She sways on her feet. "You, of all people, don't get a say in anything anymore! You made your choice. You picked her. Just like Big picked Bink. All you assholes find someone better than me. Someone you can love. Oh, I'm good enough to spread my legs for you. I'm good enough to let you stick your dick in my ass. But I'm not good enough for love. Not that. Never fucking that."

Okkkay... I didn't see that one comin'.

Niki's right, though. But we've never lied about it. Not once. Club whores often become club whores 'cause they desire to be claimed, to wear a "property of" patch. It's their way into the fold, to feel special. The sad truth of it is, we don't want long term with a woman who'll open her legs for everyone. We want our woman to be ours. One we connect with. Sure, my brother, Brew, claimed a club whore. Lots of other brothers have put babies in 'em. They still won't commit. Most of 'em end up deadbeat dads. If they claim one, they usually stray, and end up with an entire fuckin' harem of whores beatin' on their door. There's too much drama in that game.

Still, none of what I've done was ever meant to harm anyone. Just 'cause I can't love you, doesn't mean I don't care. Obviously, I give a shit, or I wouldn't be standin' here havin' this conversation. Make sense? I think so.

"I am sorry that hurts you. We've always been honest about our intentions," I explain as nicely as I can, knowin' it'll likely mean fuckall to her.

My suspicions are confirmed when Niki's eyes narrow into tiny slits. "You can lay in bed with me for hours talking. Fuck me time and time again. Face fuck me on your bed, looking in my eyes like you care. Like I matter. Come down my throat. I swallowed you. All of you. But nooo… I don't deserve your fucking love." Spittle flies from her lips.

"I don't love. I can't love. Not like that. You wouldn't want it if I could. Nobody would." Truth. Every. Single. Word.

Niki growls in frustration. "Lies! You love her!" She throws a hand up.

"It's not like that," I defend, 'cause it's not.

"Stop lying! Just. Stop. Lying!" She slaps one side of her bald head on repeat as if she can't stand to hear me speak another word. "You went to her after the warehouse! You held her hand and you comforted her. Not once did you hug me. Not once did you stay long enough to see if I was okay!"

Fuck. This isn't going anywhere.

I inhale a long, deep breath. On my exhale, I do my best to set shit straight, calmly, yet to the point. "Niki, please. I'm sorry I hurt you. Let's go drink some water, maybe grab a bite of somethin'."

Whipping her head violently back and forth at my suggestion, Niki plucks her purse off the ground, still using the wall as her anchor. She hooks the leather strap over her shoulder, reaches into the brown bag, and pulls out the small silver handgun I bought her years ago. Swaying on sock-covered feet, she points the thing straight at my forehead.

Fuckin' goddammit.

Glancing over my shoulder to make sure nobody's around to witness this, I put both hands up, palms out. "Niki —" I start, only to be cut off by the red-faced, sweat-coated, tits bouncing with each pissed-off breath, woman.

"I don't want to go anywhere with you." Niki punctuates each word with a firm shake of the gun. "I. Don't. Want. Your. Water. I. Don't. Want. Your. Food… and I sure as shit don't want your apology!"

I say nothing.

This has gone from bad to epically fuckin' worse.

She's not done.

On an endless inhale, Niki's chest expands, and she blows out a loud breath. The bottom lip I've sucked a million times wobbles as tears well in her eyes. I know this is hard. Maybe I should've gone and checked in. Bein' shot isn't an excuse. I could've done better.

Tears cascade down her blotchy face.

"I hate you."

I deserve that.

I dip my head in understanding.

"You're the only person I've ever loved."

Fuck.

My stomach clenches.

I say nothing.

"You get me, in here." She taps the handgun to her heart.

Christ. What can I say to that? She's not the first woman to fall in love with me. That's why I don't do feelings. Why I don't date. No matter how much I like them, their inevitable heartbreak isn't a prize to be won. I shield them more for their own good than mine. Sorry fixes nothing, no matter how many times I express it. Facts are facts. I want her to be happy, healthy, and not mixed up in this horrible mess. But I can't give her something that isn't mine to give. This fickle, fucked-up organ in my chest doesn't like people. The bastard doesn't even like me. Who does he seem to like? Kit. That's all I know. He wakes up when she's around. He beats and feels a whole lot less heavy in her presence. It's new. Terrifying. Confusing… and… so… so… so motherfuckin' terrifying. Yeah, the latter needed mentioning again. Terrifying. There, a third time.

Doin' my best not to make the situation any worse than it already is, and to make her relinquish the weapon, I put out a hand. "Give me the gun, Niki. Please." I speak cool and slow, palms up, feet planted, steady eyes on hers.

She steps back.

Once. Twice.

I remain still.

"Niki, please."

Staring at my proffered hand, her head shakes in tiny, sharp bursts. Tears drip one by one down her cheeks. Reaching her chin, each free falls to the floor. *Plop, plop, plop*.

"Why? You don't care. None of you care." Her words are a mere whisper, barely heard above the thumping of the common room speakers.

"I care. I'm here. This is me carin'." Wiggling my fingers, I nod toward my open palm. I don't wanna be a problem for her. I don't want her havin' to carry all this grief by herself. I just want her to put the gun down and get help. That, I can do for her. That, I can give.

"Can you love me?" Her bottom lip trembles.

No.

The look on my face must be answer enough. Niki sucks back a sob as she lifts the gun to her temple. Before I can do a damn thing, say a damn thing, she flashes me an ugly, broken smile and pulls the trigger. Brain matter sprays from the opposite side of her skull, bathing the hallway walls in crimson.

No!

Not giving a damn about my own injuries, I dive forward to catch her body before it crumbles to the ground.

I cradle her limp form in my arms as I sit on the floor, my back against the wall, my legs out, her blood coating us both. My wound throbs in time with my frantic heart as I rock her still-warm body against mine.

"I'm so sorry," I whisper, a frog lodging itself in my throat, making it hard to breathe. "You deserved better. So much fuckin' better." I hug her tighter to my chest, wishing I could have done more, could've been more.

Fuck.

I swallow thickly.

Fuck!

Niki, why'd you have to go and do something so goddamn stupid?

I can't believe this is real.

Hot liquid blurs my vision.

A large form casts a shadow over us as it blocks out the overhead lights. "Gunz…brother… What the hell's goin' on?"

Of course, Big would be the one to find us.

Unable to form words or look my brother in the eye without gettin' choked up, I gesture to the handgun lying in the middle of the floor, near the sole of my shitkicker.

A low rumble leaches outta Big. Knowin' my brother for as long as I have, it's a sad sound. "Damn, woman." He kneels and picks up the weapon, his long, brown hair dropping like a veil on either side of his skull.

Doin' what he does for family, Big pockets the gun and drops his heavy ass on the floor beside me. He lifts Niki's legs and drapes them over his lap, to bear this weight together. His thick shoulder and arm rest against mine.

"It's been a shit month," he grumbles.

Tell me about it.

Emotions paint my face in salty remnants of pain.

I can't believe she's gone.

In my arms, dead.

Forever.

Gone.

We sit in silence for what feels like decades before Prez speaks again. "This is not how I saw shit goin'." He sighs. "Remy's gotta be put to ground."

Fuck that piece of scum. "We need to get our women help," I choke out. That's what's important. Picking up the pieces. Fixing what he's shattered, one shard at a time. I don't care how long it takes. I don't care if I gotta be the one to sweep up each piece and glue them back together myself. I'll do it, for them. All of 'em. Nobody will end up like Niki, lying still in my arms as the familiar scent of death floods the air.

"The pussy doc is comin' tomorrow first thing," Big comments as if that'll somehow help.

A dry, humorless laugh releases itself as I side-eye my brother. "That's not what I'm talkin' about."

"I know."

"She's dead, 'cause of us." My embrace tightens around her form.

Big delivers a nod... slow and heavy, as his shoulders hunch forward. "I know that too... and I'm sorry for it. We didn't start this war with Remy, but we gotta be the ones to end it. We don't need any more of our women or children, or anyone for that matter, goin' through this. Think about it, brother. Janie went through what Niki did, for longer, and there are more Janie's out there." Big strokes Niki's shin with a single finger.

I've thought about it plenty. It's one of the reasons I took Janie and Dom under my roof. Why I put in the work and helped. Why I give a shit.

Glancing down at the woman in my arms, I gently rest Niki's body on my thighs, yank my shirt over my head, and use it to cover her bare chest. The last thing anyone needs to see when we carry her outta here is her naked body. She deserves at least that much dignity. Not that she'd care. Hell, she probably wouldn't care at all. But I do.

Pickin' up what I'm puttin' down, Big doesn't say a thing when he climbs off the ground with her legs in tow. I follow suit and we do what needs to be done.

Heart heavy, we head into our clubhouse infirmary and lay her body upon the cold, sterile, stainless-steel table. A table all of us brothers have been stitched on dozens of times before. The night Big got shot on the compound by a crazy bitch, we brought him here. Now it's where we leave Niki's body to rest. I adjust her head to the side, to hide the biggest part of her trauma. Not everyone has guts of steel. It takes years to handle brutal deaths without bein' squeamish.

Beside each other, Big and I stand back, our arms crossed over our chests, and look... at her, at the bruises, at her discolored skin. My gaze turns bleary once more. I wipe the wetness from my eyes with both fists. Big clasps me on the shoulder and squeezes. I grumble in response. This is not how I pictured our homecoming playin' out. Now that they're safe, I thought the worst was over.

Goosebumps pebble across my skin as I inhale the deepest breath and blow it slowly out of my mouth, to get a grip on the darkness that wreaks its havoc on my shuddery insides. It's been too much for far too long. Bad day after bad day. Dead ends and death. Exhaustion and stress. I'm barely home an hour, and I've got duties to deal with, people to see, wars to fight.

Shaking my head, I sigh and continue to do what I do... take care of what needs taking care of. I adjust the shirt over Niki's breasts and grab a white sheet from our stash on a nearby shelf. I flick my chin and eyes at Big to help me. Together, we drape the cotton over her form. The last thing we need is any of our women or children comin' in here for a bandage only to see this.

Before we leave, I expose Niki's petite hand beneath the sheet and deliver the smallest of kisses upon her cooler, firm flesh. "I'm sorry," I whisper, more for myself than her in a final farewell. May she rest in peace.

Big follows me as we exit the infirmary to reconvene in the hall. "I'm gonna get our prospect to clean up the mess." Prez gestures to where the scene took place.

Defeated by the day, I nod once, tired to the bone.

"You go home," Big orders. "Be with your woman. I'll have someone pick up Niki and do the same as they're doin' for Runner."

"Her family?" I know there are some. Not many. But a few. They disowned her when she became a club whore. Apart from her cousins, we're all she's had for years.

Prez leans a shoulder against the wall. His head tilts to the side to rest against the smooth surface. "I'll take care of it. You've done enough." His eyes close for a beat.

"Didn't seem that way today… at Church."

"I know. Fuck." He massages the nape of his neck. "It's been a lot on all of us. The club needs you. I need you. With Kai bein' new, he's—"

"Learning," I tack on for him.

"Sure. We'll go with that. Take the next forty hours. Be with your family. We can survive that long without you."

"You know things aren't gonna crumble in a week if you take a breather, Prez." He deserves as much downtime as I do, if not more. Sure, I was on the road, but he was here, dealin' with all that entails. If you think running a national motorcycle club is an easy feat, you'd be wrong. Dead wrong.

"I wish that were true."

"It is. Give Kai some credit. Tell him to handle the deaths. Give him more responsibilities. He will handle 'em, or you'll hand him his ass… No, we can both hand him his ass if he fucks it up. He's part of this club now. Sink or swim, baby. That's how we roll. Go spend the night with your old lady and your kid. I'm gonna do the same with mine. We're too fuckin' old to run ourselves into the ground."

If only I could take my own advice. Easier said than done. But Kai has kept this place together alongside Big. He's green, but he's capable. That much is clear, even if he's out of his depth half the time. Big doling out duties to the kid—shit he would have given to Steel, our former VP, in a heartbeat— is how he's gonna show his salt, his value to our brotherhood. A man can't lead if you've shackled him. That's why he's here. To step in and step the fuck up.

Absorbing my wisdom, Big tips his head in a quiet form of consideration. "I'm sorry about Niki," he says, scrubbing the two-day-old scruff on his jaw.

Not wantin' to talk about her any more than we already have, I run a palm down my bare abs and nod a couple times. "Me too," I mumble, eyes focused on my scarred boots.

"The doc will see Kit in the morning, to sort her out."

"I appreciate that. What about the rest of the sisters?" Jonesin' for a Dum Dum to ease whatever's ragin' inside me, even a little, I stuff both hands in my front pockets and rock back on my heels instead. My dumbass figured the few I already ate were gonna be enough for Church. Everyone jokes about the bowls of 'em around the clubhouse. What good do those do when I'm stuck in the hall, unable to get my fix when I'm talkin' to Prez.

Christ… I sound like an addict.

Eh.

Call a spade a spade. I am one.

For suckers.

For sex.

For Kit.

At least those are healthier vices than some.

Yeah, I know, also something addicts say. Sue me. I am who I am.

Big heaves the world's noisiest sigh. "Doc's visitin' Loretta and Jade at their homes. White Boy and Blimp are already with 'em, keepin' an eye out. Doin' what they need to do for their ladies."

"And Beth?" My poor, innocent friend who got tangled up in all this mess.

"Whisky drove up an hour ago and took her back with her."

Wait... What?

Taken aback, I crinkle my forehead and nose in confusion. "She's gone?"

"Yeah. Beth... had a breakdown after Runner and all the other shit went down. We're not equipped to handle that kinda stuff when we've got a war at our front door. She's safer with your brother and the other survivors."

And I'm informed of this now? Not beforehand. Not... I don't have time to get into the details as to why they didn't say jack shit. If Big thinks she needs better reinforcements and support, then fine. I'm too tired to fight him.

"And Jonesy?" I ask, because she was caring for him, and he's too old to look out for himself.

"After they kidnapped her, I paid to have him put in a nice home."

"Was Beth good with that?"

"Dunno." He shrugs as if it doesn't matter to him one way or another. "But it's closer to where she's livin' now and safer for him to live the rest of his days, chasin' tail, not worrying about his granddaughter."

True.

"I guess that's, that… huh?" I lift and drop a single, exhausted shoulder.

Big claps his hands together. "Yeah. Seems it is. Now get your ass home. Sleep. I better not see your ugly mug for the next forty hours."

To be an ass, I cock a lopsided smirk and salute my best friend.

He flips me off.

Then we come in for a hug. Both arms. None of that one-armed, we're too manly to embrace, bullshit. Huggin' a thick, giant ain't the easiest, but I pound his back, and he returns in kind. The familiar earthiness of his leather cut in my face sets me at ease as I finish our embrace with a final thump.

Havin' joined our hallway festivities, Viper whistles lowly, "Awe. Brotherly love," as he approaches.

The fucker opens his arms wide to Big and gets a punch in the shoulder. "Fuck off," Prez rumbles, not at all impressed by our drunken brother's antics.

As if just now realizing shit's off-kilter, Viper sees the dried ruminants of blood on me and our fearless leader. His eyes widen, and he points. His mouth moves without words. Big slaps the green-haired punk between the shoulder blades, his massive mitt covering more than half the span.

"What happened?" Viper sputters out.

Annnd that's my cue to get the fuck outta here.

I thumb by way of the incident for him to go check out if he wants, then bump shoulders with Big, slap Viper on the shoulder far harder than I should, and escape out the back door of the clubhouse before anyone tries to rope me into the welcome home party or attempts to blow me.

Forty hours with my woman.
Forty hours of bliss.

CHAPTER TWENTY-SEVEN

GUNZ

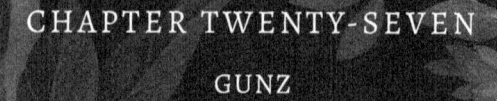

With my son fast asleep on the couch, and clothes commandeered from my closet, I've showered, towel dried, and rebandaged my wound. Standing naked in front of the bathroom vanity, I'm minutes from getting shut-eye. I tug on a pair of ratty gray sweats, sans boxers, and brush my teeth as my phone vibrates on the counter with an incoming call.

Expelling a groan, I flip the thing over. Bonez's name is scrawled across the screen, along with his request for FaceTime.

Only because he's my brother, I hit connect, and prop the device on the back of my sink as I continue to do my business.

"What do ya want?" I grunt good-naturedly when his face comes into view.

"Checkin' in." He's lounging in bed, phone held on his chest, just below his big, hairy pecs. I can see up his nostrils from this angle, and it's not the best view.

Speaking from the side of my mouth, I resume my dental hygiene. "Didn't I already see your ugly mug this week?" I wink and waggle my eyebrows like a cartoon character.

This yields an eye roll and snort from him. "Yep. When I was sewing your gut back together."

I pat the bandage. "Healin' up."

"That's good. Listen…" My brother's eyes morph from normal, to glum, I've-got-important-feelings-shit-to-discuss—the edges go soft, a deep crease forms across his forehead.

Fuck.

I should've known.

Not pleased by what's about to go down, I grumble under my breath, "Big called you."

"Yeah."

Thought so.

"I'm fine." And I am.

"You sure? 'Cause it'd be understandable if you're not."

I'm not doin' this. Not now. Not tonight.

Toothbrush propped in the corner of my mouth, I smile wide around it and pat my living, breathing, still standing, albeit old-as-fuck body. I smack my biceps and my abs. To drive my point home, I dance around in a circle, twerk for the sake of makin' him uncomfortable, and bow at the end of my small enthusiastic show. Toothpaste runs down my chin into my beard. I use a tissue off the back of the toilet to wipe the mess away and discard it in the trash when I'm through.

The dim face on the phone is none too impressed with my conduct. Bonez opens his mouth to therapize me as pain-in-the-ass brothers often do. Well, mine.

I arch a brow, testing him.

He returns the exact sentiment, his lips smashing into a firm, unpleasant line.

"You got somethin' to say?" I press, doin' my best to curb a smile. No need to piss him off when he's obviously callin' because he gives a fuck.

"Nope," is his simple, far-too-calm reply.

Good.

To ease the tension, I go about my post-shower routine of shaving, balming the beard, lotioning the tattoos, nail clipping, and shit like that as I ask him about life, how things are coming along there, and any new stuff I might have missed. Bonez is a talker, so it doesn't take much to get him going.

"Whisky hired more survivors to work at her bakery. They're takin' online orders now. Shipping anywhere in the US. Mags and Cas have been teaching classes daily on general car maintenance to the survivors. They've also taken in multiple survivors, not only to work at the shop, but Mag's and Smoke have 'em livin' in their home."

Not surprising. My brother's club is solid. Their old ladies are top-notch.

"They're good people," I comment.

He nods in agreement. "They are. The entire club has stepped up with the influx of newbies. Whisky especially."

That woman is a saint. A curvy, firecracker version of one, but still the best of humanity.

"Take good care of Beth, please," I express, not because it needs to be said, because I know better than to think they'd let her fall through the cracks. I say it because... guilt. The ugly kind. The kind that keeps ya up at night. I don't feel it much. But for those I care for... those who matter in my world, there's not much I wouldn't do for them. Her included. Beth not ending up like Niki is goddamn paramount.

Bonez's expression goes soft along with his tone. "You know we will. Big wouldn't have sent her to us if he didn't trust we would."

He's right.

It's just hard not havin' a say in something like this. Not seein' Beth and helpin' her myself doesn't sit well. I dunno if it ever will. Especially after Runner died. I was the one she vented to when he did what he did. The one to help pick up the pieces of her broken heart.

We talk longer about life before he seems convinced I'm doin' well enough to hang up.

When we're through, I palm my iPhone, quietly exit the bathroom, and join my woman in our bedroom. The flashlight on my phone works wonders in the darkness as I navigate around our bed. Kit's asleep on her side, curled up like a burrito in the blue comforter. Not sure of the protocol of us sleeping together after what she's been through, and knowin' I don't wanna wake her to ask, I pull my pillow off the side of the bed and grab a blanket from the top shelf in the closet.

Having slept in worse places, I lay my pillow on the floor, close to the nightstand, and spread out by Kit's side of the bed, in front of the door, not only as protection but in case she needs me. I leave enough space to keep from being stepped on should she need to pee in the middle of the night, as I often do. The blanket keeps my legs warm as I turn off my light, tuck both arms behind my head, and let my eyelids drift closed. Within seconds, I'm dead to the world.

CHAPTER TWENTY-EIGHT

GUNZ

Pacing my living room like a caged animal, my arms down at my sides, biceps flexed, jaw ticking, I pump my fists open and closed, open and closed, sucking furiously on a root beer Dum Dum. This is not okay. This is…

"Gunz." Debbie sighs my name as she and Candy Cane, two of the Sacred Sisters, give me a wide berth, watching as I wear a hole through the floor with my bare feet.

This morning, Adam woke both his mom and me up when he knocked on our bedroom door to inform us he was headed to work at the Sacred Sinners' auto shop and that the doc was here. The one Big told me about. The one who's in our bedroom right now with my woman, doing God knows what to her body. The doc, a nice brunette close to my age, I've met multiple times before, as she's a regular 'round here to treat the sisters whenever they need. Them… not Kit. Not my female. Not…

Goddammit!

I'm losin' my mind. That much is certain. My nightmares last night don't help matters either. An hour of sleep, two tops, most of it riddled with visions of Niki, of the women, of Kit, of Runner, of blood, death, and decay. Drenched in a cold sweat, I woke briefly to check my lady was safe, only to once again be dragged back into the abyss, where the creepiest of terrors thrive, hungry for a midnight snack. Again and again, they came. Nightmares morphing into uglier versions of themselves. Tangible entities as real as you and me, breathing life back into the horrors like the resurrection of Frankenstein's monster. We spoke—Niki and Runner, fragments of themselves.

I shiver at the memory.

"It's gonna be okay," comes from a concerned Debbie.

Logically, I know she's right. Try telling my brain that. He is not on board.

Muscles aching as they contract, the vein in my forehead throbs in time with my pulse. I swallow hard around the sucker stick. It does fuckall to quell the racing thoughts. There's no sound comin' from the room. No words. I can't hear or see a thing. All I can picture in my head is her, not here, but there, in the warehouse... on some table, tied down against her will, and those fucking pieces of vile shit raping her. They touched her in places I haven't even been able to touch. Places that I don't even know if she'll be able to give me after what they've done. Not that I care. I'm not goin' anywhere.

I'm pissed.

Scared.

Sick.

Gut churning somethin' fierce, bile surges up my throat.

I force it back down.

It feels like hours since they entered the bedroom. Debbie and Candy Cane came with the doc. She greeted us. Even shook mine and Kit's hands before taking her into the bedroom for an examination, with a medical bag slung over her shoulder. I know I need to give 'em privacy. I understand this is irrational as fuck. But I'm spiraling like I've been spiraling for weeks. It's getting worse. Not better.

Debbie crosses the room and rests a fresh mug of tea on the entertainment stand for me. She gestures to it to let me know it's there to drink whenever I want it. I mouth, *thanks*, unable to articulate legit words.

Sweat drips down the sides of my face, collecting in the hairy beard/goatee shit I have growing on my face. The hair on my chest curls from perspiration. Droplets trickle down my abs and into the waistband of my sweats. I should've put a shirt on.

"Gunz, why don't you tell me what kind of food you'd like us to pick up for the house…to get you both settled in." Again, Debbie changes tactics, clearly worried about my state of mind as Candy Cane types away on her phone, likely alerting the brothers to my outrageous behavior.

I say nothing because I don't know what food Kit wants at home.

Our home.

Christ.

Home.

She's here.

Ugh.

Massaging the knot in my chest, right above that damn erratic organ, a tidal wave of realization crashes down on my shoulders about what's happenin' here… I'm a dad, but more than that, I'm someone's old man. I've never been anyone's anything. Not like this. How do you meet someone one day and end up here? I haven't a fuckin' clue. The universe is laughing her fine, stubborn ass off at me. The man who had his head on straight. The man who doesn't fall in love. I wouldn't know the first thing about what it felt like until now. I'm sure I've said this before, but the intensity is unlike anything I've experienced. I'm protective. I've loved. This is not the same. It's watching the sun rise on the horizon for the first time after a millennium of nights.

Knowing I can't keep this up without worrying Kit half to death, and none of us need that added to our heaping pile of bullshit, I stop dead in my tracks, about-face, and meet Debbie's gaze with determination set in my own. "Cheesecake for Adam," I blurt before more word vomit ensues. "Fried pickles for her. They're her favorite." I recall from our walk by the dog kennels.

The edge of Debbie's mouth kicks up as if I'm amusing her. Candy Cane nods along with my words as she types on her phone, focused on me.

On a roll, I take care of my family the best way I can at the moment and focus less on what's goin' down in the bedroom. A list of shit flows out. Shit she might need, shit she will need, and food I wanna cook for her because I'm gonna feed my woman well. Get some weight back on her bones. On mine too.

"Clothes—" I begin, only to be cut off by the slim, big-breasted brunette running the show.

"We've got that sorted," Debbie explains. "The sisters already cleared out her place. Everything she'll need from there is inside labeled storage bins in your garage. Jez and Bink are picking up more clothes today before they come home from Jade and Loretta's. I'll leave them and the groceries on your porch later."

That works.

These women are lifesavers.

We men are damn lucky to have 'em.

Bypassing the sisters, I head into the kitchen and grab the first rag in the drawer. It's got ridiculously bright hearts and flowers on it. I use the thing to wipe the sweat from my face and body. A damp, stinky mess ain't attractive to anyone. I don't need my lady thinkin' I'm some slob when I just got her home safe, under our roof.

Now that that's handled, Mrs. Doc better get her ass in gear. She's got ten more minutes before I'm pullin' the plug on this whole up-inside my woman's vagina visit.

But before that, I've got one last thing I wanna discuss with Debbie.

With a half-assed toss, the damp rag meets the empty sink, before I rejoin the sisters for a little chat before they leave.

Nine minutes and counting.

CHAPTER TWENTY-NINE

KIT

Dressed in a fresh pair of pajamas, well, Gunz's clothes, I make the bed, pick his bedding off the floor, and return the blanket to the closet where it belongs. His pillow rests beside mine on the mattress. I can't believe he slept on the floor when there was plenty of room next to me. I know, he's too considerate to assume I'd want him there after all that's happened. But I do. He's safe. I want safe. I want him. Plus, his nightmares kept waking me. Every hour, his tossing and turning became violent. Once, he kicked the bed frame so hard I was worried he'd broken a foot. Seems we are both experiencing, for lack of a better term, stuff. Stuff we should wade through today, ya know, if he has time.

My new gynecologist left a little bit ago. The examination was your standard fare—a peek inside, a swab, and a blood draw from my forearm. No frills. No real discomfort. No flashbacks or triggers. It's still weird to me that the Sacred Sinners have an actual gynecologist on their payroll, and she does house calls like it's the 1800s. It was nice, though. She was nice. Accommodating. Informative. With far better bedside manner than most physicians.

Collecting Gunz's Sacred Sinner ring from the nightstand, I pocket it for safekeeping and exit the bedroom. The place is still. Peaceful. In the living room, I find the man I was hoping to see seated on the couch, his elbows perched on his knees, palms cupping either side of his skull as he leans forward, brooding. Or so it seems by the tension radiating from his bare, heavily inked shoulders and bestial grumbles he emits to himself.

Hands stuffed in the pockets of my oversized pajama pants, I pause at the arm of the sofa, not wanting to invade his space. "Gunz?" I whisper, hoping not to spook him.

The handsome man looks up slowly and blinks as if he's surprised to see me."Love?" Lines accentuate his eyes as they rake my form from head to toe, assessing every inch.

Butterflies wreak havoc in my middle at his... attention.

Unsure how to respond, I force a smile that looks more constipated than genuine and deliver a shy, two-finger wave. "Hi." My greeting's too high-pitched and awkward even to my ears. Heat singes my cheeks in embarrassment, but I refuse to look away.

"Hi back." The shirtless man sits up and once again does a full once-over of my body. "You look..."

Growing even more uncomfortable by the second, I reach up and tug the edge of my beanie down to further cover my head.

"Sexy as fuck," he finishes with a low, flattering whistle.

Oh.

Wow.

That's not what I was expecting.

A deeper blush suffuses my checks at the flattery.

Worried he was gonna say something else, like how tired I look, or the weight I've lost, or how visible my bruises still are, I inwardly sigh in relief. This is far better. This is open, no-holds-barred attraction, like it's the first time he's seeing me, the real me, no makeup, no bullshit, no frills, and he's savoring it.

More butterflies take flight, losing their minds.

I press a palm there to calm them.

Giving zero fucks, those intense blues continue their perusal as Gunz pats the seat beside him. Right. Next. I glance at the spot I curled up in yesterday when Adam visited and back to him. Like a hawk, he watches my every move. Noticing everything. Missing nothing. Again, he pats the cushion inches from his thigh —slow and deliberate, coaxing. Okay. I can do this. Going along for the ride, I follow his lead. If I'm uncomfortable, I can always move.

Wordlessly, I lower myself into the seat, hands on my knees, heart pounding a million miles an hour, like I'm some nerdy lovestruck teenager, and he's my mega-hot high school crush. Sheesh, this is pathetic.

Ever the gentleman, Gunz snatches the same blanket I had yesterday from the back of the couch and drapes it over my lap with practiced ease, his muscles flexing with every movement. Then he gets close. You know the kind—where you can smell his cologne, sense the radiant warmth, and see every intricate line on his forearm tattoo as he relaxes back into the cushions. Acutely aware of my own reaction to his proximity, I note his too—his labored breathing. Out of my periphery, I catch his Adam's apple bob when he swallows. He's frowning. Not the angry sort, but in concentration. He adjusts something in his pants. It's long and massive. You get what I'm referring to. If I had the gall to say it aloud, I would, but I'm a chicken shit.

Hands folded into my lap primly and far too proper, we sit like this for what feels like ages. I fix the blanket over my legs. He fidgets. I mimic his discomfort with a brand of my own. I'm not sure why this is so difficult. It's not like we haven't kissed before. I've had his tongue in my mouth. I bore his child. Obviously, we fucked, decades ago, but it still counts. There is no reason for this skin-prickling hyper-awareness.

Staring straight ahead, to not focus on him any more than I already am, I watch a black television screen. When that becomes too monotonous, my gaze wanders to the picture on the wall beside the television—of a younger Gunz and his club brothers standing beside a shiny row of bikes, their arms spread wide, as the giant of a man, Bink calls hers, stands front and center, pointing to the president patch on his chest. It's sweet. A real snapshot of their life and the joy being part of this family brings.

Before I get a chance to ask about the photo, Gunz breaks the pregnant silence with a string of colorful under-breath expletives that ends in a grumbled, "I'm sorry."

What does he have to be sorry for?

"For?" I reiterate aloud.

Shifting in his seat, Gunz massages the nape of his neck. "Everything?... Fuck. I don't... I don't know how to do this."

"Do what?" I seek clarification because he's acting stranger than I feel, and that's saying something.

"Sit next to a woman..." He clears his throat and even that's sexy. "No... *My*... woman," the man emphasizes.

Oh.

Damn.

"I'm *yours*?"

"Yeah. Of course. We already agreed on that."

Sure. In the middle of a traumatic moment, we did. People say and do all sorts of things they wouldn't normally do in times of crisis. Right? *Riiight?* Are you nodding in agreement? I sure as hell hope so.

"And *that's* why you're acting weird?" Again, more clarity is needed.

His too-handsome face scrunches into an equally too-handsome scowl. "No. I'm actin' this way... 'cause I don't wanna cross lines."

Now we're getting somewhere.

"What kinda lines?" I ask.

"Christ." On a sigh, Gunz's drops his head back onto the sofa, his eyes focused heavenward. "Okay... We're doin' this now... huh?"

Excuse me.

Huh...

What?

What?

Did he just say what I think he said? *We're doing this, now?* He started this. Yes, I wanted to have a talk...eventually. That's what you do as an adult. Talk. Communicate. But he's fidgeting more than a kid hopped up on sugar, and I'm over here sweating in places I shouldn't be sweating.

Taking the high road, my tone remains neutral as I pretend this is normal. That we've done this dozens of times before. "Sure. Why not? You have anything else you have to do today?" I shrug to appear indifferent, to play it cool. On the outside, the façade is effective. On the inside, I know I'm the biggest liar, liar pants on fire.

"Besides be with you... no."

"Then have at it." I gesture for him to let it all out.

"Do we sleep together, as in next to the other?" he blurts in a rush as if the words are gonna light his ass on fire.

Again, I play it cool. "That one's easy. Yes."

"See." He speaks to the ceiling. "I didn't *know* that. You ... you know what you just went through... I need to be respectful of that. As a man... part of my anatomy... that finds you insanely fuckin' sexy... wants to... ya know. do *things.*" He motions toward his manhood. "But I get we won't be doing any of that for a long while. Understandably so, which is why I need you to tell me what's acceptable and what's not. You set the boundaries. I respect the boundaries."

That's fair. Sweet and fair.

When I thought I couldn't adore this man any more than I already do, he proves me wrong.

See, I told you, good guy.

Pulling a hand from underneath my blanket, I rest it on his thigh. The man shivers, literally freaking shivers on contact. I pretend not to notice. To set his mind at ease, I explain what I'm comfortable with. "Hold my hands. Touch my hands. All okay. Hugging me, also fine. I'm not gonna break, Gunz."

"Erik. Please call me Erik."

Oh.

"You sure?"

Cue a round of awkward nodding. "Yeah... Yeah. I'm sure... You sure I can touch you?"

"I said so, didn't I?" To cement my words, I bump his shoulder with mine and chuckle.

The simple gesture does little to allay Gunz's concern. Leaning into my arm, bare skin on shirt, he takes my hand into his, weaves our fingers together, and squeezes, before resting them on his thigh. "Yes," he notes, looking at me out of the corner of his eye. "But this is... fucked. You had a doctor up in you, and I wasn't there. Then I was worried somethin' was gonna happen 'cause I wasn't. I don't wanna fuck this up. I want you to stay. If you don't want to, I get it. My club's responsible for what happened to you. Then there's the matter of my son. I wanna see him and get to know him... I... fuck... This is... a lot... and I don't know how to... ya know... talk about it... How to... see... I'm a goddamn mess." Once more, his head meets the sofa's back. A lofty sigh imparts his lips.

The man needs to give himself grace. This is new for all

of us. A total life-altering event. Nothing could have prepared me for what's ensued since the night I showed up at their gate. Neither of us have the answers. Life is messy. Our situation is messier than most. But he's here. I'm here. We're breathing and talking. That's a win in my book.

"You also haven't slept much." We could both use respite. Nothing will be solved in a day. It's gonna take time.

"That too," he agrees.

"Why don't we lay off the heavy for a bit? Just be here. You and me. We don't have to talk about everything right now. How about we put on a movie since I know how much you love those?" I laugh, recalling how much he dislikes television. "We can relax. Veg out on the couch. Eat food. Cuddle." The perfect compromise, in my not-so-humble opinion.

"That... works." He sounds skeptical.

"You sure?"

Rolling his head in my direction, Gunz meets my eye. "Truth? I've never done that before."

"Ever?"

"Ever."

Shaking my head in astonishment, that a man in his fifties has never taken a day to unwind in front of the television, cuddle with a female, and gorge on food, I set out to make this day the best for us both. We deserve it.

First, I untangle from Sir Hotness, get my lazy bum off the couch, and grab the remote from the entertainment stand. I hand it to Gunz with specific instructions to find us something to watch. Anything he picks is fine by me. I haven't watched anything good in ages. Next, I raid the kitchen cupboards and come up empty, unless you consider salt, sugar, half a bottle of ketchup, and a giant bag of rice proper sustenance. He has nothing to eat. Definitely, nothing to veg with—like buttery popcorn, chocolate, maybe chips, or some other version of bad-for-you-but-tastes-too-good junk.

"The sisters are bringin' food later today," he calls from the living room.

That sounds perfect.

"Janie and Dom moved to a new trailer while we were gone. So, the cupboards are probably bare, love," he tacks on as I hear him surf through the channels.

Bare is an understatement.

Working with what I've got, I make us tea and carry the hot mugs into the living room to sip on as we watch... "*John Wick?*" Genuine elation bursts from my lips.

Looking out of his element, Gunz shrugs up one shy shoulder. "You said it was good, yeah?"

"It is." I reclaim my seat beside him, hips touching, and offer him his drink.

Blanket strewn over my legs, mug cradled in my hands, I rest my head on Gunz's shoulder as he presses play.

See, we can do this.

Netflix and chill.

The literal kind, not the naughty version.

Get your filthy mind out of the gutter.

CHAPTER THIRTY

KIT

Somehow *John Wick* morphs into a marathon of action flicks —*Terminator 2* and *The Transporter*, to name a few. Tea long forgotten, Gunz spoons me on the couch as I use his thick bicep as a pillow. Time and time again, we siesta whenever the desire strikes. Hours pass with his arm draped across my middle, his dick against my ass, as he draws comforting circles onto my belly over my shirt. Every now and again, he pecks my head, then snuggles his nose there, inhaling my scent as if he doesn't give a damn I notice.

It's wonderful. Every minute. Every touch.

"Glad you're here, love," he whispers against my beanie, coaxing a warm-and-fuzzy grin to the surface.

"Me too," is my simple reply.

Dragging his damp lips across my neck, he kisses me there, soft and oh-so-sweet. "Wanna kiss you all better."

I hum, fully on board with the sentiment. He can kiss me all he wants. Anytime he wants. Wherever he wants. Gunz is safe. Sexy and powerful. I snuggle into our embrace, communicating as much without words.

A palm flattens against my belly, and he sucks a mark

onto my neck. Light flicks of his tongue coat my skin, setting it ablaze, between deep pulls and nibbles. My toes curl as I push my ass back, feeling his length hard and thick against me. His palm presses harder into my abdomen, melding us together. "Is this okay?" he mutters.

"Yes," I croak, praying he doesn't stop. I can't remember the last time I've felt this good... this cared for and desired.

"I won't do anything more, love. I promise. I just wanna feel you..." He clears his throat. "I need to... mark you." Gunz laves across the mark he finished, drawing circles around and around with the tip of his tongue, tasting me, his breath hot on my flesh, his groans low and sensual in my ear.

"Okay." I shiver.

"I promise it won't hurt."

"I trust you." And I do. Without a doubt.

"Need to erase them..." *with marks of my own* is left unsaid. Yet somehow, I understand.

One by one, each imprint is replaced. I roll onto my back as he leans up onto an elbow to kiss and taste another before sucking the bruise away, replacing its ugliness with a creation of his own.

Unable to stop my body's reaction and not wanting to, I grow wet, goosebumps pebbling across flesh as Gunz nudges my chin with his. Rolling my head toward him, I nuzzle his bicep and relish in his scent—all man, spice, and yum.

His beard scraping the best of ways, my hot biker peppers the gentlest of kisses upon the last fingerprint. "You're beautiful," he mutters before tasting me there. "Salty." He hums in satisfaction.

Teeth scrape flesh.

I gasp.

He moans, turned on by my reaction.

Undulating against my thigh, Gunz sinks deeper, pulls deeper. Reaching across my body, he grips my hip with his free hand. Fingers imprint flesh. In time with his sucks, he tugs me harder against his form, fucking my thigh through his sweats. Eyes rolling back into my skull, I free-fall into the moment, not the past, not the future. Here. Now.

Pleasure pounds through my veins.

Arousal soaks through the cotton of my pajamas as I squeeze my legs together, to quell the ache there.

Gunz inhales deeply as if he can scent my excitement. Moaning, broken and sexy, this glorious man ravages my neck. Teeth sink deeper, and I let him because I want more. More of this. More of us. Just more.

Following his lead, I taste and suck his bicep. Each pull on my neck elicits one of my own upon his flesh. Like a buoy in the ocean, I reach out to him, to tether me as we float into a maelstrom of ecstasy.

There is where he protects me.

Covets me.

Fisting the fabric of his sweats in my right hand, I saw my legs together as he continues to roll against my hip. In unison, we lose ourselves, sucking welts into flesh. Quivering in the best of ways, my back arches off the couch as the pressure builds.

And builds.

Gasping for air, I teeter on the precipice.

"Let me help you." Gunz nips my chin.

Before I can ask how, a palm slides down my hip to the side of my thigh. "I've got you." His dick wears an impression into my opposite thigh as he squeezes my legs together for me.

That's it.

All I need.

Succumbing to pleasure, sparks roar to life—violent and beautiful as my eyes slam closed. Moans pour from my lips.

Heat consumes.

Everything coalesces.

My nipples harden. My clit throbs.

And he's there.

Stoking the flames, higher and higher. Whispering encouragement in my ear. Taking me to the brink, where breath ceases to exist.

"That's it." He squeezes me once last time... and...

I rip apart at the seams.

Digging my heels into the couch, my back bowing, ecstasy ravages me, and I let it.

Want it.

Need it.

Time ceases.

When I moan, Gunz moans.

When I shudder, he shudders.

When I grab for him... he's there...my anchor.

"That's it, beautiful." He nibbles my shoulder.

I gasp, almost climaxing again from the touch alone.

Everything feels tight.

Sensitive.

Awake.

Catching my breath, I open my eyes and look at him. His face is red, those eyes lazy—bedroom sexy. The hard cock at my hip bucks with need. Biting my bottom lip, I flick my gaze to where he is and back to Gunz's face. He shakes his head slow and firm, brooking no room for argument for what he's about to say. "Ignore him. This isn't about him. This is about you."

But I want to help... I open my mouth to say but I'm shut down when Gunz delivers that same, no-nonsense shake as if he knows what's going on in this head of mine.

Reaching up, the handsome man brushes the backs of his fingers over the fresh, achy marks around my throat. "That's all I need... for now."

"Marks?"

"*My* marks."

This man.

Oh. This sinful man.

Turning onto my side, so we're face-to-face, I brush my fingertips down the center of his pecs, across the bumps of his abs to the edge of his pants, where I tease a finger there just above the waistband. He groans a heady, please-don't-do-this-to-me kinda sound. I love it.

"No," comes out as more of a croak.

I bite back a pleased smile. "Why?"

"Because I'm gonna wanna fuck you. And when that part of me comes alive, he can't be trusted."

"What part?"

"The deviant."

"You're not a deviant," I argue on his behalf.

Head shaking as if I know nothing, Gunz cackles dark and dangerous, without humor. "Wrong. 'Cause if you knew what I really wanted to do to you, you'd run away screaming."

My stomach swoops. "Tell me," I whisper in anticipation.

More of that firm-head shaky shit. "There's no fucking way that'll ever happen."

Fine.

I sigh far more dramatically than I should. Sure, I don't want sex. Truthfully, I don't even know what I want. But this right here works for me. He works for me. All the yucky stuff doesn't exist when we're in our bubble, just the two of us.

Respecting his wishes as he does mine, I relent, not because I don't wanna help him complete, but because I respect him. My fingers draw upward, my palm flattening to his sternum, right above his heart and the old-school tattoos inked there. Gunz rests a hand of his own upon mine, holding us in place. His skin's hot. His pulse a reckless thud against my fingertips.

Eyes boring into mine, he mutters, "That's better."

"It is," I agree, enjoying this closeness far too much. "Now, please tell me more about this deviant of yours."

Again, with the head shakes. "Lord have fuckin' mercy, woman. No." The smallest of smirks awaken as if he's amused by me but doesn't want it to show.

What can I say? I'm inquisitive by nature. Have been my entire life. Once I find something I like, I need to know all about it. Humans, hobbies, your mama's award-winning spinach dip... makes no difference. Fascination is fascination, and this creature is the most fascinating person I've come across.

"Please." I'm polite, not pushy.

Throwing his head back into the cushions, Gunz bites out a frustrated, "Christ."

"How are we gonna get to know each other if you don't talk to me?" The same goes in reverse. I don't expect this to be one-sided.

"I talk to you," is his simple reply.

Tugging on the tip of his beard so he'll look at me, I offer an olive branch whenever he's ready. "I'll make you a deal. Whenever you wanna talk about this deviant, I'll tell you about what happened to me." All the parts. Even the worst of them... the ones I compartmentalize, and those are the scariest of them all.

Eyes on mine, Gunz huffs the cutest, frustrated laugh. "Love." He ends with a you're-driving-a-hard-bargain groan.

I smirk. "Yes?"

"That's not fair."

Sure it is.

"How's it not? Trading personal information for more personal information."

"Do you wanna talk about what happened?" he tests, as if he's hoping I say no and that'll be the end of this discussion. It's not. I'm all in. If he wants to share, I'm gonna share. That's that. Pain happens. Talking about said pain is part of life. You wade through it like mud in a swamp, where alligators lurk, and mosquitoes the size of small dogs suck blood from your soul. It might be scary, with a healthy dash of agony. But... eventually, the sun comes out, and there you stand, with its warm rays beating down on your dirty, insect-bitten face, smiling because you're still alive.

In response to his question, I'm as honest as I always am. "With you. I would... *If* you want to know."

"Fuck."

Gunz

With you. I would...

Jesus Christ. Kit's words turn over in my skull. Look at her. All that barefaced openness. All that goddamn sexiness. I can still taste her arousal on my tongue as if I made her come with my mouth and not a little leg help. This has been an insane fucking day. Watching her watch me. All those gaspy breaths and smiles. Those marks around her neck. A necklace of my doing. Deep purple. Gorgeous. Mine.

All fucking mine.

Depravity scratches the surface, testing my will, seeing if I'll cave. I won't. Not now. Not with her.

Again, I watch her as she watches me, hoping I'll give her something. But I have nothing of real value to give. My mother saw to that. Not once in my life have I laid on a couch with a woman, watching movies, that I paid little attention to because she's here... with me of all fuckin' people. Wanting to be here 'cause I'm here. How's that for a mindfuck?

She didn't push to touch my cock.

They all push.

They all want and need. They beg. They submit.

But not her.

Not this one.

She's content to look up at me with these big, expressive, honey-colored eyes and ask me to let her in. To share. How in the hell am I supposed to do that?

My brother told me long ago this would happen. It'd be unexpected and knock me flat on my ass. He said a woman would come along and want inside. To get to know the real me. Care about the real me. Not the outside strength. Not the façade. The gritty, ugly, broken bits. I laughed at him. Obnoxious laughter. Said he was a fucking fool because we weren't born to fall in love. We weren't worthy. Hell, I'm still not worthy.

This is new.

Still just as terrifying.

But fuck it all to fuckin' hell if I don't wanna give her something. Just a taste of real. A taste of me.

"Why do you think my name is Gunz?" I ask, more as a test to myself than her, to see how far I'm able to go. To see how much she can handle.

An adorable wrinkle forms between her brows as she looks deep in thought. I caress the side of her face, waiting for a reply, my stomach tight.

This is it.

Time to rip the bandage off. A lifelong bandage that only Bonez and I know the damage beneath. The scars. The hallow wreckage.

He's gonna laugh later, in that cocky, dickhead brother way, when I tell him his punk-ass was right. Fuckin' bastard.

"Honestly, I don't know..." Kit shrugs a single shoulder up to her ear, suspends it there as she ponders the question, confusion etched in her features, then drops it when she's formed an answer. "Because of *guns*?"

Nope. That's what they all assume.

"You want another guess?"

"Not really." She nibbles that sexy bottom lip a beat. "If you're not comfortable sharing, Erik, I'm not gonna pressure you for more. I just figured we're here, we have nothin' else to do today, *and* we barely know each other."

Damn. She used my name. It sounds perfect comin' from her, light and sweet. *Erik*. I couldn't tell the last time anyone called me that out loud.

"You want the good, the bad—" I begin.

"And the ugly," she finishes.

Alright.

"Let me ask you this. What does a gun and bone have in common?"

A solid minute passes of lip-chewing contemplation before she replies, "I... hmmm... I don't know."

"They're both words that can be used for dick."

Head rearing back in surprise, Kit's eyes widen. "Wait. What?"

"Everyone assumes Bonez is named after bein' a chiropractor. Ya know, crackin' bones? He even tells people that's how he got his name, which is a load of horseshit. People assume my name has somethin' to do with guns and they leave it at that. Case closed."

"Ooo-kay? So now you're telling me you're named after a penis? Like Big Dick is?"

"Big isn't named after a dick, love." Snickering, I nudge Kit's beanie up with my thumb, so it stops tryin' to hide her eyebrows. They're expressive. I need to see 'em. "His name *is* Richard. He's huge. It fits." I boop her on the nose, enamored with her cuteness and the way she's looking at me like I've lost all my gaskets. To be fair, everyone assumes the same with Big. That his name's a play on the fact he either has a big member or is the world's biggest asshole. The former might be true. The latter, not so much, unless you get on his bad side, which usually ends in a trip to the shed. Rightfully so. Still, he isn't named after a dick.

"His real name is Richard," Kit reiterates in disbelief.

"Yes."

Unable to control herself, Kit breaks into laughter, full-on grab-her-belly amusement, which ignites the same response in me. The couch quakes as we lose it together. She snorts like a pig. I bark a deep, gruff laugh, trying to catch my breath. This woman sure is somethin'.

Grabbin' hold of her so she doesn't fall off the couch amid her delight, Kit basks in the moment, and I soak up every nuance of her childlike fun. The reddened cheeks. Her stomach trembles against mine as my dick takes notice. It all fits into the perfect package that is Kit. My stunning woman.

Tears cling to Kit's eyelashes when she calms long enough to speak. "His name is Richard... Oh my." She covers her mouth with her hand. "Please don't tell him or Bink I laughed about this... But that's a horrible name for him. No wonder they call him Big..." She pauses a beat to gulp air. "Okay... Okay... Sorry... Go on... Explain why you and Bonez have penis names."

I lean in and peck her nose.

Caught off guard, a shy blush saturates her cheeks.

Here goes nothin'.

You're not gonna be prepared for this either. Brace yourself.

Knowin' damn well this will ruin the mood, I clear my throat in preparation. "It started when I was a pre-teen, and throughout my teen years. My mother sold me and my brother to the neighborhood sick fucks."

Soaking up the information, Kit's face pales, and her mouth hangs ajar, but I don't back down. She asked. We've already opened this can of disgusting worms. I'm gonna let this truth see the light of day once and only once. Then I'm takin' it to the grave. 'Cause I'm not talkin' about it again.

I keep on. "Bonez got sold to both men and women, but they always used me for the ladies. When they were requesting us, they'd leave voicemails or notes in the mailbox, requesting the names my mother gave to us."

"Bonez and Gunz," she guesses.

Bingo.

"Yeah. She would tell me the ladies needed my gun or my brother's bone. It started as gun and bone. They'd say what they needed. She'd put it on the family calendar in the kitchen—times, locations, who was requested."

"Your mother sold you."

"Yes."

"For sex."

"Yes."

Magnificent round eyes delve into mine. "Holy fuck."

"Do you want me to go on?" I check.

Kit bobs her head in rapt fascination. "If you are willing to. Absolutely. I'm so sorry this happened to you." Her fingertips draw random shapes across my abs.

"It's in the past, love." To convey this doesn't haunt me as you'd expect, I drop a quick peck to her beanie-covered forehead, wishing I could take her hat off to rub and kiss her bald scalp. There's no need to hide it.

Appreciating her outrage, I drop a second kiss there before I continue. Leaving little to the imagination, I fill in what I think she can stomach. How Bonez hated it at first, then became addicted. How I loved it. The power. The pleasure. How I hated my mother for being an awful cunt who never really loved us, but never hated her for selling me for sex. I learned so much from those experiences. Sure, it warped my perception of sex and women. It made me want to consume more. To fuck more. To chase that addictive high. The worship. The praise. It was nothing more than pleasure in its purest form. No connection. No consequences. It was and has always been freedom.

"I... I have nothing to say," Kit sputters when I've divulged the bulk of it.

Needing to touch her, I caress Kit's cheekbone with the pad of my thumb. "You don't have to, love. You asked for real. I gave ya somethin' I've never given to anybody else, just like watching movies on the couch with you, or reading books in bed, or sharin' my home."

Looking at me like I'm some hero, she utters, "You're amazing."

I shake my head repeatedly to cut that shit right the hell off. "I'm not, love. I'm really not."

"But you are." Kit reaches up to touch me, slow enough I could stop her if I wanted. I don't. On my shoulder, she rests two fingers at first to test the waters, then her full palm comes to rest. Sparks ignite beneath her warmth, an electrical charge to the system, standing the hairs on the back of my neck on end. I shiver down to my toes. My abs flex as I gasp softly at how this woman affects me. Even my cock tingles. Balls ache. Oblivious to her voodoo, she keeps talking as if my heart isn't pounding its way outta my chest. "You can't see it. But I can... So... Okay... Um... If she, ya know, used those as references for her... I can't even say the words. How did gun and bone turn into your names with the z?"

Focus, Gunz.

Expelling a leaden breath, I will my heart to calm before I speak.

"My father, who was also a Sacred Sinner at the time, came home after some long drunken gambling binge, demandin' money from my mom. She always took the calendar down when she expected him home. Ya know, to save face. We lived in your standard single-story suburbia, where all the houses looked the same. My mom might have been a former club whore, but she had a reputation to uphold. Everything was always perfect, including the illusion that her husband and kids were the same. When he found the calendar, he saw the names, and demanded to know what it was all about. Me and Bonez listened from our bedroom that night. Dad came in after, said he knew what she'd done, made no apologies, congratulated us on our sexual aptitude, and bestowed us with our road names right then and there."

"Gunz and Bonez," she verbalizes for me.

"Yeah. They stuck. My brother hated his for a while. I used mine to my advantage and became a Sacred Sinner early on. The less I gave a shit about bangin' club whores in front of brothers, the more they respected me. The more successful and helpful I became to the club, the more they wanted me here. It didn't take long to rise up the ranks and get my father kicked out."

For Kit's sake, I omit the gory details. She doesn't need to know my father visited the shed. That Big stood and watched me strip him of his patch with my knife before I lit his cut on fire, then beat him to death with nothing more than my fists. He deserved it. As children, anytime the bastard came 'round, he was always fuckin' my mom in front of us. We tried to hide, but he made us watch. The older he got, the less it appealed to him, the less he came around. I vowed, even before I had hair on my nutsac, I was gonna be the one to end his life, someway, somehow. And I did... in my early twenties. My third official kill. It took hours and I was sore days after. Was it worth it? Hell yeah.

Busy digesting my past in her own way, a companionable silence falls upon us. Because I'm a slut for my woman's touch, I snuggle her up in my arms. Her head rests against my chest, listening to my heartbeat thrum as I press my lips to the top of her head. Eyes closing of their own volition, I revel in the moment, in her soft warmth, in the weight off my shoulders.

Fuckin' Bonez.

Always gotta be right.

Contentment settles in my gut. Happiness blooms in my chest.

When Kit speaks, her lips graze my pec with every word. "I'm proud of you."

She's proud of me.

I want to ask why. Tell her I don't deserve it. Yet, I somehow understand. So, I don't act like a fuckin' tool and undermine her conviction. I take it into me. Soak it in like a sponge. Her pride. Her affection…

and I…

Almost cry.

Because… fuck.

Nobody's ever said that to me before.

Not like that.

Not…

Fuck.

I love this woman.

CHAPTER THIRTY-ONE

KIT

Dressed in a clean pair of my own clothes Gunz found in the garage—purple leggings and an obnoxious Grateful Dead t-shirt—I rub my distended, full belly in circles as we sit around the kitchen table. Not just the two of us, Adam, too. Like a bunch of hens, they can't stop clucking—trading one story for the next. It's as if I'm invisible. Well, that's not entirely true. My foot happens to be resting in Gunz's lap. He also happens to be massaging it as he carries on with our boy. The hot biker squeezes my big toe whenever Adam discloses something he likes, communicating without words how much he's enjoying our uninterrupted family time. It's too damn sweet. I can't stop smiling.

Leaning over his plate, elbows on the table, Adam shovels a second piece of cheesecake into his mouth. I had a slice earlier. It was perfection—rich and gut-busting. Where Adam fits an extra slice, I do not know. In his hollow leg? Sheesh.

When Gunz said the Sacred Sisters would drop food by tonight, he underplayed it to the nth degree. The number of groceries I helped him put away was insane. The bags filled the entire kitchen floor. Literally. Not plastic bags, either. Larger mesh totes with sturdy handles. After we finished, the man did something no man has ever done for me before and made me shower while he cooked. In those bags was an ungodly amount of women's stuff—From razors to lotion to expensive shampoo from a salon. So, I did as the man of the house instructed and spent an obscene amount of time practicing self-care as he fried me pickles.

Pickles, y'all.

Yes. You heard right.

Fried freaking pickles.

My favorite.

He remembered.

I got teary that he cared enough to request them. We hugged. I sobbed. Then that was that. Case closed. No more tears from this gal tonight.

"Love?" Gunz pinches my big toe affectionately.

"Yes?"

"You good?" Arching a brow, the hot man looks at me, reading every cue my body gives off.

"I'm great," I reply truthfully.

"You want some tea?" His blue orbs swap from me to the open doorway of the kitchen.

"Maybe before bed." After they've gotten their fill of father-son bonding time. Not that they can't have more later. Any day, for that matter. But this is a first. Pivotal. To me, at least. Another sacred memory I'll lock away to unwrap again and again as the years pass.

Satisfied with my answer, Gunz nods once, then winks, wearing the sexiest smirk before carrying on with Adam about the club's automotive shop he's been working at.

"How's it goin' for ya?" Gunz asks.

Adam shrugs his indifference. "I like it fine."

"But it's not your *thing?*" comes from his father, as a set of talented fingers knead my arch. I bite back a pleasured groan.

"Truth. Not really." Adam swallows an enormous bite of cheesecake and washes it down with half a glass of milk. "But I am learnin' a lot from Tripper and Deke." Like a Neanderthal, he swipes the remnants of liquid from his mouth with the back of his hand and discards it on the top of his jeans.

Keeping my expression neutral and my motherly opinions to myself, I ignore Adam's choice of napkin in favor of listening to them chat. At least he does his own laundry.

"Did you talk to Big about doin' somethin' else?" Gunz asks.

"No. This wasn't even his idea. He didn't want me liftin' a finger, but I got bored sittin' around doin' nothin'. Bink musta saw how restless I was and talked to Deke. He was the one who offered me the job."

That was kind of Bink. Remind me to thank her later, along with the other sisters, for packing up my apartment, settling Janie and Dom into their new home, getting Adam this job, and supplying all our groceries. It's the least I can do. I should make a list. There are bound to be more things they've done I can't remember right now.

"When I get back to work, you wanna work with me instead?" Gunz throws out as if it's a normal, everyday, off-the-cuff offer.

Pressing my lips together, to not give anything away, my insides go hay-fucking-wire.

He just asked our son to work with him.

Holy... crap on a cracker.

"Seriously?" is the only word Adam forms as he looks to his father with round, expectant eyes—those of a kid. Shock and awe.

I can't say it doesn't hit me right where it should, because it does. My heart thuds against my breastbone as I watch their interaction unfold.

Not one to take credit, even when it's due, Gunz does what he always does and remains casual, relaxed in his chair, pretending not to notice he just handed our son a wonderful gift. "I'll run it by Prez. He's not gonna care as long as you plan on… ya know." Twirling a Dum Dum between his sexy, beard-encircled lips, the man side-eyes me.

I give them nothing to work with. He can say it out loud. I'm not stupid. Adam likes it here. The only way he can stay is if he becomes one of them. Do I want my son running with an outlaw motorcycle club? No. Does any mother ever want that? No. But I trust Gunz to keep him safe, as safe as he can, given the circumstances. All I want is for my son to be happy. To feel wanted. To belong. It's clear that means here with the Sacred Sinners.

When I focus on Adam, he, too, is eyeing me much like his father.

Slinking back in my chair, and crossing my arms over my chest, I sigh. "Come on, guys. Just say it."

"I wanna prospect for the club," Adam admits around another mouthful of cheesecake, his strong, cut jaw contracting with every bite.

To keep my hands busy, I fiddle with the hem of my shirt. "Then what's stopping you?"

"You."

I frown, confused. "How? You're grown. You make your own choices."

He always has.

"Because he cares what you think," Gunz throws out in our son's defense.

Adam nods—once, twice. Slow and observant.

"That's a nice sentiment, but Adam's never cared what I think. He marches to the beat of his own drum."

"This isn't the same, Mom."

"And why's that?"

"Because you're stayin', right?"

Without knowing my thoughts on the matter, Gunz answers in my stead. "Yeah. She's stayin'."

Pressing my lips together to stave off a reaction, I let Gunz think or say whatever he wants because I refuse to discuss our situation in Adam's presence.

Let's be honest. We haven't known each other long enough to decide if I'll stay or go. I can't... No. I *won't* make rash decisions like that. Not now. Not ever. Staying here for the time being is a godsend. Am I enjoying myself? Yes. Without a doubt. Does that mean I plan to live here indefinitely? Not at all. I'm an independent woman. I can think and act for myself. If I've learned anything in my forty-plus years on this earth, it's you only have yourself to rely on. Being with Gunz makes me happy—right now. But it's fresh. You and I both know what happens when you first fall for a guy. It's magical. You're the lovesick puppy, jumping through hoops to keep your fella interested. He's as equally infatuated. It's middle school all over again. The excitement. The hormones. Kisses and hand holding. Butterflies. No matter how old you get, that doesn't seem to change. The cycle remains the same. Eventually, the honeymoon phase wears off, and reality sets in. The things you once found endearing, you despise. It was the same with Jeremy.

I thought it was cute that he liked to pick out my clothes until it became controlling. Until the fairytale wore off. He wanted me to pack his lunches for work and cook dinner every night. Again, I adored domesticity. I found it, for the lack of a better term, nice. But, once again, I grew resentful as the years passed. Jeremy only ever wanted to eat what he wanted, never caring what I liked. Hell, he probably never knew a single dish I loved. He definitely didn't know fried pickles were my favorite. Had I told him, he'd have forgotten the same day.

I know what you're thinking. This kind of attitude isn't helpful. Gunz isn't Jeremy. Trust me, I'm aware. Just as I'm aware, I don't fit in here as Adam does. I'm not a badass biker chick like Bink or even Loretta. I don't ride Harleys, and I've never even been on a bike. Trust me when I say it takes more than tattoos, the love of loud music, and a jacked-up pickup to fit in with a motorcycle club. Gunz will learn soon enough, just as Jeremy did, I'm not worthy of his time. Thankfully, that's never been my goal. All I want is for Adam to be happy. He's here, with his father, talking. They're laughing and having the best time. That's what matters. That's what makes my heart soar. This is what I've hoped for his entire life.

Refusing to address what Gunz said about me living here, I focus on Adam instead. "Prospect for the club."

There. Done.

I dust my hands together to let things fall where they may. It's out of my control now. Not that it was ever in my control to begin with.

"For real?!"

"Yes."

"You're cool with that?"

Even if I wasn't, I want him happy. "If you're willing to put in the work *and* put down roots here, then do it. Commit." *For once in your life*, I tack on in my head because Adam lacks stability. He's practically a vagabond. Here, with the club, at least he'll have brothers, his father, and a support system in place for whatever life throws at him. There will be structure and expectations. It might even keep his ass out of jail for once. That's one hell of a bonus.

Adam cleans the fork with his tongue like he's done since he was a child when he eats cheesecake, savoring every morsel. "I want that." He pulls a disposable napkin off the table, wipes his mouth, and drops the wadded paper onto his plate.

"You sure?" Gunz double-checks.

A round of eager head bobs ensue from our kid. "Yeah. I'm positive."

His father tips his head in respect as I articulate my consent. "Then you have my blessing."

Thrilled by the news, Adam shoots out of his seat, races around the table, and yanks me into the fiercest hug. Torn from my chair and into his arms, my son crushes me to the point I can barely breathe. "Thank you, Mom. Thank you!"

"You're... welcome," I croak between shallow breaths.

Gunz chuckles from the comfort of his seat as I dangle from our son's arms. The tips of my toes sweep the floor.

Loving his innocent affection beyond words, I let Adam's hug linger as long as he wishes. Turning my head to the side, I rest my temple against his collarbone as he carries on a conversation about the club with Gunz. It isn't until he notices the time from a clock on the wall that he sets me back on solid ground and steps away, stuffing his hands into his front jean pockets.

A broad smile varnishes his handsome face. "Thanks again, Mom."

Happy to have made his day, I chuck his dark, stubbled chin. "Don't thank me. You're puttin' in the hard work."

"I am, which means I gotta jet." He thumbs toward the door. "Deke said I should drop by his place tonight to talk shop."

Seeing our son to the porch together, Gunz types on his phone, then stows it away before giving Adam a one-armed man hug. Our son reciprocates the gesture. It's quick and contains a single back slap. On his way back inside, Gunz drops a single kiss on the side of my head and squeezes my shoulder before leaving us for a private mother-son goodbye. Taking advantage of the moment, I embrace my son again, my arms around his muscled middle. This one I am left on the ground for. Resting his chin on top of my head, Adam rumbles an emotional, "I'm glad you're happy, Mom."

Grinning into the cotton of his shirt, I whisper, "Me too, baby. Me, too." I'm afraid to let the realness seep into the universe. Afraid this could evaporate at any moment.

"He's good."

I nod. "I know," comes as another whisper.

"I like him."

My grin stretches at his admission. "I know that, too." I pat my son's back in understanding.

Having said what needs said, Adam breaks away and trots heavy-footed down the steps of the porch in a new pair of black leather boots. Jogging over to Deke's, he throws a quick wave over his shoulder as I lean against the house, my arms tucked over my chest, watching him go. My boy is not a boy anymore. That mop of dark, styled hair and broad, muscled shoulders are not the body of a kid. He's all man now. A man who needs to buy bigger clothes or he'll be hulking out of that t-shirt in no time.

As if he knows I'm watching, Adam turns, throws me a brilliant, all-tooth smile, and wave, before disappearing into Deke's. I wave back, fondly recalling the times we did this when he was a kid. I'd stand on the porch as he ran his little heart out to the bus stop down the road. Halfway there, he'd slow, wave to make sure I was still watching, then carry on to join his friends. Right as the bus would pull to the stop and turn on its lights, he'd look again, we'd meet eyes, and he'd smile, too cool to wave to his mom in front of the other boys. Not wanting to embarrass him, I'd smile back.

Scrubbing a palm down my face, to clear such memories, I push off the house and turn to head back inside when I'm met with a different person—Debbie crossing the street. In her arms is the pooch I have a soft spot for.

"Hey," I greet, offering a small wave.

Stopping at the base of the stairs, Debbie lets Chibs down on all fours. Either remembering me or being a total affection slut, he clambers up the steps to sit at my feet. Debbie removes a backpack she's wearing and sits it on the bottom tread just as I hear the front screen door open and Gunz's voice. "Thanks, Deb."

"Anytime. Everything he'll need is in the bag." She gestures toward it.

Wait. What?

"Anybody gonna fill me in?" I glance at Gunz standing beside me, then down to Deb, as she props a foot on the bottom step, her hand curved over the porch railing.

Kneading the back of his neck, a Dum Dum between his lips, Gunz jerks his chin at the pup. "You like him. I'm gonna be back to work soon. You'll need someone here to keep an eye on things. Figured he could be yours."

Holy hell.

"You got me a dog?"

Removing the paper stick from his mouth, Gunz points to Chibs with it. "No. I got you *that* dog."

"Chibs," I comment for no other reason than I'm gobsmacked.

"Yeah. That gremlin-lookin' one with the smooshed face." Again, he points to the dog with his sucker.

"You said smooshed," I blurt out of nowhere, before mashing my lips together to keep from saying anything else stupid.

We have breached the twilight zone.

Giving zero damns about what he said, Gunz shrugs one shoulder. "Well, look at him."

I blink a couple of times and do as I'm told. "I can't

believe you got me a dog." With blue eyes, like his and Adam's. Not the exact shade, but similar. Big, bright, and beautiful. Kinda buggy, but I love that. It adds charm.

Once again, not one to take credit for anything, Gunz explains, "Well, technically, he's a gift from Debbie."

Lips sealed, I stave off a smile, knowing he's full of absolute shit as those butterflies from earlier run a conga line in my stomach. To save face, I pretend this is normal, that I'm not affected, and that this isn't crazy.

Shaking her head at Gunz's obvious BS, Deb chimes in, "He got you a dog." She huffs in barely concealed laughter, refusing to take credit for this unexpected creature sitting patiently at my feet, looking up at me with those oversized eyes, his speckled bat ears standing proud.

See… he got me a dog.

A French bulldog named after a sergeant-at-arms, just like him.

Gesturing for me to take the furball inside, Gunz speaks to Debbie a bit longer on the porch, as I enter the house with the cutest pup. Chibs heels the brief journey, ears and eyes on high alert. In the living room, I sit on the couch, and he roosts between my feet without a single command. I'm speechless.

A few minutes later, Gunz returns, and takes one look at me and the dog before a smile the size of California breaks across his face. Then he's gone, disappearing into the kitchen.

I watch him leave because I'm not sure what else I'm supposed to do. I'm afraid to touch Chibs because what if this isn't real? What if I'm still in that hellhole, dreaming? What if the handsome man now dressed in ovary-exploding jeans and a fitted Harley shirt is a figment of my imagination?

Stuff like this doesn't happen in real life. Not in mine, anyhow.

See. I know I shouldn't have said those words aloud. Admitted the truth.

A handful of minutes later, the same man reenters the living room, wearing the same pants and shirt, looking just as yummy. "His food and water bowl are in the kitchen, love." A body lowers beside mine on the couch. A strong hand guides my shoulder back until my spine connects with the sofa. A furry snort box is lifted off the floor and deposited onto my lap. The same animal fits itself along the seam of my legs, turning into a loaf of dog, butt against my belly, speckled paws on knees.

The sexy biker pats the top of the pup's head. "Deb said he doesn't need a leash. She said he'll sit by the door when he needs to go to the bathroom. Just let him out. He'll come back when he's done."

Right. Let the dog go out by himself.

When I don't respond, a pair of soft lips meet my temple. Dropping a simple kiss there, heat permeates the cotton of my beanie when Gunz speaks. "You tired, love?" Whispered concern weaves through his words.

I shake my head.

"Do you not like the dog?" he questions next, trying to get a bead on how I'm feeling.

Unable to do anything but, I stare at the aforementioned pup—at the single white spot on his right butt cheek. The lack of tail. Nothing more than a tiny tootsie roll of a stub. It's cute. His shoulders are broad and muscular, like you'd expect a biker's dog to be—brawny.

I've never had a dog.

Not one.

Not ever.

My ex refused to let us have any pet. He said they were

too much of a hassle. As a child, my parents barely cared for us, let alone any kind of animal. My apartment complex didn't allow anything with fur, and I'm not much of a fish or bird lover.

Carefully, I lift both hands and just as carefully lay them on either side of this living creature. He breathes, his body moving up and down beneath my touch, fur soft. Chewing my bottom lip, I blink away tears, knowing damn well I promised myself I wouldn't cry again after the silly pickle incident in the kitchen. Or the shower one... which we don't need to mention.

Dammit.

"Sweetheart." Gunz thumbs away a lone tear as it descends my cheek.

Sliding my palms upward, I finger Chibs' soft bat ears at the tips and work my way down to give them the best scratchy scratches. They twitch and I smile because how could I not? They're cow print, a stark contrast against the rest of his body. Out of my periphery, I note Gunz's smile, too. It's reserved as he watches me with laser focus. Not wanting him to get the wrong idea, I swallow down my pride, my fear, and my concerns, to say what he deserves to hear, even if now's not the perfect time.

"I don't know if I can stay with you."

When Gunz opens his mouth to respond, I raise a hand to stave him off. If I don't get this out now, I'll chicken out later. "When you said I was staying... I don't know if that's true or will ever be true. I... I've never had a dog. I want this dog, but I can't keep him if there are conditions." I don't think I could take another thing being torn from me. Another thing I care about gone. *Poof.*

Resting a hand on my thigh, Gunz chuckles warmly as if he finds me amusing or something else entirely. "He's yours whether or not you stay, love. I told our son you're stayin' 'cause you are, for now. Even if it's only for another week or a month. He needed to hear that."

"He did," I agree with a shallow nod.

Gunz keeps talking. "We both know if he joins the club and works with me, he'll be a helluva lot more successful than he would be on the streets. I'll make use of his talents. Keep him out of jail."

That's all I could hope for.

"Thank you." There's no way I could ever repay Gunz for what he's done. What he's taken on with grace and maturity. A thank you isn't sufficient, I know this, you know this, and deep down, I hope he knows this too, but I have nothing more to give.

Squeezing my thigh, Gunz knocks his shoulder into mine, expelling a grumbled, "No, love. We're not doin' that." He pauses, inhales, and exhales before carrying on. "No thank yous. No misplaced appreciation. I'm helpin' our kid because I wasn't there when he was growin' up. I'm keepin' him close because I wanna get to know him. It's selfish on my part. And… Chibs is your dog. He was your dog the moment you held him. You stay. You go. You never wanna speak to me again. None of it changes the fact he's yours if you want him."

"I want him." Without a single doubt, I want him.

"Good. 'Cause he suits you, and I don't want you here without protection when I'm gone."

This man… Always one step ahead. I need clothes. Gunz produces clothes. I need food. We have food. He wants me protected. A dog literally shows up at our doorstep. I'm worried about Adam. He swoops in and offers our son a job to work with him at his club, without knowing Adam more than a few days in person.

Rubbing our dog's back, I rest my head on Gunz's shoulder. "He's gonna protect me?"

Another kiss is deposited onto my beanie, reigniting all the warm-and-fuzzies inside. "Maybe not as well as Deb's other dogs, but hell yeah, he'll guard the house." Alongside me, Gunz pets the pooch with a single finger. "He could put the hurtin' on someone if he wanted to. Deb trains these dogs to fight. There's a booklet in the backpack with commands you'll need to learn."

Okay.

I guess that's that.

I now have a dog with fancy instructions, an attractive man seated beside me, and a son pledging to be a Sacred Sinner, or whatever they call it when a person tries to join a motorcycle club. Prospecting? I think that's what they call them. Prospects.

What's next?

My head still resting on Gunz's muscular shoulder, I peek up at his face. Well, the side of it and the gray scruff mixed with goatee there. Out of the corner of his eye, he's watching me watch him. Our eyes meet. He smiles, soft and sweet. I return the sentiment with a shyer version of my own. Warmth pools low in my belly. He winks.

"Another movie, babe? Or book two in bed? Your pick." Ever so gently, the sexy man brushes his fingertips over my cheek, down to my throat, and over the marks he made there, eliciting goosebumps in his wake.

I shiver. "Book."

Decision made, Gunz urges me to sit up, thumbs one of his markings around my throat with a quick admiring sweep, then heads to the bedroom as I take Chibs out to potty. Standing on the porch, I watch our lil guy make quick work of his bathroom duties in the front patch of grass before we both join Gunz in the bedroom.

With the bed turned down, pillows fluffed, the sexiest biker alive spreads out on his side of the mattress, arms tucked behind his head, elbows out, ankles crossed, in a pair of boxers. Only boxers. Tight boxers. I can see everything. Every. Freaking. Thing.

Nearly swallowing my tongue, I stand at the edge of the bed and stare. It's impossible not to. This is the most I've seen of his skin. Chest hair, defined abs, his bullet wound patched, solid pecs with a valley down the center, tattoos for days, including the skull tat poking out from the top of his low-slung boxers. The outline…You know what I'm referring to is… semi-hard. The tip, there's a definite impression of a hoop or barbell of some sort there. I wanna ask if he's got a dick piercing, but I won't. Those legs—long, defined, dusted in hair, and covered in more ink. Where my tattoos are vibrant, full of color, his are darker. Black and gray, with other shades thrown in here or there. Roses and skulls in more places than one. The same symbol the men wear on the back of their vests.

Pulling an arm out from behind his head, Gunz rubs a palm down the center of his stomach to his bulge. He squeezes there and groans, his eyes locked on mine. That wicked tongue samples his bottom lip, leaving a wet sheen behind.

"If things were different, I'd ask you to sit on my face," he admits out of nowhere, continuing to massage his erection to full mast, not an ounce of discomfort or remorse to be seen.

Shocked by his brashness, I swallow hard but remain poker-faced. There's no need to show how much I'd love to try that. Not that I have any experience in that field.

He's not done. "Then I'd tongue fuck you 'til you couldn't walk straight."

My knees almost give out at the thought. "Erik," I breathe.

The sexiest I-wanna-eat-you-alive smirk hooks at the corner of his mouth. "When the time comes, and you decide to pick me back, I'm gonna do that. Right here. In our bed.

I'll devour your pussy 'til you beg me to stop. But I won't, love. 'Cause you'll be mine… and I ain't never had anythin' be all mine."

Oh.

"Erik." I open to mouth to say… what? I don't have the slightest clue. But he cuts me off before I can say something I'll regret.

"Don't say anythin', love. Just get your fine ass up here." He pats my side of the bed. "Take that stupid hat off first, so I can see your sexy head for once, and then read to me. I wanna hear all about Rhage and his old lady."

Doing as instructed, I throw the beanie onto my nightstand with flourish. Gunz chuckles. Refusing to let my lack of hair own me, I do one better and remove all my clothes, down to my sensible blue lace panties. No bra. Nothing. Emboldened by him and my faux confidence, I pretend I'm just as sexy as I was when we first met. When my tits were perky, and I didn't have tiger stripes across my abdomen. When cellulite was just a word other women had to deal with. Then I crawl into bed beside the man who turns my world upside down. Chibs joins us, making his own kneaded doggy bed at the end of ours, in the corner, facing the door.

Ignoring the fact I'm mostly naked in front of Gunz for the first time since Adam was conceived, I coolly collect the book from the nightstand, prop my back against the wooden headboard, stretch my bare legs out, and read.

By page three, I gather enough courage to glance over at a quiet Gunz. Propped on his side, he stares at me. Pupils dilated. Breathing labored. Cock straining the cotton of his boxers. A dot of precum soaks into the fabric, changing the gray to a darker color in that spot. I turn back to the book before I do or say something stupid.

"Love?" His voice sounds like chewed-up gravel.

I keep my attention focused on the book. "Yes?"

He draws a single digit down the side of my arm. "You're fuckin' perfect."

Oh. Damn.

I blush down to my toes, my heart pounding a thousand miles an hour.

Gunz

If the Devil was real, Kit would be his muse. He'd protect her from everything. Fuck her for eons. Worship the ground she walked upon. Drink her fucking bath water. Because this is what perfection looks like. This is what men go to war for. What men die for.

Christ.

Locked in a fucking trance, I listen to the goddess read. Words don't permeate, but her tone sure does—light and airy. Articulate. Smart. She knows what she's doing. So fuckin' brave. So fuckin' exquisite.

Soft, handful-sized tits hang the slightest, with big ripe nipples, needing to be sucked on, chewed on. I gorge on her form as Kit pretends I'm not as hard as a rock over here. As if I'm not ready to suffocate in her pussy. As if I'm not fucking addicted.

Keeping my hands to myself, for her sake and my own, I listen, and I savor, every inch, every second. Colorful ink coats her body in a tapestry of art. Legs and arms, part of her side. Jeweled lace beneath the breast, making those tits even more mouthwatering.

In the warehouse, I caught a glimpse of this. But it wasn't the same. Years ago, when I fucked her into oblivion, it wasn't the same then either. That was the girl. This is the woman. A grape turned into wine. A road map of life... of experience.

For hours we hang. Every now and again, I lean in and kiss her thigh, liberating the smallest of sighs from her—a soft, throaty, content sorta sound. On her side, in the juncture between hip and ribs, I drop another kiss, atop one of her biggest stretchmarks. Not wanting to pull away from her peaches-and-cream scent and her warmth, I linger there, needing to remain close. To touch her in any way she'll allow, without crossing lines.

Cupping the back of my skull, Kit presses my head to her stomach. "Rest."

Curling up to Aphrodite incarnate, I relax a cheek on her belly and slide an arm underneath her legs to get extra comfy. My hand cups the meat of her ass cheek on the opposite side. I open my mouth to ask if this is alright, but her slight shiver and a pat on my hand communicates all I need to know. This is good. She's happy. I'm fuckin' happy. Rhage is fuckin' happy.

I could do this shit for eternity.

And I will.

Come Hell or high water, this woman will stay mine.

If I don't fuck it up first.

CHAPTER THIRTY-TWO

KIT

Six Weeks later

Standing in front of the kitchen sink, sipping the last bit of tea from my favorite hand-thrown mug, I rest a hip against the countertop, and watch Gunz load our dishwasher. "Would you just talk to me?" I beg. "Please tell me what's going on." My voice cracks alongside my poor, achy heart.

He says nothing. He won't even look at me.

A person clears their throat.

I blink and then frown, trying to remember why I'm here.

Centering myself, I draw circles across the arm of the couch I'm seated on.

"How has everyone's week been? Is there anything you'd like to discuss?" our dark-haired, lean, pencil-skirt-wearing, group therapist asks from her seat beside me on Loretta's hideous, well-kept 1970s autumn-colored, wood-trimmed velour couch. If you're old enough to know, you know the one I'm talking about—wheelbarrow and trees. Odd texture,

A sofa someone in your family likely had growing up. Only this one is in Loretta's sitting room. A space she's designed to look like the '70s came for a visit and puked all over the space. Wood-paneled walls, orange shag carpeting, geometric printed curtains, with plants on every surface, including a few hanging from the ceiling. It's a trip. Literally. I'd hate to be high in this place. Not that I've lit up since college. But I'm willing to bet this is Blimp's favorite room.

We're here for our weekly therapy session. Five weeks ago, Big, ordered we attend these together at Loretta's house since it's next to Jade's and easily protected. Jennifer's our therapist. She's about as nice as you'd expect and has experience with women who've been sexually assaulted.

Jade hates her.

Loretta's indifferent.

I'm ready for the next five weeks to be over with, so I don't have to deep dive talk about my feelings anymore. Trust me when I say, I appreciate therapy. I also appreciate what this woman is trying to do. But it's apparent to the three of us, her experience with rape victims doesn't include kidnapping, murder, or motorcycle clubs. The first thing we covered was Niki's death. That I didn't find out about until a few days after I was living on the compound.

The following week, we had her wake along with Runner's. A two in one, if you could call it that. It felt like more of a party, with drunken antics and club whores, than a celebration of life. It was nothing more than a reason for men in leather to screw whatever available pussy they could get their paws on. Gunz and Adam both stayed for the bash as I, and most of the women, left the men to their devices. I wanted no part in it. Neither did they.

Especially when a van load of young, topless women wearing short, schoolgirl skirts rolled in carrying six-packs of beer. I heard one of the brothers say this would have been

Runner's wet dream. Another said Niki would have loved it. I can officially say I've never attended a wake that resembled anything of the sort. Nor would I want to attend another like it again.

A single look at the topless women draping themselves all over Gunz, my son, and the taken brothers, I thought I was gonna be sick. Two days later, I began searching for apartments. Every one of them I've called to get a showing has bailed. Said they had no vacancies, or I wasn't approved. Except for the one I'm viewing this afternoon, thanks to Bink and her influence.

I wish I could say the past six weeks have been a glorious, life altering cuddle fest with a particular sexy biker. Sadly, the honeymoon bubble has exploded, and along with it, my childish fantasies of romance and belonging. Each day that goes by, it's more apparent I need space, as does Gunz. Sure, we still sleep in the same bed. Still eat at the same dinner table with our son each night, trading off cooking duties. We spend time with his granddaughter, Harley, the most adorable one-year-old on the planet.

But we don't touch anymore.

The forehead kisses and hand-holding have left the building.

He's gone.

The night of Niki and Runner's wake, the man I knew disappeared, and in his place is this new zombie of a person I don't recognize. He smiles little, works a lot, and comes home drunk more times than not. It's early to work, dinner, then disappear into the clubhouse. By midnight, he's crawling into bed, reeking of alcohol. I've asked him what's wrong repeatedly. I've tried to figure out why things have changed. All I can deduce is he doesn't want me there anymore, but he doesn't have the courage to ask me to leave. Even if that's not why, he still won't tell me what's going on.

So, I'm taking matters into my own hands, for both our sakes and my sanity. Because if I have to attend these therapy sessions to deal with my own trauma *and* live with him like I have been, I won't survive another week, let alone a month.

Seated on an overstuffed brown chair, Jade plays on her phone, paying Jennifer no mind. The fierce, tatted-up, curvaceous beauty I call friend has little patience for these visits. She'll sit, say a handful of words, and disappear back into her phone for the rest of our hour. Today, she's wearing a black-and-white polka dot dress, black chucks, and a beanie.

True to her eclectic tastes, our hostess, Loretta, is rockin' a new wig to cover her still mostly bald head. Well, she's decided to keep hers that way. Easier to wear wigs, she says —now that she's bought a dozen different kinds in assorted colors and styles. Today's is long, sleek, and black—akin to Cher's hair. It pairs well with her leopard-print shorts and slouchy, off-the-shoulder tank.

I wish I could say I look as good as any of these women, but my lack of sleep, abundance of stress, and boredom, has caught up with me. Holey jeans, a band shirt, and flip-flops. No frills. Only mascara. Not even a hat. I'm starting to embrace the baldness in my own way. This quarter-inch hair is the starting point to doing just that.

When none of us reply to her questions, Jennifer cuffs both hands over her knees, an irritated tell, and tries a different tactic. "Have any of you begun exploring sex again, like we've discussed?"

Eyes rolling to the heavens, Jade snorts, and Loretta does as she always does when sex is the topic of conversation. She overshares. Tuning her out, because I don't wanna hear about her and Blimp's sexual exploits, I join Jade in playing on my phone. It's a gift from the sisters. A new, secure line, with all the modern advancements—the latest iPhone.

A couple of weeks ago, Jennifer asked about our sex lives

during one of our sessions and encouraged us to take baby steps to see how we feel about sex now, in the wake of our trauma. She said it's perfectly normal to explore our boundaries and triggers. The thing is, Jade is celibate. Has been for ages. I might as well be labeled the same. I haven't had consensual sex in forever. With the current state of my life and hers, neither of us are going to be exploring our boundaries and triggers anytime soon. This leaves Loretta, who has jumped feet first into the deep end with her man—fucking like rabbits.

This isn't helpful.

Or healing.

It's an hour out of my week, spent talking to women I already talk to daily, about shit we already talk about, if that makes sense. Except it's with a therapist who, no doubt, reports her findings back to Big. We are under no illusion there is any sort of confidentiality here.

My phone vibrates with a text through our collective sister thread.

> Jade: If I gotta listen to Loretta talk about her sucking Blimp's dick one more time, I might scream.

> Me: She's your best friend.

> Jade: I know.

As if on cue, Loretta sweeps her hair over her shoulder and starts talking about blow jobs, using graphic hand gestures, and making slurping noises.

Refusing to encourage her behavior, I stifle a laugh. Jade does the same as she looks up at me, arches her brow in a see-I-told-you way, and returns to texting.

> Me: I think this is so Jen will report back to Big.

Jade: Look at her. The woman is blushing.

> Me: Loretta has that effect on people.

Jade: This is ridiculous. Did she just make a choking sound? As if this woman has a gag reflex. I've known her forever. That's not a thing.

> Me: Maybe we should have Loretta run these sessions from now on.

Jade: Agreed. I'd much rather talk to you both when I've had a nightmare than to Jen. Do you remember the day she cried when we told her about the woman who died and was left to rot in the closet with us? I don't want a therapist who cries. I know what we went through was fucked up. I don't have to come to terms with that. Healing takes time.

Jade's right. Session two was heavy on Niki's suicide and Julia's murder. We didn't get far before Jennifer had to take a moment to gather her composure.

While these sessions haven't been the most productive, something positive to come from the last six weeks we've been home has been my relationship with the sisters. We talk each morning and before bed each night. They know about Gunz, just as I do about White Boy living on Jade's couch most nights, and Blimp's hovering. And it's not just them. I've gotten closer with the sisters on the compound, too. Bink, Deb, and the others I've been introduced to—Jezebel, my wild, across-the-street neighbor. Pixie, the colorful-haired, petite, tattoo artist, who owns the shop Jade works at. Daisy, Bink's sister-in-law. Jo, Bink's half-sister. Candy Cane, another OG of the club. You also can't forget the kids—from Leech, Deke's daughters, Deb's sons, to Jezebel's kids, Tati, the teen I first met, and Janie and Dom.

On our same chat thread, Bink chimes in.

> Bink: Not to rain on your parade, Kit... butttt the apartment today is a no-go. Just got a call from them.

Ugh. Another one bites the dust.

> Me: Why does this keep happening?

> Bink: I'll give you two guesses but you're only gonna need one.

I figured as much. After the first two apartments fell through, I started to get suspicious. Now I know it must be the case—*Gunz.*

He won't let me leave.

But he doesn't want to keep me either.

This man needs to make up his mind.

I refuse to live like this anymore.

In limbo.

Miserable.

If I can't move into a local apartment to stay close to Adam, then I'll do the next best thing. A hotel. I'm tired of sleeping next to a liquor store and waking up to an empty bed.

I'm just... tired.

Not wanting to be rude, I sink into the couch, suck up these warring emotions to deal with later, and pretend this isn't that bad.

At least it's not the warehouse.

At least I'm alive.

At least my son is safe.

> Me: Thanks, Bink. I'll figure something out.

> Bink: We got you no matter what.

> Jez: Gunz needs his ass kicked.

Jade chuckles at Jez's message as I hide a private smile. They have me. Have. Me. A woman they barely know. A woman who doesn't deserve their loyalty. Jez is ready to commit violent crimes of the foot-to-ass variety. These really are my people. Women I don't deserve, but I'll cherish all the same.

Mind made up, I tell them my plans. They're minimal and off the cuff.

Pack. Give Chibs to Jez for temporary safekeeping. Leave after dinner. Hotel.

What do they do?

They have my back.

Bink books the hotel under a fictitious name to keep my identity a secret. Jez is excited to have Chibs for a while. Pixie will open the gate when I'm ready to leave because nobody would expect her involvement.

In less than the hour it takes for our therapy session, everything is mapped out, and I'm ready to take the next step.

Freedom is finally within my reach. No more limbo.

CHAPTER THIRTY-THREE

GUNZ

Closing my eyes for a beat, I massage the bridge of my nose, tryin' to stay on task and focus for a solid minute without a fuckin' problem. My head's pounding, stomach churning. I'm runnin' on a couple of hours of shit sleep, and once again, I've had to run interference on another apartment Kit has tried to move into.

That's not happening.

Not now.

Not fuckin' ever.

For the second time in less than five minutes, the vision that continues to plague me paints the back of my eyelids. I try my damndest to force it away. I don't wanna see her. Not now. Not again. But the bitch won't stop haunting me. When I'm awake. When I'm asleep. She's there. I can feel her breath on my neck. Her tongue on my balls.

Blood coats her naked form as she masturbates, begging me to help her come.

Fuck.

This all began the night of her wake.

When I said goodbye and I threw a handful of her ashes into the fire.

Conjured out of thin air, she was there, dark hair spilling over her shoulders. Those nipples I've sucked hundreds of times before on display, cunt ready and willing. Except she was wearing the hottest schoolgirl skirt, offering herself up to me. How could I say no? I couldn't. I took her. Right there. In front of the brothers. In front of my own son. Drunk off my ass, I bent her over a picnic table, threw up her skirt, and violently fucked her sloppy wet pussy... The same picnic table I've fucked her on before. The same one I've shared her on at many club parties. She fucking loved my cock. Begged for it. Took it like a champ. It was like old times. Her smiling over her shoulder at me, gripping my shaft with her tight walls. She fed him. The gluttonous beast thrives on depravity. He finger fucked her tight little asshole. Bruised her pert little ass in a punishing grip. Bit her back. Licked up her spine, tasting salt and all that was her. She moaned my name. Told me she loved me.

I came calling out to her, filling the condom I somehow remembered to put on.

That's when it happened.

Reality flooded in.

The woman beneath me was wrung out, her legs quaking. But those weren't *her* legs. Her skin was too pale. Hair, the wrong shade of brown. She had a lip ring. I fucked this woman, this whore, in front of my entire club, like I'd done hundreds of times before, but... this female wasn't mine.

She wasn't the woman I'd screwed for years and she sure as hell wasn't the woman I had at home, sleeping in our bed, waiting for me to come join her like I should have done hours before. The woman I love. Cherish. Made a goddamn baby with.

"Leave me alone," I whisper to the ghost, hoping it'll work this time.

As always, she smiles—bright, full teeth, tits still coated in blood. She steps forward, licks those same teeth, slow and sexy as fuck, then beckons for me to join her with the crook of her finger.

Refusing to let her win this time, I chug my third bottle of Bud. Then another. And another.

The drunker I am, the quicker she vanishes. Day after day, from the moment I wake, she's there… forever lurking. At night, I drink her away for just a little while, only to stumble home, so I can watch my woman sleep. For hours, in the quiet of our bedroom, I watch. Niki isn't there, but the guilt remains, gnawing at my guts like termites in a house, destroying the foundation little by little. I understand I'm fucking everything up.

Each day I push Kit another inch away. I see it. I feel the yawning distance grow. She no longer looks at me as she did before. She's grown quiet. Niki fucking revels in that. Knowing I can't have the thing I want most. To love and worship the only thing I've ever loved. When I was a kid, my mother told me I wasn't worth anything more than a quick fuck. That nobody would ever love someone like me. That my cock was the only thing of value. She was right. I should've known the bitch would always be right. She created this monster.

On the stool next to mine, Mickey bumps his shoulder into my arm. "It's about time to stumble home. Yeah?" He shudders in laughter, watching me swallow the last bit of my sixth beer before grabbing my seventh from the growing row of empties. Ten should do it. I'm almost there.

This bastard's on babysitting duty. Each night, Big has sent another brother to keep an eye on me, as if I'm some child who needs looking after. Mickey drew the short straw this time. Bet he's hating life right about now, not able to partake in libations, per Big's orders. No, I didn't ask if those were the rules, but I notice shit. Seein' as though my babysitters remain sober, I know it's under Prez's orders. They'd be as trashed as me otherwise.

So, what do I do? I drink another fuckin' beer because I can. It pisses Mickey off. His under-breath complaints are evidence enough.

Smirking wickedly against the lip of my Bud bottle, I explain, "You could tell Prez to mind his own fuckin' business, and you could just go home." I gesture toward the front doors with a flick of my chin, hoping he'll take the bait and get lost. I'd rather do this alone—wallow in my own hell, without company.

Shaking his head as if I've lost my mind, Mickey rolls his eyes. "I like my body parts right where they are." He pats his flat stomach and dick as if those are the most important parts.

"Then report back I'm A-Okay." Fingers fanned out, I form an okay sign and look at him through the hole, my elbow perched on the bar.

My brother delivers an amused smile. "Right." He snickers. "'Cause that's not a lie or anything."

"I'm good." I waggle my brows for show. The last thing I want is a fucking babysitter having to put their life on hold because of me. If I could drink at home, I would. But then I'd have to face Kit and show her who I really am. I'd have to explain what's happening. I'd rather carve my heart out with a dull spoon than pull her through the depths of my darkness. Especially after what she's been through.

What can I say? I'm a weak bastard.

I didn't even have the courage to tell her Niki died. She found out through Bink. When she asked about what happened, because Kit knew I was there, I lied. Told her I found her dying on the floor in the clubhouse. She cried so fuckin' hard, it tore me in two to watch her break down on our couch. Like I was gonna tell her what really went down. Not likely. Big doesn't even know. And it's gonna stay that way. Forever. Ya hear me? For...ever.

"Ya know, you're gonna have to come clean sometime." Mickey motions to my line of beers.

Giving zero fucks, I finish one and crack open another. Out of the corner of my eye, I watch my brother watch me as I relax my throat and down this motherfucker in record time. It sloshes in my gut, makin' we wanna wretch. I burp and pound my chest to give it space to settle. The alcohol will soak in soon enough. Once I can barely walk, I'll have a few hours of solace, if you could call it that. Watching your woman sleep like some goddamn creeper lurking in the night, unable to touch her, kiss her, or say what you wanna say, ain't the best, but it suffices. It's all I've got.

I'll take what I can. Even if it's nothing more than stolen moments of time.

When I close my eyes again and focus on what matters most—seeing Kit... I wait for Niki to emerge. For her ghostly fingers to send shivers down my spine. For her mouth to wrap around my cock, making it painfully hard, even though there's nothing touching him. I wait for her to call me every name under the sun for not loving her. For not saving her. For being the biggest piece of shit before she gets on her knees and rubs her bloodied tits against my shin.

When she doesn't surface, and I'm finally at peace, at least for a little while, I slide off the stool and leave. I don't wait for Mickey. I say nothing. On a mission to do what I've done every night for weeks, I stumble through the clubhouse to the backdoor. The night air invigorates me as I navigate through the back grass, onto the pavement, and past the concrete wall that separates the front of the compound from the back estates.

Using the railing, I drunkenly lumber up my front steps and open the door, making as little sound as possible. I kick off my boots by the couch and leave them, along with most of my clothes, to pick up in the morning. The last thing I wanna do is wake my love.

On the way to see her, I make a quick pit stop in the bathroom to piss, wash my hands, and brush my fuzzy teeth before I sneak into our bedroom and snick the door shut in my wake.

Padding my way to our bed, careful not to trip over any of Chibs' bones, I glance over to Kit's side of the mattress. It's vacant, as is the spot where our dog sleeps.

What the fuck?

"Love?!" I call out to her, my voice hoarse.

Silence.

Dammit.

Flicking on every light in every room, I search the house. In our spare bedroom, her clothes are gone from the closet. Not a single note is to be found. The shower and under the bathroom sink is void of all female shit—like she was never here.

Freaking the hell out, the organ in my chest pummels my sternum in a vicious boxing match as air pumps in and out of my lungs. Sweat blooms across my entire body as I frantically search for any clues she might have left. Afraid I'll miss something, I tear open every drawer and cupboard, leaving them wide open as I move on to the next.

In our bedroom, I dump all my clothes onto the floor and rip shirts from their hangers. Bed pillows hit the wall before they, too, join the mess. Our comforter goes next, into a heap on the floor. Gripping the edge of the mattress, I grunt as I flip it off the box spring. It lands in front of the open door, its corner caught on top of our nightstand. Our lamp slides to the edge and hangs there for a beat before crashing onto the carpet.

"Where did you go?" I sigh in misery, still coming up empty.

Climbing over the disaster, I stumble into the hallway and use the wall for support as I make my way into the living room. I find my phone discarded on the couch.

Desperation clogs my throat as I fumble with the screen to check her location. It's gone. Our tether was there this afternoon when I checked to make sure she was safe at Loretta's for her weekly therapy session. It was there when they went to lunch with White Boy and Deke at the bakery in town. White Boy even texted to say she ate a giant salad and a chocolate croissant. I was relieved she indulged. Kit's appetite has been a rollercoaster of late. Some days, she eats like she should, while others, she barely touches her dinner. I've been keeping an eye on it, worried she'll lose the progress she's made.

When she drove home today, her dot moved. I watched as I always do every time she leaves, afraid something will happen if I'm not there to protect her. As if my brothers can't take care of my precious cargo.

When I'm working, I keep the app open so I can see everything in real-time—for peace of mind. Adam, who now has a desk in the corner of my office, likes I keep tabs on his mom, too. It's a joint effort. 'Cause we give a shit.

Running out of options, I connect a call and pace the living room.

It rings, and it rings, and it goddamn rings. She doesn't pick up.

"Fuck!" Pissed off at the world, I chuck my phone at the couch. It bounces off the back, and lands face down on the floor. On an ugly, lip-curling growl, I flip the piece of shit off.

A heavy knock resounds at the door. Marching over, I don't bother looking through the peephole as I throw the thing open, hoping it's her but knowing damn well it's not.

On the opposite side of our screen door stands Big, a deep-set wrinkle between his brows, frowning at me, his tattooed arms tucked across his chest over a plain white t-shirt.

"Where is she?" I demand, nostrils flaring.

He cocks his head to the side and drawls, "She's... safe."

"Where?"

"Safe," he repeats, refusing to relinquish any information.

This stubborn goddamn dick bag.

"I asked you a fuckin' question, brother," I snarl.

"And I gave you a fuckin' reply, brother," he growls in return.

"You won't keep her from me," I warn. Over my dead body.

Ejecting a loud, irritated sigh the entire compound can hear, Big explains, "I'm doin' what she requested. That's the least I could do."

She requested? I don't believe that. Then again, I didn't think she'd leave. Even if our homelife hasn't been the greatest, I've been... nice. Never once have I been a jerk. I've cooked dinners. Even paid close attention to the food she likes, so we have more of it in the cupboards. After dinner, before I head out, I make her a cup of tea and turn the television on to something I think she'll like. I even load the dishwasher most nights.

"I—" I begin, only to be cut off by the asshole.

"I'm not tellin' you jack." Big's no-bullshit gaze bores into mine. "You fuckin' know that. The brothers aren't gonna tell you shit, either. Including your boy."

"Adam knows?" I seek confirmation.

"Yeah."

Sagging against the door, I sigh. "Thank fuck... Okay. She's safe."

"Yeah, dumbass." Big snickers.

I scrub a hand over my bald head. "I fucked up." Big time.

Pursing his lips, Prez nods in agreement, his tone far softer than I expect. "Yeah. Ya did. I told you this would happen if you kept it up."

He did. He also made me switch from hard liquor to beer a few weeks back. Said I needed to take it easy. If I wanted to kill myself, there were better, far cheaper options. Ha. Ha.

"I don't have a choice," I explain, not wanting to go into the specifics.

Not buyin' my shit for a second, Big unfolds his arms and scratches his forehead in agitation. "We all have choices, brother. I kept my distance from Bink for-fucking-ever... my choice." He points to himself.

This isn't the same situation. Not even close.

"Really? We're goin' *there*. Big, that wasn't your choice. Don't pretend like it was. The shit Lindy Sue found out coulda put you down for a long time." I can't think of a single instance Bink's mom wasn't a piece of work. A bitch to her rotten core. If I didn't know any better, I'd say she and my mom were cut from the same cloth.

Knowin' I'm right about this, Big relents, "True. But I could've said fuck her, took what I wanted, and hoped she didn't throw me under the bus."

Right. Like that woulda happened.

"Then you would've gone to prison and where would Bink be?" Oh. We know where. She'd have grown up and married some small-dicked, prissy-bitch, non-biker. Together, they'd live in suburbia with their 2.5 kids, a dog, and a white picket fence. He'd sell insurance or something equally boring, while Bink catered to his every whim. On

Tuesdays, after he watched the news, they'd *make love* missionary style with the lights off.

"Exactly," Big grumbles, pulling me from my messed-up musings—the same ones he's probably considered over the years. "That's why I made the choice I did. To wait it out. Did what I had to do to get what I wanted. Worth the wait, even if it killed me. The choice you're makin' by pushin' away the woman you love... solves what?"

Licking the front of my teeth, I try and fail to summon a simple reason he won't shut down in two seconds flat. "It's complicated," is all I come up with. It's late, and I'm half-drunk. I dunno what he expects me to do. Pour my heart out? Not likely.

"Then simplify it for me," he offers. "You're a smart man. You can use words. I got ears." Tucking errant strands of long hair behind his ears, Big then taps those same ears with exaggerated fanfare. "They listen quite fuckin' well."

Heaving a sigh, I stare up at the ceiling in my entryway, hoping for... I dunno what... divine intervention? Or for Kit to put me outta my misery by somehow Dorothy-ing her fine ass here with the click of her heels. When that doesn't work, I *thunk* my head against the door at my back and mutter, "Not happenin'," hoping Big will let it go and leave me to handle the Kit situation by myself.

Not a fan of my pigheadedness, Big grumbles a slew of laughable bullshit under his breath. "Then you're not gettin' your woman back," he throws out, as if that's a foregone conclusion.

I snort. "We both know that's not true."

"Do we?" Big scratches his chin. "'Cause from where I'm standin', I'm your club president, and she left your ass of her own free will."

That might be true. She might have left of her own free will... But... "Rank or not, brother, she's mine." Yeah. There's that. She's my woman. My old lady. The mother to my son. Wham bam, in yo face motherfucker.

"She got your patch on her back?" He levels me with a look like he somehow wins with this one. The asshole's itching for a fight.

Lucky for him, we're not built the same.

"No," I answer honestly, calmly, and not at all in the mood to punch him in the mouth for baiting me with this crap. He's trying real hard to make me crack under pressure.

"She gonna get your patch on her back?" Big challenges next.

"Yes." That's a dumbass question. Deb's already on it. I commissioned Kit's cut the day after we got back. The same day Deb took mine to patch over the bullet hole and wash all the dried blood off. Still, that's none of Big's business. It's mine and Kit's… and a bit of Deb's, considerin' she's the one puttin' in the hard work.

"How's that gonna happen if you won't fix your shit? You think she's just gonna wait around for you to decide to get sober? To explain what the hell's doin'? If she were Bink, and I was pullin' this crap, would you tell her to put up with it? Or would you tell her she deserved better, then help her, like you did when my woman left me the first time?"

When I open my mouth to mention, once again, this isn't the same situation, he keeps yappin'. "Thought so. Now you gonna let me in, or am I gonna stand out here all night?" He kicks the steel of the door, impatient as ever.

"You can come in, but I'm still goin' after her."

"It's funny you think you can leave." He smirks, his head shaking in laughter as if he could stop me.

What's funnier is he thinks he has that much power.

Sorry, brother, ya don't.

Crossing my arms over my bare chest, lips thinned, I blink up at Big slowly, unimpressed by his level of fuck-around-and-find-out. "I. Can," I grind out through clenched molars. It might involve violence, but I've proven on a regular I'll do what I gotta do to handle my own. Stand in my way and see what happens.

Reading the air thickening between us, the smirk wipes clean off Big's face. "Why don't you go sit your drunk ass down and let's have a chat." He jerks a chin toward the inside of my house. "You're not goin' anywhere tonight."

"She's not in my bed. I'm goin' to hers." We aren't sleeping apart. Drunk or not, I've made it to bed every single night since we rescued her from the warehouse. I don't plan on changing that ritual anytime soon.

"No, brother." Big's shoulders lift as he inhales a bottomless, chest-expanding patience-imbuing breath. On his exhale, the man expels a dramatic, long-suffering sigh. "The sisters are with her, Gunz. She's safe. What *is* your plan? Bang on her door in the middle of the night, professing your love, beggin' her to take ya back?"

That's not how I'd do things.

"No." I haven't thought that far yet, but that's none of his business, either.

"I didn't think so," Big cocks off.

Unlatching the screen door to get this over with, Big grabs the steel frame and swings it wide open. I step back to give him space to lumber his giant ass into my house. He claims a seat at the small dining room table. In Kit's spot. I wanna order him to get the fuck up, because that's where she sits, but think better of it. Across from him, I drop into Adam's vacant chair. Big eyes me and does a thorough once-over. I know I look like dogshit. I've lost more weight since we've been home. Nothin' tastes good anymore. Not even the alcohol. It's a means to an end.

"Adam told me you've been talkin' to yourself," Big blurts

out of thin air, catapulting us into a conversation I don't wanna have.

Here we go.

"I'd suggest you leave my son out of this," I warn, unimpressed with the low blow, but not surprised by it either. I'm sure Adam doesn't enjoy hearing me beg Niki to leave, any more than I like having to argue with a ghost. It makes sense that he'd talk to Big about it. I can't blame the kid. I might do the same if I were in his shoes.

A deep rumble bangs around Big's chest, as he attempts and fails to conceal his laughter. "I'd suggest you quit bein' a prissy bitch and tell me what's doin'. Not as your brother or your prez, but as your friend, asshole."

"I told you. It's complicated," I reiterate, in case he forgot.

"And I've got all night." Big leans back in his chair to get comfy, causing it to groan in protest. Tucking his arms across his chest, a cocky smirk locks in place, then there's that stubborn gaze daring me to start somethin'—'cause he's ready.

Have I told you how much I hate havin' a meddlesome asshole for a best friend? Yes? No? Well, consider yourself told. This prick is worse than any woman. At least, with a female, you can remove yourself from the situation, no worse for the wear. Big doesn't roll that way. If it's important to him, he's not only obnoxious, he's also relentless—quite the combination. Bein' King-Kong-sized and a national president, nobody gets to just walk away if he don't want you to. Normally, I'm cool with that as long as it don't involve me.

Obviously, I'm involved.

I scratch my pec to give my hand something to do. "We're not doin' this."

"Oh. We are. 'Cause I didn't pound a fuckin' Monster energy drink for nothin'."

Fantastic.

I open my mouth and start to tell him to fuck right off, but a slew of emotional word vomit pours from my lips instead. Everything from Niki and what went down, to her haunting me. Followed by what I did to Kit, by screwing that club whore, when I should've controlled my cock. Then onto the wonderful gift that just keeps on giving—guilt. I omit my childhood because that's for my woman to know. The rest I unleash in a torrent of ugliness. He takes it. 'Cause he's my best friend. Nodding along as if he gets it, Big remains quiet 'til I've laid myself bare. By the time I'm through, I'm slouchin' in my chair, bone tired, legs spread wide, sweatin' through my boxers.

Big clears his throat and blinks a handful of times before words form. "Holy hell. That's a lot."

No shit.

I shrug, not sure what he expected. "You asked."

"I'm glad I did. You need help. 'Cause you and I both know she's not really haunting you. You're doin' this to yourself." He taps the side of his skull, indicating it's all in my head.

"I know," I agree.

If I believed in hauntings, I would've already hired a witch to cleanse my house and the compound to get rid of her ghostly ass. But I don't believe in that voodoo hoodoo mumbo jumbo.

"You think it's the guilt?" he asks.

"It has to be." That's all that makes sense to me.

"This ever happened before?"

"Nope." My head shakes. "We both know I've killed a fuck ton of people, but I've always slept like a baby after. Seen some vile shit, too. Never got nightmares from that either." Not after baggin' up a room full of dead kids, courtesy of Remy. Not even after scooping brains off the side of the highway, when a brother played sleepy chicken with a semi. May he rest in peace.

"You're hallucinating." A statement, not a question.

"Yep… and when I'm around Kit, it's worse. Niki comes out for longer periods of time. I can't focus. At work, it's not as bad." It's manageable when the erections go away, but I'm not about to admit that.

"She here now?" He looks around the space as if he expects Niki to float into corporeal existence.

"No. I'm too drunk."

Big nods as if he gets what I'm puttin' down.

Rubbing my sore flank, thanks to my wound not healin' as it should, I tilt my head back and stare up at the ceiling. "Niki loved me. I should've expected someone I cared about dyin' because of me would turn up this way."

"Then what's your plan?" Big's foot taps against the leg of the table, jiggling the entire thing.

"Bring my woman home."

"How you gonna manage that?"

Good question.

Completely out of my element with love and relationships and all those intimate feelings and stuff, I shrug for the millionth time. "Talk to her, I guess. Ask for forgiveness." That's about all I can do. I'm not like Big or some of the other brothers. I'm not gonna lock her away. I'm not gonna force her to fall in line. She's gotta want me as much as I want her, and if she doesn't, I'll survive. That's what I do.

The table stops moving, and Big sits forward, his elbows resting on the table, fingers steepled in front of him, pressing against the center of his chin. "Does she know about the club whore?"

"Not that I've heard." If someone mentioned it to her, it would be their right. I did it. There's no use denying it.

Big hums to himself. "Then maybe it's better she doesn't find out."

"Maybe it's better for me, but it ain't right. I fucked around on her."

"Not on purpose," Big somehow justifies.

I fuckin' despise how easy it is for some people to rationalize their indiscretions. You screw up, it hurts someone, and instead of manning or womaning up and owning it... You do what? Lie? Deflect? Or my personal favorite—lie by omission. That one's a doozy.

Since Big and I don't see things eye to eye, I set him straight. It won't be the first or the last time. "Men don't stick their dicks in willing cunts on accident. Don't be stupid, brother."

I didn't accidentally fall, with a condom and a hard-on, into a willing cunt, bent over a picnic table. Whoopsie. My bad.

"Yeah. But you haven't claimed her yet." There he goes again, trying to let me off my own hook.

"But I have." We've already established this.

"Not officially."

Christ.

In hopes Big sees the light and knocks off this nonsense, I hit him on his home turf. "That's like sayin' Bink wasn't yours before it was official. You threatened all the men she dated before you. You even paid some of them off. You made her life hell half the time. Sorry if I don't take a fucked-up page outta your relationship playbook, brother."

Nodding as if it clicks, the giant asshole snorts. "Alright. I'll give ya that. You do what you gotta do. But I'd say you need to see Doc and get checked out. Have you told Bonez about this?"

"He's been busy." That's code for I haven't told him.

"Not that busy."

Not givin' me a chance to talk to my brother on my own time, the pain in my ass pulls out his cell and dials.

"Fuckin' asshole," I hiss when the call connects.

Sitting up straighter, Big smiles broadly, proud of himself.

Rubbin' sleep from his eyes, Bonez's pillow-wrinkled face appears on the screen. He squints at Prez, then looks at me, assessing. "What's wrong?"

"Nothin'," I growl at the same time Big begins to fill in every detail of what's been happenin' the last month.

As expected, like takin' a bucket of ice water to the face—this wakes Bonez right up. Leaving his bedroom, he pads to the kitchen to get a drink.

He fills a mug at his fancy-ass fridge as I comment, "You got company? I can call back later." There was someone in his bed. I saw a flash of hair.

Big's eyes tip all the way back into his skull as he focuses the phone on me.

Rubbing my temple with my middle finger, I flip the man off.

He chuckles, far too pleased.

"Bullshit." Bonez drops onto his couch and yawns. "Company or not, we're doin' this now. I can't believe you didn't tell me." He sips from a literal penis mug. The cup portion is flesh-colored, shaped like two nuts. The handle is the shaft with a fat mushroom head. It's ridiculous, and he gives zero fucks when he raises his eyebrows, before taking another long drink.

Loving this far too much, that cocky smile of Big's grows, his eyes crinkling at the edges. Annoyed by this entire night, I scowl at the intrusive prick, then at my brother for good measure. Fuck 'em both.

Knowing I can't get out of this even if I tried, I yield to my brother's interrogation.

One by one, he fires off a list of questions, from what I've been eating and drinking, to sleep patterns. Typical doctor stuff. Since he can't check my vitals, he makes me stand and give him a slow turn.

Bonez whistles. "Jesus, brother, you've lost a lot of weight."

My eyes roll.

I know.

"Remove your bandage." Having already cleaned and redressed it this morning, I peel back the tape for Bonez to inspect.

The moment it's revealed, he sucks back a curse. "Gunz, hospital, now."

With two fingers, I prod along the edge of my injury, studying it myself. "What? Why? I'm already on a new round of antibiotics. Doc gave 'em to me last week." When I called to let him know I was runnin' a low-grade fever for like a day, maybe two. He knew what was up. Sent over a script. Done and done. No muss, no fuss.

"You're hallucinating." Bonez states the obvious.

"So?"

Big pans in the camera, to give my brother a better view. "There could still be bullet fragments in your abdomen. It's too red, and I can see the crusted puss. It's infected." Bonez squints. The lines around his eyes deepen, as he plays concerned doctor to a T.

"It's better than it was last week." I push along the edge that oozed last week, and I'm happy to report there is no such ick this time 'round.

Still squinting at the site, Bonez licks his lips. "It's not."

"I've been shot plenty of times before, brother." And never had a problem healing. To emphasize my point, I pull down the back of my boxers to show the scar on my ass cheek, where I was last shot. Then another on my left bicep. Onto the outside of my right forearm. Right thigh, covered by ink, and the same calf. All there to be seen in their scarred, healed glory. Tada.

Irritated by my showmanship, Bonez speaks directly to Prez. "He needs a hospital."

Two sets of worried eyes stare at me. "I'll take him," Big promises.

"He won't," I volley, glaring straight at Prez.

"Do you know without a single doubt this isn't happenin' 'cause you're a stubborn motherfucker? That there isn't an infection there? That your odd behavior isn't because of that?" Big two-finger points to the scab.

Dropping back onto my chair, I shrug because I don't know shit anymore. My woman left me. Gone. No goodbye. I can't sleep more than three hours at a time. Besides a piece of fruit in the morning, I don't eat 'til dinner. Even then, I have little appetite. Yesterday, during a bathroom break, Niki came for a visit when I was takin' a piss. I got so hard I couldn't finish leakin' without jackin' off. Christ. Even thinkin' about it makes me wanna puke. It was… gross. I don't do that. Yankin' my cock 'til I spill cum into a wad of toilet paper. Childish stuff. It felt like I was back in elementary, readin' Dad's nudie mags all over again. Not something I wanna relive.

"We're going tonight," Big declares as if he's made up his mind, and I don't have a say in the matter.

Tired of fighting him, I relent. It's obvious what I've been doin' isn't workin', and I'm sick of Niki livin' rent-free in my head. Our hospital is, how you say, friendly to our breed. They don't ask too many questions. The care is always top-notch.

Gettin' my ass in gear before these two meddlesome assholes bark orders, I push out of the chair, using my knee as leverage. On a groan, I shuffle to the bedroom, climb over the mess I've made, and throw on a new pair of sweats from the pile, a t-shirt, and a pair of crew socks before stuffing my feet into my least-worn boots. I leave them unlaced. I don't give a damn how I look. All I want is sleep. Hours of it. Days. Weeks.

But what I want more than that is…

Kit.

In my life.

In our house.

Pussy on my face.

To accomplish that, I gotta get this head screwed on straight. Niki's gotta go.

Operation get-well, woo-my-woman, and eat-some-pussy is officially underway.

Wish me luck. I'm gonna fuckin' need it.

CHAPTER THIRTY-FOUR

KIT

Fuck.
 Shit.
 Damn.
 Damn.
 Dammit.
 Using both fists, I rub blurring wetness from my eyes as I navigate a long stretch of sidewalk, careful not to trip and fall on my behind.

I left him. I left Gunz in his time of need. I'm the world's biggest bitch.

Racing to the hospital in the literal middle of the night, the doors retract. Just beyond is the brotherhood, pacing the halls in leather. Hot on my tail, a tired Jade and Loretta enter alongside White Boy and Blimp, our babysitters tonight.

They escorted Bink and the rest of the sisters home, to keep an eye on the kids. Don't worry, they're not alone. Deke and three others were left to protect the compound. I didn't ask. Adam told me when he called to make sure I was doing okay, after Big called in the middle of girl time to explain

Gunz's in surgery for bullet fragments, an infection, and as if the first two weren't bad enough, internal bleeding.

It's been quite the evening.

Three conjoined hotel rooms at the nicest place in town and girl talk. Hours and hours of it. We had a bar of chips and dip to pair with our hours of chatter. We were just finished dressing for bed when the call came through. First to me, then the rest of the sisters.

Every moment since the news broke has been a blur. My focus singular. On him and getting to the hospital as fast as possible. Not that it does much good. His family is already here for support.

Adam breaks through the crowd, heading straight for me. We don't speak as he leads me by the arm through a throng of men, into a nearby waiting room, teeming with even more males—a stark contrast of denim and leather versus the sterile white walls and tan chairs. In the center of the space, there's a cart full of snacks and coffee. One brother gets up and offers me their seat. Swallowing down my ball of nerves, I offer him a tight, grateful smile before I take it, my hands trembling.

Acting far beyond his years, Adam kneels in front of me and rubs his palms up and down my thighs. His smile's watery, his eyes rimmed in red, when I meet them with my own.

"He's in good hands, Mom." He attempts to comfort, his voice hoarser than usual.

Scratching my nail along the chair arm, I bob my head, so he knows I'm paying attention.

In good hands.

Right.

A surgeon's hands in the middle of the night. It doesn't take a genius to know they don't operate at three in the morning unless it's life-threatening.

Like Moses parted the sea, if the sea was bursting with testosterone, Big lumbers into the space. Somehow, he swallows most of the air before he stops close to my chair, his attention on us. I tilt my head way back to look at him at this angle. If he reached up, I bet his fingertips would graze the ceiling.

"Just so you know, he asked me not to call you." Their president rocks back on his boot heels as if this conversation is just as uncomfortable for him as it is for me.

Wind fully knocked out of my sails, my shoulders deflate. "I understand." I left Gunz. He has a right to feel betrayed. Maybe I wouldn't have wanted to call me either if I were in his shoes.

"Fuck. Don't look at me like that," the giant rumbles. "It's not 'cause you left. He doesn't want you to worry. Here." Big shoves his phone into my hands and strides away. On the screen, looking straight at me, is the familiar face of Bonez, drinking from an actual dick-shaped mug. Caught off guard, I try my best to suppress a smile and fail. The size of that 'ahhem' *thing* and the crinkle of exhausted humor in his gaze, as he sips from it, draws a tiny giggle to the surface. One I didn't know I needed until this very second. It lightens the mood a smidge, and for that, I'm thankful.

I adore this man.

"Sooo..." Bonez drawls, then grins, despite the terrible circumstances. "I guess this is the part where I get to betray my exceptionally stubborn brother in favor of his woman."

Oh.

"It is?... I mean... *Right.* It is," I fumble.

Sipping from his mug, Bonez winks over the rim. "Good girl... Hey, Adam, why don't you get Mom somethin' to drink while we talk?"

Without a word, Adam pats my thigh twice, then sets off to find me something to drink as his uncle fills me in on what the hell's going on. The last I knew, Gunz was healing. Then again, the last I knew, we were in a good spot. That was before the funeral. Before the alcohol and tension. Before we stopped communicating.

When Bonez is through explaining the Niki suicide, guilt sex, infection, drinking, hallucinations combination, I'm full-on sobbing. Adam sets a box of tissues in my lap. I collect a wad and wipe the snot from my face, not caring who sees this hot mess.

"Thank you," I croak, dabbing my swollen eyes.

Incredible as always, Bonez offers a contrite, singular nod, that says it all—you're welcome, and please don't screw over my brother, among a dozen other sentiments.

Before long, we hang up with the promise to keep in touch, and I return the phone to Big, who's hovering on the outskirts, eavesdropping, and chatting with a man named Kai. The giant with a ponytail down his spine plucks the phone from my palm and deposits his cell into his back pocket. Not wanting to be a nuisance, I return to my chair. Adam pulled up another beside mine. He hands me a Styrofoam cup of tea. I accept it with a sad but gracious smile.

Then we wait.

And while we do, I overanalyze every morsel, down to the minutia, of what I've learned.

Gunz is visited by Niki. Seeing her. Feeling her. Explicitly.

Sucking on my bottom lip, I shiver at the thought.

That isn't something you hear every day.

I close my eyes and try hard not to picture them together. I try not to think about him coming inside her. It's futile. Because it's all there. In vivid color. Them. Their relationship —the kissing, the fucking, the bond. Bile surges up my throat as the spike of jealousy does what it does best—takes root and poisons you from the inside out.

People have pasts. I understand this. That's not a problem.

It's the woman he screwed at the fire. The one with Niki's face. The one he thought was her.

Bonez omitted most of the details but told me just the same. He's probably concerned Gunz wouldn't share, since he hasn't been the most forthcoming, or maybe he wanted to take the heat off his brother. Perhaps a little of both. If I had a sibling I was as close to, that's what I'd do.

Truth? From me to you... I don't know what I'm supposed to do with all this information.

If you could help a lady out and give me your thoughts, I'd appreciate it. Because now I'm not just worried about him. I'm hurt even more than I was before. I'm...

Dammit.

I'm tired.

Resting my head on Adam's shoulder, he drops a kiss there as I shove all these icky feelings down, way, way, way down, to deal with later. I'm done crying tonight.

I'm just... done.

Throughout the night, Loretta and Jade stop by to check on me before they leave. In and out, I doze, resting on my son—fifteen minutes here, half an hour there. For hours, we linger with no update. Apart from a nurse stopping by to see if we need our cart refilled and to flirt with the remaining brothers, we're left in the dark.

Light filters through the tall windows as the sun rises.

Finishing what's left of my now cold tea, I stretch a bit and massage a kink out of my neck. The surrounding chairs are filled with snoring brothers, most of who could use a trip to the ENT to get checked for sleep apnea. Their poor partners. I sure lucked out with my guy.

I sigh inwardly.

My. Guy.

Gunz.

Erik.

Less than six months ago, I was eating chicken over the sink for dinner, so I didn't have extra dishes to wash. I spent my nights watching television and grading papers. On occasion, Adam and I would have lunch together.

Now look where we are.

My son's wearing a leather vest with his name on it—Oz.

That's what the brothers have named him. Oz. Adam and Gunz explained it to me over dinner one night. Something about it meaning strength. Also, Adam's a bit like Dorothy, according to them. There was something in there about him following a path, making friends, encountering some witches, whatever that means, and making it back home—to the Sacred Sinners and his father. It's poetic in its own way. Weird, too. When you've been calling your son Adam all his life, and now everyone around you calls him Oz, it's an adjustment. Just as I've become Kit. No longer Melanie. That woman died the moment I rolled onto the SS compound in my jacked-up truck.

Life is…in the wise words of Forrest Gump, *like a box of chocolates*. You never know what you're gonna get.

And so, we wait to see what the next gooey filling has to offer.

Let's hope it's a good one.

CHAPTER THIRTY-FIVE

GUNZ

Monitors beep quietly. The cuff around my bicep tightens. Everything's heavy—my skin, bones, teeth. Fighting against sleep, my eyelid cracks open, one and then the next. Pale light seeps through the slits as I dampen my dry lips with the sweep of my tongue.

"You're one stubborn asshole," a familiar voice complains.

Ejecting a heavy breath, I blink.

"You hear me?"

Yes, I hear you, fucker.

Another blink—difficult and slow.

My surroundings take what feels like decades to focus.

Lulling my head to the side, a large form stands near me. His hand cuffs over the plastic railing of my bed. I look down at the giant, sausage-sized fingers, and the light dusting of hair on his knuckles.

Blink.

"You with us?"

I groan in response, phlegm caught in my throat.

I'm alive.

With every pump of my heart, heaviness bears down like

gravity. The harder I try to stay awake, the powers at be work against me. Unable to stop them, my eyelids wilt. In the darkness, I'm alone, in the recesses of my own mind. In my own body. A first in over a month. To test the theory, I draw memories of Niki to the surface. Happy ones. Of our sex-sharing days. Before the emotional crap. When it was fun. When the only thing I worried about was Bink, the club, and endless days of fucking.

Wearing a crop top and boner-inducing daisy-duke shorts, she smiles at me.

I smile back.

Then I release the thought. It goes along with the woman, fizzling to nothingness.

I'm free.

Finally fucking free.

Melting into my bed, no longer bogged down by the past, I let go. Of her. Of the drinking. Of my mom. Of my father. Of… all the fucked-up bullshit I let stand in my way and hold me back. All of it. I can't live like this anymore.

Where has it gotten me?

In a bed. In a hospital room. Recovering from wounds. And I'm not talkin' about the bullet or the infection. That's nothing more than a physical injury I've survived before.

Crackin' a single eye open, I search out my brother, who, no doubt, has been livin' here since they brought me back to recover. He's an overprotective one. Not that I don't get it. Despite all the shit I give him, I'd do the same for Big. We've been through a lot over the years.

When I can't see him, I grumble, my mouth as dry as the Sahara.

"You need somethin'?" Big stands, so we can see each other.

"Her," I rasp.

"You want your woman?"

I nod the best I can. It's slow and takes a shit ton of effort.

I don't want her. I need her. Now. I need to apologize. To make amends. To fix the past six weeks. She needs to know how sorry I am. That I'll do whatever it takes to get her back. To bring her home.

She's mine.

And it's about damn time she knows it.

CHAPTER THIRTY-SIX

KIT

Following the club president through an endless maze of monochromatic hallways, we stop beyond Gunz's hospital door. Nobody has been permitted inside except Big and medical personnel. President's orders. It's been three days since Gunz's surgery. Three days since he woke the first time, and he's been fading in and out of consciousness ever since.

For those three days, I've slept sitting up in a hospital waiting room, and only left twice to shower and check on Chibs. Jez and her little ones are doing a bang-up job keeping him company. Turns out, our bat-eared boy loves kids. More specifically, the human snacks they keep feeding him. Our Frenchie has become a cucumber and cheese stick slut, or so I've heard.

Opening the door like a gentleman, Big waves for me to go inside. Bowing my head in silent appreciation, I do as I'm told. Sitting up with the help of his hospital bed, Gunz watches me enter the room. Skin paler than usual, scruff extra sexy, he's wearing a blue gown that makes his already attractive eyes pop. There's a white blanket strewn over his legs and pillows behind his head. Sock-covered toes with those little grippies on the bottom peek out from beneath the covers.

Tracking my every move, his smile's lopsided and tired as I approach. He pats the bed for me to sit. I perch on the edge, my butt nudging his leg.

"I've missed you," he says. Stealing one of my hands, he sandwiches it between his own. Warmth encases not only my skin but my heart. He's alive. Breathing. Here. Looking right at me.

"I missed you, too." I sigh, happy to be present and see him face-to-face. I didn't know how much I needed this.

Gunz strokes the inside of my wrist with the pad of his thumb. "I'm sorry."

"It's okay," I reply honestly. It's been a long week, and he's been through a lot.

Frowning at my words, a crease forms between Gunz's brow as he growls, "It's sure as fuck not."

"You need to focus on getting better. The rest will work itself out." If he's healthy and on the mend, that's all I care about. Adam has been sick with worry, as have most of the brotherhood. The rest doesn't matter in the scheme of things. It was a fleeting moment in life. A mere blip. I'm not excusing his behavior. We've both made mistakes. Life is about learning from them. Growing and not living in the past. I know that's far easier said than done.

Accepting my words at face value, Gunz says nothing as he tugs my arm up to place my palm on his heart, just over the hospital gown. Both of his hands lay on mine, holding it in place. Our gazes catch, and there we pause. His chest rises, and I breathe along with him, somehow in sync. An affectionate smirk hooks at the corner of his mouth, and he shakes his head. "You're somethin' else, love... Will you marry me?"

Will I... What?

Will I... Do... What?!

Replaying what he said, my eyes widen to the size of tractor tires. *Will you marry me?*

What is happening?

With his heart beating wildly beneath my touch, even faster than my own, I sputter a frantic and not-so-cute, "Wh-what?!"

Amused by this, the sexy-as-fuck man has the goddamn audacity to laugh. At me. At my reaction. As if asking someone to marry them is a normal, everyday request. As if I wasn't scared out of my mind the past three days, wallowing in my own guilt for leaving. The bastard takes it a step further and pats my hand as if that's somehow going to calm my nerves. To take the cake, he smiles as he does it.

"Love." Gunz pauses a beat to rein in a chuckle. It's a half-assed attempt because one still slips out. "I didn't stutter. I said, will you marry me?" There goes that smile again. Wider this time.

Ugh.

Why's he doing this? I don't even know what to say.

"Erik... I—"

He interrupts me. "Is that a no?"

Not knowing much of any-damn-thing, I massage the center of my forehead and breathe, so I don't end up hyperventilating. "That's a...ugh... we've been through a lot... um... you're in the hospital. Let's focus on that." I wanna focus on normal life stuff. Like getting to know each other better and getting back on the track we were on after the warehouse.

Not on the same page as me, his firm, "No," brooks no room for argument. "My head's better now, and I know what I want. I've known what I want for a long time now. I want you in my bed. In my life. Ridin' on the back of my bike, on my face and my cock, for the rest of our lives."

Oh. Boy.

This man doesn't half-ass anything, does he? I show up out of the blue and drop the Adam bomb on him. What does he do? He accepts the knowledge with far more grace than anyone else would. Then he spends days not only in my presence but wanting to get to know me. If that wasn't already enough, he wanted to visit our son in jail. No hesitation. That's all before the kidnapping. He got me a dog. Brought our son into his own personal office to work alongside him. Now... marriage.

I guess I should have expected this would happen... huh?

Gunz's choices are cut and dry. There is no sway. No indecision. He knows what he wants and who he is.

"Erik," I begin, so we can have an open discussion about his proposition.

Once again, the stubborn man cuts me off at the pass. "Do you wanna be my wife?" His steel gaze is one of determination. Intention finite—yes or no.

"I... I can't believe you're asking me this..." Today of all days.

Gunz lifts my hand from his chest and kisses each of my fingertips one by one as he speaks. "Why? I love you. I ain't never loved anyone before. I get I fucked up, but I'll spend the rest of my life makin' it up to you. Takin' care of you and our son, and our smooshed-face dog."

There go those weird butterflies again, beating up my insides.

He loves me. He loves our son. Our dog. His actions have shown as much.

"I... I... I..." Unable to form words, I clear my throat to bide me some time, to focus less on the wild emotions going batshit crazy in my head, and more on the logistics.

"When?" I ask, just to see where he's at.

"In twenty-three days."

"What?!" I half-scream, hating the shrill, nervous tone. Mortified by my outburst, I turn my head away, but keep touching him, because I can't stop. It's been weeks since we've been this close. This engaged. I missed him so damn much.

"Love." Gunz jostles my arm, encouraging me to look at him. I do. Chewing on my bottom lip, tapping my foot on the floor anxiously. Satisfied with my attention, he continues, "We spent twenty-three hours together the first night we met. If you say yes, we'll get married twenty-three days from today. That's enough time for you and the sisters to plan a little somethin'." There he goes, offering more direct decisiveness, I wish I possessed even a quarter of.

"You're serious?" I double-check… because… internal freakout. Who gets married in twenty-three days who isn't part of a reality TV show? Well, I guess some people who elope do. Huh?

Warm, smirking lips kiss the tips of my fingers a second time. "As a heart attack." He winks, far too charming for me not to half-swoon. He's pulling out all the stops today.

This damn man. I don't know what to do with him.

"You don't think this is… quick?"

A simple shake of the head. "Nope."

"You want to marry me?" Yep, I'm checking a whopping third time to give the man an out.

Enjoying this far too much, Gunz's entire body vibrates in barely concealed laughter. "Yeah, love. I wanna marry you."

"But we haven't even had sex yet… ya know… again." What if I'm bad at it? What if he doesn't like my… ya know… parts? I'm not as youthful down there as I once was. You and I both know sex is part of any healthy relationship. These boobs reside in Sagville. My vagina isn't visited by the moist fairy as often as it was way back when. She sometimes takes a little extra help in that department. Then again, this is Gunz. She likes him. She likes him a lot.

"So?" He shrugs, not at all reading between the lines.

"What if I'm…" Lousy at it? Cry? Fail to meet his expectations after years of kinky fuckery?

The man rolls his eyes. "I know what you're gonna say. That's not fuckin' possible. To prove it to ya, why don't you climb on up here." Using my own fingers, he taps them to his mouth, then uses my pointer to caress his bottom lip before drawing his tongue across the pad. My stomach shudders, and my breath falters from the simple touch.

I swallow hard. "I'm not… we're not…"

"Love, might not be able to fuck you right now, but my tongue works just fine." To prove a point, the devil draws the tip of my same digit into his mouth and sucks.

Holy hell.

"Erik," I croak, knowing darn well my cheeks are flaming hot, that I'm… bothered.

"Take off your pants," he states around my fingertip.

"Erik."

"Wife. Take off your pants and sit on my fuckin' face." His laser-beam stare locks onto my pants like he's willing them to disintegrate to ash.

"This is silly. We're in a hospital," I reason… because logic.

"I know. What's crazy is you haven't sat on my face before this. Now get your fine ass up here and let me taste my woman's pussy. I'm an injured man. Give me somethin' to live for." Gunz releases my hand and juts his chin at my clothing.

"You're ridiculous." I chuckle awkwardly, far too charmed by him.

"And horny," he tacks on.

Legs shaking, I stand and slowly unbutton my jeans, my eyes focused on the door, my back to him. What if someone walks in? What if they catch us? In my twenties, I didn't care who saw us screwing. The more the merrier. It was nothing more than a youthful rite of passage. This is a hospital room after he underwent major surgery. We're older now. It's not the same thing.

Gunz clears his throat. "Come on, love. Just a little taste. If you don't like it, we can stop," he reassures, and I adore him even more for it.

I think I can do this. I want to try.

Ignoring any reason to chicken out, I unzip my fly and shuffle my tight jeans to the floor as Gunz lays the bed flat with the button on his bed. Now pooling around my ankles, I slip my jeans, shoes, and socks off at the same time. Left standing in my barely there lace thong, I cup my hands over my privates, not caring Gunz can see my bare ass. He's seen it before. Hell, he's seen all this before. A long time ago, but still.

Chewing the inside of my cheek, I spin to face him.

With an arm tucked behind his head, he winks at me in the naughtiest fucking way that leaves me squirming. I've never done this before. No man has wanted me to ride his face. Not once. I wouldn't know the first thing to do. Like, how do I keep from suffocating him? Sure, I'm not a big woman, but I'm not small, either.

Perhaps this wasn't such a good idea.

With the crook of his finger, the hottest man I've ever met urges me to join him. My feet stay planted where they are. Every now and again, I steal a glance at the door before watching him watch me with interest, with desire. His chest expands between every laden breath. The white blanket tents in his lap, highlighting his arousal as the mid-morning sun streams through the floor-to-ceiling windows. I shiver, knowing this turns him on... and if I'm honest... me, too. I'm already wet.

"Love?" He samples his bottom lip, then nibbles it as if he can't wait to taste me there.

"Y-yes?"

"Take off those panties." Gunz jerks his chin at said undergarments.

Right.

Panties off.

I can do this.

It's just a little fabric.

We can stop anytime I want.

I release a pent-up breath.

Hooking my thumbs into the delicate waistband, I gather all the courage I can and do as instructed. Down my thighs, they glide, ever so slowly, until they, too, join the discarded clothes on the floor. Then I'm bare. For him to see. A short, well-kept bush at my sex, shaven underneath. At least he hasn't asked me to take the rest of my clothes off.

Uncomfortable in my own skin, I rub both arms up and down to stay warm, despite the fact we're in a temperate room.

"On. My. Face. Wife." The man taps his mouth with two fingers.

Wife.

Holy hell.

I'm going to be his wife... in twenty-three days.

Kneeling one knee on the mattress, I use his guardrail to help me up. Afraid to look him in the eye, I stare at the tan wall above Gunz's bed as I carefully maneuver around him until I'm straddling his head. With his help, he guides me where I need to go. His nose nuzzles my folds as he inhales deeply and emits a heady groan.

335

"I've been wanting to do this forever, love," he whispers against my flesh.

With a hand on my knee for stability and the other wrapped around the bed railing, I quake in response.

I can't believe we're about to do this.

I can't believe…

All thought fades into oblivion as the wet tip of his tongue glides through my lips. Closing my eyes, I drop my head back and relinquish control.

I trust him.

My future husband.

Gunz

Holding my woman's soft, tattooed thighs in a vise, my face smothered in delicious-smelling cunt, I taste every inch of her. Giving zero fucks about how loud she gets or my recent surgery, I gorge. Lashing her clit with my tongue, she shakes the entire bed, moaning. High on her scent, I revel in our excitement.

My woman's palm cups the top of my head as her body does what it wants and rides my face. Undulating hips grind wet flesh against my mouth, my beard, and my tongue. Focusing on her little nub, I suck it into my mouth, and she screams. Knowing what she needs, I deliver light flicks and sucks, followed by sharper, more intense care. Wetness floods my face as she loses herself in pleasure.

That's right, love. Drip all over me.

Her sharp nails bite into my skull, and my cock bucks, begging for attention. I ignore him. This isn't about me. This is about taking care of what's mine. It's about showing her desire. My desire for her and only her.

"Erik," she wails, her legs trembling.

That's it, love. Take whatever you need.

Back arching, her chest thrusts toward the ceiling as I tongue fuck her sexy little hole. Another rush of sweetness floods my mouth, and I gulp it down, eager for the next hit.

"Erik… I'm…" Kit grinds against my face in the hottest fucking way. My nuts draw up, wanting to unload inside her. To bury myself to the hilt and fill her with cum. Again, I ignore the urge. Another time. A different day.

Latching onto her clit, I brace Kit's legs with my arms and hold her pussy against my mouth. I stop messing around and give her exactly what she needs. Higher and higher, my tongue drives my woman to madness. She babbles incoherently, trying to squirm away, to make me let her up, to give her a breather. Do you think I listen? Hell no. I double down. Tightening my arms until my biceps ache, I force her to succumb to ecstasy. I force her to endure the pleasure. I force her to pant so hard, to shudder so goddamn hard, she can't think of anything other than gettin' off.

Closing my eyes, I revel in the power, in her softness, in her perfection, and when she comes screaming my name, her nails leaving claw marks in my head, a lone tear sneaks out of my eye, because this is what I want. This is what I need. I've never been happier in my entire fuckin' life than in this moment.

Licking her clean, because I can't help it, I release the grip on my woman, hoping I didn't leave bruises. Kit almost collapses in half but grasps the guardrail at the last second before she pitches off the top of my bed, headfirst into the wall.

"Love, you okay?" I scoot her down my chest, so she can sit there, her ass on my pecs, so I can keep an eye on her.

Blinking, as if she's drunk, Kit sweeps her thumb across my bottom lip, then top. "That was…"

"Good?" I wink, loving how wrecked she looks.

"The best." She giggles. "I think you're gonna have to wash your beard." To cement her point, Kit tugs lightly on the gray hair.

"I probably should. Huh?"

"Yeah. I made a mess."

"Messes aren't always bad, love."

"It's gonna smell like my pussy."

"Maybe I wanna smell like it."

She blushes deep red, and I fuckin' adore it.

"You gonna let me do that again soon?" I test.

She nods.

"You like me eating your pussy?"

Another shy nod.

Gorgeous.

"One of these days, I'm gonna fill you with my cum, too. You gonna let me do that?"

Nod.

"You like that idea?"

Nod.

"Might fill your mouth with cum, too, love. That work for you?" 'Cause I can't help myself, I reach up and brush my thumbs over the nipples protruding through her band t-shirt.

A nod and slight shiver.

"You gonna marry me in twenty-three days then? Make me your old man, officially?" 'Cause I can't wait to have them in my mouth, I play with her nipples a little more. Perfect size. Perfect everything.

Her "Yes," comes out breathy.

"Good. That's real fuckin' good. Now, why don't you lie your sexy self down beside me and rest for a bit?"

Together, we guide her form down next to mine. Resting on her side, I position her head on my pec and draw her arm across my ribs for a cuddle, far enough from my stitches it won't be an issue.

"Rest." I peck her forehead and nuzzle my nose there. "I've got you."

Eyes sinking shut, Kit yawns as if she hasn't slept in days. Maybe she hasn't.

"I'm glad you're okay," she whispers, absentmindedly tracing circles on my ribs with a single finger.

"I'm glad we're okay."

Her cute, noncommittal sound is all I get before my woman drifts off. For hours, I nap alongside her. At some point, I wake to Big draping a blanket over Kit's exposed bottom half. Not even that rouses her.

"Thanks, brother. She's tired," I mutter to him, offering a sleepy, appreciative smile.

Standin' beside my bed, freshly showered and shaven, Big chuckles. "I figured, after her livin' in the waitin' room the past couple'a days and that loud as fuck show you just put on for the entire hospital."

Eh. What can I say? My woman comes like a champ and I'm not gonna apologize for it.

"I asked her to marry me, and she said yes," I announce.

He grins. "Congrats, brother."

"Thanks. 'Cause you're the best man, and we're doin' it on the compound in twenty-three days." Figured it's best he knows now than when I break outta this joint. The doc said I could go home tomorrow or the day after. A few extra hours to let it sink in will do him good. Big ain't keen on weddings. Never has been. He shows up because it's required, but he's never liked the legal ball-and-chain ordeal. Before Kit, I wasn't keen on dating, much less anything else. People change.

Prez's head shakes in a fun blend of I-wanna-murder-your-ass and you're-lucky-I-love-you. "Christ. Alright. Fine. As long as I ain't gotta plan the thing or wear a tux," he growls.

"No tux. No plannin'. We'll leave that up to the sisters."

"Not the sisters. You mean, Bink… Fuck. That's all I'm gonna hear about for the next three weeks. Wedding shit. I hate you right now." He flicks my shoulder in retribution.

Not wanting to wake Kit, I curb a laugh and deliver a bright, toothy smile instead, ya know, for Big's benefit. "You'll get over it." To further drive him up the wall, I bounce my eyebrows for effect.

He heaves a long-suffering sigh. "Yeah. Sure. Over it. Fuckin' bastard."

"Leech will make a pretty flower girl."

He nods. "True."

"This will also make your old lady very, very happy, after all the shit that's gone down. A little light will do everybody some good." After all the death and funerals, any slice of happiness is better than none. I'm willin' to bet even the brothers will like this reprieve. It's the perfect excuse to get shit-faced.

A round of absentminded nodding ensues as Big digests my words. "Fuck…I know you're right."

"I usually am." That's why he keeps me around.

Fixing his ponytail, Prez rolls his eyes into the back of his skull. "Asshole." A smirk ticks up at the corner of his mouth.

"Thanks for bein' here, brother."

"Don't," he grumbles, hating the kindness.

"I *can* thank you."

Nostrils flaring, Big's head shakes. "No. Ya can't. We don't do that shit. You can get your stubborn ass healed, and I guess… *married*… I can't believe…" Again, he shakes his head, this time in disbelief, his eyes focused on the back of my lady's head and my arm curled around her body. "Anyhow…

do your thing. I'll report back to the brothers you're whole and let that little one run the show from here on out. Whoever she wants in here can visit. Her word goes."

"Th—"

He cuts me off at the pass. "Shut the fuck up, Gunz."

"Yeah. Yeah. See ya around, Prez." Not wanting to move any more than necessary, I lift my chin in farewell.

Throwing a middle finger over his shoulder, Big exits in spectacular heavy-footed fashion.

Once the door comes to a suctioned close, Kit whispers, "He loves you, too," and nestles her cheek against my pec like a kitten.

"I know." And I do. Big might be rough around the edges. Hell, all of us Sacred Sinners are. But he's genuine. A real brother. Blood. No blood. He's as real as it gets. Ride or fuckin' die. Been that way since the moment I punched him in the nose for cockin' off when we were kids.

Here's a little back story… ya know… since I've got time.

Both of us grew up around the compound. Him far more than me. We didn't like each other at first. His dad didn't like mine, and the feeling was mutual with bad blood between 'em. As it often goes, sons worship fathers when they don't know any better, and we looked up to ours. Day in and out, we heard the bullshit they spewed about each other. Big was, as you'd picture him—big for his age and mouthy. A brute of a boy. I was how you'd picture me. An average kid. Darker hair, blue eyes, nothin' special. Not one to be pushed around, but also, not one to start shit.

Big knew that. So, he did what the man still does, and let his temper flare. The issue was about a girl. He liked her. Thought I did too. One thing led to another, and he ended up with a bloodied nose and two black eyes. I don't even remember landing the punch, only that I laid him out. He shed a few shocked tears, I helped him off the gravel parking lot, dusted off his pants, 'cause I'm a nice guy, and the rest is history. He didn't retaliate. For whatever reason, it made him respect me, and we've been brothers since.

It might not be the most exciting story, but I'm layin' here with my woman, no longer tired, I figured, what the hell, I'll share a little of my past with ya. A slice that doesn't include my mother.

Kit mumbles my name, and I pepper kisses along the top of her head. "Sleep all you need, love," I reassure.

"'Kay." She yawns and draws the blanket up to her shoulders.

I kiss her again for good measure and relax. The worst is over. She's here. I'm here. We're gettin' hitched. Life's good. Better than good. Even with the war looming overhead, 'cause that fucker ain't about to end anytime soon, I haven't been this content… ever.

This time it had better last.

At least for a little while longer.

Come hell or high water, I'm gonna make sure it does.

CHAPTER THIRTY-SEVEN

GUNZ

"Erik!" Kit giggles as I lift her fine ass off the kitchen floor and plop her on the countertop. I step between her legs and do what I've wanted to do all goddamn day. With my thumb, I shove her cute little heart-printed panties to the side, exposing her smooth pussy, and massage her needy little clit. Grabbing my shoulders for support, she squeaks on impact, eyes shuttering closed as she relishes the attention.

"That what you need, love?" I tease, 'cause I can, knowing she's just as hungry for this as I am.

She babbles adorably as I work her up to full, uninhibited moans. I woke up this morning, hard as a rock. Hell, I wake up most mornings hard as a rock. Can you blame me? Look at my woman. Unfortunately, Kit was still asleep, and I didn't have the heart to wake her. Sure, we haven't fucked yet. I'm actin' like a responsible adult and waiting for the Doc's a-okay before we go that far. But I've been home for a week. Between goin' back to work with my son, and her talking about wedding details, I give absolutely no shit about, but listen anyhow, I make her come like a champ as often as I can. If I can't get mine, she can get hers. Oh, and she does. As much as I offer.

Latching onto the side of her neck, I suck a couple well-placed welts and slip two fingers into her wet cunt. Curving them upward, to hit that G-spot just right. Her legs quiver, and her sex squeezes around my digits.

That's it.

She never takes long to finish.

Like a depraved fiend, I finger fuck my woman until she gasps my name. Tiny nails bite at my shoulders. Legs squeeze around me. I nip her throat before licking a long strip of silken skin up to her ear, where I nibble the lobe.

"You gonna come for me?" I whisper there.

A broken sob is her response.

I smile wickedly, 'cause there's nothing more powerful than owning your woman's cunt. And own hers, I do. We've become well acquainted. It's ready and willing anytime I wanna give it attention. Last night, it was on the couch, when we watched movies. I relaxed behind her. The big spoon to her little and rubbed my aching cock along her ass as I massaged her clit to completion over a pair of tight, cotton shorts. She's magnificent when she climaxes. Her face flushes, and lips part. A light sheen of sweat coats her forehead. The noises she makes are enough to almost tip me over the edge.

Nipping her lobe one last time, I add another finger to her sex. She gasps at the stretch. Wanting her mouth on mine when she comes, I attack her lips in a brutal, unrelenting kiss. My tongue penetrates, and she tries but fails to keep up as I fuck her on my hand and with my tongue as hard as I'd fuck her with my cock.

Knowing she's on the precipice, Kit stiffens, and her kiss falters. I suck her bottom lip into my mouth as her breath ceases and wetness splashes my wrist. Fuck yeah. A first.

Making her squirt. Emboldened by this new revelation, I curve my digits more, and finger her rougher through the climax. My woman doesn't disappoint. Grasping at anything for purchase, her toes curl, as a second gush of liquid bathes not only my wrist but the front of my jeans and the floor.

"That's right, love. Come on my fuckin' hand. You're so hot." Stepping back to watch as I continue to ruin her, I press down on Kit's lower stomach to see if I can get her off a third time.

"Erik… I… Oh… My…" Nearly slipping off the counter, her shoulders resting against the top cabinets, Kit's entire body shakes as a third, less violent squirt dribbles down the front of the lower cupboards.

What do I do? I massage her cunt through the final stages of orgasm. Then, I kneel and lick her clean. Starting with my fingers, I suck her juices off before drawing her little nub into my mouth. She hums in satisfaction as I lick every inch of her, not wanting to miss a single drop.

With the heel of my palm, I press my erection down. He'll get his when it's time. When I'm ready to have her kneel before me and stretch her lips around him. When I'm ready to thrust into her mouth and fill her with cum. But I'm not ready yet, and it has zero to do with my stitches and healing and everything to do with opening a can of worms that can't be resealed. Each day, we take things a step further. Each day, I scare myself a little at how much I love this woman and, more importantly, how much I don't want to hurt her. Not again.

I refuse to treat her like a club whore. I know how I am when the darkness unleashes. What it'll do without the restraint. They raped her. The last thing I want Kit to do is relive those atrocities with me, because of me. So, for now, oral sex and finger fucking will have to do.

Helping my woman off the counter and back onto solid

ground, I hold on to her as she wobbles on unstable legs. Resting her head on my shoulder, she catches her breath. "I made a mess."

I peck her forehead. "I know, don't worry. I'll clean it up."

She sighs dreamily. "I've never squirted before."

"It won't be the last," I vow because that might very well be my next kink. One we can share.

Knowing I gotta meet Adam at the office to go over club financials and the new compound security systems being installed today, I escort my woman back to our bedroom, where a nosy Chibs waits at the door. He sniffs me and her as we enter, then climbs onto his corner of the bed to chew on his bone. Kit pats his head as she passes before picking a pair of clean clothes from the closet we now share.

I snag a Dum Dum from the nightstand and pop it into my maw as I watch my woman undress, down to literally nothing. The curve of her tattooed spine, shapely legs, and an ass that would bring any man to his knees. Breasts, perfect in both size and shape. Ink, everywhere. More than my own and far hotter. She smirks uncomfortably over her shoulder as I watch, soaking up every inch.

"You're staring." She rolls those honey eyes and dons a coy smile.

Giving zero fucks, I shrug one shoulder. "I'm a man with a hot old lady. I'm always gonna stare."

This awards me the sweetest blush, and I feel ten feet tall for making Kit realize how irresistible she is. Trust me, her looks are only a small portion of what I love.

I trace the flowers on her arms with my eyes as a thought pops into my head. "Ya know, we should get tattooed together sometime. Add some new ink to our skin." It's something I've never done with another woman. Honestly, it's not even something I thought I'd do until now.

Buttonin' up her jeans and tugging on a skintight Harley

t-shirt, Kit spins to face me. "You wanna get tattooed together?" She sounds skeptical, and her wrinkled forehead reiterates that sentiment. That's been normal as of late. Probably has to do with our yo-yoing over the past two months. We're good. Then we're not. 'Cause, ya know, me. Drinking. Niki. All that. We've been over it already. Plus, the proposal. This likely feels like warp speed to her. One minute, I'm pushing her away. The next, marriage. In my head, it's always been there. The desires. The reality of my feelings. But she doesn't live in my skull. For that, I'm grateful. It also means I gotta help her catch up. Get on the same page, or, at the very least, in the same zip code. The more I talk, the more she knows, the less overthinking she can do.

"We're gettin' married. Might as well make it more permanent with ink," I explain.

"I'm always down to get tattooed, but what kinda ink?" Kit grabs the lotion from her nightstand and slathers it on her exposed arms, making her tattoos come alive.

"Rings?" I suggest, 'cause it makes the most sense. Couples get matching tattoos sometimes, but what's more personal than getting rings? I can't think of anything.

Kit's head rears back in surprise. "You wanna get wedding rings?" she double checks, which she does a lot.

Not wanting to push her into something she may not want, I play it cool. "Sure. Why not?"

"That's not a good omen, Erik. We're not gettin' rings." My woman's firm on her stance. I smile on the inside, loving her willingness to stand up to me, but also thinkin' she has any real say in what I put on my body. It's cute. Real cute.

"Allll-right." I speak around my sucker stick, not wantin' to rile her up. "Then you get whatever you want, and I'll get a ring." See. Compromise.

"A wedding ring?" she triple-checks, her voice shrill, eyes blown wide, like I would get any other kind.

"Yeah. Our wedding ring. Nothin' says forever like a black band around this finger." For emphasis, I hold up my left ring finger. Sure, I've got the club ring I wear. It's a heavy son of a bitch. But that can be removed anytime. I can't take that with me in the afterlife. See, I'm well past middle age. I'm past sowing my wild oats, finally in my right mind, and showin' your forever devotion to a woman you love is to get a symbol of that love on your flesh. I did it when I got the Sacred Sinner roses. I did it when I got a B tattoo on my thigh, for Bink… so why wouldn't I do it for Kit with a ring?

Knowing by her scrunched-up, sourpuss expression, Kit's about to unleash a torrent of reasons that's a bullshit idea, I pull the half-eaten peach Dum Dum from my mouth, march up to my woman, and push it into hers. Before she gets a moment to scold me, argue, or whatever else she's conjuring in that intelligent overactive brain of hers, I kiss her cheek and get the hell out of dodge.

Just as the front door comes to a close, I hear Kit yell for me. Head shaking, wearin' a big ol' grin, I keep goin', back to the clubhouse. Tonight, at dinner, I'm sure she'll have thought of a thousand things to chat about. Until then, I'll live in peace, with our son.

Openin' the door to my office, Adam's busy at his computer. A plate with a sandwich and chips rests on my desk.

"Hey, Oz," I greet my kid.

"Hey, Pops. Mom's blowin' up my phone."

I chuckle. "I'm sure she is."

My kid throws a lopsided smirk over his shoulder. "Bink dropped that off a little bit ago." He gestures to my food. "I got one too." Adam lifts his empty plate.

I pop a chip into my mouth and chew. "We on—"

Knowin' what I'm askin', my son interjects, "They'll be here in an hour." The installers we hired to up the compound security. New cameras, motion detectors, sirens, hidden weapons, and escape routes. You name it, we're gettin' it. From spike strips outside the main gate, to tear gas vents outside the walls.

"The strip club?" I take my seat and power up my computer.

"Moved and cleaned."

"Good." Adam's proven to be a quick learner. The Sacred Sinners, or more specifically, our members, own businesses. Most of them operate within legal parameters with one caveat—we launder money through them. The money we earn through less than reputable ways, we filter through their systems, and voilà, cleaned. Their profits continue to climb, as do ours. It's how most of our chapters make money, and our nomads stay in the loop. Deke was one of our nomads before he patched in with the mother chapter. Now he runs our body shop down the road.

"The tattoo shop?" I ask, referring to Pixie's place.

"Moved and cleaning it now."

Good kid.

I check my emails, noting one from Big and him cursing me out, because of Bink and wedding stuff. "The church?" I ask Adam.

"I handled the rest of that yesterday. We are now the owners of a new church. The building you said to buy, I purchased under the new name. Bonez called to say they took possession yesterday. All the accounts are legit, tax-free, and set up to help with all the survivor expenses. The government would be hard-pressed to find anything to sniff at with the way I set things up. Especially with their judge friend helping me navigate the legalities."

"Kellan's a good man." He came recommended from not only Bonez but Whisky. Since my head wasn't screwed on straight, I asked Adam to handle the ins-and-outs of the legalities this past month, and as you can see, he's kicked ass. Not that I had any doubt. If I have any say in the matter, Oz will be a patched brother in no time.

"Agreed. He is," Adam remarks, and we do what we always do, get back to work. Every now and again, we talk numbers or business shit. He doesn't mention what Mom texts about because we keep that separate unless it involves her safety. When she leaves our house to go to Bink's, I watch her location move on my phone screen.

Then I chuckle, knowin' damn well I will be hearin' the ring complaints not only from her tonight, but Bink too. The sisters and their gossip. As much as it should piss me off, it doesn't. I wouldn't have it any other way. My woman fits in. They accept her as one of their own. Even my grandbaby has taken a shine to Kit. So, they can go on and gossip all fuckin' day long. As long as they're safe and happy, that's all I give a damn about.

Before I meet the men out front to start the walk-through of the compound, I text my woman.

> Have fun with the sisters, love. I look forward to eating more of your sweet pussy tonight and you reading me more BDB.

If I have it my way, she'll read while I'm eating her pussy. That's something we haven't tried yet. Bet we could make it work.

Tonight, I'll give it the good ol' college try.

Pressing the heel of my palm down on my unwanted erection, I inwardly scold the thing for gettin' riled up when all I'm doin' is thinkin' about her. He's a fuckin' menace. The motherfucker gets harder more now than it did when I was a teen. I get a whiff of her peaches-and-cream scent. Boner. I think of her naked. He's awake. I kiss her. Stiffy. If I didn't like the fucker, I'd be embarrassed by his constant appearance. Then again, I can't blame the guy. He's as much in love as I am. The only difference is, I get to indulge in what's mine, while he sits the bench.

Pattin' his head for takin' one for the team, I promise him action soon enough, when I'm ready. Until then... achy balls are how we roll.

CHAPTER THIRTY-EIGHT

KIT

Barefoot and thoughtful, Bink paces her living room, phone in hand. "I say go for it." She's talking about the tattoo I'm supposed to get with Gunz. After another successful oral session with my partner, I'm starting to refer to him as the magic man, I went over a bit of work at home before dropping by Bink's place for another wedding planning party. We've had three so far. Yes, you heard me. Three. Bink's a firecracker, on top of every little detail. She also cares far more than I do about the wedding. I couldn't care less about what flowers we have, the cake, the food, or my dress. I'd be happy to elope somewhere. It was Gunz's idea to get the sisters involved, and involved they are.

Jade, Loretta, Tati, Debbie, Janie, and Jezebel are all present, spread around Bink's living room.

Each sister was given a folder with the Sacred Sinner emblem on the front. Hot pink ones, as Bink is obsessed with the color. So far, we've gone over the stack of papers within the folder. Since I'm against the traditional wedding party of bridesmaids, she's decided the sisters are going to coordinate clothes for the occasion. They were given a selection to choose from. Apparently, Big is ordained, so he'll not only be Gunz's best man, but our officiant. That's news to me. I'm pretty sure it's news to her old man as well, as she's fielding texts from him that range from amused to downright fuming. Bink's been sharing them with the crowd.

She's having a ball.

I'm happy she's happy.

Gunz was right when he said the sisters needed something to occupy them since everything's happened. Jade is more present today than I've seen her in weeks. Loretta is still... Loretta. Wild and fun as ever. Tati's playing with Dom, as she doesn't care much for planning things. Few teens would. I'm doing what I do best, sitting on Bink's comfy leather couch, conversing with a talkative Harley. Well, I'm listening as she babbles nonsense that I pretend to understand. Then I reply like I do. This thrills her to no end.

Sipping from a travel tumbler I brought from home, Harley pats the side of my cup, eyeing it like she needs a sip. Not wanting her to share my germs, I rest it on the floor to keep it out of arm's reach.

The one-year-old grumbles at me, wearing the cutest scowl, which I imagine is more her father than mother.

"If you are thirsty, Miss Lady, I'm sure we can get you something to drink," I explain.

In response, the blonde cutie babbles.

"Oh. Right. You want water too?" I pretend to understand, and she nods as if she's following right along and agreeing.

Carting the toddler on my hip, the way moms do, we leave the sisters to their devices and seek a sippy cup for Miss Lady. Not wanting to disturb Bink, and knowing she isn't gonna care if I go through her kitchen cupboards, I open them one by one until I find what I seek. With the cutie's help, we fill her butterfly cup with water from the fridge, tighten the lid, and I hand it to her. All the while, Harley babbles on, telling me her life stories.

"I think I like water that much, too," I comment as we return to the living room to find their pitbull named Pretzel on the couch cushion we vacated. I shoo him to the side, and he listens as well as Chibs, and gives us just enough room to retake our spot before his head ends up on my lap. His little owner rubs the spot between his floppy ears with one hand as she uses the other to hold her sippy in place to drink until she's gasping for breath.

I massage her tiny back. "Big breaths, big girl. I can get you more when you're done." I chuckle, remembering times like this with Adam. Him and his blue dinosaur sippy. They were inseparable. He wouldn't drink from anything but that sippy for a year.

When Miss Lady is done, she hands me her empty cup, and I rest it on the floor beside mine. As she plays with Pretzel, I dial back into whatever the sisters are discussing about my pending nuptials.

In front of an enormous fireplace, Bink continues to pace as she speaks. "Debbie already has the cuts complete." She's talking to Jezebel, our clipboard holder. Jez's hands move quickly, taking in notes or checking things off as Bink commands attention. I owe her for this. Planning my first wedding was more about my ex's family and their expectations than anything he or I wanted. It was too large, with far too many guests I didn't know, and about as traditional as you could get. In a church, white gown, black tux, fall colors, a fancy meal, three-tiered all-white cake. I went along because that's what's expected. You're quiet. You're submissive. Only I've never been any of those things. It took a lot of years of fitting myself into a box for everyone else before I realized I couldn't do it anymore.

This I can do. I can marry Gunz. I can watch my son, *our*

son, work with his father every day. I can eat dinner with my guys each night. We can go through shit, ugly shit, and he'll still have my back. Gunz doesn't expect me to bend, to fit into whatever perfect, little box he's designed. He has no expectations. Sure, things are sometimes messy. Nothing's perfect. But I've never been happier.

Speak of the devil, my phone chimes with a new text. This one's not from Adam. Since I might have told him to slap his father silly for suggesting the ring tattoos, right after he ran away. Silly man. I'm still not gonna bend in that regard. A tattoo, sure. Matching rings. No thanks.

> Have fun with the sisters, love. I look forward to eating more of your sweet pussy tonight and you reading me more BDB.

Biting my bottom lip, I smile like the lovesick teenager I've become. My stomach gets all wonky as I reread his message.

A chorus of womanly awes rings loud and clear. I glance up from my screen to see the sisters staring at me, all smiling. Jez makes googly eyes. Jade winks. Bink does a small dance in a circle, flapping her hands.

"I can't believe he's getting married!" she cheers.

"I can't either." Debbie's kind, aged smile mimics my own. Except she's not blushing. My cheeks are on fire. I'm not used to being the center of attention.

Not knowing how to take this intense sisterly love without wanting to cry, I fuss with Harley. I comb my fingers through her silken hair, massage her back, and scratch the pup to distract myself.

Knowing me as well as she does, Loretta pulls the same crap she does at therapy to take the heat off. Sex talk. Only this time, she talks about…

"Did you guys know Gunz likes kitchen sex?" The bitch cackles, making eye contact with me.

Oh. Shit.

Fixing the beanie on her head, Jade snorts.

"I heard some really loud sounds comin' from his kitchen today, when I stopped by," Loretta illuminates.

I drag a hand down my face, mortified. Why didn't she tell me she was gonna stop by? Then she wouldn't have heard.

Pleased as punch by this, Loretta keeps talking. "If I didn't know any better, I'd say he knows how to make his woman come. Multiple times." She shimmies her shoulders, her eyebrows waggin'.

Ugh.

"Oh. My. God. Shut. The. You. Know. What. Up." I glare at her, not wanting to curse in front of the kids.

"You've been holding out," Loretta scolds good-naturedly as Bink and Debbie cover their mouths, trying their best not to laugh. I love them even more for it because Loretta's downright ridiculous.

Okay. So, I haven't told them about the sexual stuff. It hasn't been that long since we started, and we're in such a good place, I didn't want to talk about it and someone jinx how mind-blowing it's been. There's nothing wrong with a dirty little secret between me and my man.

"Well… he likes to be helpful," I clarify.

Jade barks a laugh, smiling wider than I've seen in weeks. "Helpful."

"Yes. We haven't done the deed. He just likes to… you know… help." Get me off and other things, too. Like laundry and dishes. Cooking. Making tea. But he mostly likes to help with orgasms. I'm not complaining.

"Would you say he's a master at his craft?" Loretta's salivating for more details on my sex life. As much as she shares about her and Blimp, this woman's life force runs on depravity, and I love that for her. What I don't love is her wanting my sexual exploits to fuel that life force.

Hoping this shuts down any further prodding, I explain, "Don't pretend like you haven't seen him in action before." They all have. It's no secret Gunz has always been into sex and gives no actual fucks where he performs. Except maybe with me. Time will tell if that remains true. When we met all those years ago, let's say he didn't care where we fucked then. In front of his brothers. On his bike. In a bar. There wasn't a surface he was opposed to. We had our fun.

A round of bobbing heads is their response.

See. Like I said.

"We just want you happy," comes from Bink.

"I am." Very.

"And I wanna know when my sister is getting some after what we went through," Loretta clarifies, her tone more serious than before.

"Well, I am getting some." A lot. According to this salacious text, I'm getting even more tonight.

I clench at the thought of having him in there again, in just a few scant hours. The magic man. His tongue. His fingers. That voice.

I miss him already.

Geez, I'm pathetic.

"Sooo…. how do we feel about burgers at the wedding?" Bink throws out, changing the subject.

Heaving an internal sigh, I mouth *thank you*. Bink flashes me a knowing smile and nods in understanding.

As they finish whatever details are needed for the wedding, I text Gunz back.

> Me: I look forward to tonight.

> Gunz: Me, too. I miss you, love.

> Me: Miss you, too.

> Gunz: Pizza tonight?

> Me: Sure. That sounds great.

> Gunz: I'm gonna run into town later. If you need anything else, let me know. I'll pick it up. Mushroom and pepperoni pizza? Breadsticks with extra garlic?

Grinning far too wide to be considered sane, I stare in awe at the words on my screen. This man remembers what I like. Down to the extra garlic. This never ceases to amaze me. We haven't even had pizza together yet. It was only a topic of conversation we had with Adam one night over dinner of all our favorites. Of course, Gunz would file it away to use later.

> Me: Sounds perfect. Thank you.

> Gunz: You're perfect. Now I gotta get back to work. New security system to go over. See you tonight at dinner. I'll bring you some chocolate for dessert. Since you'll be mine.

This man.

Oh. This man.

Wanting to share a snapshot of my day with him, I hug Harley up close, press my cheek to hers, and take a selfie of us together. I send him the text with no words and stow my phone away. He's gotta work, and I've got a one-year-old to chat with. I should also help Bink with the wedding details. It's the least I can do. Though, cheeseburgers sound like fine wedding food to me. I'm not picky.

CHAPTER THIRTY-NINE

GUNZ

Seven days 'til the wedding.

Relaxed in my office chair, I read through the new church documents, including the new name my brother, Bonez, bestowed on the damn thing—Sacred Chaos. I get it. It's a play on our two clubs. But why he didn't pick something less conspicuous, like Holy blah-blah-Jesus-Lover-Mary-Amen or whatever the hell else that would sound far more religious, is beyond me. We set this up for him. To give him more space to spread his bleeding heart wings. He's pleased with the purchase, even if I'm not keen on the name. His business. Not mine. I'm nothing more than a glorified bookkeeper when he's on the front lines doing all the heavy lifting with the survivors and their recovery.

There's a tap at my office door, as quiet as a church mouse, I barely notice the thing.

"Yeah?" I call out, knowin' if it was Adam, he'd come in, and if it was my woman, she would've texted first.

"We need your assistance," comes from a shaky female voice I don't recognize.

Laying the pages face down to scour later, I push from my chair, round my desk, and open the door just enough to see who's on the other side. It's a young woman. From the looks of her clothes—a club whore I've not seen before. Why she's here during the day doesn't make a lick of sense.

"How can I help you?" I arch a curious brow and keep an eye on her hands. Woman or not, I don't know her, nor do I trust a single soul I haven't scouted. We're at war. My idiot brothers would do good to remember that before they let stragglers stay the night.

The brunette chews her fat bottom lip. Whether that's cause she's nervous or she's tryin' to entice me, I don't give a single fuck either way.

"Well?" I prompt, growing impatient.

Her brown eyes swim with unshed tears. "My friend—"

The woman's words cease as my son jogs toward the office and stops feet from the brunette, breathin' heavy. "Pops, we got a situation." He waves me to follow, and I do, but not before I lock the office door, and urge the woman to join us.

In the hallway outside of Mickey and Gypsy's clubhouse bedroom, brothers have gathered. Adam pushes them to the wayside to let me pass. They keep the brunette back as I enter the room to find a pale, buck-ass-naked Mickey, shakin' like he's hopped up on somethin' as he stares at the unmade bed and the naked woman there. The dead, naked woman—on her side, curled in the fetal position, her long, blonde hair plastered to her face. She must be the brunette's friend.

In the darkened corner, a fully clothed Gypsy leans against the wall, watching his best friend lose his mind.

"I didn't mean it." Mickey gestures to the blonde.

He never means it. This isn't the first dead club whore we've come across, thanks to his particular brand of fuckery.

Nor will it be the last. When he first joined the club, they were plentiful. A few a year. That was a long while ago. With Gypsy as his constant companion, he's smartened up and picked better candidates.

Ya see, Mickey doesn't screw conscience women. Something happened in his childhood. It's not my story to tell. So, he micks his sexual partners in the safety of our clubhouse then fucks their asses. That's his thing. He's always careful with the women. Never brutal. Gypsy oversees every bit of it. How he missed this, I don't know.

Dallas and Axel swallow up the doorway, keepin' everyone and their prying eyes out. I overhear Kai speak to the girl's friend in the hallway as I get to the bottom of what happened here.

"Talk, brother." Wanting the poor girl to keep whatever dignity she has left, even in death, I cover her naked form with a sheet as Mickey does his best to explain.

Fisting his hair, he pulls the dark strands on end. "I met her at the club party last night. She was into me. I micked her drink and straight up told her what I did to it. 'Cause I'm tryin' to be more upfront about that kinda shit, ya know? I told her what I wanted to do to her. That she probably wouldn't feel a thing. Even asked her what tie she wanted around her wrists when I took her ass. I was upfront. I did what Gypsy told me I should start doin'. Let 'em have a choice. If they don't wanna do it, they don't have to drink it."

See, he's turned a corner. Makin' better choices.

"She drank it," I guess.

"Yes. She drank all of it and was happy to do so."

"And you gave her your normal amount?" I glance over my shoulder at Gypsy, who corroborates Mickey's story with a slow, solitary nod.

Eyes buggin' out of his skull, my naked brother's head

bobs the affirmative. "The same drug I always give 'em. Same amount. Same everything."

"Then how did she die?"

"She was breathin' when I took her." Mickey points to the blue tie on the floor. "I used that on her wrists. Gypsy was there for all of it. He watched me. He saw she was alive. After I came, I cleaned everyone up. Like I always do. I untied her. Then I went and found her friend she'd left with Viper. They were done, so she came back here to be with her friend 'til she woke up."

"And, where were you?" I ask.

"Here. With everyone else. We let 'em have the bed. Me and Gypsy took the couch." Mickey jerks his chin at the blue sofa covered in blankets and pillows, beneath the only window in their room.

"Then what?"

"We all went to sleep, and she never woke up," he explains.

"They took drugs before comin' here last night," our VP calls from the hall.

Ah. That makes far more sense. "She probably OD'd, Mick. That's not on you."

Expelling a pent-up breath, Mickey's shoulders deflate in relief as he turns to face his best friend. Gypsy opens his arms and Mickey comes in for a long, far too intimate hug for me to bear witness to. I give them my back to do whatever works for them.

"You know who to call," I yell to Kai, referencing the person who's gotta come, pick up, and then dispose of the body in whatever manner necessary for her family to get closure, but so nothing can lead back to the Sacred Sinners. The only actual issue is the friend. The club whore who could talk. Will talk. She's worked up. That's what they do. Then comes the cops breathing down our necks. All of it's such an ugly thing. Dealing with war and then this, seven days before I marry Kit.

"Already done," Kai responds.

Good man. Kai's come a long fuckin' way. Stepped up and took charge.

Knowin' Kai and I gotta have a sit down with Big to discuss how we wanna handle this new club whore predicament, I exit Mickey and Gypsy's room, and go straight to church, to get this meeting over with. 'Cause I've got more pressing matters to handle, like feeding my woman my cock, among other things.

CHAPTER FORTY

KIT

An awfully sexy man straddles an equally sexy piece of steel in front of our house. Booted feet on the ground, he revs the engine. "Come on, love. Let's go for a ride." He smiles, revving a second time for show.

Standing on our porch, arms tucked over my chest, my head cocks to the side. "I didn't think that was allowed." The *we're at war and don't wanna die* is left unspoken.

The hot biker double taps the *Sergeant-at-Arms* patch on his chest as if that somehow negates the rules. As if he's above club law. What do I know? He might be.

Gunz thumbs to the back of his bike and the seat there just for me. I glance down at my clothes—jeans, t-shirt, no shoes. The norm as of late. I spent half the morning working in the compound's shared garden. Soiled knees aren't exactly all the rage.

Flicking my eyes to him, then my bare toes, I wiggle the pink polished things for emphasis. What does the man do? Smiles wider. Full teeth, shining between a thick, graying beard. He fusses around with his saddlebag and produces a pair of women's black leather boots out of thin air, like Mary

Poppins's bag of wonders. Laces tied together, he drapes them over his handlebar, wearing the smuggest expression I've seen in ages.

"*Those* for me?" I clasp my hands together at my breasts and pretend to swoon like a damsel in a fairytale.

Playing right along, Gunz puffs his chest out. "You'll have to put 'em on and see." He winks, ever the flirt.

Knowing I can't try anything on without socks, I gesture to the front door. "I'll grab—"

Before the words can leave my mouth, that damn man produces a pair of black crew socks from his Mary Poppin's bag and drapes them over the bootlaces.

"Are there any other surprises you'd like to share from that bag, babe?" I double-check because it seems someone's come prepared for whatever it is he has up that sleeve.

"Not yet. Now put 'em on, so we can blow this popsicle stand."

Dancing down the front steps, his arm then curls around my waist as I snag the new boots and socks from the bike. Gunz draws me in, and I do what any sane woman would—I plant a big, sloppy, grateful kiss on his lips. Gunz chuckles on impact before slating our mouths together and claiming me like a beast. Tongues dueling for dominance, my brain turns to mush, and my panties catch fire. Lost in the moment, I claw at his clothes, not giving a single damn where we are. The quicker we're naked, the better.

Wrenching his lips away from mine with a pained groan, Gunz's hooded gaze stares down at me as I force air to enter my lungs. He boops my nose with a finger. "You're gonna be the end of me."

"You say that like it's a bad thing." I slide my hand over Gunz's thigh, into the juncture, right alongside his erection. Teasing the tip through his denim, I innocently bite my lip as he gasps, then growls, when he realizes what I'm trying to do. He pries my hand off before we get ourselves into trouble.

I need to see it.

I need to play with it.

He goes down on me... Every. Single. Day.

Not once has he let me do what I want. To explore and taste him. It's driving me crazy.

"Get dressed, love. We've got places to go. People to see."

Grumbling a slew of unpleasantries, I stomp dramatically over to the steps of our house, boots in hand, plop down, and proceed to do as instructed, all the while glaring at him—partly because I'm sexually frustrated and partly out of fun. What can I say? I love this man.

Gunz watches me pull on the socks and the boots, wearing the sexiest smile known to mankind. What I did to deserve this guy, I'll never know, but I'm gonna appreciate every minute.

Sufficiently dressed for a ride, I use Gunz's shoulder for support as I swing my leg over and mount the back of his Harley. He downs the pegs for me to place my feet on before reaching into his bag of wonders and handing me a matte black half-helmet. I strap it on as he slides a pair of black sunglasses over his eyes.

"You ready to ride?!" he hollers over the rumble of his bike.

"No helmet for you?"

"I'll be fine, love."

"Erik." That's not gonna work for me.

"Kit," he mocks.

"Helmet."

"Love, we're not goin' far."

I don't care. "We're at war. You need a helmet. You've already had two surgeries. I'm gonna guess ridin' wasn't in the doc's approved notes, but we're doin' it anyhow. Helmet, babe."

It's the least he can do to protect himself.

Gunz nods stiffly in agreement, unhappy with my demand. He pulls out his phone, fires off a text, and less than a minute later, Adam comes running from the clubhouse with a helmet similar to mine in hand.

"Hey, Mom," he greets, delivering the protective shell to his father.

"Hey, back. Thanks for bringin' it."

"No problem. Stay safe." Adam taps the side of my leg and gives a chin lift to his father before jogging back to the clubhouse.

My guy secures the helmet on his head. "There. Better?" he grumbles, knocking the side with his fist.

From behind, I squeeze him around the middle, careful not to get too low and bother his stitches. "Thank you."

"Yeah. Yeah." He pats the back of my hand before repositioning my hold around him.

Settled on his Harley, I relax the best I can, given I haven't ridden on one of these in forever, as Gunz heels up his stand and gets us rollin'. White Boy opens the front gate for us to leave, and before I know it, we're cruising on the open road. Cool wind in my face, warm sun on my back, and a beautiful man in my arms.

The longer we ride, the more my muscles ease. The stress I've been carrying for months fades, replaced by a calm I've never felt before. This is where I belong. Each day, I heal a little more from what happened. Each day, I'm accepted into a world I never realized I needed. In a week, I marry this man.

Chin resting on his shoulder, I close my eyes and fly. A mishmash of happy, sad tears paint my face, disappearing just as fast as they come. Their remnants a memory on the wind, and with them goes the past, the pain, and the fear of what was or is to be.

Reaching town, Gunz rides through streets I've never been down before until we pull up to a large, concrete building at the city center. He parks in the only space available, drops his stand, and cuts the engine.

"What're we doing here?" I ask, taking in my new surroundings—there's a water fountain on the lawn and bright, colorful flowers planted everywhere. Old, well-kept brick buildings line the street, each filled with cute mom-and-pop shops.

"Gettin' our marriage license. To make this legal." From his bag of wonders, Gunz procures a manilla envelope and hands it back to me. "All our documents are in there."

Oh.

I unclasp the packet and peek inside. He wasn't lying when he said all our stuff's here. Down to my previous divorce decree. Even my driver's license. Sneaky, sneaky man.

With his help, I dismount Gunz's bike and remove my helmet on the sidewalk as he does the same seated on his Harley. We rest our safety gear on our seats before climbing the courthouse steps hand-in-hand to make things official. Less than fifteen minutes later, we're walking back down those same steps an envelope richer.

Next to his bike, Gunz pulls me in by the waist and nuzzles the side of my throat. "How ya feel?" His facial hair brushes over my flesh, making me shiver.

"Like I'm about to be married." I swallow hard at the truth as nerves bubble in my gut like a witch's cauldron.

A pair of sexy lips drag up my neck to the shell of my ear, where he whispers, "To me."

"To you," I whisper in return.

My man pulls back to look me in the eye. "You ready for that?"

"Yes. Are you?" I am ready. Nervous, but ready. Scared, but ready.

"We wouldn't be here if I wasn't." Somehow reading my unease like he always does, Gunz extracts two Dum Dums from the inside of his leather vest, removes both wrappers from the orbs, and offers them to me to pick from.

Knowing it isn't the polite thing to do, but not caring either way, I steal both and stick them in my mouth anyhow. One in each cheek. Cherry and strawberry.

Amused crinkles at the corner of Gunz's gorgeous blue eyes surface just before a chuckle emits, accompanied by a head tilt and a lopsided smirk. He boops me on the nose then leans in to kiss me there before extracting another Dum Dum for himself. He pops it into his mouth. "It's gonna be okay, love. We're gonna get through this."

I know.

Oh. I know.

I suck harder on the sugar, hoping the mysterious powers work on me the same as they do him. I signed legal documents today to make things official. Less than a month ago, I was living a lonely existence in the house with him. Now look where we are.

In need of a hug, I wrap my arms around Gunz, underneath his vest, and rest my cheek on his pec. A sigh escapes me as his big, strong arms tighten around my shoulders. He kisses the top of my head. "Take all the time ya need, love. I'm not goin' anywhere. But I do got another thing I wanna show ya."

For however long we stand in front of the courthouse, wrapped in each other's embrace, people pass by, but nobody says a thing. For a suspended moment, the world stops as his heart beats steadily against my ear. The spice of his cologne mixed with cinnamon, leather, and soap curl into my nose, making me feel the safest I've felt in ages. The defined muscles in his back are firm to the touch as I trace them with my fingertips. What's better, is Gunz's true to his word. He lets me take all the time I need. So, I do. I hug him and savor him until my worry is replaced with contentment. Until the Dum Dums enact their superpowers. Then and only then do I pry myself away from his touch. Far enough to look up and meet his eye. Gunz hooks two fingers into my belt loops to keep my front plastered to his—tits to abs.

"I love you, so fuckin' much," he growls, igniting those weird tumultuous butterflies in my middle again. They pair nicely with the ridiculous smile that lights my face.

He smiles, too, watching my over-the-top girly reaction.

"I love you, too," I admit aloud for the first time. Even to my ears, it sounds foreign, but good. Damn good.

"I know." Gunz pecks my forehead. "Now, love, let's get on to the second part of my plan."

I nod in agreement.

The second part. If this is the first, I can't imagine what comes next.

Instead of asking, I follow his lead, excited to see what else he has in store. No man has done anything like this for me before.

Thoughtful, thoughtful man...

My future husband.

Pinch me.

I can't believe this is real.

CHAPTER FORTY-ONE

GUNZ

Where do you take your woman to romance her? If you asked the brothers, they'd say the bedroom. Those fuckers are no help. Not even Big. And there's no way I'd ask the Sacred Sisters for help in these matters. They're as goo-goo for romance as the next female, and I'm not here to fulfill their fantasies. I'm here to create memories for one woman and one woman alone.

Kit.

The one who has my balls aching nonstop.

The one who smiles, and nothing else matters in the world but her lookin' at me like I'm the center of her universe. Alert the press, I'm turning into a fuckin' sap.

To put the nail in the sappy coffin, I brought her to a park on the outskirts of town. A place few frequent. A place we'll be safe.

Hand in hers, a drawstring pack strung over my shoulder, I escort a quiet Kit through the wooded area. We step over fallen limbs and through overgrown brush until the tree cover breaks into a place I've visited once before. The clearing. Only it isn't clear. Surrounded by a centuries-old forest is a meadow of wildflowers in full bloom. Bees buzz, birds swoop overhead, as butterflies dance flower to flower, living their best, temporary lives. It's a place most women would love. Especially the one who's spent so much time tending our club garden and planting flowers around our house in her free time.

Her stunned gasp says it all.

Her squeeze of my hand fills my heart with so much fuckin' pride.

I did good.

My woman loves flowers. Her arms are tatted in them. This place is flowers on steroids.

Leaving my hold, Kit wanders into the awaiting meadow. Colorful blooms brush against her calves as she bends and sweeps the tops of her hands over their vibrant caps. Wading further into the growth, she dances around like a child. Equally excited sounds fill the air with joy as a smile the size of the earth fills her face, crinkling the edges of her honeyed eyes. Her short hair shines in the sun, highlighting the beautiful grays and whites she's yet to dye another wild color.

To capture the moment, I snap pictures of her with my phone to look back on later. As she explores, I set up shop. Opening the bag, I pull out a thin picnic blanket large enough for two to lie on. Not wanting to ruin the oasis, I find the least flower-populated area I can find and spread it out. A frozen water bottle, sunscreen, a bag of fresh fruit, my gun, and a few other odds and ends remain in the sack as I remove my shitkickers and knife to stretch out on the blanket and await my frolicking future wife.

Face red from exertion, little beads of sweat on her brow, Kit flounces over to our spot and flops down beside me, breathing heavy. I rest on my elbows, legs out, as she curls onto her side, propping her head on her arm.

"This is beautiful," she pants.

"It's a local secret few know about. Your tattoos reminded me of it."

"Thank you for this. For everything."

Lips pressed together, I nod once, not wanting the praise for somethin' I'm supposed to do. "That's what one does for their old lady."

"Like the new gardening tools and gloves that randomly showed up on our porch." Brows bouncing in fun, she all but calls me out for something I haven't admitted to doing.

"Yep. Like those." Ya can't blame me. She needed them. Kit would rather dig hard, clumpy dirt with her bare hands than ask for anything. The last thing I want is her getting blisters because she was helping around the compound without proper tools. You take care of the females under your protection. If my grandbaby needs diapers, she gets diapers. If Bink needs a night off, she gets a night off. If Janie needs a new car seat for Dom, she gets a new car seat. If my woman needs gardening shit to garden shit, then I'm gonna make it happen. It's not hard showing up for those you give a damn about. It's as natural as breathing.

Kit rolls onto her back and stares up at the blue, marshmallow-clouded sky. "If you keep this up, you're gonna end up with your dick... living permanently in my mouth. Once you finally let me suck it, that is." She sighs as if that'll never happen.

"Love." I groan, throwing my head back in agony. "That sounds like... fuckin' perfection. But I don't do this shit to get anythin' in return. That's not how this works."

"I know. Which is why I wanna do it."

"We will... get there." *When I know it won't trigger you.* I've read books. I've done my research. Givin' my woman pleasure is one thing. Taking it in return is another. Baby steps.

"Today. We will get there today," she announces, shocking the hell outta me.

"Love... It'll—"

"Go in my mouth today, Erik," she finishes in my stead.

I drag a hand down my face. "Christ."

Tilting her head my way, batting those eyelashes the way women do, Kit juts out her bottom lip. "I wanna see it. Please." She pleads all cutesy and far too adorable.

A lot of headshaking ensues on my part. "Love. No." I'm firm in my response, but not a dick.

"Please. There's no one here. I just wanna see it." Kit flicks her gaze down south and lingers long enough my cock bucks against the fly of my jeans, desperate for attention. Wetness blooms through the denim before her gaze drags up my body. Goosebumps sprout like phantom touches upon my skin.

"Fuck." Unable to say no to this woman, I relent because I want her to see it too. Sure, I'd planned on gettin' her mouth on me sometime soon. After we talked about it. I'd planned on eatin' that sweet pussy here in the meadow. But I didn't plan this.

Unbuckling my belt, I unfasten my jeans, unzip, and scoot the denim down to my knees. Sans boxers, my wet-tipped, hard-as-steel cock bobs in the late afternoon sun. Curling back onto her side, Kit watches it in fascination. The fucker I am watches her lick her lips as I move my piercing and smear the precum into the fat head to keep it from makin' any more of a mess. He has a tendency of doin' that. The guy loves to perform.

"That's nice," she groans, scissoring her legs together.

Fuck.

"Love, could you not do that?" I jut my chin at her, tryin' to get friction on her clit.

"I can't help it."

Fine. Then we'll both be exposed. "Take off your bottoms," I order.

The gorgeous minx does as she's told, and off goes the boots, socks, jeans, and sexy little thong. She tosses them all into a pile in the grass and turns to face me, her teeth sunk into her bottom lip, pupils blown. I wanna consume this woman. Drown her on my cock. Cupping the back of her head, I lead her forward to do just that. She wants to see him. She wants to taste him. This is her fuckin' chance because I'm not gonna say no. Not anymore. I fuckin' hope this doesn't backfire.

Curling over me, she wraps those lips tentatively around my pierced head, and I nearly explode on contact. Grippin' the back of her neck, I thrust into her mouth, just enough to graze the back of her throat, but not enough to hurt. The darkness I'm afraid to unleash ripples through my body as Kit moans around my cock, taking as much as she can like it's a goddamn Olympic sport. The depraved part of me revels in her sounds, in the wet heat, in her potent eagerness. It's sweet and salty—beautiful and addicting.

Knowin' the shackled part of me can't yield much longer, I grasp the blanket in my fist as my other continues to encourage her to suck, to take, to draw him in, to drink his offering.

"Love, I don't... fuck... I don't know if I can... I'm... I'm gonna lose control... You're—"

Somehow understanding me unlike anyone has before, Kit hums around my fat cockhead, then crawls up and throws a leg over my body to straddle my face. Met with my favorite taste in the world, I dive in and ravage her wet cunt. Gripping both of her thick, ass cheeks in my hands, I smother my face in her pussy, suck on her little clit, and tongue fuck her hole. Lost in her heady scent, I get high as she sucks me and uses her hand to stroke whatever doesn't fit.

It's sweet fuckin' relief.

To feel. To fuck. To savor and consume what I want most as she cups my balls. I groan, snapping my hips to get deeper, to fill her. My fuckin' toes curl when she gags on my prick. Likin' my reaction, the minx does it again, gettin' the same response. Eyes closing, I suffocate in her pussy as she wrecks me. Tongue slidin' over my piercing. Throat closing around my sensitive glans. The darkness ebbs and flows. One moment, the urge to destroy her has me thrusting into her mouth. The next, I submit to her ministrations—lying still as she explores and tastes to her heart's content. When I can't take it anymore, the internal chains snap. Before I realize what's happening, she's on her back, and I'm straddling her chest, feeding my cock between a set of rosy, red lips.

Kit takes me—honeyed gaze on mine, nostrils flaring between each thrust. She swallows me down, her hands gripping my ass as I cradle the back of her head, feeding her more and more until tears spill over, and she's shaking. Not from sadness but need. From desire. From me owning her mouth as I take what's mine. Forever.

Without warning, my nuts draw up tight, and I come, growling her name. Fillin' her mouth and throat. It spurts out of the sides of her lips, and I fuck it back in. Beautiful eyes closing in ecstasy, she moans, and swallows what she can of my offering.

"That's it, love. That's it," I encourage as she consumes whatever I give, licking and sucking every drop from my shaft.

When I pull back, my dick falls from her mouth with a suctioned pop. Because I can't fuckin' help myself, I smear my cockhead over her wet mouth, painting my cum over the last pair of lips I'll ever wreck. Kit's tongue sneaks out and teases my slit, a devilish glint in her eye.

"You like this, love?"

A small, innocent, hot-as-sin nod.

"You did so fuckin' good," I praise because that was the best blowjob of my life.

A blush consumes her cheeks at the compliment.

To take it a step further, I hook my thumb into the corner of her mouth. She opens for me, and I dip my softening head back inside, where she suckles him. I caress her cheek with the backs of my fingers. "So fuckin' beautiful. So fuckin' good at that. You look fuckin' perfect with my cock in your mouth."

She hums in agreement, continuing to taste what's hers.

"This what you wanted?"

Another nod, her hooded eyes on mine.

"You gonna let me take your mouth whenever I want?"

Another nod.

"You sure?"

Blink. Nod. Suckle.

"You ready for me to eat your pussy?"

Her tongue swirls around my piercing as she delivers a subtle nod as if she's happy to just sit here and suckle him all damn day.

Only, I'm not down with that. Doin' what I do every single day, sometimes twice a day, I scoot down her body and open those fine-ass legs. The sun highlights everything. The wet sheen of her arousal. The light dusting of hair. Her sexy little clit hiding under its hood. Kneeling between her legs, I lick my lips at the sight and groan. I fuckin' love this pussy. It's pretty. A pretty pussy just for me.

I drag a finger through her folds, and she arches her back, hands fisting on either side of her body. "You want me to get you off, love? Make you squirt on my face?"

Another one of those sexy nods is my offering. As much as I love her words, her little cues are just as hot. I don't make her wait. What kinda fiancé would I be if I did? Lying on my stomach, bare legs half in the grass, I dive in.

As always, she doesn't take long to come.

Once.

Twice.

Soaking the blanket in her essence.

I drink up what I can, as my cock hardens a second time, ready for another round. Knowin' it ain't the right thing to do, but givin' zero actual fucks, I get my woman off a third time, then crawl between her legs and rub my wet cockhead all over her cunt. Pressing it against her clit, she squeaks in pleasure.

"You like that?"

"Yes," Kit breathes, wigglin' beneath me, skin all glowy.

I tickle her entrance with him. "How about that?"

Her eyes widen as those legs follow suit, to give me better access.

'Cause I'm a bastard, I don't ask for permission when I nudge him inside, just the head, and rest him there, my eyes on hers, so she knows I'm the one there, not those bastards in the warehouse, not her ex, or any other unworthy piece of shit who's taken what's mine before.

"I'm not gonna lie, love. I wanna fuck you right now. But I won't. I'm gonna kneel here, and I'm gonna let you feel him. You good with that?"

A shallow, nostril-flaring nod.

"Words. I need the words, love."

Her eyelids flutter. "Yes."

"You want more?"

"Yes."

Doin' as requested, I push him in halfway. Her walls contract around my girth, gettin' used to his size, and piercing. Kit sucks in a sharp, sexy breath. I watch him there, fascinated by the bare connection. It's been decades since I've gone without protection, and damn, is it fuckin' awesome. Not wanting her to freak out and go to a dark place and lose what we have right now, I gesture for her to give me her hand. She does so without pause, and I place it between us, right where my cock is, inside her. Delicate little fingers touch our connection. My shaft, her entrance.

"You good?" I check, proud of how brave she is.

"Yes."

"You want more?"

"Yes."

Keeping her hand where it's at, I glide myself inside her body. To the hilt. Kit's eyes widen at the fullness, at the stretch, and she moans like the perfect woman she is.

"That's it, love."

Massaging her little clit with my thumb, she cries out in pleasure, her cunt squeezing me in a vise. I don't move. I let her adjust as I give that little nub just what it deserves. When she comes, her throat elongates, back arches off the blanket, and cunt flutters around me. When she's through, I back out, still hard as steel. Curling onto my side, I rest next to my woman and draw her into my front. Throwing her leg over my hip, I cup Kit's bare ass, to keep us close, as my cock folds between us, wetting her stomach. Needin' a bit more, I nudge my woman's lips with my own, and she opens as she always does. The kiss is soft. It's everything and more as it lingers for minutes, hours, days, I dunno which, and I don't care. I melt into her, our invisible tether twining around us like a cocoon of our own making. Her palm upon my cheek. The sweetest of tastes on my tongue.

For the rest of the afternoon, into the early evening, we laze in our own world, just like this. Half-naked, together. Never apart. Always touching. Always kissing or sharing.

We speak of the future. Of the wedding and what we'd like our lives to look like together. She explains how happy she is to be where we are in our lives. And I vow to myself, to make damn sure she remains this happy, this satisfied, for always.

We suck on Dum Dums, eat the fruit I packed, and make sure she stays hydrated with the water I brought.

I play with her pussy a few more times, and she's nice enough to swallow down a second batch from my cock. I couldn't think of a better day, nor a better person to spend it with.

When we're through, we pack up together, and she takes a final stroll through the meadow, that same sunny smile playing on her lips before we navigate through the woods, and back to my bike. Before I take her home, we hit the final stop. Dinner in town, at a biker-friendly café, where our conversation never ceases, and we play footsie like teenagers under the table.

The new compound gate yawns open as we arrive home. After today, I know, without a shadow of a doubt, I made the right choice to marry this woman. I should've known she was the woman of my dreams all those years ago, but I wasn't ready then. Hell, I didn't realize I was capable now, until she showed up, banging on the gate, demanding I help our son.

In a week, it'll be official. My property patch on her back. Her in my bed, *our* bed, until I draw my last breath.

I don't check in at the clubhouse when I park in our driveway and help Kit dismount the bike.

For the rest of the night, we carry on as we always do—shower together, read in bed—naked this time, because who in the hell needs clothes when you can look at that smokin' hot body instead.

Truth, no matter how long we're together, i'll never get enough...

Because love like this is once in a lifetime.

Kit's reading about Z and his lady when I pluck the book

from her hand, rest it face down on the bed between us, and take her mouth hard... to pour all my love and appreciation into.

When she pulls back, panting, I peck her cute little nose. "I love you."

Eyes on mine, Kit cups my cheek. The warmth of her connection soaks right in, as it always does. "And I love you more. Thank you for today."

I turn my face and kiss the inside of her palm. "Anytime, love. Any-fuckin'-time, yeah?"

"Yeah." She smiles—shy and soft, and oh-so-mine.

Seven days.

Seven more fuckin' days.

CHAPTER FORTY-TWO

KIT

Life on the Sacred Sinner compound is anything but traditional. I don't know a single person who can say their sisters live beside them. If you need a cup of sugar, you don't call, you walk over and get the sugar. They're here for everything. From movie nights in Bink's basement to shared recipes, to male bitching hour via text, no matter the day or time, they're there.

Most of us grow up hoping to fit in. That's part of the human condition. To want to be wanted for who you are. Not for what you bring someone else. Not because you serve them, like I did my ex.

Every day here is a new adventure.

Whether it's Bulk pissing Jez off, Deke running after his daughters, or Loretta and her sex tales with Blimp, it's always entertaining, to say the least.

Today, our small house is full of those very sisters.

Not just one or two.

All of them.

It's my wedding day.

I can't fuckin' believe it.

My. Wedding. Day.

The entire compound is buzzing with people, all of them draped in leather. From Adam and the brothers setting everything up with the guidance of Debbie and Candy Cane. To Bonez, helping us ladies get ready for the big day. Well, maybe not ready, but he sure is helping dial down the crazy. To be honest, I think Gunz sent his brother to make sure I don't get cold feet. As if that'd ever happen. There's not a stitch of cold goin' on in these boots. The same boots he bought me last week. The same ones I wore on our ride, and I took off at the meadow. Our meadow—is what I've begun calling it. Because that was the most magical day I've spent with any person in my life, and the most I've connected with another person.

All of my new sisters are ready to take on the day, including Whisky, the fiery redhead, who rode in with Bonez this morning for the party.

Most of the sisters are busy getting dressed throughout my house. Why they decided to get ready here and not Bink's is beyond my comprehension. Our place is way too small to host this many bodies.

On the couch, the picture of calm, Bonez lounges in jeans and his leather vest as the horde of females dress and undress in front of him. The man doesn't bat a single lash. If I didn't already respect him before, I'd respect him even more now. He's got Leech on one leg as Dom sits beside him, playing with an alligator toy.

"Does anyone need hairspray?" Jez calls from the bathroom, where plumes of toxic fumes cloud the air.

Hot footing a fresh cup of tea from the kitchen into my bedroom, to get dressed in peace, I escape the madness. At the end of our bed, I pat Chibs' brawny head and take the world's longest sip of hot chamomile. In through my nose, I breathe. Pause. Count to five. Then out it goes. Chibs nudges me with his flat nose, and I plop down beside him for a quick cuddle before dressing.

We are T-minus one hour to wedlock.

"It's crazy out there, huh?" I talk to my pup.

He snuggles against my side in response.

"Dad and I are gonna be married today. You might need to sleep in the living room tonight. Dad and I don't wanna scar ya for life, bud." I scratch behind his ear.

Our Frenchie doesn't seem to grasp what I'm saying, and I don't care either way. This room is a refuge and has been since the night I first wound up on the compound. The day I read the first vampire romance in here. The day I found out bikers can be into romance books. Though, Gunz would still argue that to this day. Don't worry, I'll keep his secret, as I'll keep all the rest of them.

A double knock sounds at the door. "Kit, you need anything?" comes from Jade.

"No. Thanks. I'll be out soon." More like last minute.

The sisters are donning denim skirts and red tank tops for the wedding. Those who have an old man are wearing their property of vests, too. I'm... wearing... this...

Standing from the bed, I finger the edge of my band t-shirt draped across the dresser. A tight skirt pairs well with my Tom Petty and the Heartbreakers top. It showed up yesterday, out of the blue. Gunz handed me a package and said, "Wear this tomorrow."

Oh, I'm wearing it.

I'm gonna wear the hell out of this shirt. It's freaking awesome.

Doing my best not to let my anxiety win the day, I drown out the chaos in the house, finish my tea, and get dressed. My t-shirt slides over a sexy lace bra. The black, skintight skirt keeps my panty-less pussy under wraps. The leather bracelet from Adam adorns my wrist, and as a last little somethin' somethin', I slip the black garter Bink bought up my leg. It's exposed for everyone to see. I can't lie. It looks hot with the skirt, boots, and tattoos. Not too shabby, if I say so myself.

Knowing I gotta slap on some makeup to be more presentable, I kiss Chibs' head before I exit the room. Out of the frying pan and into the fire we go.

"Woo! Woo! Hot mama!" Jez cheers when she sees me.

With long, blonde hair braided down both sides of her head, Bink approaches and squeezes my arm. "He's gonna lose his mind. You look hot as fuck."

Wrinkling my nose at the compliment, I squeeze her arm in appreciation.

Bonez whistles his agreement from the couch as Leech scrambles to get off his lap and does her best to toddle over to me. By her second plop to the floor, I swoop in for the save. Hooked on my hip, she pats my nose with her palm like she's seen her grandpa do with his finger many times.

I chuckle at her adorableness and pat her nose, too, nicely with a finger. "It's good to see you, too, young lady."

Dressed in a frilly red dress and matching headband, Leech babbles an entire story before I hand her back to her mama so I can finish getting ready. Jez is nice enough to fan out the bathroom before I enter, so I don't die of sticky aerosol lung.

In the mirror, door open, I give myself a once-over. My hair's grown a bit since the warehouse. Not as much as I'd like, but I'm rockin' the shortness anyhow. I'm just lucky I have the head and face for it. Not everyone can pull off bald.

From the small bag under the sink, I cart out the necessities. A dramatic smokey shadow, eyeliner, and va-va-voom mascara. I smear on dark lipstick for effect. Normal pinky blush and a bit of shimmer finishes the look. It's not much, but it's far more than I wear on the daily.

From the doorway, Loretta watches me, in her red, denim, and a sexy black wig. When I turn to face her, fat droplets cascade down her cheeks. Not wanting to lose my shit, I wrap the woman up in a big hug. Because I get it. This is a big deal for us. All of us. Something we didn't think could ever happen when we were there. With them. When real life and happiness was a distant memory. Two of us are dead because of those bastards. We lost a bit of ourselves in the darkness, but we also gained each other. Before I know what's happening, there's a circle of sisters surrounding us, all wrapped up in each other's arms, smelling of perfume and soap.

Resting my chin on Loretta's shoulder, I refuse to cry. I won't drown in those memories. I refuse to go back there. Those fuckers won't win. Caught up in her grief, Loretta trembles against me as I recall our hands clutched in the cold, listening to the screams of our sisters, begging for mercy. Of the intense hunger and fear. We did it, though. We're breathing. We're alive. Loved by men. Loved by our sisters. Loved by our families. We made it out. We made it to today.

One by one, the sisters release their holds until all is left is three—Jade, Loretta, and me—our foreheads pressed together.

"Thank you for being here," I whisper.

"Always," Loretta vows on a sniffle, and Jade nods.

"I'm getting married today." As the words fall, a sense of awe reaches into my chest and squeezes its tight fist around my heart.

I'm getting married today.

To my son's real father.

To a man who accepts me.

Who saved me.
Who loves me.
Today, I become a real Sacred Sister.
Today, these women will be by my side for always.
Today, I am freed.

CHAPTER FORTY-THREE

GUNZ

Since the moment I woke this mornin', alone, in Big's clubhouse bedroom, after an impromptu bachelor party of club whores and booze, everything's been a fuckin' blur. I'm here, but I'm not. And before you worry your pretty little head, I didn't partake in any of the whores or libations. I was sober the entire time. I learned my lesson. My dick belongs to one woman and one woman alone. When Jizz tried to get me a lap dance, I declined. When they tried to get me to take a shot from a woman's big, luscious tits, I spun her around and made them take the shot. Not my thing. Not anymore. This man is taken. This man is also about to burst out of his fuckin' skin.

Marriage jitters are a real goddamn thing.

I'm livin' proof.

Since the moment I opened my eyes, I've had ants in my pants—like I took a line of the finest coke. It's been decades since I've lived that wild, and let me tell ya, the feeling's the same as I remember. Only I'm stone fuckin' sober, all sweaty, and unable to sit still. So, I've kept busy, helpin' Debbie set shit up for my wedding.

She wasn't keen on it at first until I explained what's doin', and she relented. We've got potted flowers every-fuckin'-where. Tables for food. Damn, good food. Our chairs are full of brothers, many of who rode in from out of state to be here. Some of their old ladies tagged along, too. The compound's burstin' with family.

My woman isn't here yet.

Chewin' a hole through the side of my cheek, I'm standin' at the head of some aisle we made. Debbie rolled a red runner thingy down the center. Big's up here with me, wearing his cut and a dumbass clerical collar he fashioned outta somethin'. You know what I'm talkin' about. The white piece religious men wear when they're men of God. Only, Big ain't a man of no god. He's a sarcastic fucker, who's takin' his reasonability of marryin' us far too seriously. If I hadn't nixed the idea early this mornin', he planned on wearing a large wooden cross attached to a leather strap around his neck. That's Big for ya.

Every eye in the crowd is on me.

I adjust the neck of my cut, hopin' it'll somehow calm these nerves, then roll my shoulders a handful of times to loosen them up. Kit's takin' forever. The sisters have already taken their seats, apart from Bink, who's got my blonde grandbaby and the adorable redheaded Dom, at the start of the runner, ready to do their part as ring bearer and flower girl.

Tati and Janie kneel at the other end to help wave the kiddos thisaway. A chorus of laughter rings out when Leech turns to Dom and boops him on the nose with her palm. He staggers a step back, flashing her an offended stink-eye. When she doesn't get the smile she's after, Leech turns to her mama and pouts. Bink boops her nose in return, and my grandbaby breaks into a fit of tinkly giggles. The sound alone makes me forget my own chewed-up nerves for a beat as the first smile I've brandished all day rises to the surface.

For a suspended moment, everything is peace in my world until my son comes into view, and on his arm... her.

Big clasps me on my shoulder when I forget to breathe.

He squeezes me there hard enough to bruise and slaps a white handkerchief to the center of my chest when he catches me welling up. This is straight up happening.

The boy nobody gave a shit about. The man incapable of doin' anythin' more than pleasure a woman is gonna have a wife. A mighty fine, tough-as-nails wife. A wife who beams at me every day for no reason than she wants to. A woman who listens and cares. Really cares. Who spends time asking questions—deep, meaningful ones. A forgiving woman who sees my flaws and doesn't stop lovin' me anyhow.

And beside her is my kid wearing his cut.

Mine.

Flesh and blood. Same eyes. Same hair. Or at least what it used to look like when I wasn't as old as dirt.

My first child, not of blood, the one who gave me a reason to live, to care and give a damn about somethin' other than sex, booze, and bikes, escorts my grandbaby and Dom down the aisle. Or attempts to, as they stop to greet half our guests. I make eye contact with my honey-eyed goddess. The tattooed beaut winks, far more confident than me, as my pussy-ass lets the waterworks flow. I don't give a shit what anyone else thinks. A sweet, lopsided smirk ticks up at the edge of Kit's luscious red lips before she mouths, *I love you.*

Christ.

Swallowin' thickly, I rub the handkerchief across my eyes to stop this cryin' shit.

"Fuckin' breathe," Big growls, not a fan of feelings. "Breathe."

Through my nose, I draw in a chest full of air, before

blowing it out through my mouth. It does fuckall to quell the nerves, and I can't think of a single reason it matters. Stepping side to side, I fiddle with my SS ring, but I don't stop watchin' my woman.

Once Leech reaches us, little basket in hand, I kneel to kiss her cheek before I ruffle Dom's hair and untie Kit's ring from his little pillow. I slide it up my pinkie for safekeeping. My baby doll, all grown up, steps before me, her bright, blue eyes shimmering with unspent tears. I do what I gotta do and pull her into my warmth. Her head against my chest, arms around my middle, she utters so only we can hear, "I'm so happy for you both."

Doesn't that just take the fuckin' cake? She's happy. I'm happy. I kiss the top of her blonde mop and say as much. "Me, too, Baby Doll. Me, too."

When we've gotten our fill, Bink steps back, rockin' a bright watery smile, and finds her spot to sit in the front row, a blanket stretched out on the grass in front of her for Dom and Leech to play.

Returning my attention to the reason I'm here, Kit and Adam step onto the runner, white-and-black flower petals scattered before them. The mice in my gut start to gnaw like feisty bastards. Fuck, that's my wife. Yep, this is real.

Music starts from a speaker I had Blimp set up for this moment, to the clip of the song I pictured her walking down the aisle to. The idea came to me last week, when I ordered her shirt, sittin' in my office, listenin' to my old records.

"Here Comes My Girl", by Tom Petty and the Heartbreakers, serenades the crowd as my woman nears, her arm linked in our sons. She's breathtaking—black skirt, t-shirt, boots, and that hot-as-sin garter I'll remove later with my teeth.

'Cause here comes my girl.
Yeah, she looks so right.
She's definitely all I need tonight.

Big doesn't bother with customary shit when Adam hands off his mom and takes the vacant seat Bink saved for him.

I don't bother with customary shit either when I draw my woman in for a kiss before we get started. She falls into me, her dainty hand between my pecs, mouth on mine. The brothers crow their approval from their seats. I grin against her lips as Kit laughs, light and sweet, full of life.

Sipping from lips I'll never tire of, cupping an ass that makes me rock hard, I take what's mine and then some. What's better, Kit lets me. Her tits mashed to my abs, I grip the back of her neck and consume.

Growin' uncomfortable, Big gruffly clears his throat. "Brother."

Fine.

Fun sucker.

Discharging an impatient growl, I separate me and my woman to make this official. Kit's lips are swollen, her cheeks the perfect shade of pink, as her chest heaves for air alongside mine. Knowing we can't do this boring, hand-in-hand, leave-a-space-for-Jesus-between-us bullshit, I fit us together once more. I'm polite about it. For the families here. Even though I know she can feel the steel length of my cock on her belly as I cuff both hands around the sides of her neck. Gaze locked on gaze. Just the two of us doin' this.

"You ready, love?" Caressing the underside of her chin with my thumbs, I make sure, 'cause after this, she can't back out. It's done. We're bonded for life.

Those expressive, steadfast eyes speak without words. She's ready. I'm ready. The club is here as our witness.

Standing tall, as if he isn't already large enough, Big clears his throat. "Dearly beloved—" he starts, and I cut him a swift, unimpressed stare.

The asshole winks, far too pleased with himself. "As I was

saying…" He clears his throat again and imparts a wisdom only the sarcastic fucker himself could bestow. I ignore the lot of it, too focused on Kit and her amusement at his ridiculousness. The crowd eats his antics up in spades.

Our vows are simple. A blur of I dos and promises to give her orgasms, 'cause Prez needs to be thorough. Hers comes after, same as mine. Only sucking my cock is involved, and I suppress the urge to roll my eyes at this level of marital promises.

"You're a fuckin' dick," I whisper under my breath, only it's not a whisper. It's a growl, and Big loves it, as do the brothers.

Yucking it up, the man shrugs up a single, innocent shoulder. "You wanted me to marry you. I'm marryin' you." Big's long, brown eyelashes flutter, ever full of shit.

Havin' the best time, Kit's lips smash together to keep from laughing. Those eyes dance in absolute delight at how much of a mockery this has become.

Looking up to the heavens for a bit of divine intervention, I shake my head, ready and willing to kick Big's ass. *I* didn't want him to marry us. Bink did. She set this up. This was her livin' out some girlish fantasy where Big would do the proper, adult thing, like I would have done, had this been their wedding and I was marrying them. Only Big and I are two sides of the same coin. His side—the ass side. If it looks like a duck and quacks like a duck, it's a duck. He isn't somehow gonna wake up one day a different man.

Tamping down my irritation, I follow along with Big's instructions and remove Kit's ring from my pinkie. The square, red ruby center and halo of diamonds around it suits her. Sliding it up her finger, it fits as it should.

She gapes at the ring, her finger moving around like women do when they wanna see it sparkle… and sparkle it does. "Erik, it's beautiful."

The tight spot in the center of my chest unravels a bit, knowing I did good.

"Like you," I remind.

As Kit's gaze lifts from admiring her ring to my face, those expressive eyes and mouth round in horror. "I... I didn't get you—"

Before she can say another word, I cut her off at the pass. "I told you I handled it." And I did. After the ceremony, we will handle my ring.

"Okay. You're sure?" She worries her bottom lip, and her nose wrinkles adorably with unnecessary concern.

"Yes, love. I'm sure." To ease her conscience about this not workin' like normal weddings do, with the customary exchange of the rings, I slide my SS ring off, turn her hand over, and drop the heavy metal into her palm to slide on for me. She does so, repeating whatever Big says. It doesn't fit my left finger like it should, since it wasn't meant for that digit, but it's enough of a replacement to relieve her distress.

"And now, by the power vested in me, the Sacred Sinners National President, I pronounce you, ball and chain. You may kiss your old lady." In spectacular fashion, Big bows at the waist, his muscled arms spread wide.

The crowd stands from their seats. Brothers and sisters alike whoop and holler like they do, as I take my woman's mouth in a brutal, soul-crushing kiss. Tongues collide, and my anxiety fades to dust in the wind as I claim what's officially mine. Palming the back of Kit's neck, I dip her over my leg, like I've seen men do in the movies we watch. My woman gasps in audible shock, gripping my cut for balance. I smile wickedly against her lips, knowin' I've got her and would never let her fall. To prove as much, I growl against her mouth before pushing back inside once more. Aching to slide my hand up her silky thigh, into the heat meant for me, I grip her ass instead, as hard as I take that mouth, and she moans. My dick relishes the sound, knowin' damn well it won't be long before he slides inside what's ours.

Before that can happen, I must give myself to her fully and make this final, as real Sacred Sinners do. Our way. Since the beginning.

Righting Kit on two feet, I tuck her against my side as we both return to reality. She blinks up at me dreamily. I lean down to kiss the tip of her nose. "You're the most beautiful woman," I rasp.

Nibbling her swollen bottom lip, Kit's shyness bubbles to the surface at my declaration. Fuck if I don't love the softness. The innocence.

Debbie taps me on the shoulder. "Gunz."

Step one—marry my woman.

Done.

Step two—her property cut.

Turning around, I accept the new leather from Debbie, knowin' it's perfect without havin' to examine it. Brothers who choose to claim a woman give their old ladies cuts to show who owns them. Not only for their safety, so other men and clubs see who they're claimed by, but also as a sign of respect. A declaration. A promise. Sure, some assholes who patch their women don't stay faithful, but the lot of us who respect the ones we love, do.

Knowin' what this signifies, Kit turns to and faces the crowd. In slides one arm and the other before I glide the cut onto her shoulders. Stitched on the back is the SS patch and the words I've longed to see there—*Property of Gunz*. When she spins back around, tears glitter like diamonds in her gaze. A single nomad drips down the crease of her nose, as she caresses the name patch stitched into her chest—*Kit*—the name I bestowed her all those years ago.

"I don't even know what it means," she whispers, clearly feelin' a little out of her depth.

Stepping up to Kit, I caress her jaw, then the name patch, where I trace each letter with the tip of my finger. "Do you remember the Kit Kat bar commercials in the '90s?" I ask.

Thinking for a beat, Kit frowns in concentration before her eyes widen when realization hits. "Break me…"

"Off a piece of that Kit Kat bar," I finish for her, smiling like a goddamn lunatic because, yeah, I saw her at the bar, all sweet, dark-haired, and innocent, gettin' hit on by that low-rank biker, and I thought to myself, break me off a piece of that. When we came together, literally, it stuck. I was younger then. Sue me.

"I'm named after a candy bar." She blinks in shock, fingering the patch on her cut.

Not wanting to upset my lady by making a joke, I smother a chuckle. "Yeah, love. You are."

Looking up at me, Kit's smokey gaze narrows, full of piss and vinegar. It's cute. Far too cute for that face. "And you're tellin' me on our weddin' day?"

"Technically, I'm tellin' ya after we're married. But yeah." I shrug, not sure what else she expects me to say, given the circumstance.

"A candy bar." There goes that overthinking brain of hers again, dissecting the name, why she got it, and how she never knew. I recognize that introspective, Imma-start-shit look. It takes hold far more than I'd like. Then again, I wouldn't change her for the world.

Still standin' beside us, Big snickers. Rockin' the smallest of grins, I shoot him a fake death glare, not wanting him to open his mouth and fuck this up. She's gotta process. Had she asked sooner, I would have told her. It never came up.

Watching the entire revelation play out, Bink sidles up to us, fake punches her man in the gut, and bumps shoulders with her new sister. Blinking a handful of times, Kit glances over to Bink and points to her name patch. Bink points to her own as other sisters gather 'round. "I'm named after a binky," my baby doll explains, giggling to herself.

"A binky?" Kit reiterates in surprise.

"Yeah. Big's Bink," Bink states proudly.

Not knowing how to take the news, she glances over to Big, who smiles coyly and shrugs up a single shoulder, communicating, *I dunno what to tell ya. It's true.*

Jez steps up next. Giving them time to do the chick thing, I give them space but don't stray far as each sister joins the group to explain how she got her name, to commiserate with their new sister.

Jezebel for bein' a former sex worker.

Debbie 'cause she and Dallas fucked all the time—ya know, *Debbie does Dallas.*

Pixie, 'cause of her size. Small and petite, lookin' a whole lot like a woodland creature.

And the list carries on… short and sweet.

The look Kit shoots me after the sisters have shared is one of open appreciation and adoration. I flash her a grin and a quick wink. We don't get to pick our names. They're bestowed upon us. Good or bad, they're ours. Kit's an excellent name if I do say so myself. 'Cause break me off a piece of that. Alright. Maybe it is a tad ridiculous. But I'd prefer she got one by innocent means than how Bonez and I acquired ours.

"Gunz, we're ready," Blimp and Dallas call from the firepit.

Step three.

Knowin' this next part is gonna suck, I approach my woman, secure her hand in mine, and escort her across the grass to do what I gotta do. What Dallas and Tripper and a whole lot of the brothers endured before me. It's tradition. A sacrifice.

Standin' beside a chair they used during today's ceremony, Tripper gestures for me to take a seat next to the fire. I turn to Kit and peck her cheek before makin' you-know-what-to-do eye contact with Bink, who trailed us here. I already told her what's doin'. My baby doll nods in understanding and hooks an arm through Kit's just as our boy takes the opposite side of his mother. Kit will need support. She won't like this. Nobody does. But it needs done. This is how we roll. This is what we do.

Unclasping my belt, not caring who's watching, I drop my pants and boxers to my ankles, exposing my dick and balls—freshly waxed for this occasion. Those who wanna stand witness gather 'round, as those too squeamish find the row of kegs to tide 'em over before the feast.

"Erik, what are you doing?" Kit's voice is shrill as I take a seat and spread my legs, ready to get this over with.

Blimp grasps my shoulders from behind, to keep me still.

"Erik?!" Kit takes a step forward in concern. Bink and Adam do as I instructed them and hold her back.

I can't let her interfere.

"This is for us," I clarify, not wanting to make this any more difficult for her than it already is.

"What's for us?" Growing far more uncomfortable, Kit twists her wedding ring around her finger on repeat.

Out of the firepit, Dallas pulls a red-hot branding iron.

I flick my chin at the glowing metal. "That, love."

"What're you doing, Erik!?" Kit struggles to get closer. Bonez slides up from behind, just in case he needs to step in.

"What needs done," I clarify.

Beside me, Big kneels in the grass and holds my knee to keep it from moving as Tripper does the same from the other side. Hands fisting, jaw locked tight, my nostrils flare in anticipation. We're doin' this.

My brothers speak in hushed tones. Words from our brotherhood, from the beginning, as Dallas steps before me.

I stare at the grass beneath his feet.

"Erik! Look at Me! Please! Stop and tell me what's going on!" Kit screams over the crackle of the fire, over the whooshing through my ears, and the music pulsing from nearby speakers.

I listen because she's been through enough.

She deserves transparency.

I twist my head and give her my undivided attention.

Fat droplets trek down her reddened face as I speak the truth. My truth. "You are the last woman I will ever be with. You are my old lady, my wife, my forever. You wear my ring. You wear my patch. You carried my son. I will wear this for us. As a reminder. As a promise. Just like the other brothers."

"The ones we read about?" She speaks of the vampires we spend our evenings caught up in and the old English scars on their backs of their woman's name.

"Yes, love. Like those brothers, but also mine."

To show her what I mean, Dallas reinserts the iron into the fire and faces Kit. He undoes his jeans and shoves the side down, just above his dick, where a circular D&D is branded, decades old.

She stares at the scarred flesh. Dallas gives her all the time she needs to comprehend what this means before buttoning back up. This is new for my lady. Club life is nothing like normal life for people outside these walls. I get it. My brothers get it. Hell, half of us fell in love with women outside the life. Women who saw the world a certain way before we rode into their lives with our leather and loud pipes. It's a lifestyle we've grown accustomed to. A life some of us grew up in. It's all we know. For her and my son, everything's fresh—a culture shock. Bink and Debbie have only begun welcoming her into the lifestyle, by showing her the ways of the Sacred Sisters and what it's like to be the property of a one percenter.

Leaning in, Bink whispers something in Kit's ear, and she nods, sucking back tears. Half a beat later, my beautiful old lady straightens her spine, no longer overcome with emotions. It's a goddamn relief. Kit shrugs Adam's hold off, as Bink lets her go. Still kneeling in the grass at my side, Big removes himself from the spot, and Kit takes his place. She holds my thigh open and looks up at me with such respect my heart clenches.

"If you need to do this, I'm gonna be right here." She pats my knee in support.

"Okay, love." Removing a Dum Dum from my cut, I peel the wrapper off and toss it into the fire as Dallas retrieves the iron. I push the ball to Kit's lips. She smiles and takes the gift, shoving it into the side of her mouth.

"Where do you want it?" my brother asks.

Wanting her to have a choice, I lift my chin at Kit to decide. She touches the inside of my thigh, right next to where my dick lay. Not wanting it to get branded, she grasps it in her soft palm, and pulls him to safety, tucked against the opposite side of my leg. Tripper pulls my thigh wider to give Dallas better access for a clean mark.

The warmth of the iron heats my skin as it nears, hovering above its intended spot.

"Ready?" comes from Dallas.

I suck in a sharp, readied breath and nod my approval. It lands firm and sizzles. White-hot pain rips through every nerve ending. Clamping my eyes shut, abs tensing, neck elongating, I breathe through it, growling lowly in my chest as the scent of burning flesh abrades my nostrils. It lasts forever, yet not long enough.

When Dallas pulls back, air hits the wound, and I almost crack a tooth.

The brothers cheer.

Salve is slathered on by delicate hands. One's I don't even

have to look at to know who they belong to. When I do, she's there, kneeling between my legs, tending to me as she always does. I brush my thumb along her cheek as she applies a white bandage over the fresh, circular G&K brand.

Despite the throbbing pain, my dick twitches when she looks up at me, full of love and a whole lot of other shit I don't have time to decipher.

Kit throws her empty sucker stick into the fire and playfully slaps the top of my knee. "You're an asshole. You could have told me you were gonna do this."

My eyes roll on a smile, 'cause that's a lie, and we both know it. "Right. Like when I told you I was gonna get my wedding band tattooed, and you didn't like the idea."

She levels me with a blank stare. "I still don't."

"Too bad. 'Cause that's next on the list." Step four.

"It's what?" Still kneeling between my legs, Kit's palms rest on my exposed kneecaps.

I set one of my hands atop hers, to keep us connected. "Where do you think Jade is? She didn't disappear, love. She and Pix set up a sterile tattoo station in the clubhouse infirmary." I planned that too. Sure, Bink did the heavy lifting with the help of Debbie for most of this shindig, since I could give a shit how I married my woman. That being said, I took care of the things that matter to me. The music, her ring and shirt, the brand, and our tattoos, to name a few.

Kit's brow arches in question. "To tattoo your ring," she guesses.

"Yeah, and tattoo whatever you wanna get." Together. The point is to get inked side by side, on our wedding day. Building memories and shit. That's what you do, right?

"You're frustrating." Her growly conviction is mild at best. The tiny nose wrinkle, and lopsided grin she sports is far sweeter.

"Yet, you married me," I tease.

"I know. I think I've gone insane."

"Yeah. Yeah. Yeah. Now get up here." Pulling Kit from the ground, not carin' who's watchin', I drape my woman over my lap. To distract her from the crowd of bikers doin' post-wedding celebratory shit, I focus on us. All they're gonna do is get drunk, eat, and maybe fuck. Big already pitched a bunch of tents over by the dog kennels and playground for anyone who needs a little privacy or time to sleep off the booze, since we don't have enough rooms to house all our visitors.

I slip my hand up my woman's shirt and palm her tit over a lacey bra.

Her mouth rounding in a gasp, Kit glances down at my naughty hand, doin' whatever he wants. "Erik." My name's a curse upon her tongue, yet she doesn't pull away.

At the mere sound of my real name comin' from that pretty, little mouth, I get hard. To show her as much, I pull my erection between her thigh and my belly as she sits across me. As always, the fucker drips with precum. My woman doesn't hesitate to rub her finger across the head to smear in the wetness before it makes a mess.

"I can't believe you're..." she trails off with a sigh.

"We've fucked a lot of times in public, love. Or don't you remember?" I toss out, smiling at her and how much she likes to play with my cock. Even now, she continues to twirl her finger around the head, her nails painted black.

"That was a long time ago," she counters.

"Yeah. It was. Now we're married." To further prove my point, I tap her ring finger and the ruby there.

She stares down at the gem. "We are."

"You think anyone is gonna care where I fuck my old lady?"

"I don't know." She shrugs, all innocent and cute.

To show nobody gives a damn, I move Kit around 'til

she's straddling my lap, my dick, hot and hard between us, her skirt bunched around her waist. Scootin' her back just a smidge, I reach between us, push her lacey thong to the side, lift her up, and glide her walls down my cock. Stuffing her face into the side of my neck, she moans on the way down, stretching perfectly around my shaft, takin' him to the hilt. I palm her ass cheeks and rock my dick in and out of my old lady's perfect cunt.

"Erik," she breathes hot and heavy in my ear.

"You okay?"

"Yes." A shiver ripples through her body.

"You wanna stop?" All she has to do is say the word, and this ends.

"N-no."

Good wife. Perfect wife. Sexy wife.

I rock her more, just enough to hit her G-spot with my piercing. "You wanna come all over your old man's cock in front of all these people?"

Kit trembles at my words. "Erik."

"Tell me, love. Tell me what you want."

"The kids. I don't…"

"There are no kids, love. They're gone." I wouldn't have taken it this far otherwise.

"You… you sure?" she mutters.

So fuckin' sweet.

"Yes, love. I'm positive." When the parties start, the kids go home. Nobody here wants them subjected to adult content. Especially me.

"Adam?" she checks.

"He knows how this works, love. He's not gonna be around to see anythin'." That's code for, I talked with him, told him what's doin', and he was more than cool with it. I've got a good kid.

"Promise?"

I chuckle lowly at how worried she sounds, even though she's turned on. What a heady combination. To ease her mind, I kiss the side of Kit's neck and drag a hand down her spine. "Yes. I promise. If you wanna take this inside, we can. But I don't wanna move. I wanna fuck my wife for the first time. Right here. Our brand throbbin' on my thigh. You lookin' sexy as fuck by the fire."

Sittin' back to look me in the eye, her fingers laced behind my neck, Kit doesn't say a word when she slides both hands into my cut, to peel it off my shoulders. Givin' her space to drape it over the back of the chair, she then takes it a step further and lifts the hem of my t-shirt, pulling it over my head. Tossing it to the ground, she exposes all of me to her. The firelight casts a warm glow over her face and my pecs. Scraping her nails across my chest, she rocks her hips and squeezes around my girth. Turned the hell on, I groan as she undulates on my lap. To help her along, I palm her ass—one hand on each cheek. She tweaks my nipples and twists them hard. I snarl, my legs tightening as I fuck into her depths.

"You like that?" she taunts, her nails biting into my sensitive flesh.

"Yes," I growl darkly and dare her with my eyes to take it further, to give me more.

What does the minx do? She stands, leaving just the tip of my cock inside her wetness. Looking down upon me, Kit cuffs her delicate fingers around my throat, forcing my head back, to look her in the eye. And fuck do I look, 'cause I've never been so turned on in my life. My fingertips embed in her ass cheeks as a feral snarl rattles in my throat.

"Who's in charge?" she goads.

"You," I croak, trying to swallow as she applies pressure.

"Now, why don't I believe that?" Her curious head cocks to the side, judging, assessing.

I don't understand why she doesn't believe it. Because

she's in charge. She owns me, and I fuckin' own her, so does the depravity. It loves her the most. Craves her the most. When I open my mouth to explain, she leans down and whispers in my ear, "Come out and play. You know you want to," her sultry voice beckons.

I blink, and my wife's bare back is against the brick wall of the clubhouse, her legs around my naked waist, nails embedded in my shoulders as I rut her like an animal. My teeth sink into her neck, sucking deep, hungry welts into flesh as I claim and claim and fuckin' claim what's mine.

Her thighs tighten around me in a vise as Kit moans. "I'm gonna come."

And she does. Wetness splashes my dick and runs down my legs as I pound into her cunt. Not even close to done, I put my woman down gently, pull out, spin her around, plant her palms on the rough brick, and enter that slick heat from behind. On her tippy toes, she meets me thrust for thrust, takin' everything I give like a goddamn angel. I nip and bite at her shoulders, bruise her hips, smack her fine ass, but I don't stop. Pleasure licks up my spine, setting my teeth on edge. My breaths expel in sharp pants. Sweat drips, muscles contract. The world fades, leaving only us and her and... soul-aching hunger.

Needing to be closer, to feel more, to crawl inside this perfect human to live for eternity, I splay my hands over hers on the wall, pressing them together, my front against her back, her ass jiggling with each potent thrust.

"Erik," she sobs in pleasure.

I want to apologize for taking her like this... but I can't...

I fuck her.

Brutal and goddamn unrelenting.

I shatter her into a million tiny pieces and glue them back together over and over again.

Her cries are music on the wind.

Her heat, heaven on earth.

Her scent, maddening.

This is mine.

Forever.

For me.

Only me.

And I make every inch of her feel it as I consume what's mine.

I drag my lips against Kit's ear and nip the lobe enough to sting. "How many times can this husband make his old lady come tonight?" I torment.

Kit babbles in response as I grip her hip and fuck deep, balls slapping that ass.

The dark, insatiable hunger unfurls in my belly, stretching itself wide, filling in all the spaces.

I blink, and my woman's on her knees in the grass, sucking my fat cock, taking as much as she can between shiny, swollen lips. Wanting it all, I cup the back of her head and push in. Swallowing around my shaft, she holds her breath 'til it's gone, all of it inside her, nuts against her chin, my skull tattoo kissing her face. Kit's eyes widen as I pause there, tears dripping down her cheeks, but I don't pull back, nor does she ask me to. She endures until her body quakes. She endures until her eyes roll into the back of her skull. Only then do I relent, and she collapses forward, gasping for air.

I drop to the grass beside her to rub her back. "You good, love?"

Still coughing, she nods on repeat, spittle flying from her lips.

Hooking my finger under her chin, I force her to look at me. Kit smiles, blissed out and gorgeous as hell.

Knowin' exactly what I need, what we need, I guide my woman onto her back onto the grass, feet from the clubhouse wall, and kneel between her tattooed legs. Licking my lips, I swipe a finger through her swollen, wet folds. Her back arches on contact. Those fat nipples stand at attention through her lace bra.

I chuckle at how sensitive she is. "You still want more, love?"

Eyelids hooded, a sweet, lip-biting nod is her only reply.

Not one to deny my woman's needs, I hook Kit's legs over my shoulders and glide my heavy cock right back inside. It goes with ease, fitting right where he belongs. We groan together, touching, connecting, gettin' our fill. Fuck, if it doesn't make me wanna blow. I take a beat to let him calm. We're not done yet. Hell, I feel like we haven't even started.

Those honeyed eyes locked on mine, my body looming over hers, I pound into my woman's heat and wreck her. Own her. Take and take, and fuckin' take. Her eyes slamming shut in ecstasy, Kit cries out as she explodes for me. It's sexy as hell as I pull out, and she sprays me in cum. I slam back in only for her to climax again, her legs quivering as another orgasm crests. I revel in it. The squeeze and release on my cock. The hoarse, needy moans.

"That's it, love," I encourage, my voice wrecked.

"Erik."

"You've got another in you."

"I… I don't know."

"You. Do."

To prove I'm right, I show her. Pulling out, I help Kit onto her knees, doggy style. Dusting the bits of grass off her back, I pull her ass tight against my cock. It slips down her crack and nestles itself between her dripping folds. I tease him there, watching as I dip inside just a fraction. Desperate to have him back where he belongs, Kit swivels her ass, grinding against me.

Spreading a luscious cheek with my free hand, I spit on

her little pink pucker. It's there, all cute and tight. That one's mine, too. Maybe not today, but tomorrow or maybe the next. To show her as much, I tease its rim with a fingertip. Kit pitches forward onto her elbows, a fluttery moan imparting those lips. Oh. She likes this.

Around and around, I coat her rear entrance. It opens just a fraction as if saying hello. Not wanting to disappoint my new friend, I dip the tip of a finger inside. Far enough to feel, but not enough to hurt. Kit's spine goes stiff at the intrusion, her legs quaking. Refusing to push her too far too fast, I pause a long beat for her to adjust. On an audible exhale, the muscles in my woman's back relax. I push forward, fitting the first knuckle inside. Again, she breathes, accepting me, accepting it until I'm there, fully encased in her tightness.

"Does that feel good, love?" Slowly, I fuck her on my finger, in and out, watching in fascination as it disappears and reappears—smooth and warm.

"Yes," she croaks, squeezing around my digit.

So fuckin' turned on by my woman, my teeth sink into my bottom lip as a low, hungry growl rattles in my throat. Look at how hot she is, on her knees for me, resting on her elbows, that juicy ass on full display and that curve of her back… fuck, I could sip wine from it. "I'm gonna fuck your pussy and finger your ass. Does my old lady want that?" I ask to be certain.

"Yes," she croaks.

"Tell me."

"I want you to fuck my pussy and finger my ass," is her perfect reply.

"Mmm. You do, do you?"

"Please."

"Show me."

Thrusting her hips backward, my woman grinds herself against my awaiting cock. Not one to deprive such a needy pussy, I slide right back in and, fuck, if that's not goddamn bliss. My eyes roll into the back of my skull, my nuts drawin' up tight as my ass clenches in ecstasy. The minx doesn't stop there when she opens and closes that tight, little hole—the best invitation if I ever did see one. I drop spit onto her opening and press two fingers inside until I feel my cock through the thin wall between pussy and ass.

Kit's long guttural moan is heaven on earth.

That's it, love.

That's it.

And so, I show her how it's done. I show her what it's like being married to me. What it's always gonna be like.

Taking my woman to new heights, I fuck her 'til her knees give out. Then I fuck her some more. When she unintelligibly begs me to stop because she can't come another time, do I listen? Hell no. I fuck her 'til every muscle in my body aches. 'Til I'm wrung out. Only then do I collapse on her prone form, chest to back, sweat-slicked between us, and let go.

Teeth sinking into her shoulder, blinding ecstasy tears through me like a bolt of lightning as jets of cum explode from my cock, filling her pussy. Kit's walls contract, sucking every last drop from my body. Spent, I collapse onto my side in the grass, staring up at the darkening sky, the incoming moon blotted out by clouds. Not one to stray far, Kit rolls onto me—her head heavy on my chest, a leg strewn across my hips as we both come down from whatever miracle I just performed.

"How do you feel?" I ask, rubbin' her arm, hopin' she doesn't have too many bruises or pain. The grass burns on my knees are gonna be a bitch tomorrow.

"Good. Really good," she mumbles, tracing designs across my chest and around my sensitive nipples.

Goosebumps pebble to the surface. "I feel like I ran a marathon."

"You did. That was grade A, top-tier, sex, husband." Kit giggles like she's higher than Blimp. Hell, she probably is. That was a fuckton of orgasms. If she's not mush, livin' in a vat of female euphoria, I didn't do my job right.

I toss an arm across my forehead to wipe away the sweat. "I'm too old for this shit." I sigh in exhaustion.

"Doesn't seem like it to me."

"I've been wantin' to do that for-fuckin'-ever."

"I could tell."

On a groan, I palm my face. "Should've gone down on ya, though. Kinda forgot that part."

Play slapping my chest, Kit snorts. "You're ridiculous. You went down on me last night."

"Yeah. So? I fuckin' love your pussy." I'm addicted to it. So fuckin' addicted.

The minx flicks my nipple playfully. I capture her hand, so she doesn't do it again. "I know." She giggles all quiet and cute and shit.

"And I fuckin' love you even more than that," I explain.

She kisses my pec. "I know that too."

"Good. 'Cause once I recover, we're gettin' inked, then I'm eatin' that pussy." Her hand still in mine, I drag it down my chest to my dick, where I leave her to hold him instead of tormenting my nips.

"You think so?" Nuzzlin' her cheek against my pec, Kit massages my empty sac.

"I know so," I declare.

"Ohhhhh... really?" She laughs.

"Yeah. It's mine." To show her just how fuckin' serious I am, I roll Kit onto her back, climb back between those legs, and rub my semi-hard, cum-soaked cock all over her puffy, cum-soaked pussy.

Palming her tits, stretchin' like an oh-so-satisfied cat, she hums in pleasure, not complaining in the least.

"See. It's fuckin' mine." I slap my piercing against her clit, and she practically purrs.

"Oh. I do, babe. I do," she husks.

"Good. Now let's get you cleaned up, tattooed, and fed."

"In that order?" On a groan, she stretches her arms up and dances her fingers in the grass.

"Yes, love. In that order."

The softest expression morphs Kit's face as she reaches out to cup my cheek. "Kiss me."

Givin' her anything she wants, I lean over and kiss my woman, languid and full of unspoken emotions. Her heart thuds against my breastbone as I meld our bodies as one. When I pull back, just enough to look into her eyes, she smiles lopsided and endearing as always. "I'll always be yours, Erik, and only yours."

Not wantin' to go there after I just got off and all the walls are down, I swallow thickly. "I know."

"And nobody can ever change that."

Christ.

The little boy in me rears his head back, and stares in wide-eyed wonder at the precious gem we've found. A woman who finds us worthy.

Words could never express what Kit brings to my life. Not really. I could never do them justice. Actions are where I thrive. They always have been. Emotions are too goddamn messy.

Pealing us off the ground, I gather our discarded clothes by the fire, shield my woman's bare body from the onlookers the best I can, and escort her inside the rear of the clubhouse. The air is cool as we navigate the halls to Big's bedroom to wash up, pull the grass bits out of my beard and from her short hair, before we redress.

In the mirror above Big's sink, Kit washes off her smeared makeup as I watch from the doorway, my shoulder leaning against the frame. Our gazes clash in the reflection. "Can I help you?" She blushes, not fond of bein' the center of anyone's attention.

"You're breathtaking."

Looking away, uncomfortable, Kit says nothing.

"I mean it."

Off goes what's left of the smokey eyeshadow with the swipe of a washrag. "I know you do."

"I'm really happy you let me fuck you at the bar the day we met."

"Me too," she whispers to the sink.

Not wantin' to get too mushy for both our sakes, I remain quiet, contemplative, as Kit finishes cleaning up. When she's through, she turns around, looks me up and down to make sure I'm not a mess, then steps up to me. Her front against mine. Head tilted back to look at my face, she tugs on my beard. I grin, angling my head down to give her what she wants without bein' asked.

She comes in first, dropping a simple kiss upon my lips. Sweet. Just enough to tide us over, for now. Until later. Ya know, when I have time to say hello again, to all the parts of her anatomy. Especially the one my mouth neglected tonight. Don't worry, he'll make up for his lapse in judgment.

Taking her hand into my own, I dust a final piece of grass from Kit's short hair before departing Big's bedroom.

In the infirmary, Jade and Pixie await us. They're chatting on stools as we enter. Knowin' Pix has my stencil ready, I take the steel chair next to her as Kit drops next to Jade to discuss their options.

Together, on our wedding day, I watch my woman get inked as I think about what my life might look like had she not shown up that day, at the gate.

The pain in my finger is nothing compared to the pain I felt when I thought I might have lost her before we even had time to know one another.

My wedding band is black and gray, interwoven with a thin red line—Celtic in style. Three strands—one for me, one for her, and one for our son. A symbol of our family and what it means to have them in my life forever. Even if we missed over two decades together, they're here now.

Lying flat on the steel infirmary table, Kit gets a tattoo on her hip as the music from the party outside serenades us.

Pix finishes my ink first, gives it a good wipe down, and a coating in cocoa butter to heal. I join Kit when I'm through. Head lolling to the side, she looks over to me, wearing the softest, most serene look I've ever seen on her face. She holds out her hand to me, and I weave our fingers together as Jade continues to draw onto flesh.

"What'cha gettin', love?" I ask.

Jade pulls back long enough for me to see. My stomach dips at the sight, and my expression must turn some sorta way when Kit's voice rises with concern. "Babe?"

She. Wow. I didn't expect that.

I massage my breastbone.

"Babe?" Kit repeats.

On Kit's hip, Jade's tattooing a sucker. A Dum Dum, like the ones we share. On the white stick is our wedding date.

I'm speechless.

Unable to say anything with tangible words, in fear I'm gonna get choked up when I don't wanna do that shit, I lean down and drop the softest of kisses on my old lady's mouth. She hums in satisfaction. When I pull back, Kit watches me to makes sure I'm alright.

"I think he likes it." Her hand squeezes mine, and I squeeze it right back in confirmation.

I don't like it. I fuckin' love it.

"Of course, he does," comes from Jade, watching me watch her handiwork.

A knock sounds at the infirmary door. Through the window, the wild mane of Kai is visible.

"Yeah?" I call out.

"Can I come in?"

"Yes," Kit replies for me.

Pullin' the door open, yet not stepping inside, Kai gives me a hardened look I've seen a million times before.

"We have a problem," I say before he gets a chance to.

Massaging the nape of his neck, Kai chooses his next words carefully. "Yeah. We do. Viper and Oz already brought all the women into the clubhouse as a precaution."

I glance down at Kit and expect her to be overcome with worry. She is female, after all. New to this life. Only, all I see is trust in her eyes. An expression of love and acceptance.

"Go." She releases my hand, and I've never been more grateful to have picked this woman as my partner in this life and the next. Not wanting to leave without a proper kiss, I cup the back of her neck and plant a quick, hot, and heavy one right where it belongs. When I pull back, she's a beaming soft-eyed vixen. Absolutely gorgeous.

"I love you." I boop her nose. "I'll be back as soon as I can. Do not leave the clubhouse. Any of you. Yeah?"

"Yeah... and I love you too," Kit replies, more than willing to follow my orders without a fight.

I picked a damn good one.

Knowin' if I don't take care of business now, they'll have to tear me away by my teeth, I shut the door in my wake and stop in the hall to get briefed by Kai on what's doin'.

"We have a breach," he explains.

On a nod, I reply, "I assumed as much."

"It's not what you think."

"It probably is." You don't have a wedding with a fuckton

of Sacred Sinners in attendance when you're at war if you don't expect shit to pop off. Big and I knew what could happen. That's why the new security system got installed. That's why I called our brother's down at the Texas chapter and requested they send Kade and Rosie to stake things out during our wedding as a precaution. We're not stupid. We knew the risks. Sure, I wasn't about to disclose any of that to Kit, or she'd had wanted to postpone our nuptials or elope. I wasn't gonna let that happen.

We're as prepared as we've ever been.

"Weapons?" I prompt Kai on the way out of the rear clubhouse door, into the middle of my wedding reception, or what's left of it. Chairs have been shoved to the side. The aisle is gone. Flowers scattered across the grass. The fire's still roaring and tinkly lights the women strung illuminate the backyard. Brothers have gathered in a circle. Around what? That's the question.

They part down the middle to let me and Kai through.

In the center, kneeling in the grass, bawling his prissy-bitch eyes out, is a naked Malcolm—our longtime prospect. The one we took in out of respect after Bink was kidnapped by her mother, and he helped get her out The southern motherfucker who rocks a cowboy hat. The man Big despises and refuses to patch in as a brother.

Behind him, pressing the tip of a gun to the back of the asshole's skull is our prez, far calmer than I expect him to be in situations like this. Grinding his jaw, Big pulls a flip phone from his front pocket and tosses it to me. I catch it midair and scan through the messages giving details to an unknown number about our compound, the people who live here, and the security systems.

Ah.

He's the reason we were infiltrated months ago.

A rat.

A nasty piece of shit rat under our very noses.

A…

I come across an address.

A familiar address I sent flowers to once upon a time.

"You're the reason my woman got kidnapped and raped and…" The vein in my forehead pulses as I take a step closer to the traitor. He's the reason Niki is dead. He's the reason Beth lost her innocence. He's the goddamn reason Jade and Loretta…

Red clouds my vision as I slam my fist into Malcolm's jaw, sending him sprawling into the grass. He lands on his hands and knees, blood flowing freely from his mouth. Not givin' a single fuck who sees me, I kick the slimy bastard in the ribs. Dropping onto his back, clutching his side, Malcolm cries out in pain. Looming over the piece of shit, I step on his throat and apply pressure, not enough to do much, but enough to communicate he'll die soon. Very, fucking soon.

"How long have you known?" I rumble, speaking directly to our prez.

Re-holstering his gun inside his cut, Big widens his stance and crosses both arms over his chest. "I've had my suspicions for a while." He lifts his stubborn chin.

"And you didn't tell me." Fury thrums through my words.

"No. The less you knew, the better."

"Why?"

"'Cause you weren't ready."

Right.

"Ready for what? The truth?" I thunder.

Ever the mediator, Bonez steps out of the crowd into the open circle and spits on the rat. Then he turns to face me. "The club was attacked, brother. The day after, you find out you had a kid you never knew about. Then Kit was kidnapped while you're on a run, along with Niki and Beth. You were fucked up. You didn't see what you were like at the farmhouse the night shit went down. Or what followed for weeks after. Then you were shot when they were rescued. Not to mention Adam, Niki dyin', the infection, Kit healin', and all the other shit."

Look… I fuckin' get it. It was a shit show. I was a mess.

"Fair. But what does that have to do with this?" I gesture to the traitor. The goddamn narc.

"I couldn't tell you," Big explains as if that's somehow okay. It's not. None of this shady shit is. He kept this from me on purpose.

"So, you tell me on my wedding day, instead?"

Big nods toward the phone in my hand. "Look at the last message he sent."

Goin' back through the burner, my foot still on the asshole's throat, I read the latest text aloud, *"They're riding in today. Wear the cuts to blend in. After the ceremony, you know what to do."*

Shouldering his way through the crowd, Kade enters the party with his old lady in tow. Decked out in all black, her blonde hair covered in a matching black beanie, Rosie dumps a small trash bag upside down next to the rat. Four human hearts bounce across the grass. One hits him in the ribs, leaving a bloodied mark on his flesh.

Malcolm trembles in wide-eyed horror as he observes the gifts they've brought.

Ever the showman, Kade extracts a still-bloodied knife from its sheath and twirls it between his fingers. "We had fun together, me and my old lady. It was a great bonding experience, wasn't it, Swan?"

Not one to show emotions, Rosie nudges the organs toward the rat with the tip of her boot. "These belong to you."

Malcolm moans in distress and tries to squirm away from the body parts.

Fuckin' pussy.

I press down harder. He starts to choke and gasp for air. It's annoying. I let up when I tire of hearing the disgusting, pitiful sounds.

"And soon there will be five," Kade cackles like a sadistic motherfucker, pointing to Malcolm with the tip of his blood-caked blade.

"Remy sent four men?" I ask Rosie, the saner of the two.

"Seven," Kade replies, bouncin' on the balls of his feet, jacked up from his kills. "But I—"

"He got a little too carried away," Rosie answers, side-eyeing her man.

"Whoops." Wearing the widest and craziest of smiles, Kade mimics what he did with the other hearts by squeezing his fist together and shaking it in the air with manic flourish.

I nod once. "Right." Kade had a little too much fun like Kade usually does. Not surprising. Leaving that as that, I face Big to figure out what's next. "So, Prez, what are we gonna do with the rat?" Since he's been keepin' this from me, perhaps he's already got a plan.

Prez shrugs as if he doesn't give a damn. "That's up to you and Blimp. Your old ladies were the ones taken. He had a hand in it. I already killed the men who fucked with Bink. He's yours."

Alrighty then.

"What about White Boy?" I throw out, 'cause Jade was taken, and she's family to all of us. Especially him.

Apparently, Big has already thought that through too, when he explains, "Jade's not his old lady, and Loretta's his mom, who's already been claimed by Blimp."

Lumberin' his way into the circle, a glowing blunt between his lips, Blimp points toward the shed where the torturing goes down.

Sure. That works for me.

"String him up," I order to whoever's listening. "Don't forget to stuff, then tape his mouth shut to keep him quiet. We're not touchin' him tonight. I've got a new wife to feed and dance with. He'll survive 'til morning. That work for you?" I gesture to Blimp so we're on the same page.

Plumes of smoke rise from Blimp's lips as a far-too-happy smile parts his long, overgrown beard. "Perfect, brother. Sounds perfect," he singsongs.

Doin' what brothers do, they peal the naked dickbag off the grass as I remove my foot from his throat. Malcolm begs like a little bitch, then screams for mercy as I depart to make good on my promises to my woman.

Next on the list.

Feed my woman.

I didn't request we have fried pickles and homemade ranch for just anyone.

Malcolm will die in the morning.

Ya know, as a post-wedding present to me.

CHAPTER FORTY-FOUR

KIT

I'm a married woman.

Sitting on a couch in the clubhouse common room, I'm keenly aware of my new reality as my *new* sisters pull up chairs to chat as if the lockdown is a normal, everyday occurrence around these parts.

Welcome to the life as a Sacred Sister.

Seated beside me, Bink pats my raw, grass-stained knee. "Everything's gonna be fine," she attempts to reassure.

Across from us, lounging unladylike in a plastic chair, Jez nods twice as if agreeing with Big's old lady. "No gunfire is good news. Plus…" trailing off, the rhinestone, pantyhose-wearing woman, points to the double front doors and the two Sacred Sinners standing watch outside of them. "They're talking. Not armed. With Gunz's new security system and with as many brothers we have here for the wedding, if it was a big deal, we'd be locked in bedrooms, and they'd be ready to kill," she explains, as if this is an ordinary conversation.

Out of my depth, I nod to express I'm following along

because what else do you say? I'm glad nobody's shooting. I mean... There are no words.

Not finished, Jez points to my son, standing guard by himself at the hall exit. "Oz is only there to keep us from leaving the room. Some of us don't listen to orders." The feisty big, boobed sister cuts Bink a knowing look.

The blonde beside me shrugs as if she's not about to argue. "Not all rules and orders are meant to be followed."

Debbie snorts from her spot at the bar.

Loretta cackles from the pool table, where she plays a round with Jade.

And I observe because I have nothing else to add. The sisters lapse into mini conversations about times like these. Bink reminisces on the time a crazed woman shot Big. There's something about food poisoning. Another from her childhood.

Getting up from the couch, I leave them to their stories and approach my son.

Swallowing up the entire doorway with his size to keep all of us in and everyone else out, Adam looks far beyond his early twenties in his new leather vest, tight, dark denim jeans, and plain white t-shirt. My boy sure has grown up.

Not knowing protocol when we're on lockdown and not wanting to get him in trouble for disrupting his duties as a prospect, I pause a few feet from him. He is a brother, and I'm an old lady. Not his mom. Not right now. Even if that is a load of crap. Still, I know my place, or at least I think I do. I'm trying.

Hands clasped in front of me, I'm the first to speak. "Do you think you can reach out to yo—Gunz?"

Amused by the way I've addressed him, Adam mashes his lips together, and straightens his shoulders before schooling his features and replying, "Mom, I'll text Dad. Did you forget your phone?"

I sweep a hand down the length of my body. "No proper place for it. Plus, I didn't think I'd need it today."

Adam's head bobs in understanding. He pulls out a phone from his vest to fire off a text.

Looking around for eavesdroppers, I lean in, so nobody else can hear, and whisper, "I don't know how I'm supposed to address you and stuff… when you're… ya know…" I point to his official vest. Somewhere beneath all that leather, he's packing a gun. The men talk about it over dinner sometimes. Apparently, Adam has a decent aim. Not sure a mother wants to hear those things about her son when it pertains to illegal activities. Then again, I'd rather he be safe than sorry.

A smirk lifts the corner of Adam's full lips, highlighting a dimple I don't see often. "I am your son." His blue eyes dance with mirth.

"I know."

"You can always address me as your son, Mom."

Alright. Good to know.

"And… Gunz?" I check, still whispering.

"He's my dad. I'll worry about what I need to call him and when. You don't need to worry about that stuff."

Okay.

Also, good to know.

"Unless I'm in the middle of club business, you can talk to me whenever ya need or want to," Adam tacks on.

"This isn't active club business?" Again, I indicate where he's standing. He escorted the women in here for a reason. He's standing in the doorway for a reason.

"Not the kind I'm talkin' about, Mom."

"Right." Of course.

Adam reads a message on his phone. "Dad's on his way inside now."

"Is he okay?"

"I'm fine, love." Gunz's voice carries from the hall, his

bootheels scraping the floor with each step. Our son steps to the side to give his dad room to pass. He clasps Adam on the shoulder, sharing a quick moment before he's in front of me, red-faced and… I glance at his hands as he opens and closes them in tight fists down at his sides. The right one is jacked up. There's blood on the top of his boots.

"What happened?" I ask, looking up at his face for answers.

Fitting my front to his, his feet on either side of mine, Gunz slides a muscled arm around my waist and brushes his lips across my forehead before kissing me there. "I can't tell you, love." His hot breath fans across my skin, making me shiver.

Lookin' down, I finger the edge of his belt buckle. "Club business. I get it. I watched—"

My biker cuts in with a groan. "*Sons of Anarchy*," he deadpans.

Ever the observer, Adam snorts a laugh.

"You don't have to sound so grumpy about it." I poke his rock-hard abs.

Emitting the world's heaviest sigh, Gunz's body relaxes against mine, his tension deflating like a balloon. He draws tiny circles across my lower back. "I'm not, love. They're cleanin' up outside, so we gotta wait here for a few minutes. Big will come get us whenever they're ready."

Cleaning up outside. I wanna ask what they're cleaning up but think better of it. Club business. Not my business.

"But we're okay?" I need to hear him say it. Over his cotton shirt, I trace the valley of Gunz's abs with my fingertip.

His boots nudge the outside edges of mine. "Yes, love. We're safe. We're okay."

"Are you?" His fist doesn't look okay. Those boots are dotted with blood. I have two eyes. I notice shit.

"Yes."

Tilting my head back to look him in the face, I eye him skeptically. "Promise?"

"I promise." He pecks the tip of my nose and smiles like he wants to kiss me a thousand times more.

The lovestruck fool I am smiles back, despite my unease. He's been through a lot. We've been through a lot. I don't want anything to sour our wedding day if I can help it. Not for me, but him. This is a first for Gunz. Whether he'll admit it to me, let alone himself, this was a giant step for the forever bachelor. Not to mention the brand and the tattoo that came after.

Trust me, I'm gonna give him shit for it later. At the right time. Who burns their skin and never tells their partner they're doing it? Apparently, him. The tattoo I get. The other, he'll have to explain. Bink said it was a tradition when she urged me to pull up my big girl panties and stand by my man even if I didn't like it. I did. I stood by him like I always will.

I mean, it ended in an incredible round of sex. My pussy is sore. The pleasant kind of sore. Tomorrow morning, we'll have to see the level of damage Gunz wrought. The bite marks and hickeys across my shoulders and neck are already brands upon flesh. The number of fingerprints on my ass are sure to paint an interesting picture. Perhaps we can play connect the dots with them, after Gunz spends an hour apologizing for getting carried away. That's how it typically works.

Apologies, followed by orgasms.

I can't decide if it's the guilt that makes him atone for his actions, thus wanting to bring me subsequent pleasure. Or it's his marks that turn him on, and the orgasms are a byproduct of his arousal. Perhaps it's a smidge of both.

A set of soft, warm lips encased in a delicious beard drag across my sensitive neck. "You're thinkin' an awful lot, love."

Laughing quietly at how attentive my husband is, I inhale and get a high-octane hit of all that is Gunz—leather, spice, cinnamon. Cupping the back of his neck, I hold him to my flesh. "Of course I am."

His hand slips up my skirt and grips my ass. "Should I make good on what I forgot?" Gunz yanks me flush against him. His thick cock, ready and willing, prods my belly through the denim—a naughty promise of what's to come.

Fisting the front of his shirt, I shudder. "Not right now."

He nuzzles beneath my ear. "You sure?"

"Yes. I'm sure. Don't we have food to eat? And… maybe you'll dance with me." I tack on the last part, timid but hopeful. We never discussed dancing together.

Never one to let me down, Gunz pries himself away on a disappointed growl. Rubbing my hands up and down my arms, I glance around the common room. The sisters have left, and Adam too. Guess we were a little too preoccupied in our bubble to notice. Not that I'm surprised. It's a common occurrence.

Gunz hooks his thick, muscled arm through mine and escorts me from the clubhouse common room through the halls and out the back door. Only then do I realize how many brothers are in attendance—over fifty or sixty I've never seen before. All of them busy drinking and chatting with various women and each other.

Now dark outside, the fire and a few outdoor lights illuminate the large outdoor space. It's cozy. Intimate.

Gunz pulls me to a group of long tables filled with food in various covered containers. He hands me a plate before he grabs one for himself. I gather our black-and-red plasticware and napkins. Together, we scope out the spread. Fried chicken is first up. He tongs a thigh from the pan and drops it on my plate.

"Thanks, babe."

As we go, my husband serves us both. The things he knows I like, which is most of the food, he gives me little bits of. The foods he doesn't know for sure, he asks, and by ask, I mean he points, and I either nod or shake my head. It's simple and easy, as it always is. Honestly, it's not much different from nights at home.

At the end, he drops one of Bink's famous chocolate chip cookies next to a brownie on my plate. I grab us two water bottles from a cooler and follow him to a picnic table.

We sit next to each other and eat in companionable silence. I watch him out of the corner of my eye, takin' in how handsome he is. Gunz winks when he catches me. I wink back, takin' a sip of water, not at all ashamed I'm ogling my husband.

As usual, Gunz finishes first.

"Do you like it?" he asks.

"It's awesome," I mumble around a bite.

"I thought so, too. You wanna dance after this?" He lifts his chin at a brother passing by. The man pats Gunz's shoulder, then keeps on walkin'.

Swallowing, I watch the man join a group by the fire. "Um… sure? If you want."

"You're transparent, love. You get that, yeah?"

"Maybe you're just observant."

He ponders that for a minute. "Could be. But you wanna dance. We're gonna dance."

"If you're—"

He cuts me off. "Stop that shit."

"Stop what?"

"Say what you want, love. Period. None of this, if you want bullshit. If I don't wanna do somethin', I won't. We're married. Man and wife. You are my old lady. My name is on your back. If you ever want or need somethin', say it. I love you. You love me. It's that simple."

I stare at him in wonder. "Okay."

"Okay, what?"

"I'll say it." It won't be easy, but I will. I still can't believe he's real.

"Then say it," he challenges.

"I want to dance with you."

"Good. I wanna dance with you, too. But it's gotta be a slow one."

"Sounds perfect."

Pulling his phone from his back pocket and a Dum Dum from his vest, Gunz peels off the wrapper as he types away on the screen. I finish the delicious pile of food on my plate. Or most of it. It's a lot of food. Not wanting to be bloated when I got hitched, I didn't eat much this morning. More like toast and tea. That was hours ago. This is perfect. Crunchy, salty, fried pickles with ranch. Corn on the cob, though messy, it's mouthwatering good. Whoever cooked for our wedding is wicked in the kitchen. I'm gonna go out on a limb and say it was the sisters. All of them.

A song changes on the outside speaker.

It's slow.

Looking over to Gunz, he's staring right back at me, his lips split into the sweetest smiles as he hands me a red napkin. "Wipe up, love. We've got a song to dance to."

Just like that, I'm done for.

Owned.

Blissfully happy.

Together, standing next to the picnic table, we dance. My head on his shoulder. Gunz's strong heart beats against my ear—a soothing lub, lub, lub. Tom Petty serenades us, drowning out the boisterous brothers having the time of their lives. Once again, the world fades, and here we remain, safe, in our bubble.

One slow song turns into two, then three. By four, my

eyes drift closed in the comfort of his warmth, in the strength, in our gentle sway.

Gunz whispers sweet nothings to the top of my head, and I melt. This is what I dreamed of as a child. A man like him. Not perfect, but perfectly imperfect for me. An amazing father and husband. An equal.

We don't say thank yous or goodbyes to any of our guests when Gunz takes my hand in his, and we leave our own wedding.

Up the stairs of our home, we ascend side by side, his hand in mine. Gunz opens our front doors and places his back against the screen to keep it open. He waves me to come to him, and I do. He places my arm around his neck before sweeping me into his arms in a…

"Are you carrying me across the threshold?" I giggle.

"I sure as fuck am. We just got hitched."

"We're old, Erik. This isn't necessary." My stomach swoops in girlish ways. I laugh as he grumbles, maneuvering us through the doorway, careful not to bang my legs or head on the doorframe. He doesn't stop there. Through our house, Gunz carries me as if I weigh nothing. Reaching our bedroom, he sets me on the edge of the mattress and kneels at my feet to remove my boots and socks. And I let him because this is sexy.

Placing one of my feet over his shoulder, Gunz kisses the inside of my calf. Kiss—inside of my knee. Kiss—inside of my thigh. Fisting the bed covers on either side of me, I squirm, watching the hottest man I've ever met reach the garter. With his teeth, he snags the black fabric and smiles like the devil. Those expressive blue eyes swirl with promises of filthy things to come. Ever so slowly, he drags the band down my leg, to the tip of my big toe, where it drapes.

"I'm gonna make good on what I promised, love."

My pussy clenches at his vow.

He pushes my other leg to the side, and my skirt rides up, exposing the scrap of lace covering my sex. With a single finger, he pushes the gusset of my panties to the side, giving him the perfect view of my pussy. Gunz licks his lips and inhales as if he's scenting me in the air.

"I can't believe you're mine."

"I am."

"Only mine."

"Yes. Only yours."

Pressing his thumb between my folds, my husband massages my little nub in circles. On a throaty moan, I collapse onto the bed, my back arching, tits thrust toward the ceiling as I revel in his addictive touch. Gunz drops my leg, and the garter falls to the floor as he settles himself between my spread thighs, where he fits like a glove. Just the right weight. The right feel. The right everything. He drapes one of my knees over his shoulder and then the other before burying his face in my pussy.

I'm a goner.

For him.

For this.

For us.

Gunz

Devouring my woman's cunt, I tongue fuck her 'til my face is covered in her sweet essence. The minx screams through a second climax, her fingers tearing at the comforter. I fucking love it. Ripping my belt buckle open and tearing down the front of my jeans, I don't bother asking questions when I slam straight into my woman's body. Her neck elongates, her eyes rolling into the back of her head as she shatters beneath me, oversensitive from our previous fuck. Like the bastard I am, I suck another welt into her throat, next to another beautiful mark I put there.

Kit's legs squeeze around my hips, as her pussy holds my dick in a death grip, and I give my wife exactly what she needs. Because I love her. Because this is what men like me do.

Throwing my cut onto the top of the bed, I tear my shirt over my head, ball it up, and throw it on the floor. Kit struggles to remove her own clothes. Her cut joins mine on the pillows, but her shirt gets stuck. I reach back into my boot, pull out my knife, and I slice the fucker from her—hem up through the neck. Kit's pupils dilate as if this turns her crank. Takin' it a step further, I lift the thin scrap of lace at the center of her bra, and I cut through that too. And would you look at that, my foxy old lady is naked, breathing heavy for me, skin all flushed with desire.

To think this is the first time I've fucked in this bed. Our bed.

It's a good thing Jez has Chibs for the night. We don't wanna scar our poor pups with what I'm about to do to his mom.

I'm gonna ruin her.

Sure, the grass fuck was intense.

But this is our house. Our bed. Our new life.

She can scream and beg here without shame. She can come on my cock as many times as I want, and nobody but us will ever know.

To prove this theory, I pull out of my woman's perfect fuckin' body and drop onto my back. I return my knife to its home and remove the rest of my clothes. We're gonna be naked for the rest of the night. No more fabric between us. Not anymore. Blinking as if she's floating in another world, Kit rolls over and looks at me, unsure what to do.

Knowin' my woman is gonna need help rememberin' her name come morning, I do the gentlemanly thing, and I help her undress the rest of the way. I stand at the side of our bed to drag both her thong and skirt down her legs. I toss them onto the floor to deal with later. All splayed out for me, perfect nipples beckoning to be sucked, my old lady scissors her inked legs together, as if she's ready and more than willing to come for me again and again and fucking again. Trust me, she will.

"Play with your nipples, love," I encourage as I leave her to root around in the bottom of our bedroom closet. Right on top is what I seek. When I return to my squirming, deliciously hot wife, plucking and twisting her nipples, I lay the first book we ever read together on her belly. Then I climb onto the bed beside her, our shoulders touching. I stroke my cock as she plays with her tits. Precum slickens my shaft, mixed with the remnants of her climax. Damn, if it doesn't feel good to jack off beside my woman. Don't ask me why it's hot. It just is.

"Whenever you're ready, love. Sit on my cock."

Not needing to be told twice, Kit's tits bounce as she straddles my hips, grabs the base of my erection, and slides down him. We both groan on the descent, and it's fuckin' magical. I snatch the book she let fall onto the bed and hand it to her.

She looks at me funny.

I set it on my chest.

"Read to me," I instruct as I grip her hips and fuck her in shallow strokes.

"Now?"

"Yes, love."

Dainty fingers brush over the black-and-red cover of the first book we ever read together.

"You want me to read to you…"

"Yeah, love. I want you to read to me while I fuck you."

Kit bites her bottom lip, equally turned on and contemplative. "You know it's romance, right?" She giggles, so proud of herself.

"It might be. But you know what's better?"

"What?"

"This. Us." I grip her hips to express so fuckin' much.

Tears well in Kit's honey-colored depths as she looks down at me, on us, on our rings and her fresh tattoo.

I rock her on my cock.

A tear spills over, and I reach up to swipe it away with my thumb. "I love you." I brush the backs of my fingers down between her heaving breasts to her belly button.

Picking up the book we both love from my chest, Kit shivers and sucks in an emotional breath, her gaze never leaving mine.

I mouth the words I'll never tire of saying, *I love you*.

Another tear spills as she mouths the same in return.

This is my forever.

Right here.

Riding on my cock. Reading to me with that perfect voice.

The mother of my son.

The woman I never knew I needed.

This is mine.

For always.

Until my dying breath.

Kit will always be enough.

The End

PLAYLIST

- Paint it Black - The Rolling Stones
- Don't Come Around Here No More- Tom Petty and the Heartbreakers
- Fire It Up- Black Label Society
- If You Want Blood- AC/DC
- Sad But True - Metallica
- Lay Down Sally- Eric Clapton
- Here Comes My Girl- Tom Petty and the Heartbreakers
- Sabbra Cadabra- Black Sabbath

Printed in Great Britain
by Amazon